PRAISE FOR THE AUTHOR'S 'V2V' HISTORICAL SERIES

Mary Anne Yarde – Author of the Du Lac Series

"These are not dry dusty books whose historical characters are one dimensional. Hughes has brought these men and women back to life with her quick wit and beautiful prose. The stories she tells are fabulously descriptive, as well as at times profoundly moving. She pulled it off beautifully."

D.K. Marley – Historical Fiction author of *Blood and Ink*

"What an incredibly fascinating walk through history with such in-depth historical research. I applaud Trisha Hughes for this immense undertaking, as well as the beautiful imagery and story-telling quality of her voice. I highly recommend taking this ambling journey into the pages of this historical series"

David Baird – David's Book Blurg

"Trisha Hughes did a great job of bringing each of these Kings and Queens to life. This is the kind of book that gives you the juicy, interesting facts and ignites the flames of passion for history"

Tony Riches – Historical Author of the *Tudor Trilogy*

"I wasn't disappointed as Trisha's lively and engaging style takes us on a grand tour of those who enjoyed wearing the crown. As Trisha Hughes says 'these stories span hundreds of years of lust, betrayal, heroism, murder, cruelties and mysteries.
What more could you ask for?"

Renny DeGroot – Author

"Hughes creates a fascinating ride with her remarkable talent for dressing the bones of history in body and soul.
A definite 5 stars"

Lyn Horner – Author

"Written in a lively, never boring style, I thoroughly enjoyed this historical epic. A definite 5 stars."

Paul Bennett – Author and Book Reviewer:

"Detailed research is evident throughout the book giving the reader a full picture of the events and the larger than life people who sought for the crown of a kingdom seemingly in constant turmoil and uncertainty. A fascinating tutorial of the period from Canute to Elizabeth. I'm looking forward to the next book.
5 stars"

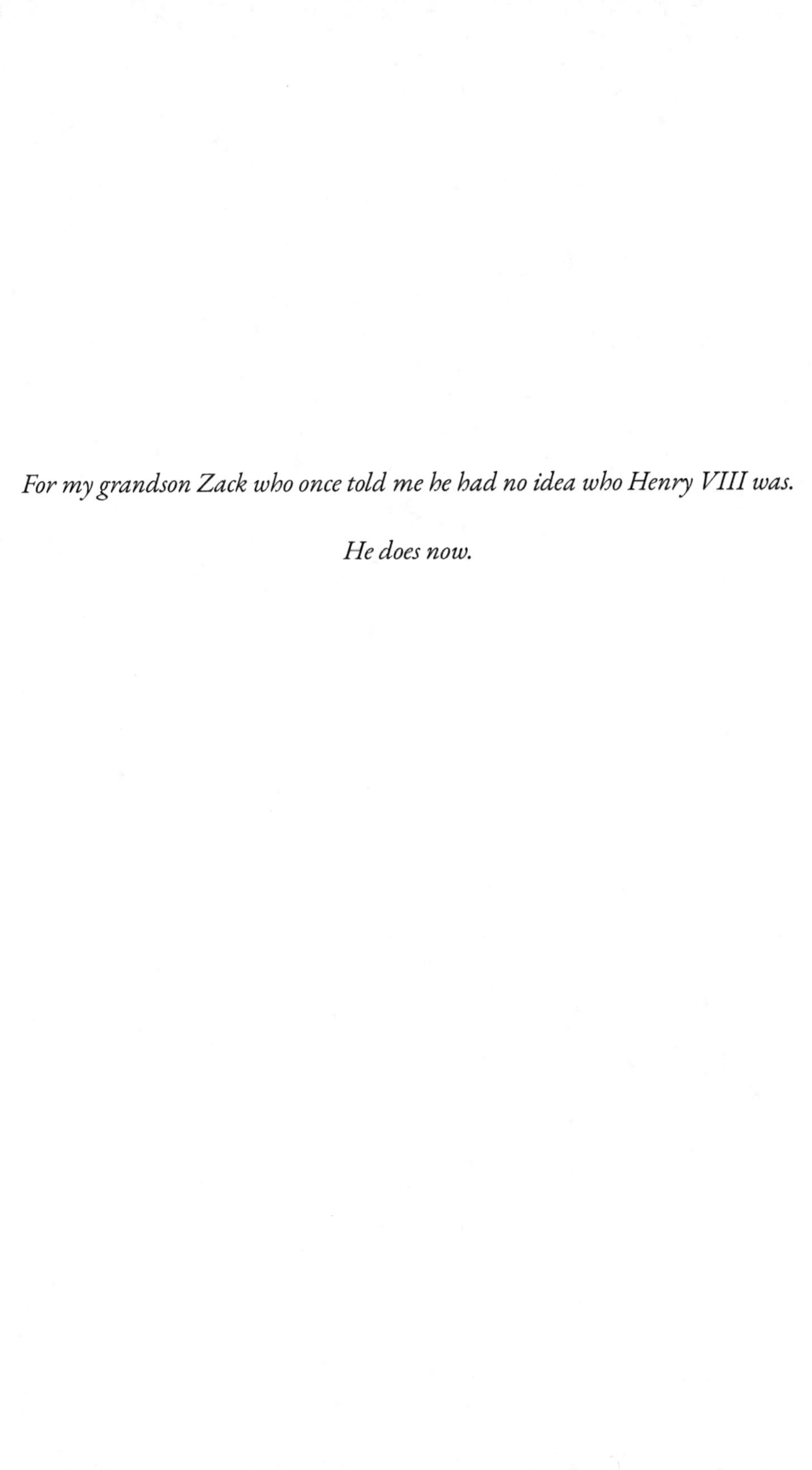

For my grandson Zack who once told me he had no idea who Henry VIII was.

He does now.

VIKINGS TO VIRGIN

THE STORY OF ENGLAND'S MONARCHS FROM THE VIKINGS TO THE VIRGIN QUEEN

SECOND EDITION
BOOK ONE

TRISHA HUGHES

GATSBY PUBLISHING

First published in Great Britain 2018 by
The Book Guild Ltd

This work is fiction based on real events in history.

Typeset in Garamond

ISBN 9798879249705

*'If history were taught in the form of stories,
it would never be forgotten.'*

Rudyard Kipling

CONTENTS

FOREWORD

In history, to be an English king and to be murdered was no more than a hazard of the job and there has been a vast number of kings where this has actually been the case. The story of the kings and queens of England is a wonderful drama, far more surprising than you might think.

Times were brutal and felt the need to take certain measures into their own hands, and trust me, there has been many extraordinary and various ways that royal family members have sought to delete relatives who were obstacles in the path of their own progress to the throne. Many were not averse to the odd assassination or two by poisoning, starving, burning, imprisonment, beheading or an old favourite, red hot poker up the bottom.

Many historians pass hazily over the precise methods employed to delete family members. Some choose to leave it as an insinuation of 'died under suspicious circumstances', because the entire truth will never be fully known. Some historians are not so coy. Neither am I.

Hunting seemed to have been a dangerous sport for a king to participate in as a stray arrow in the back while out hunting with a cherished loved one has killed many an unsuspecting king. In one instance, instead of helping their beloved ruler, the brother high-tailed it immediately back to the castle and claimed the money and throne for himself.

To be a king and to be murdered in one's privy is, however, to suffer a considerable indignity. Yet that is exactly the fate of at least two British royals, if certain sources are to be believed.

And then we have Edward II, a weak monarch remembered for losing the Battle of Bannockburn to the Scots and who had been deposed earlier on in the same year by his own wife, Queen Isabella and her lover, Roger Mortimer. According to some historians, he was subject to extensive indignities including being starved and thrown into a pit of rotting corpses. That will certainly do the trick.

It is not possible to write everything about each king but I have tried to bring you juicy snippets about every king from the Viking, Cerdic, to Elizabeth 1, the Virgin Queen. It is not meant to match historical works of professional historians, but is rather my own personal and sometimes rather quirky view on how the British monarchy has persevered and developed over the centuries. Some chapters will be scant as little information is available while others will send your head spinning with the atrocities of the times.

I have sourced those early years relying on information from various documents: the most notable was the Anglo-Saxon Chronicle. It is partial and not always correct but it is invaluable as a guide to show us people and events that shaped British history. They were often written quite a while after the event based on hearsay and therefore leaves room for historians to debate what is correct and what is not. As well as this, only fragments of the original documents have survived through the centuries so early historical events are often circumstantial and some of the chroniclers had axes to grind so their information is sometimes not entirely accurate.

Many 'facts' were pure guesswork such as birthdates, spouses who appear and disappear and the number of children. The latter is understandable as the infant mortality rate was high until relatively recent times and life expectancy among infants and children was much shorter than it is now. Additionally, life expectancy among adults varied as well with kings leading their men into battles and even a minor wound could cause death due to gangrene and septicaemia.

I have adhered to the facts as best I can and hope that it will make it easier to visualise these past monarchs as flesh and blood characters and not simply eccentrics in a history book.

Having said all that, I sincerely hope you find my rendition every bit as enjoyable as I have enjoyed researching for it.

PART I

THE VIKINGS

When we speak of Britain's monarchs, most of us would agree that early periods of time are clearly muddled. Many of the early British kings are hidden in the mists of time while some, the ones who lost crucial battles, have almost completely disappeared when the victors erased their rivals from all surviving records. There are kings who ruled for only a few months and there are some who ruled for over fifty years. There are also some who should never have ruled at all. They include, among their number, the vain, the greedy and the downright corrupt as well as adulterers, swindlers and cowards. Yet this group also shares one thing in common. In their own lifetimes, they were the most powerful individuals in the land. Their stories span 1500 years and are full of lust, betrayal, heroism, murder, cruelty and mysteries.

The men, and a couple of women, who triumphed made sure that the records showed their better claim to the throne, their better prowess in battle, and their greater magnanimity and consequently love and support of their people. Kings needed to prove their strength in battle, and they almost never reached middle age. Many times, a young boy was left as the heir and he could not possibly hold his own against intense family members. More often than not, this resulted in invading armies, not just from local clans, but also from warriors across the seas. For example – the Vikings.

But Britain's history goes back much further than that. They were a race of people who were struggling to survive. Copper and tin was discovered and the Bronze Age began when men with bronze could easy beat up other men who only had sticks and stones to protect themselves. Being simple farming people, they were not organised for warfare.

Then the unimaginable happened. Bronze was dumped when iron was discovered and it could not be disputed that for smashing skulls, iron was certainly best. It was a time of huge transformation in Britain and a time when tribal leaders began to believe they were more than just chiefs. They were kings. Tribes were beginning to rub up against each other with only one consequence: hostility.

This new age was a ferocious time throughout Europe as local tribes tussled for power and the country descended into bloody conflict where the need to fight and defend became the main focus of their lives. So the fighting and defending increased. It was a time when men who could wield swords could also expand their territories. It was the age of warriors and Britain was becoming the land of ancient myths and folklore with warrior heroes on horseback armed with highly decorated, glittering Celtic swords. They built forts and everything about these forts said 'KEEP OUT'.

But, for all their hard work to survive, the Celts came up against an incredible force and Britain fell to the greatest empire the world had ever seen. The Romans were on the march and things had turned ugly.

If ever there was a time when the Britons should have stood together, shoulder to shoulder, this was it. The trouble was some of these tribes hated each other more than they hated the Romans and while many Britons banded together, some sided with Rome seeing it as an ideal opportunity to get rid of their rivals.

But if there was one thing the Romans quickly learned, it was that you don't stand still when a Briton was coming at you on his horse waving his sword. Always duck.

The Britons were very proficient with their swords but it just wasn't enough. They fought – and lost – and they were to find that Rome's rule was more violent than their own. If you got in the way, heads would be cut off and put on spikes for all to see just what would happen if you didn't do it the Roman way.

By the time the Romans left Britain, they had changed everything:

governments, laws and taxation. They built towns, cities and roads and they introduced the written language. But if the Britons thought that they could finally live in relative peace, they were wrong. It was all coming to a terrifying end. There was a new enemy surfacing and life would change for everyone. The Saxons had arrived and of all the Germanic races, Saxons were the most appalling. Their very name was supposed to have come from the use of a short, one-handed sword. The English now lived under a worse menace, crueller and bloodier, coming from the sea. Wave after wave of Saxon invaders began landing on Britain's shores. These were the days of Cerdic and his son Cynric.

Saxons brought with them their structure of Germanic life: fighting for life and control against men as hard-pressed as they were themselves and only winning because of their butchery as war-leaders. With this new lifestyle came a long and intricate rivalry for leadership between various Anglo-Saxon kings and they all strived for mastery by force and savagery. To understand these days and the constantly changing monarchs, we have to understand time frames. Five years was a lot in those days. Twenty years was the far horizon and fifty was antiquity.

Up to the end of the 4th century, we see signs of fear spreading throughout the whole country. A dark time had fallen on Britain and dawn rose with a poor, barbaric and divided England. The light of Christianity burned in Ireland with the efforts of Saint Patrick, and followers of his doctrine flowed into Wales and England. But now, after 400 years where there had been law and order and a respect for property during the Roman occupation, all had vanished. Where craftsmen had once been nourished and merchants had been welcomed, now barbarism reigned. People were losing the art of writing and a form of scribbling was the only means of conveying their thoughts or wishes to anyone at a distance. Provinces were popping up everywhere and in the confusion and conflict, petty ruffians who called themselves 'kings' took over in each province. But those kings weren't content in their own kingdoms. They wanted more. It almost seemed that they were addicted to violence and savagery.

By then, after many attacks from the Picts and Scots to the north and the Saxons from Germany, the Britons had finally had enough. Instead of waiting for the Romans to help them, they took matters into their own hands and began fighting for themselves as they had done centuries before.

We can only view these early days through dim telescopes across the span of 2000 years. In this scantily recorded history, there are stories of a British knight who won countless battles in those savage times. In mythology, King Arthur and the Knights of the Round Table loom romantically. Around him and all his deeds, romance and bravery abounds. Stories of twelve separate battles (all untraceable) against people (all unknown) are told. No one can say for sure where, or even if, Arthur actually existed, although it is assumed that if there was such a person, he would have been alive at the time of the Saxon invasion in 495 AD.

But all of this savagery was just a foretaste of what was to come and York had a terrible shock coming. Britain was waking to a new nightmare, not just from the savage hordes to the north but a different force stirring beyond the seas.

The Age of the Vikings was beginning and the force moved slowly but surely towards Britain.

At the end of the Roman Empire in the 5th century, Scandinavia stood on the brink of the Viking Age. This period in Scandinavian history is important as we now see the first powerful people who were not chiefs anymore but a dynasty of kings. It is also important since this marked the emergence of a violent religion that included animal and human sacrifice. It was a reminder that this world was different from a Christian religion.

What we know about the Vikings is more myth than reality as they were basically warriors and not writers. What we *do* know is they didn't just spring out of nowhere, fully formed. They were the product of thousands of years of a cultural evolution with a dynamic and violent history.

These men had the sea running through their veins. For many turbulent centuries, the glimpse on the horizon of a square sail and dragon-headed prow churned by oars through the waves, blue water foaming around the hull of the mighty ship, must have struck terror into the hearts of medieval Europeans. These golden-haired, blue-eyed savages were shaped by the land, sea and previous civilisations and it is only by understanding their ancient ancestors that we can hope to see why and how this terrifying phenomenon ever came to be.

These Vikings weren't just expert sailors and ship builders: they were warriors in every sense of the word. Even to the dark-age standards, Vikings were very adept in the messy business of killing. Their long boats were stunning craft, packed with two dozen men, that could sail up rivers and anchor in creeks and bays and their beautiful lines and construction could ride out the fiercest storms of the Atlantic Ocean. Every male Viking had a sword, an axe and a knife on him at all times but when going to war or on a raid, equipment like shields, spears, bows and arrows was added. On top of that, these heavily tattooed men held no semblance of a moral code.

And so it probably comes as no surprise that when those first Viking raiders attacked a monastery in Northumbria, they thought they had nothing to fear from a Christian God because as far as they were concerned, he was no match for their own gods, Odin and Thor.

The Vikings arrived in Britain in 793 AD in their long boats on a cold miserable January morning while the English people were enjoying their tranquillity. The raid was planned with care and knowledge and executed with complete surprise in the dead of winter. Britain just didn't have a chance.

Imagine an icy wind ripping through shrubbery and trees after a savage night of arctic air cutting its way through cracks in walls and threatening to freeze everything. In the early morning light, no one heard the muffled sounds over the water. Everyone slept, still clinging to their dreams. Suddenly a hollow pounding was heard, at first in the distance, but gradually coming closer. This ominous sound broke the peaceful silence as people were rubbing the sleep from their eyes.

The Vikings arrived, attacking and murdering viciously, and they only left when their boats were filled with a rich booty of gold, jewels and sacred emblems.

The unprecedented violence of this raid sealed itself into Britain's very being. Now the English were confronted with a different type of enemy. They were the most treacherous and audacious type of pirate that had ever appeared.

For forty guarded years the English coast was left unravaged but in 835 AD, the Vikings returned in ferocity with three to four hundred vessels for the rest of the booty and for another thirty years, Southern England was under constant attack from Denmark and Norway. Saxon England was at this time ripe for their savagery.

In this period, there was one particular Viking who stood out from the rest. Nobody was more ruthless than Ragnar Lodbrok. He was born in

Norway and was a raider from his youth. Before attacking England, he began with leading his fleet up the Seine into Paris before a plague took an unforeseeable revenge upon the Norsemen. He then turned his interests to Northumbria. But here again, fate was hostile. According to a Scandinavian story, Ragnar was captured by King Ella of Northumbria and cast into a snake pit, dying in a coiling mass of loathsome adders. It was too bad for Ragnar that Saint Patrick wasn't around to save him.

It was a cold winter's morning when Ragnar's four sons received the news of their father's death. In the eeriness of the pre-dawn, smoke drifted lazily up from chimneys as snow floated onto the barren icy wasteland. Around a fire inside one of the huts, his sons huddled together, warming themselves while they waited impatiently for news of their father's return from the marauding trip to England and they fully expected every hull in the fleet to be laden with precious gold and gems. When the news came, it wasn't good and each son went silent in furious rage.

Legend says that Bjorn 'Ironside' gripped his spear shaft so hard that his fingerprints remained stamped on it. Hvitserk was playing chess but clenched his fingers around a pawn so tightly that blood started from under his nails. Sigurd 'Snake-eye' was trimming his nails with a knife and kept on paring until he cut into the bone. But the fourth son was the one who would seek revenge for his father's death. Ivar 'The Boneless' demanded the precise details of his father's execution, and as his face turned red, blue and pale by turns, his skin began to swell with anger. Britain was to find that the Vikings believed in vengeance and sons were expected to avenge the killers of their fathers.

It was known as the "Blood Eagle". The flesh and ribs of the killer must be cut and sawn off the spine, and then the dutiful son with his own hands would rip out the palpitating lungs. And that is exactly what Ivar and his brother Hvitserk had in mind. This conquest was far greater than anything they had attempted before and the brothers had only two things on their minds, revenge for their father's death and control of the whole of England.

In 865 AD, the two brothers planned their attack of York, East Anglia, Northumbria and Mercia. On both sides of the country nestled abbeys and monasteries, churches and cathedrals all loaded with treasures of gold and silver, of jewels, wine, food and luxuries and they wanted it all. In a world where priests were taught to turn the other cheek, England was ripe for the attack. The church made it an easy prize for the Vikings' sharp swords to win.

Not surprisingly, before Ivar arrived in York, the local rival kings forgot their feuds and united in one final effort to fight against the Vikings who they fully expected to return.

And they were right to be worried. King Ella was the first to die and Ivar was certain to make him suffer the Blood Eagle fate for his father's death. Next in line was Edmund of East Anglia who put up a good fight but in the end, suffered a brutal death as well. Ivar's men used him as target practice, tying him to a tree and shooting spears at him until he was entirely covered with their missiles, like the bristles of a hedgehog. They then cut off his head for good measure and threw his body in a bramble thicket.

This was the end of Northumbria and East Anglia, and North England took a long time to recover from the slaughter.

Rightfully alarmed, the King of Mercia called desperately for help from Wessex, the royal house that could trace its lineage back to Cerdic.

We now come to one of the greatest figures in our long history. A warrior who is said to have turned back the tide of ignorance and disaster. A man who would not only change the fortunes of the English, but his descendants would go on to build a new united English Nation.

We now come to the House of Wessex and we begin with the first of our rulers – Alfred the Great. His legend was only the beginning.

THE HOUSE OF WESSEX

essex was geographically strong with ridges facing north and none of the slow rivers the Danes used for steering their long-boats into the heart of Mercia. As kingdoms such as Kent, Northumbria and Mercia quickly disappeared, everyone turned to Wessex for help.

For years, three brothers had ruled Wessex in very quick succession of each other. Their father, Ethelwulf, died many years before after returning home from France with a new French bride. Despite her tender age of twelve and Ethelwulf's mature age of 60, he had married her on the spot when visiting her father, the Holy Roman Emperor. But with three feisty sons back home, the eldest one being a rebellious 35-year-old looking after the kingdom while his father was away, this unlikely tryst was to have dire consequences. When Ethelwulf arrived home, it was to find his son Ethelbald sitting firmly on the throne, refusing to get up and intending to oust his father off to Kent with his new bride.

Ethelwulf could, perhaps should, have mustered enough support to fight back or even evict his impatient son, but perhaps he knew that it was a wasted exercise. His sons were against him and he wasn't a young man anymore. When looking at his options, there didn't seem to be much of a choice. He could spend the last few years of his life fighting his sons for the throne, and more than likely lose, or he could enjoy them with his beautiful young wife in peaceful, picturesque Kent. The last option must have been very appealing to him because that's exactly what he did. He simply stepped aside.

It would seem he made the right decision. Two years later, Ethelwulf was dead and Ivar the Boneless and his brother Hvitserk were plundering their way across Britain. But standing firmly in their path, fully prepared for them, were the Wessex brothers.

As Ivar moved gradually towards Wessex, things took a turn for the worst when Ethelbald, always the stronger, more fierce of the three brothers, suddenly died. This left two surviving brothers of the Wessex dynasty, Ethelred and Alfred, to defend the kingdom.

In those changeable times, the brothers realised that arrangements needed to be made rather urgently for their family's uncertain future since either of them could die at any time as well. Keeping this in mind, the two brothers decided to make a pact. Whoever outlived the other would inherit the personal property that their father had left in his will, with the understanding that Ethelred's two under-age sons would only receive the riches that he, as their father, settled upon them plus any additional lands he had acquired in his lifetime. The unstated presupposition was that the surviving brother would inherit the rest of the kingdom and be the king.

Alfred was not a strong man. He was slight of build and he was fragile. From a child, he had suffered from Crohn's disease and he was less likely to live long enough to rule, much less lead anyone into battle against the Vikings. But he was loyal to his elder brother and he helped to gather their troops together from the surrounding countryside.

With success after success spurring them on further, the Danes marched confidently west towards them. Soon they were in Wessex.

On another cold bleak winter's day in January in 873 AD, beautiful Wessex turned into a battleground. The early morning fog had risen from the valley and drifted through the trees like cold grey smoke before turning to soft rain. Ivar stood with his arm raised high above his head, signally his men to wait. Behind him, his warriors waited impatiently, raising long blood-curdling war cries as they stood high on the hill overlooking the tents erected in the lowlands of Ashdown. In front of them, they held their brightly painted shields and banners as their golden bracelets glistened in the mist. As they watched, the rain lessened to a drizzle even though the vapour was still thick around them.

Ethelred's military skills were common knowledge. His very name loosened bowels and tightened throats. It was spoken in whispers and many crossed their fingers while others knocked suspiciously on wood. Every breath must have been like slivers of ice in Ivar's lungs as he remembered past raids and battles. But like Ethelred, he knew that there were no rules on a battlefield. Watching the enemy gathering below him, he must have been counting on it.

Ivar must have been feeling more than a little confident. On top of the hill, he had the better position and more men and he would have believed it was going to be an easy defeat. With overwhelming confidence bursting up from inside, he concentrated all of his force on the battle ahead.

Ethelred prayed quietly in his tent while the two armies jeered and shouted at each other. It was Alfred who was growing more anxious and impatient with his brother, who was refusing to leave his tent until Mass was finished. Inexperienced as he was, 21-year-old Alfred knew he had to act quickly before the Danes swept down the hill first, uprooting everything in their path, intent on destroying the Wessex army.

Despite this inexperience and the absence of his brother, Alfred did what he knew he had to do. Sitting high on his white horse as rain began to fall softly, Alfred sounded the horn, raised his sword in the air, and gave the command to his men to charge. On the hill above him, Ivar lowered his arm at the same time.

With a roar, both lines of warriors broke into a lurching run through the mud. The ones at the rear would have watched as their army disappeared into the mist like ghosts. They could barely have seen twenty yards in front of them. In a great clash of swords and shields, the two sides collided violently and in the hissing rain, blood flowed and men screamed.

When Ethelred finished his prayers and walked out of his tent, he was alarmed to find that Alfred had already led the charge without him. He quickly gathered his few remaining men and charged up the rear to help his brother.

Through the fog, Ivar would have seen shadowy figures moving and he would have been struggling to make sense of them. By then it would have been too late. Only as the soldiers suddenly burst out of the fog, coming straight for him, would he have realised the size of the group and there would have been little choice of what to do. In his confusion, he panicked and fled.

Despite the retreat, there were heavy casualties on both sides but for the Saxons, it could not have been worse. At only 24, Ethelred was mortally wounded and later died. Alfred was now the only brother left and the legend of 'Alfred the Great' began.

For years, the fighting swayed to and fro. But things were slowly changing. Slavery was becoming a much more lucrative form of income and Irish monasteries were ready for the pillaging of religious artefacts. This was organised human trafficking on the scale of the slave trade to the Americas 1000 years in the future with slaves being sold to Russia, China and as far as the Middle East. And Ivar wanted to be a part of it.

It must have been an unexpected blessing for Alfred when Ivar suddenly left England to set up shop and reside in Dublin.

The invaders had gone for the moment but Alfred knew he had to undertake a radical reorganisation of his kingdom if he was going to keep them out permanently. He put ideas into motion that would continue to blossom for a thousand years.

He ringed Wessex with thirty garrisoned fortified towns and constructed larger ships for the royal fleet. He created what modern strategists call a 'defence-in-depth' system and one that worked. His boroughs were not on the grand scale of Roman forts but consisted mainly of massive earthworks and large walls surrounded by wide ditches with roads linking the boroughs together. These boroughs blocked passage on the river and if the Vikings returned, they would have to row under a garrisoned bridge and risk being pelted from above with stones and spears before heading further upstream. Alfred's system was revolutionary for those times although potentially expensive in its execution. But not only was the cost of building the boroughs great, it paled before the cost of upkeep and maintenance. With this in mind, he reorganised and established a system that obligated all landowners to provide a 'fortress tax' as a means of funding.

But this is not the only thing that makes us remember him as Alfred the Great. In his youth, Alfred had no schooling and up until this time, English was mainly a spoken language. Songs, stories and poems were learned and recited but few, if any, seem to have been written down. Alfred dreamed of an England where peace, order, and righteousness prevailed, where learning flourished and important books were translated into English for all the people to read, not just the well-educated. He was married and had children of his own by then and he wanted them to govern his kingdom with a language they could all understand. He brought scholars from Europe to England and had all his children educated, even his daughters.

One final war awaited Alfred in 892 AD. A hostile Viking fleet of 250 ships appeared off the coast having already ravaged France. Alfred, who was suffering more and more from his digestive illness, was not seen often by this time. His son, Edward, at the age of 22, was the one who led his father's armies on to the field and defeated them in this third war. In the autumn of that year, Alfred's hard work paid off.

Alfred had secured fourteen years of anxious peace in which to develop Britain's defences so when this fresh wave of Vikings returned, they found a very different kingdom defended by a strong army and a network of forts. But even Alfred knew he wasn't strong enough to hold the Vikings out indefinitely so a treaty was made up as a sort of peace, which probably meant handing over an awful lot of money to them. This treaty was called the 'Danelaw' and it effectively created a separation between the North and the South, with York becoming the capital for the Vikings in the north, while Alfred and his family stayed safe and sound in the south.

Where conquest had previously been the main reason to invade England, it now became settlement and York's population exploded from 2,000 to 10,000 as more and more Vikings arrived. It was to create a new problem: sanitation. All of a sudden, 50% of Vikings were now faced with a change in life expectancy – most women only made it to 35 years of age while a man was lucky to reach fifty. It would be a continuing problem for many years to come.

Alfred's death in 899 AD at the age of fifty sparked a serious family quarrel. His bloodline gave the English a series of great rulers but with this same bloodline came intense rivalry within the family. At the time of his brother's death, Alfred's succession had largely gone uncontested because of the youth of Ethelred's two sons. But you can see that this could only be a temporary measure because as both boys grew to manhood, they naturally wanted their birthright back. Instead, on Alfred's death, his son Edward immediately proclaimed himself king before his two cousins knew what was happening.

Ethelwold had definite views as to whom should be king and it surely wasn't Edward. His younger brother had already married the daughter of a lord from Mercian lord and had stated he was not interested in the family squabble. It left the way totally open for Ethelwold.

He stood before Edward, full of righteous indignation, and hotly declared that *he* was the eldest of the two sons of Ethelred 1, and *he* was the one who should step up to the mark and take over now that he was of age. It was *his* turn now, thank you very much.

Of course, Edward refused to listen. He knew as Alfred's elder son, there was no certainty that he would succeed his father as king, but there was no way he was going to allow anyone to snatch away his prize at this stage of the game. He told Ethelwold he may be ten years older than him but it was he, Edward, who had the throne well and truly secured and he was not going to give it up without a fight.

With those words ringing in his ears, Ethelwold left for Northumbria looking for support from the Danes. His own army was small but with the Danish backing him, he was sure he could wage war against his cousin. And win.

The Danes weren't stupid. They were well aware of how much power Ethelwold would have if he were to be successful in claiming the throne so they eagerly pledged their alliance and crowned him King of Northumbria at Jorvik. With an increased army at his command, Ethelwold was ready to push south.

On 13th December 902 AD, he arrived with a fleet in Essex and attacked as Edward, itching for a fight, retaliated by devastating the southern areas of East Anglia where the Danes resided. With a thunderous charge and with swords held high, they met the Danes head on. So began the Battle of the Holme.

The course of the battle is largely unknown but in the blood-soaked field, among the mutilated bodies of men and horses, the Danes found they had suffered heavy losses. They had lost two distinguished earls, a Scandinavian baron and their own Danish King Eric. Riding wildly and distraught to the end, Ethelwold also lost his life on the battlefield.

When news of Ethelwold's death reached Edward, there was to be no mourning for his cousin. Ethelwold's death meant the way was clear for him to claim the throne as King of Wessex and ruler of Southern Britain and that's exactly what he did.

The Danes however had other ideas. They were going to finish what Ethelwold had started and within days, they marched resolutely towards central England. What they hadn't expected was Edward's feisty sister, Aethelfleda stepping into the action. She had married Ethelred of Mercia at the age of twenty (old for those times), and had become Lady of the Mercians. Upon her husband's death, she had succeeded to the throne of Mercia as his widow and at her disposal was a huge, experienced army that she intended to use to help her brother.

It is surprising how varied opinions are of these times concerning whether women were treated with respect or not. Some say it was a shining time in women's history while others say that women naturally lost their personal property to their husbands when they married. They also say they had their noses cut off if they were caught in adultery.

Considering this, you don't see many women like Aethelfleda in history. The last time a warrior queen had appeared was a woman by the name of Boudica, the widow of a king from the Iceni tribe during the Roman occupation. She was imposingly tall with wild reddish-blonde hair hanging below her waist, a harsh voice and a piercing glare. She had been angry and out for revenge at all cost after the Romans had beaten her and raped her daughters. Translated, her name meant 'victory' and she had come very close to achieving it. As the Romans pounded through northern Wales, Boudica led the Iceni people along with many other tribes in ferocious revolt. As the people of Londinium had fled their homes, Boudica attacked and burned it to the ground as well as three cities along the way. An incredible number of people, estimated at 70,000 – 80,000, were reported killed and no one was spared who had dealings with the Romans. Even Roman noblewomen were impaled lengthwise on spikes and had their breasts cut off and sewn in their mouths to the accompaniment of sacrifices and banquets.

But the Britons had one big disadvantage. They fought with long swords designed for slashing rather than stabbing, which meant they needed room to swing their blades. And the Romans knew it. With that knowledge, they adjusted their tactics with terrible results for the Britons. Like so many others, Boudica lost her life for her audacity of challenging Roman rule.

Here again, at the front of an army, stood another imposing woman ... almost a reincarnation of Boudica. Another woman with flaming hair and a piercing gaze. Another woman out to extract revenge for her country and her people. And everyone remembered well the legend of Boudica. Her wild beauty and courage had given them the strength to stand up and fight for what they believed in when for so long, they had only felt defeat. It was time to do that again.

After her husband's death, Aethelfleda went straight to work with anger rippling down the muscles of her back and shoulders, her fiery hair streaming behind her. In these savage times, a women ruler must have had extraordinary qualities and together, she and Edward, knit by blood, marched together at yet another onslaught from the Danes in the north. In Wales, she captured the king's wife and thirty-four more hostages and the Welsh, justifiably nervous, hastened to offer their perpetual loyalty. With that support, Edward's army swelled even more. The two strong families, Wessex and Mercia, were now the two ruling kingdoms of Britain.

For the next ten years, brother and sister advanced mercilessly together, strengthening towns as they went, and succeeded to heights that their father Alfred had never dreamed possible. Together, they seemed tireless in their defence of Britain as Vikings attacked them from all directions.

Finally, in 917 AD, when the King of the Danes, King Guthrum II was killed, East Anglia collapsed and the garrisons of Derby and Leicester submitted. The Danish leaders had finally surrendered. One year later, twelve days after midsummer, Aethelfleda died, followed by Edward five years later at the age of fifty.

The events that followed Edward's death are very messy. With three wives and five aggressive sons from different mothers, it was never going to be simple or easy.

Edward may have intended Elfweard, his eldest son by his second wife to be his successor in Wessex alone, but that's not what Elfweard thought. He considered himself ranked above his older half-brother, Athelstan, for succession to the *entire* English throne for two reasons. Firstly, the House of Wessex was the ruling house of Britain and if Elfweard was to be the King of Wessex, then surely he should also be the King of the English. Secondly, as Athelstan was born in 893 *before* Edward became king (and to a common-law wife, no less) and Elfweard was born *during* the reign, then Elfweard believed he should be ranked higher. But not everyone saw his logic, especially not Athelstan.

As fate would have it, Athelstan was by his father's side in Mercia when he died, so the Mercians promptly elected him as their new king. Meanwhile, Elfweard was in Wessex, and he was elected to be the new king by the people in Wessex.

And no one dared to take sides.

Whether Edward intended a division of the kingdom is uncertain and as it turned out, it didn't matter. Fifteen days later in Oxford, Elfweard conveniently and rather suddenly died under 'mysterious circumstances'. His death ended what would certainly have been a civil war between the brothers and overnight, everything changed yet again.

Athelstan took no time at all to pronounce himself *Rex Anglorum* – King of the English. He took off the traditional helmet and placed a shiny new crown firmly on his head as if he was challenging anyone to test his authority. And he wasn't finished yet. Not by a long shot. He'd only just begun. Plans were in motion and he had a very busy year ahead of him.

His father and aunt had already conquered Danish territories in Mercia and East Anglia but when they'd died, the Danes, under King Sitric Caech, still ruled the Viking kingdom of York. And it rubbed Athelstan up the wrong way. As soon as his coronation was over, Athelstan approached Sitric with the idea that Sitric should marry his sister, Edith, to make peace. At her marriage, both kings were to make a deal and agree not to invade each other's territories or to support each other's enemies. Surely everyone could live in harmony, Athelstan asked?

All very civilised and natural, you would think. A terrific outcome, you might even say. And Edith was certainly not a wallflower. She was a beauty anyone would be happy to wed and bed.

However, and there is always a however, none remembered to ask what would happen when one of them died?

In Sitric's rush to get to the altar, the question was never discussed or planned. After all, both men were still in their prime so there seemed no need to dwell any further on that nasty little subject. Right?

Until a year later when Sitric very suddenly and mysteriously died as well.

Athelstan had been itching to invade York and add another notch to his belt so as soon as the rather opportune death occurred, he wasted no time in the muddled business of mourning but gathered up his army and set off for Scotland. It would seem that England was not enough for Athelstan. He wanted the lot.

When Sitric's Irish cousin, Guthfrith, heard of the unexpected death, he had grand thoughts of his own to take the throne of England for himself. He even got as far as leading a fleet from Dublin. But Athelstan had seen that one coming and he was very well prepared. He led his army north so quickly that Guthfrith was forced to flee to Scotland, since there was no time to escape back to Dublin.

This set up a fresh wave of anger and outrage by the Northumbrians who were gathering their own forces together to defend themselves against Athelstan. By then, he had conquered York and was marching further north into Scotland to confront them. With him were three Welsh kings and six Viking chiefs, all with adrenaline pumping through their veins.

King Constantine II of Scotland had never seen an army so vast and he panicked. The way he saw it was if he was going to save his people at all, he only had two choices: risk annihilation or surrender the kingdom of Scotland. So he chose surrender.

In itself, the decision was understandable. But what irked the Scottish nobles was that he did it without a fight and they were furious that he had accepted Athelstan's victory so easily. After all, everyone knew the Scots never gave up *anything* without a good fight.

Constantine knew his nobles were right. Neither option was really acceptable to him either. But what was his choice? It was only then he realised that there actually *was* a third choice. He could still remain King of Scotland if it *looked* like he was accepting Athelstan as his overlord. By this one deception, he would save any more Scottish blood from being spilt and it would give him time to make plans of his own.

Submission had never been the Scottish style and by backing down so quickly, the nobles thought he had cowardly sold them out. While the nobles protested vehemently, Constantine took a few deep breaths and thought long and hard about what he would do next.

Athelstan's court was constantly on the move, heading wherever the food supplies were plentiful though mainly basing himself in Wessex. But despite becoming one of the most powerful monarchs Britain had ever seen, it seems that the Wessex party were still not entirely pleased with Aethelstan's leadership and his legitimacy was always in question.

While Wessex squabbled amongst themselves, in other parts of the country a conspiracy was being hatched. The plan was to have Athelstan blinded at Winchester and have him replaced by the late Elfweard's full-brother, Edwin. To do that, they had to have the full support of the Bishop of Winchester. And they already had it.

Whether the plot simply failed or was uncovered is not clear. The men of Wessex seem to have broken out into open rebellion but Athelstan was always one step ahead and ready with his army to subdue them. In the ensuing confusion, the nobles of Wessex decided to send Edwin abroad to his cousin Adelolf, Count of Boulogne in France, for safe keeping until things quietened down a little.

While on the boat to France, it seems Edwin inadvertently fell overboard and drowned.

It was yet another very opportune death for Athelstan who had found himself on rather shaky grounds since he hurriedly declared himself the king in 925 AD. A hat trick, one could even say.

By 934 AD, Olaf Guthfrithson felt good and ready to launch a bid for his father's former kingdom of York. He had succeeded his father Guthfrith as the Norse King of Dublin and had defeated his rivals for control of the Viking part of Ireland.

King Constantine had also been waiting patiently for the right time to step in. And he had a rabbit in his hat – an eligible daughter. Individually Olaf and King Constantine were too weak to challenge Athelstan, but together they knew they could succeed, and the marriage between Guthfrithson and Constantine's daughter would both seal the deal and the alliance at the same time.

As Olaf and Constantine joined with the Strathclyde Britons to invade England, Athelstan marched north to meet them again.

Neither life nor time was wasted in manoeuvres as the Battle of Brunanburh began. The armies, very large for those impoverished times, took up their stations as tempers flared and the masses of soldiers wielded their blades and shields across a narrow field.

The fighting continued from dawn to dusk and when it was finished, the field was strewn with the dead and dying, picked over by wolves and carrion birds. One of the dead was King Constantine's son.

It was a cruelly fought clash and is remembered in poetry as "The Great Battle'. This poem tells of 'hoary' Constantine, by now around 60 years of age, in this historic battle and referred to as the 'greatest single battle in Anglo-Saxon history before the Battle of Hastings'. Thousands of Scots died that day, while King Olaf escaped back to Dublin with the remnant of his forces. A large number of Saxons fell on the other side as well, including two of Athelstan's cousins, sons of Ethelweard. Athelstan, King of the Saxons and the English, along with his younger half-brother Edmund, possessed an overwhelming victory.

But this was not purely about blood and conquest. This was a showdown between two very different ethnic identities. The North Celtic alliance versus the Anglo Saxons and it was meant to settle once and for all whether Britain would be controlled by one single power or remain several separate kingdoms.

It would be difficult to exaggerate the importance of this victory. If Athelstan had been defeated, the West Saxon domination over Britain would have disintegrated and Scotland would have taken over the whole realm.

But for all the blood and suffering, nothing was solved at all.

In the weeks after the battle, Athelstan turned his attention to his own family.

In my humble opinion, any man whose parents managed to provide him with eight or even nine sisters deserves our sympathy. Like his father, Athelstan was unwilling to marry them to English nobles who might pose a threat to him in the future, so he looked outside of England for their husbands. This was the main reason for his close relations with European courts and he rather wisely married several of his half-sisters to European nobles.

Although he had established many alliances through his family, he himself never married and had no children of his own. Two years after Brunanburh, Athelstan was dead and his 18-year-old half-brother, Edmund, from his father's third marriage, took over the throne.

England would find that for all the fighting, nothing had really changed.

Life was not going to be simple after all.

EARLY KINGS OF ENGLAND

A hundred and twenty years had passed since the first Vikings had ravaged the land and for years the English had struggled to survive. During the past seventy-two years, four warrior kings had fought against the Vikings and it looked like they had finally been defeated.

When Edmund I came to the throne in 923 AD, he was only 18 years old. During his six-year reign, the revival of monasteries in England began but it was a period in time when not much happened and little is known of his reign, perhaps because of the short length of time.

While celebrating St Augustine's Mass Day in Gloucestershire, one year after the death of his wife, Edmund was murdered by an exiled thief while feasting with nobles. He spotted Leofa in the crowd and attacked the intruder in person. In the event, Edmund was stabbed in the stomach and died almost instantly.

Unfortunately for England, his death left them not only without a monarch but it also left them with the problem of who would look after his two young sons, Edwig aged 5 and Edgar aged 3, both now fatherless and motherless.

* * *

A HUNDRED AND twenty years had passed since the first Vikings had devastated the country and for most of those years the English had struggled to survive. But during the past 72 years, four kings had fought hard against the Vikings and it looked like they were finally defeated.

When Edmund I came to the throne, when he was only 18 years old and for a little while, the young man managed to maintain peace where most of his ancestors had failed. It was a period in time when not much happened and very little is known although we do know that there was a revival of monasteries in England.

Six years into his reign and one year after the death of his wife, Edmund was celebrating St Augustine's Mass Day in Gloucestershire and feasting with his nobles. The air rang with laughter and clapping as delighted guests watched beautiful women dancing as they revelled in the splendid waste of expensive wine and food.

No one except Edmund saw Leofa, an exiled thief, in the crowd. He attacked the thief in person but unfortunately for Edmund, he was stabbed in the stomach during the scuffle and died almost instantly.

After six years of peace, England was again without a monarch. Edmund's two young sons were only toddlers so the only solution was for Edmund's 23-year-old brother, Edred, to step up to the throne.

During Edmund's reign, Edred had seen the Northumbrians and the Scots finally surrender to the south and the coming years looked rosy for him. Times were peaceful and he was young and virile. In the first year of his reign, everything seemed to be going pretty well for him.

Perhaps it was Edmund's quiet strength that had kept the north subdued because for some unknown reason, within months of Edred's coronation, the Scots changed their allegiance in favour of a Viking who had the magnificent name of Eric Bloodaxe. Once again, the English became uneasy and watchful.

Like Eric's contemporaries, Thorfinn Skullsplitter of Orkney, Thorfinn the Short and Rollo the Walker, their names conjure up images of huge, hairy owners of very large axes. But it seems the Vikings had a sense of humour as well.

Rollo was called the Walker because he was so big that no horse could carry him and apparently Thorfinn the Short was quite a tall man. So perhaps Thorfinn Skullsplitter was simply a harmless old man who wouldn't hurt a fly?

Eric Bloodaxe was the favourite and probably the eldest son of Harald Finehair who had a grand total of twenty children. Harald's kingdom in Norway was very small and did not provide for much of an inheritance, especially with so many children to provide for. So as any self-respecting Viking would do, Eric took matters into his own hands. Methodically, one by one, he murdered most of his brothers (which is probably how he earned his descriptive nickname).

The only brother to escape Eric's murder spree was Haakon, because he was safely ensconced in the English court as part of a hostage-taking exercise during Athelstan's reign. When hearing of his father and brothers' deaths, Haakon promptly sailed for Norway, rather bravely I should imagine, to claim his inheritance. Surprisingly, Haakon defeated his brother Eric and sent him packing to the Orkney Islands.

During Athelstan's reign, Eric Bloodaxe had spent a lot of his time raiding northern England with a certain amount of relish until an opportunity further south, in a part of Northumbria called Jorvik, presented itself to him. Athelstan had suggested that Eric could rule as his agent to protect the land against the Danes and 'any other marauders' such as the Scots and the Norse in Ireland, as long as Eric regarded Athelstan as the overlord. This seems to have satisfied Eric for quite a while but after Athelstan died and Edmund began to rule, Eric saw the resulting power vacuum as an opportunity to improve his own personal lot and become the new king of York in his own right.

By the time Edred heard that Northumbria had made Eric Bloodaxe their leader, he already knew his grip on the north was diminishing so he reacted as you would expect. He exploded.

England had come a long way in the past few hundred years but the country was still packed with brutal men. And Edred was no different from any of them. To show them he meant business, he burned the town of Ripon in North Yorkshire to the ground. But on his way home, feeling well satisfied with himself, the Northumbrians retaliated from his rear at Castleford and once again, he was forced to react. Infuriated at their audacity, Edred replied by attacking them again as well as imprisoning the Archbishop and killing the abbot of Thetford before heading back home again.

Eric Bloodaxe's grip had been somewhat tenuous to start with but it looked like the tide had turned when five kings from the Hebrides and two earls from Orkney joined up with him to rampage through the north.

And he almost succeeded. The raids only came to an abrupt end at Stainmore in 954 AD where he met another Viking by the name of Maccus who was acting, at least partially, on behalf of Edred who was using the long-established tactic of setting one Viking leader against another. After a lengthy battle, Eric Bloodaxe was killed and the fighting in Northumbria suddenly ended.

Edred's reign spanned for nine years and for most of it, he suffered from the same persistent digestive illness as his grandfather, Alfred the Great. In his final years, he sucked out the juices of his food, chewed on what was left and spat it out. The disease would eventually kill him.

By the time he died in 955 AD at 32 years of age, his nephew Edwig was chomping at the bit to sit on the throne. This handsome young man was the eldest of King Edmund's two sons, and at 14, he was confident and active.

The inheritance that had passed on to him from Alfred the Great and Athelstan came intact and well established and it was fortunate that it did because Edwig was very adept at alienating almost everyone he came into contact with. His reign was long enough for him to acquire a bad reputation but not long enough for him to redeem it. His uncontrollable rages ripped all reason out of his mind and turned him into a child of the devil.

Edwig's short reign of barely four years got off to a shaky start when, after his coronation at Kingston-on-Thames, he quickly absented himself from the subsequent celebratory feast. The gathering of nobles and ecclesiastics were affronted by this break with accepted protocol and Archbishop Oda sent Dunstan, the Abbot of Glastonbury, together with the Bishop of Lichfield, to find out where the new king had disappeared to. Dunstan discovered Edwig in his private apartments in flagranté delicto with not only his distant cousin Aelfgith, but also her beautiful mother, Aethelgith.

As you can imagine, the ecclesiastics were absolutely horrified. Dunstan immediately ripped the bedclothes from the startled naked threesome and dragged Edwig away to fulfil his Royal obligations.

Edwig never forgave him. He waited eighteen months, until he was sixteen, to defiantly marry Aelfgith against everyone's recommendations. As expected, it did not endear him to the ecclesiastics, in particular Dunstan.

The influence of the unpopular queen and her designing mother appears to have been considerable as soon afterward, the Mercians and Northumbrians organised a revolt against all three of them. Their plan was to place Edwig's 14-year-old brother, Edgar, on the throne as the new king while Edwig would only be allowed to retain Wessex.

Needless to say, tempers flared and Edwig stoically refused to either step down or be pushed aside by his younger brother. The throne was his and he intended to keep it.

But his temper was not the only thing the nobles were worried about. Keeping in mind Edwig's rather insatiable sexual appetite, questions were being asked regarding the possibility of an heir with royal blood from both parents, however distant the connection. It seems *that* little problem was uppermost in everyone's minds, especially with the tendencies Edwig had already displayed. Without having to be asked twice, the church annulled the marriage on the grounds that the couple were related by blood.

Still Edwig refused to listen.

It would seem that British nobles had had enough of his 'push and shove' tactics and they took matters into their own hands. On 18th October 959, Edwig died under 'suspicious circumstances'.

The English people had endured much in the past hundred years with invasions and internal wars but to top it off, they had endured three rulers in twenty years. England's only hope lay with Edwig's young brother, 16-year-old Edgar.

As with most predecessors of the House of Wessex, Edgar was less than five feet tall and very small of build. He was however devilishly handsome and charismatic, as his many mistresses would have confirmed. There is a record that at a banquet at Chester, the current King of Scots, commented jokingly that it seemed extraordinary to him how so many provinces *"should be held by such a sorry little fellow"*.

Although Edgar was not a particularly peaceable man, his reign was a peaceful one. England was at its height and was unified enough that it was unlikely to regress back to a divided kingdom as it had under Edred's reign.

Like his brother, Edgar's sexual appetite became legendary and it was widely known that he was by no means monogamous. During his first marriage, Edgar seduced a young nun from Wilton Abbey in Wiltshire by physically carrying her off to Kent where their extended affair led to the birth of a daughter. This was the biggest scandal of the times especially since Edgar was still married to Ethelflaed who was sitting at home patiently waiting for him.

And then a son magically appeared and a cover up began. This little boy was a very precious child since Ethelflaed had not been able to fall pregnant up to then and a legitimate male heir was essential to the royal line's continuance.

Some stories tell us that the young nun was in actual fact the baby's mother while others state the mother was definitely Ethelflaed, although she had somehow failed to show any signs of a pregnancy. This confusion would play over and over in the very near future. If anyone could have given us a glimpse of the truth, it was Edgar. But he wasn't telling.

In any case, the nun disappeared from the scene and our story continues to when Edgar heard of another great beauty, Elfrida, a woman of 'tarnished' reputation. His plan was to divorce Ethelflaed so he could marry Elfrida but he was persuaded not to make such a hasty decision by Ethelwald, an Ealdorman from East Anglia.

Rather foolishly, I would think, and not considering the actions of past royal generations, Ethelwald found her so stunning that he promptly married her himself and settled down to a family life in distant Devon.

Hearing that Ethelwald had married, but not to whom, Edgar insisted the newly-weds visit him at Court to celebrate their nuptials. As you can imagine, when the pair walked in together, Edgar was livid.

It would seem that Edgar thought long and hard about his next move. With his brother's past actions still vivid in his mind, he had to be careful. His plan was to invite Ethelwald to join him on a hunting trip in Harewood Forest to discuss the matter. And rather stupidly, I would think, Ethelwald accepted the invitation.

This grave mistake earned him a wayward javelin in his back.

Historians can only presume that Ethelflaed had died in the meantime because by then, she had disappeared without a trace. Her disappearance was rather timely because it allowed Edgar to do what he had thought to do in the first place. He married Elfrida himself.

With Edgar's help, the 10th century in English history produced an increase in English fortunes as it slowly stepped out of the Dark Ages. Shires were reorganised, each with its own sheriff who was a royal officer directly responsible to the Crown. A beginning of native English literature began and although slow at the beginning, England advanced quickly with contact to the Continent.

All in all, it was a quiet time for England, earning Edgar the title of Edgar the Peaceful. Under his rule, squabbles between different houses diminished and his dynasty was firmly established. Highly conscious of the importance of sea power, Edgar built up a navy of 3,600 ships by the time of his death, which were used to guard England's shores from the invasions of the Danes.

Edgar died suddenly at only 32 years of age by all accounts of a natural death at the summit of his power. As both of his uncles had died from a terrible digestive illness, it would seem likely that he had succumbed as well.

His actual plans for succession can only be conjecture, as he died still a young man leaving two sons, neither yet an adult, and taking the secret of his first son's birth with him to the grave. When Edgar died in 975 AD, his eldest son Edward was almost thirteen and his half-brother Ethelred was probably only nine.

But the decision of succession to the throne was not to be so cut and dried. The contradictions regarding the identity of Edward's mother still continued and in the foreseeable future, it would cause more violence than anyone could ever imagine. As a consequence, Edgar's reign was to be the last of peace and harmony in the Anglo-Saxon world for many generations and from his death until the Norman Conquest a hundred years later, there was not one single succession to the throne that was not hotly contested.

Perhaps it was in his genes but 13-year-old Edward was a terror. He was full of adolescent attitude and prone to violent and uncontrollable fits of ferocious temper, much like his uncle Edwig. Many high-ranking officials were shocked by his behaviour and language and as a result, they refused to accept Edward as Edgar's legitimate heir. Anyone was better than this little upstart.

So while some supported Edward's claim, others supported his younger brother Ethelred, using the question of Edward's illegitimacy as their excuse to be rid of him.

It was at this stage that Archbishop Dunstan intervened and persuaded everybody to back off, although for a time it almost looked as if there might be civil war. Dunstan's power was remarkable and with his support,

Edward's supporters were successful and the throne was allowed to pass to the fiery boy because of a lack of evidence to either prove or disprove his legitimacy.

In earlier days, a king was judged by his warriors as fit to lead in battle. If the same was said for the right to sit on the throne then neither of the princes would have been a worthy king and the government would have looked beyond the House of Alfred the Great for their new ruler. But no one was prepared to go that far and if anyone had entertained such ideas, they were certainly smart enough not to voice their opinions. What had been seen as high-spirits of a young prince was now seen as tyrannical bullying by a king and many men preferred to absent themselves from court, taking their wives and daughters with them, away from the lust of Edward.

As many times in the future, Edward's reign began ominously when a brilliant comet flashed red and gold across the skies of London and to those uneducated superstitious people, it was seen as a sure sign of change in the future. Everyone prayed for a good change after what they had endured for the past twenty years. When a famine soon followed, people began to grow nervous.

Far from being thankful or even overawed by the Archbishop for his support after his father's death, Edward dismissed Dunstan to Canterbury and declared he'd do things his own way, thank you anyway.

The kingdom could only stand by and watch as the young boy mishandled his inheritance without the solid guidance of Dunstan. But far from improving, he went from bad to worse and we begin to see Edward's stepmother step into the picture.

Elfrida was beautiful, there's no doubt about it, and she was still not much more than 30 years old even though she'd buried two powerful husbands by then. She fascinated everyone with her strange intensity and many knew that beneath the appearance of the dutiful, charitable and a loving supporter of the church was an ambitious schemer with the viciousness of an alley cat. Her sole interest was putting her only son, Ethelred, on the throne.

Elfrida hated Edward and she had seethed when he had been elevated to the throne, not only because of his viscous temper that made him feared by most of the court, but because he had been elected king when she had hoped her own son, Ethelred, would take the throne.

However safe she felt in her home at Corfe, she knew she lacked any power to resist Edward. She also knew that whatever his father had given to her, it could easily be taken away by Edward and she could be driven into a nunnery at his will to end her days. As a consequence, she was more than a little afraid of her stepson.

And so Elfrida was tempted on to a very dangerous path. A sudden end to Edward's reign would remove all difficulties and her son would be crowned king. After all, Anglo-Saxon kings had a habit of dying suddenly.

Dawn brought a cold, grey harsh light that March morning and the Palace of Corfe, in Dorset, where Elfrida and Ethelred were staying, was never the most welcoming of places. That bleak morning, as fog drifted through the trees, Edward was hunting nearby. He had been riding too fast and his horse had already stumbled on half buried roots a few times. Being weary and thirsty, Edward turned away from his hunting party and rode off to drop in on his stepmother and half-brother to take a rest.

Elfrida saw him emerge out of the mist as the autumn leaves fell softly from the trees.

There is a point of no return in most stories where the characters have made their way on stage and the drama is unfolding. Elfrida's entrance in history is well known but up to then, she had only been quietly present. As she watched Edward approach, she realised it was now or never. With Edward being alone, the opportunity and timing was perfect. She had come this far and there was no going back.

When he rode up to the palace gates, Elfrida must have been shaking with nervousness and anxiety. It was one thing to plan a murder but it was another thing to actually put that plan into action, especially when the success of the plan not only depended on her own ability but on one of her trusted servants. She had already chosen her most loyal servant and he had agreed to do whatever she requested. Knowing the consequences for both her son and herself, it was a huge undertaking when at any time, anything could go wrong.

Bracing herself, she sent Ethelred inside and away from his half-brother so he could not see what was happening. Then she put a smile on her face and greeted Edward with a kiss on his cheek.

It turned out to be a Judas kiss. Without dismounting, Edward asked his stepmother for a drink. Elfrida sent her servant inside for a cup of wine and the exhausted Edward drank eagerly. But as he drank, Elfrida gave a sign to the servant, who stepped forward and drew his dagger. Before Edward knew what was happening, he had been stabbed in the back.

Edward cried out in pain, but managed to set his spurs to his horse in an attempt to escape to the safety of his comrades. In agony, he slipped off with his leg caught in the stirrup and he was dragged along behind the horse. The combination of the knife-wound and inflicted head injuries killed him.

Edward had disappeared from her sight after the stabbing but Elfrida would have been stupid not to know the result. And she was anything but stupid. As he disappeared from sight, she sent her men out to follow the bloody trail and retrieve the body before others in the hunting party became aware of his absence.

Edward's body was, at first, hidden and then hurriedly buried in an attempt to hush up the murder. She had his body buried in Wareham Priory and sent word to Dunstan that her servants had found Edward's dead body and because of the heat, she was forced to bury it.

Anybody would have seen holes in this story. While some were highly suspicious, many were angry that his family were not avenging him and had not arranged a more honourable burial for him. While Edward's body was dug up and given a more befitting burial in consecrated grounds in Shaftes-bury Abbey, no one truly believed in their hearts that Elfrida was blameless. They knew how much she hated Edward but could she actually stoop so low as to murder her stepson?

If Elfrida thought that Edward's death would resolve the power struggle, she was sadly mistaken. It was well over a year later that Ethelred was finally crowned due to the suspicious circumstances of his brother's death. Eventually, everyone realised that there was quite literally no one else left and Ethelred was the only person who could realistically and legally become king. His accession was inevitable no matter how shady the lead up was.

England, so magnificent in stress and danger, so invincible under valiant leadership, now saw another child, a timid 13-year-old succeed to the throne of England. It was to be a momentous era in English history.

At the time, when his mother had ordered Edward's murder, Ethelred had been unaware of his mother's plot even though he had little regard for his half-brother. There had been times when Edward had laughed at Ethelred who didn't join in with his drinking or womanising and Ethelred had left the festivities in abject humiliation. So the fact that his brother was dead would not have caused him a great deal of anguish. In fact, he would have been a little relieved and quietly elated at the unexpected rise in his situation.

Ethelred's epithet, commonly said to be 'Unready,' dates from sometime after his reign. It has nothing to do with being ill-prepared, but means 'Ill-Advised'; a name for which he was well suited. It was a punning name, a kind of play on words that the Anglo-Saxons loved, so that he became King Aethelred Unraed, King Noble Counsel Lousy Counsel.

During his teenage years, his mother went along with Bishop Aethelwold and Ealdorman Aelfhere who guided him. However, when these last two died, new influences came into play, and you guessed it: a woman. Aelfgitha was a distant cousin and the daughter of Ealdorman Thored of Northumbria. She was beautiful and scheming and Ethelred was smitten.

Elfrida could see the writing on the wall. She had enjoyed her place in court as the king's mother but that would soon come to an end if the strong-willed young woman stepped into the picture. As much as she tried to dissuade Ethelred against the marriage, he was determined to have her and two years later, Aelfgitha was his wife.

As Elfrida had expected, with Ethelred's forceful young bride settling in nicely, she was forced to withdraw from his court. With his happy bride by his side, Ethelred then turned his thoughts to the great task of converting the Danish settlers and repairing the damage of previous invasions.

With his mind fully occupied, greedy counsellors had plenty of time to plot. It had been an easy task to persuade Ethelred, logical to him at the time as well, to confiscate lands from the Danes and redistribute them amongst his loyal and faithful barons. As greedy hands went out, things began to heat up.

While much of the Dark Ages of Europe had been shaped by the civilisation of Rome, the Vikings in Scandinavia were a unique culture not exposed to things like written law, life in towns or even belief in a Christian God. It's not just what they did or thought but what they believed in. The Vikings gave us a part of our DNA that is wild and mysterious. But back in Denmark, things were beginning to change.

A Viking by the name of Harald Bluetooth had converted to Christianity and the focus of Valhalla shifted to a fear of the afterlife. But just because Harald had been converted to Christianity didn't stop Harald from seeing everything that was happening in England and wanting a piece of the action. He knew that the Britons had established 70 mints throughout England and were minting silver coins and he knew that England had a sophisticated and well-organised tax collection system. Unfortunately for Harald, Denmark had neither. He also didn't see a need to bother changing Denmark's system when he had a neighbour who could do it so very well for him. His intention was to head off to England and exert his authority. But around 986 AD, things changed dramatically for Harald.

Harald's son, Sweyn, was born a buccaneer and indulged by his father. From very early in his life, his father could see that Sweyn was smart and he encouraged him to watch and learn everything, which he did with amazing ability. As he soaked up knowledge, Palnatoke, a Jomsborg Viking who was a staunch pagan, enters the story.

Palnatoke was out for revenge against Harald for killing his grandfather but Sweyn's story is more basic. He just wanted to be ruler and he wasn't prepared to wait until his father died. Together, the two young men waged war against Harald. Palnatoke had willing soldiers ready to fight and Sweyn had the determination to be King of Denmark. Together they saw them-selves as invincible.

For six years, battles raged until finally, Harald was killed. Sweyn, now called Sweyn Forkbeard because of his long cleft beard, fired up the long boats and headed off to England to get a share of the action for himself.

Meanwhile, wave after wave of ships carrying marauders from all parts of Scandinavia and Ireland were already entering England and Ethelred couldn't keep up with their demands. He tried to resolve his Viking problem by paying off some of these pirates with gold and giving them property in England. And he wasn't the first to have done this. In an earlier century, after long years of battling the Viking plague, Alfred the Great had made treaties with his enemies, granting them land in northern England around York. A century later, the folk in Northumbria still followed Danish laws and language, even though Ethelred appointed their political and religious leaders for them.

Ethelred had no idea how to stop the invaders. He had begun paying the invaders £10,000 in the hope that they would leave but instead, within two years, Viking attacks grew worse despite further payments of £16,000 and £24,000. It seemed that the more he paid, the more they wanted.

Unfortunately for Ethelred, one of the Danish leaders who was taking some of the coin for himself was a man named Pallig whose wife just happened to be the half-sister of Sweyn.

When Sweyn arrived in England, his brother-in-law, who should have actually defended his new English home against this Danish threat, gathered men and ships and joined in the pillaging and burning.

Who can say what motivated him? Did Sweyn call on kinship to persuade Pallig to his side? Were Pallig's shipmen surly and combative, in need of some more strenuous occupation than farming? Was he just bored? Or was it merely a case of once a thief, always a thief?

Ethelred must have decided that it was the latter, because even though he eventually bribed Sweyn to depart and then bribed Pallig (again), to go back to his own estates, Ethelred apparently began laying more involved plans of his own. He'd finally had enough. In Anglo-Saxon England – as in most of the medieval world – the game of thrones was a deadly serious one.

It was at this time, after eleven children, that Ethelred's wife died. Ready to remarry for a second time, he chose Lady Emma, the sister of Duke Richard II of Normandy, as his bride. His plan was to draw the Duke away from his Viking allies, who were using Normandy as a base from which to attack England. And of course, Emma was very pleasing on the eye.

It was a well thought out plan, and so successful that it made Ethelred feel secure enough that one year later, he put his plan into action to rid England of the Vikings once and for all. It was to be a serious mistake.

Friday 13th November 1002 was one of the most infamous events of English history and it would prove to be an unlucky day if you were a Dane in England. This drastic step was not taken on a whim, but was the product of 200 years of Anglo-Saxon frustration and fear. Vikings, who had long plagued the Isles with raids and wars, had taken over the north and were settling in permanently. Ethelred felt he knew beyond a shadow of a doubt that they were growing stronger in the north and that they had designs on his southern realm as well.

In actual fact, these were people whose families had lived in England for generations and who regarded themselves as English. They had worked hard and they had made a life for themselves in England.

But they stood out from society and every one of them became a target. Ethelred was convinced that the Danes had sprung up in England *"like cockles amongst the wheat"* and they should be exterminated.

And that's exactly what he did. They were butchered while they ran into a church seeking sanctuary and refuge.

The story of the St Brice's Day Massacre has been told again and again in English history, written two years after the event, and there is no question that the massacre turned out to be a spectacular example of lousy advice born out of fear and desperation.

It's doubtful that the killings were intended to reach into the long-settled region of the Danelaw where residents of Scandinavian descent probably outnumbered those whose bloodlines were Anglo-Saxon. The population targeted for execution would most likely have been more recent arrivals in the south and west, for example shiploads of young warriors who were troublemakers and who considered themselves outside the law.

Pallig was certainly among the victims, as were his wife and young son. 11th century collateral damage. And while it is impossible to know exactly how many were executed that day, we know this much: it did not accomplish the result that Ethelred intended. It was meant to preserve his kingdom from the hands of the Danes but it did just the opposite. And Ethelred knew it. He knew that Sweyn Forkbeard would try to avenge his family's deaths as every Viking before him had done with terrifying precision and planning. And he was right.

The Viking attacks kicked in and continued with a vengeance. No longer were the savage attacks random with the aim of accumulating wealth at the expense of the English. They were motivated by the dual goals of revenge and the complete annihilation of England.

Ethelred put all his efforts into beating back his enemies before they even reached English shores but unfortunately, another huge Viking army led by Thorkell the Tall, struck and the Norsemen ravaged most of Southern England for the next three years. Before he could regroup, Ulfkell Snilling attacked as well and Ethelred was totally overwhelmed.

Snilling attacked and ransacked Canterbury, kidnapping and then murdering the Archbishop, and Ethelred was frantic. After all, he knew Sweyn Forkbeard was still coming and he had every right to be scared.

Desperately, he resorted once more to paying the Vikings to stop. But with one important condition. He would pay them £48,000 if they would offer their services to him and him alone to fight against Sweyn Forkbeard.

Finally, in August 1013, Sweyn Forkbeard and his son Canute landed at the mouth of the Humber. Even with his paid help, Ethelred was still failing to hold back Sweyn's vast army as they ransacked, raped and murdered their way through the North.

It was a brutal time and Sweyn was not one for mercy. He burned women alive, children were impaled on lances and men died suspended from their private parts. But really, he was no different from Ethelred, who was guilty of very similar atrocities, which had started the whole situation in the first place.

Beyond Watling Street, a major Roman road that crossed the River Thames in London and linked it to Dover, Sweyn and Canute began to ravage the countryside to such an extent that East Anglia and Wessex soon followed the Northern example and quickly submitted. Unhindered, they continued on through Oxford, took hostages, and then went on to Winchester before travelling further south on to London itself.

Ethelred & Thorkell managed to hold out for a while only because Sweyn turned his attention to Mercia. It gave Ethelred the opportunity to send Emma and their children to her brother in Normandy to escape the invasion while he himself fled to the Isle of Wight.

By Christmas 1013, Sweyn simply took over England unopposed.

Sweyn had only just begun his rule. He had only just started the process of organising his new kingdom and finding trusted and worthy supporters. Five weeks into his reign, on 2nd February, he was murdered.

His death leaves many unanswered questions but above all was the question, who killed him only forty days after his accession?

One whimsical story is that the ghost of St Edmund, who was himself killed by Sweyn's Viking predecessors, murdered him. This ghost is said to have risen from the grave in the dead of night during Candlemas and killed him. The only problem with that theory is that ghosts can't hold axes.

A grave dug up at Roskilde Cathedral on the site of an old church where Sweyn is thought to have been buried may hold the secret of *how* he died but not who killed him, although we can all hazard a guess. When discovered, the grave held a skeleton of a large man with a sizeable portion of the skull removed. No ghost had done that.

The English nobles quickly sent word to Ethelred in the Isle of Wight, seizing the rather opportune moment of Sweyn's death to rid themselves of his equally brutal son Canute. In their letter to Ethelred, the nobles declared *"no lord was dearer to them than their rightful lord, if only he would govern his kingdom more justly than he had done in the past"*. It would seem that a weak king was by far better than a savage one.

Ethelred sent his reply: he *"would remedy each one of the things that they all abhorred"* and it was a triumphant return for Ethelred as he once again resumed the throne. With the sword of Damocles swinging towards him, Canute beat a hasty retreat back to Denmark.

But in all this glory, family squabbles led to Ethelred's final downfall as he began deciding who would be his heir.

By his first wife, Ethelred had a very large family, with a total of eleven children, and by his second marriage to Emma of Normandy there were three children. The grand total was fourteen children, and there were more than a few who were desperate for a piece of the action. It was an incredibly messy period in history.

Ethelred's eldest son, Athelstan, by his first wife had long been recognised as heir apparent, and evidence shows that Edward, the eldest son of Emma, ranked well and truly far behind all Ethelred's sons by his first marriage. However that all changed when Athelstan suddenly and unexpectedly died and Edmund, the next eldest son from Ethelred's first marriage, was the new heir apparent. It seems the Anglo-Saxon kings had a habit of dying rather unexpectedly.

But things were not going too smoothly for Edmund either. For some time, Edmund seems to have been alarmed by Emma's efforts to persuade Ethelred to name their 10-year-old son Edward as the heir apparent instead of Edmund. The following year, when Ethelred ordered the murder of the leading Northern barons, Edmund made his own play for power by marrying a deceased baron's widow.

It turned out that Edmund had every right to mistrust Emma. When Ethelred heard of the marriage, he was furious and Emma upped the ante. It was obvious, she argued, that Edmund could not be trusted.

It had been two years since Canute had left and returned to Denmark and a lot had happened in England since then. While everyone squabbled in England over who would succeed to the throne, even though Ethelred was still very much alive by the way, Canute had kept his eye firmly on the English throne. Finally, in 1015, he was ready to return.

On a bleak day in winter, as Canute landed with 200 ships and 10,000 men, English loyalty was still bitterly divided over who should lead them. The South rallied to Ethelred's right-hand-man and brother-in-law, Eadric Streona, while the North supported Edmund. By then, he was being called Edmund Ironside and his father Ethelred was an ill man.

Unfortunately, reconciliation between Ethelred and Edmund came too late to salvage the situation and Ethelred died before the war with the Vikings ended. Emma, however, was not to be quickly forgotten.

England's new king, now called Edmund Ironside, was altogether a different character to his weak and indecisive father and a new chapter in English history was about to begin as Edmund took over the throne and put up a heroic and fearless stand against the Viking invaders. By the new year, they had advanced into Mercia, plundering, burning and slaying all they met along the way. Hastily, Edmund begged for aid from the Londoners and between April through to November, fought as many as five major battles.

Unfortunately for Emma's son Edward, it would be his trusted earl, Eadric Streona, who would betray him and defect to Edmund's side.

In the end, it hadn't mattered. During the decisive Battle of Ashingdon, Eadric Streona fled the field with his men at the height of the battle, leaving Edmund's army depleted and in confusion.

With no time to lick his wounds, Edmund faced Canute in Gloucester-shire and challenged him to fight him in single combat. The Danish king, arguing that Edmund's great size and strength made it an unfair competition, politely declined and suggested instead that they should simply partition the kingdom between the two of them. His suggestion was that Edmund would retain Wessex, Essex, East Anglia and London while he took control of the north.

This should have sent bells clanging madly in Edmund's head as Canute himself was a very intimidating man. Not just that, but he had already defeated Edmund at Ashingdon, so realistically, most of the kingdom was already his anyway.

No one will ever know why Edmund accepted the deal. Perhaps it was because it came with a tempting caveat. The arrangement would only remain in force until the death of one of the participants of the treaty, at which time all lands would revert to the survivor.

Haven't we heard this before?

And sure enough, barely one week later, Edmund Ironside, at the age of 22, was dead.

Stories about the speedy and undoubtedly convenient nature of his death soon generated some gruesome accounts of a sticky demise at the hands of Canute.

Many historians pass almost hazily over the precise method employed, but Henry of Huntingdon, writing in the 1120s, was not so coy. His version of events states:

'KING EDMUND WAS TREACHEROUSLY SLAIN a few days afterwards. Thus it happened: one night, this great and powerful king having occasion to retire to the house for receiving the calls of nature, the son of the Ealdorman Eadric Streona, by his father's contrivance, concealed himself in the pit, and stabbed the king twice from beneath with a sharp dagger, and, leaving the weapon fixed in his bowels, made his escape.'

THERE ARE PLENTY OF PROBLEMS, it must be said, with this story as it stands. For one, in the dark, how could the killer be sure that the posterior he was stabbing was the king's? For another, could he have got close enough to use a dagger? Cesspits, after all, were often deep, and the drops to them long, and at least two variant accounts wordlessly address this problem. The first suggests that the assassin employed a spear rather than a dagger; the second, by the French chronicler Gaimar, reports that the murder was carried out by the diabolical contrivance of a 'spring-bow' – a deadly sort of booby trap consisting of a loaded crossbow that could be triggered by pressure as the king sat on his...eh...throne and was known to the French as *li ars qui ne fault,* or *"the bow that does not fail."*

According to this account (it is a late one, dating to about 1137), Edmund was shown into a privy rigged with *"a drawn bow with the string attached to the seat, so that when the king sat on it the arrow was released and entered his fundament."*

The truth, it is safe to say, will never be known. Several modern historians stress that no contemporary source mentions murder, and conclude that Edmund merely died of natural causes. This may be true, of course. Who knows what wounds the king may have picked up in the course of his battles? But the timing of Edmund Ironside's death remains highly suspicious, and I personally have always thought that it pointed to murder more likely than not, especially when it is remembered that Canute was far from averse to the odd assassination or two. After all, one year later in 1017, Canute had the treacherous Eadric Streona put to death at a Christmas feast.

But with the sudden and rather timely death of Edmund Ironside, the climax of the Viking invasion had now been reached, and Canute became the new King of England.

Hardly anything is known of Canute's life until he was part of the force that overthrew Edmund. He was the typical Viking of the time – tall, strong and handsome with a fair complexion and a fine, thick head of hair. His only flaw was his nose, which was long and hooked.

In those days, there were three principles upon which sovereignty could be determined. Hereditary right, which none could really dispute. Election, which was always dicey. And then there was conquest – Canute's strong-point. It was also the time when Emma of Normandy was to reappear on the scene.

In July 1017, Canute was quick to eliminate any prospective challenge from the survivors of the legitimate dynasty and his first actions were ruthless. The first year of his reign was marked with executions of a number of English noblemen whom he considered suspect. Ethelred's son from his second marriage fled from England but was killed on Canute's orders. Edmund Ironside's two sons, Edward and Edmund, both fled abroad as well, with Edward fleeing to Hungary.

The figure of Emma, sister of Robert of Normandy, looms large in English history especially when Ethelred married her to create a blood-tie with the most vigorous military state in Europe. Little is known of her but in fact, Emma will be remembered for having had two husbands who were Kings of England and two sons who would be future Kings of England. But more importantly, she had a feisty nephew we will see very soon.

From the moment Canute saw Emma, he had designs of his own.

To give Emma a little credit, she held out against Canute for a short while. Remember Canute had been trying to rid himself of rival claimants including Emma's brother, Richard Duke of Normandy and that little point would have weighed well and truly on her mind. So when Canute offered to spare her children's lives if they hightailed it to their relative in Normandy in exchange for her hand in marriage, there was really no question of what she was going to do. She readily agreed.

In researching Canute, it seems that he was not the brute that everyone envisages in their minds. Canute ruled England for twenty years where he dealt intelligently with situations and always acted with acute political sense. Despite his shaky start, he was a firm leader, renowned not only for his calculated actions to win support but for his attempts at reconciling the English and the Danes. He had three sons, Harold Harefoot and Sweyn by a former wife Elfgifu, and one son Harthacanute by Emma.

But for all the energy Canute put in to uniting England, when he died in 1035, his empire began to crumble. Even before Canute was buried, his sons began fighting.

Canute's children were ignorant and coarse Vikings and on his death, many believed that even though he had left his son Sweyn to rule Norway while both Harold and Harthacanute ruled jointly in England, most nobles believed that the rightful heirs to the English throne were in reality the sons of Ethelred and Emma. And Ethelred's eldest son Alfred wholeheartedly agreed with them.

From Normandy, Alfred was making plans to return to England ostensibly to visit his once-again widowed mother, Emma. Assuredly, his thoughts were with gaining support in order to claim back the throne. After all, he *was* the eldest son of Ethelred and he had a solid right to be the heir, (if you excluded the two sons of Edmund Ironside, both exiled in Europe).

At the same time as things were unravelling in England, Magnus I, a son of a former king of Norway, became hell-bent on claiming the throne of Denmark after hearing that Canute was dead. In a panic, Sweyn called for help from Harthacanute to try and keep Magnus out of their homeland.

Even though Harthacanute did not want to leave England in his elder half-brother's hands, he knew he had two choices. It was either remain in England with Harold or return to Norway to help Sweyn. The whole situation solved itself at Oxford when it was decided that Harold should have all the country north of the Thames with London as its capital and Hartha-canute could have the south - on his return. With the quarrel sorted, Harthacanute left for Norway with the understanding that Harold would only be the regent in his temporary absence.

That's not how Harold saw it.

At this time, Godwin, Earl of Wessex, was the leader of the Danish party in England and he was beginning to flex his own muscles. He could trace his own lineage back to Ethelred I in 871 (surely that counted, right?) and he had sons of his own to think about. Initially, Harold's chief supporter was Leofric, Earl of Mercia and the opposition was Godwin of Wessex. Being a smart man and knowing that the numbers were against him, Godwin soon realised if he wanted to have any influence in government at all, his best interests lay with Harold Harefoot. So Godwin switched sides.

Harold must have felt he had found a kindred spirit in Godwin as very soon, they both began to devise a plan that would exclude both Alfred and Harthacanute from the throne.

Without being aware of any danger, Alfred landed on the coast of Kent and was welcomed by Godwin. When they approached the town of Guild-ford on their way to Surrey, they stopped for the night after the long march. With food and wine in their bellies, all proceeded happily to bed.

The next morning, Alfred was woken early by the sound of confused voices as his men were dragged outside and lined up, one by one, He was forced to watch as they were tortured and murdered then he too was stripped naked, tied to a horse and led to the Isle of Ely, where he was then blinded with a hot iron. Needless to say, he died soon after from his injuries.

With the succession simplified, Harold claimed the throne of England for himself and promptly told Emma to leave England immediately. With one son dead at Harold's hands, she didn't wait to be told twice. She left for Bruges on the next ship.

Maybe the cruelty of the Vikings had scared the population in the past but the fact that Harold had no real blood-line to the English throne did not seem to make too much of a difference to most people. Within two years, Harold was generally accepted as the king. Except by Godwin, whose boys were growing up fast and restless for power.

In Norway, angered and horrified at the treatment of his mother Emma and the murder of his half-brother Alfred, Harthacanute gathered together a force of 62 warships to forcefully assert his claim, demand revenge and snatch his throne back. He was taking no chances with his half-brother and he was arriving as a conqueror with a full invasion force.

Unfortunately for Harthacanute, he was to be denied his revenge, as Harold died 'unexpectedly' at the age of 24. The cause of Harold's death is uncertain but while Harold lay dying in Sandwich, a monk reported that Harold grew black as they spoke and the word 'poison' was thrown around. Harold was only one of several youthful kings to die 'unexpectedly' following short reigns. And he would not be the last.

Harold's short reign was considered quite peaceful as nothing remarkable happened during his four and a half years. Still, he died little regretted or esteemed by his subjects and was buried before Harthacanute even landed on English soil.

But things were going to change very soon.

When Harthacanute arrived back in England with his mother Emma, his first action was to have Godwin arrested knowing that Godwin was responsible for Alfred's death. During his trial where he was being tried for murder, Godwin's only defence was that he was merely carrying out the order from Harold himself. After giving a generous gift to Harthacanute, a richly decorated ship with a figurehead of solid gold with a crew of eighty armed men, the charges were suddenly dropped and Godwin escaped punishment and resumed duties as normal.

Harthacanute's second task was to have Harold's body exhumed, publicly decapitated and then thrown into a sewer. A little excessive with a touch of overkill but there you have it.

Harthacanute had always been a quarrelsome man and being king seemed to bring out the worst in him. He spent most of his time ranting, persecuting and murdering the supporters of his half-brother Harold and was very successful at intimidating his subjects throughout his short reign. In that time, he doubled the size of the English fleet from sixteen to thirty-two in case he had to deal with other invaders in his empire. To pay for this huge expense, he increased the taxes like every self-respecting king had done in the past, which unfortunately for England, coincided in a year when the harvests were poor. During one of a string of serious riots that popped up, a tax collector was killed. Harthacanute reacted by having his earls burn the town to the ground and kill the population. Overkill again.

With the influence of Emma, Harthacanute invited his half-brother, nicknamed Edward the Confessor, back to England from exile and the three family members were once again reunited.

It was two years later again, on a bright sunny day in June 1042, that Harthacanute, Emma and Edward attended a wedding in Lambeth. The groom was a standard bearer to his father and the bride was a courtier. After drinking large amounts of wine and raising a glass to toast the bride, Harthacanute suddenly fell to the ground and died at 24 years of age. A dangerous age, it seems, if you were a Viking.

Now there are accidental deaths and there are *accidental* deaths, if you know what I mean. And by the looks of it, the male descendants of the House of Normandy had a nasty habit of dying suddenly from unexplained causes. So here's something else to consider. In 1027, Richard III Duke of Normandy, died without apparent cause. In 1035, Richard's brother Robert died suddenly after returning from a pilgrimage to Jerusalem and in 1040, their cousin Alan II Duke of Brittany died of unexplained causes. In all of these cases, no one knew the reason. The one thing that is consistent though in every single case is the fact that it was sudden and unexpected. And of course, poison was suspected because it was a pretty fool proof, convenient and reliable way to get rid of someone you didn't want around, especially if you thought no one could find out.

Keeping that in mind, we should then look to see who would gain the most from Harthacanute's death and we have only one suspect - Emma's son Edward. Edward was the brother of Edmund Ironside, the younger son of Ethelred, the stepson of Canute, the stepbrother of Harold Harefoot and the half-brother of Harthacanute. Who was more deserving of the throne than he? Add all of that to the fact that he had recently married Edith, the daughter of Godwin, who was not shy at all about scheming his way into power. Godwin had already proven his ability when he and Harold Harefoot murdered Edward's brother, Alfred, five years earlier. And don't forget Harold died from suspected poisoning, too.

With Harthacanute out of the way, Edward's way to the throne was clear with his wife Edith Godwin by his side as queen and her father standing not too far behind. To make the case even stronger, in a few years' time, Godwin would also die 'unexpectedly' after dining with said son-in-law, again pointing the finger at Edward as the probable culprit behind both deaths. One other point I would like to make is that, while not accusing Edward of any of the deaths in Normandy, he was possibly present, certainly close nearby, at every single one of them.

In any case, Harthacanute was dead and there was no shortage of discontented candidates to choose from.

With a touch of irony, Sweyn's descendants, through his daughter Estrid, continue to rule Denmark to this very day and one of his descendants, in another period of history when fierce battles would rage and countless people would die, Margaret of Denmark would marry James III of Scotland. In a strange twist of fate, after James VI of Scotland inherited the English throne and become James 1 of England in 1603, Sweyn's ancestry would once again be introduced into the English royal bloodline and Danish blood would again become rulers of England.

But for now, The House of Wessex was to rule once more with Edward the Confessor, the seventh son of Ethelred the Unready and Emma of Normandy, the sister of Richard, Duke of Normandy.

While Canute had been king, Edward had spent a quarter of a century in exile in Normandy with his brothers Edred and Alfred. We remember Alfred's sad story and equally as sad is that Edred was to die in 1042 never to return to England.

Following the death of Harthacanute, Emma was rumoured to have thought of Magnus 1 of Norway as the next successor to the English throne, perhaps even as his wife, but shocked, Godwin of Wessex, the most powerful of the English earls, stepped in. He had great plans for his own son, another Harold, and his other five sons, not to mention his daughter who was now married to Edward.

Edward took a tenuous and shaky control of the throne. Strangely enough, since it was Emma who had influenced Harthacanute to have Edward returned to England, the first thing he did was to deprive his mother, Emma, of all of her estates and reduce her to relative poverty. Apparently Edward blamed her for his miserable and lonely childhood spent in exile while his mother lived in England in the lap of luxury with Canute. Complaining that his mother had done nothing to help him, he took three leading earls and rode to her property taking back treasures that he declared belonged to his father, King Ethelred, and which naturally now belonged to the present king. Himself.

Edward's position was weak when he came to the throne. Effective rule required keeping on good terms with leading earls, especially the House of Wessex, so his marriage to Edith had seemed a smart move at a time while Godwin had strengthened his own position by marrying Canute's former sister-in-law.

All accounts of Edward's wife Edith say that she was a gentle kind-hearted woman but from the first, Edward neglected her, much to the anger of Godwin and her six brothers. Not that Edward was too concerned. Having lived so long in Normandy, Edward much preferred the Normans to the English and soon began handing out positions to his Norman friends, which didn't help his relations with his wife's family. As they complained, he introduced Norman fashions and language and instead of marking documents with a cross as past Saxon kings had, he used a great seal that was a custom in Normandy. No one in England was happy and as the Godwin family's anger flared, their support grew, which meant that Edward's popularity diminished.

It all came to a head in 1049, eight years after Edward had come to the throne. Edward's sister had married Eustace, Earl of Boulogne, and the Earl had spent some time visiting his brother-in-law.

As Eustace prepared for departure and set off with his numerous attendants to begin the trip home from Dover, they entered the quiet town in full armour demanding that they be given the best accommodation, without payment of course, due to their royal connections. One innkeeper stood firmly in his doorway and refused admission. It all blew up rather quickly when the armed attendant struck the innkeeper, and he in turn, retaliated by killing the armed attendant.

Within minutes, word had spread to Count Eustace. In a temper, Eustace and his men galloped to the house, riding over women and children in the streets, surrounded the inn, and then killed the innkeeper.

Even in these harsh times, it was a brutal thing to do and the people of Dover were shocked. But they were also angry enough to react violently. In a state of absolute fury, they killed nineteen more attendants and wounded many more before blockading off the road to the port where the men were hoping to embark. With only a handful of attendants left and knowing he had no chance of winning the skirmish, Eustace beat a hasty retreat back to Edward to inform him of what had happened. He demanded that Edward intervene on his behalf and deal out justice. Furious now as well, Edward commanded Godwin to take reinforcements to Dover and kill the inhabitants who had slaughtered his brother-in-law's men.

It was the opportunity that Godwin had been waiting for. With his sons fully prepared to fight for their father, Godwin stood his ground and flatly refused Edward's command.

If Edward had been thinking rationally, he would have stopped to consider whether he should really intervene in his brother-in-law's fight. But he wasn't. He let all reason fly out the window and demanded that Godwin stand before the court, under pain of banishment and loss of titles and property, to answer for his disobedience. Again, Godwin refused.

Instead, he and his sons Harold and Sweyn raised as many fighting men as they could and demanded that Eustace surrender to the country to answer for what they had done. The king, in turn, gathered together his own men.

Edward's aggressive countermove worked. When seeing the size of Edward's army, Godwin went into panic mode. As fast as he could, he gathered together his possessions and beat a hasty retreat to Flanders while his sons barely escaped with their lives to Ireland. Unfortunately, his daughter Edith was left behind in the rush.

Edward was beside himself with anger and the fact that there was no one to take his anger out on only made it worse. But then he remembered Edith. He seized her jewellery and with only one attendant and barely any possessions, he sent her unceremoniously off to a convent. She had been a means to an end and he had no further use of her.

With Godwin and his family out of the way, Edward invited William Duke of Normandy, the son of the Robert Duke of Normandy, who Edward had lived with while in Normandy, to stay with him in England. William willingly accepted the invitation and with more and more Normans arriving at court, Edward's popularity hit an all-time low.

But while Godwin was hiding in Flanders, he hadn't been sitting on his hands. He was busy gathering an army together and when he was satisfied with the numbers he had, he sailed to the Isle of Wight to join up with his son Harold. Together they sailed up the Thames to the cheers of the English people ringing in their ears. Before Edward knew it, Godwin was at court, demanding that his possessions and titles be restored to him.

With the prospect of a civil war looming, Edward knew he had no choice but to do what Godwin demanded. What really irked him was that Godwin insisted, with the backing of the barons, that most of Edward's Norman friends, along with William of Normandy, were to be sent back home to France. Not just that but his daughter Edith was to be released from the convent, her jewels were to be returned to her and she was to be sitting in her chair of state, as was her rightful place.

Godwin was in heaven, but if he thought that Edward was going to let him just step in and take over, he was sadly mistaken. He should have taken the time to remember the string of Edward's relatives who had died suspiciously over the years. Even his father-in-law wasn't safe. At a dinner party held by Edward, Godwin had a fit and died days later. Once again, poison was suspected and once again Edward was lurking in the background. With that little problem out of the way, Edward settled comfortably into his throne unopposed.

There was no doubt that Edward was anxious about a successor. His wife Edith had not born any children due to Edward's vow of celibacy taken earlier on in their marriage. Add that to an ambiguous sexual orientation and you have brewing family squabbles ready to erupt yet again.

Edmund Ironside's son, Edward the Exile, had the best, perhaps only, claim to the throne. In 1057, the ageing Edward heard that his nephew Edward was alive and well, living in Hungary, and he summoned the young man to return back home to England. Edward the Exile offered the last chance of an undisputed succession within the Saxon royal house and Edward promptly declared him to be the heir to the throne when he died. Preparations were made and invitations were sent out and in no time, Edward the Exile was eagerly on his way back to England.

The journey took many months but as soon as he arrived he headed straight to see his uncle the king.

What happened next is very tragic. On his arrival at court, the Godwin boys blocked him from seeing his uncle with no explanation and two days later, he was dead.

The exact cause of Edward's death remains unclear, but of course, there is a strong possibility that he was murdered. Once again, by whom is not known, but he obviously had some powerful enemies. Keep in mind it was a period in time when Harold Godwinson's power was increasing and the old king, politically weak, was unable to make an effective stand against the steady advance of the powerful and ambitious Godwin boys. The question mark was always hovered over Harold's head.

What the Godwinsons didn't know was that following Edward, and arriving days later, was his wife, seventeen-year-old daughter Christina, twelve-year-old daughter Margaret and six-year-old son, Edgar.

Edgar the Outlaw, as he would later be called, was brought to the English court and given the title 'Aetheling' by the ageing king, meaning throne-worthy, which suggested Edgar was now considered to be the heir to the throne. The Godwinsons must have been furious.

Jump forward nine years and the year is 1066, a date remembered forever in history. Edward's death at the age of 62 set into motion a series of disastrous events that would change the history of England forever. At the tender age of fifteen, Edgar had no chance whatsoever against the powerful Harold Godwinson and Harold simply took over. But from across the channel, William Duke of Normandy was watching with his full attention focused on the English drama that was unfolding.

William's claim to the English throne was tenuous at best. He was the only son of Robert I, Duke of Normandy, illegitimate by the way, and also the grandnephew of the Emma of Normandy, wife of Ethelred the Unready and then of Canute. He could trace his ancestry back to Rollo the Viking and Rollo was no shrinking violet when it came to fighting. But as impressive as his CV was, there wasn't much in the way of bloodline and he certainly did not have it in the bag.

William argued that he also had the support of Emperor Henry and papal approval and that Edward had promised him the throne when he had visited him in London fourteen years ago in 1051. He also claimed that Harold had sworn to uphold his claim to the throne in 1064, (possibly since Edgar was only 13 years old), and therefore, it was Harold Godwinson who was a usurper.

He'd certainly done his homework, I'll give him that. But Harold would have nothing to do with it and on 6th January 1066, the day of Edward's burial, Harold Godwinson had himself crowned King of England by Archbishop Aldred.

Harold must have seen the writing on the wall because he began assembling troops in England and on the Isle of Wight in readiness for William's reaction. And he was right to feel nervous because when William heard the news in Normandy, he was apoplectic.

William went into overdrive and began laying plans for an invasion. During normal times in the past, he had shown a certain degree of patience but this was not normal times and he had run out of patience. There was a war council to organise and an army to put together, so with promises of English lands and titles for everyone who supported him, his fleet of mercenaries swiftly grew to well over 700 warships. Brittany and Flanders from his wife's family also joined the fight together with smaller numbers from other parts of France and from the Norman colonies in southern Italy, and before long it was a truly sizeable force to be reckoned with. It was just a matter of time before he would be able to leave his wife, Matilda of Flanders, at home with six children under the age of twelve, and head off with his army to conquer England.

What delayed William's crossing to England by eight months was not just bad winds and weather, it was the time it took to build his ships. This delay gave Harold the much-needed time to assemble his own troops.

But it was a Catch 22 situation for Harold. While giving him more time to be ready for the invasion on the south coast, his large army was slowly diminishing by dwindling supplies and falling morale. And then, with the harvest season upon them, Harold made a big mistake. He disbanded his army on 8th September, consolidated his ships in London and left the English Channel unguarded.

What followed for Harold was an unfortunate set of circumstances. While William sharpened his battle-axe in Normandy, a Viking by the name of King Harald III of Norway, otherwise known as Harald Hardrada was heading out of Norway with a fleet of his own, ready to invade Yorkshire. And with him was Harold's younger brother Tostig.

When Harold heard the news that Tostig and Harald Hardrada had landed and had defeated the English earls of Mercia and Northumbria near York, shock waves rippled through him. Harold had been fully prepared for William's invasion in Sussex so his brother's invasion in the north meant Harold had to quickly assemble his army and make a gruelling four-day march north to catch his brother by surprise.

While Harold battled it out at Samford Bridge, the weather had changed and William finally set sail for England. To his surprise, he landed unobstructed in Sussex on 28th September. He immediately moved on to Hastings, a few miles to the east, and built a prefabricated wooden castle as a base of operations. Unaware of Harold's battle in York, he settled in and commenced to destroy the hinterland around him while he waited for Harold to arrive.

William's choice of Hastings was not by chance. Hastings was at the end of a long peninsula flanked by impassable marshes and from this position, William was not concerned about desertion from his troops. There was simply nowhere else to go. He also knew he could wait out the winter storms by raiding the surrounding area for food. It was a win-win situation for him.

At the moment of Harold's victory in York, news reached him that "William the Bastard" had landed in Sussex. The unwelcome news meant that Harold had to march his tired army back for another four days to meet William's fresh army massing in the south. By then, many of Harold's exhausted soldiers would have guessed that few of them would ever see their families again.

At dawn on 14th October, William set out from his camp and Harold, eight miles away, waited for him, his army in array.

Harold had established his men in hastily built earthworks on top of a hill in Hastings and as the sun shimmered above him, he felt prepared for the battle ahead. He knew William had both cavalry and infantry, including archers, in his army while he only had foot soldiers, but his men seemed to have caught their second wind as they stood determinately along the ridges facing the enemy in the valley below them. Then as Harold watched, an amazing thing happened. William's army seemed to scatter and to Harold, it looked like William's infantry were retreating.

In hindsight, Harold should have waited. He had fresh reinforcements on the way from London and with the added manpower; he knew he could easily defeat William. But he did not want to lose the advantage opening up before him. He raised his sword high in the air and sent his soldiers surging down the hill at breakneck speed.

It didn't take Harold long to realise that it had been a ruse. Even as he realised his mistake, William raised his helmet and his archers fired their arrows high into the air.

The Norman arrows took their toll. After losing thousands of men,

Harold's weary army made their final stand for the day just on dusk, prepared to recommence fighting in the morning with fresh backup.

Then, with less than thirty minutes from sunset, an arrow caught Harold in the eye and killed him. His two brothers Gyrth and Leofwine lay dead on the battlefield with him and as the triumphant roar died away, the shouts of victory would have mingled with the cries of the dying. Horses and riders would have lain dead on the ground as the sinking sun shimmered on helmets, chainmail, broken swords and trampled bodies.

Battles of the time rarely lasted more than two hours before the weaker side submitted, but the fact that Hastings lasted an horrific nine hours indicates the determination of both William's and Harold's armies. Historians state that had Harold waited, he would not have been killed shortly before sunset and he could have survived William's final cavalry attacks and perhaps he would have won.

With the battle over and Harold dead, the remains of the English army made their sad way back to London with news of their defeat. The events had occurred so swiftly that everyone was left dazed.

Amid the chaos, they would have remembered past wars and battles. Never since Boudica was the loss so terrible. 10,000 of William's men had lost their lives and 7,000 of Harold's men lay dead on the battlefield as well. The English would have been waiting in terror for the next English king to protect them from the Norman invaders.

In a panic, as William marched towards them, the council consisting of the most powerful surviving members of English ruling class, hurriedly assembled in London and elected Edgar the new king. Although dedicated to putting Edgar on the throne, these same men had only recently passed over his claim to the throne in favour of Harold. It seemed anyone was better than a Norman.

But at only fifteen, Edgar was far too young to be any sort of an effective military leader. Although it had previously not been an insurmountable obstacle, (the earlier kings of England, Edwig, Edgar the Peaceful and Edward the Martyr had all come to the throne at a similar age), without the help of adult relatives to back him, Edgar had no chance. The man best placed to defend the country against the competing foreign claimants had been Harold Godwinson. And Harold was dead.

Triumphant from the Battle of Hastings and Harold's death, William destroyed everything and everyone in his path as he travelled through Southern England. As his army marched through Kent and attacked London Bridge, some of Edgar's closest advisors deserted him and changed sides.

With fresh continental reinforcements, William reached Berkhamsted a few days later and with desperate refugees pouring into London, the pressure mounted for Edgar.

For two weeks, William waited for the surrender of the English throne. As he waited, the council steadfastly declared Edgar to be the rightful king. By mid-December, William's patience had run out. His next target became London and his army surged in.

With his kingdom in a mess, Edgar finally agreed to meet with William to discuss terms. But as we know, things are never that easy. William was still on a high and true to form, he captured Edgar and triumphantly claimed both the throne of England and London for the Normans.

Flush with success, William desperately wanted to gloat to his own countrymen and he set off with Edgar as his prisoner bound for Normandy.

But then a curious thing happened. One year later, William made a hasty return to England due to unrest among the nobles and with him he brought his valuable prisoner. It seems that after several uprisings in England, William had hoped to use Edgar to help put them down. And it worked. The south submitted quickly even though resistance in the north continued on for a while.

But the cosy state of affairs with Edgar and his family being supported by William was about to end.

Everyone knows you don't bite the hand that feeds you. But that's exactly what Edgar did upon his return to England. After a failed revolt of the Northumbrian earls, which Edgar fully supported, he tried to escape back to the safety of Hungary with his mother and two sisters in an attempt to outrun William's wrath. Their ship, bound for the Continent, was driven off course by gales near Scotland and forced to land in a small bay in Fife, Scotland.

Edgar had only one choice available to him. Not a good one, mind you, but the only one. With his mother and sisters in tow, he made his way to the court of King Malcolm of Scotland, begging for support.

To Edgar's relief, Malcolm agreed to help, but on one condition: he would be allowed to marry Edgar's sister beautiful Margaret.

Malcolm's wife Ingibjorg had recently died before Edgar's untimely arrival in Scotland. The story of Malcolm Canmore meeting Margaret of Wessex has been heavily romanticised. The story tells of the 40-year-old Malcolm Canmore, now a widower with two young sons, Duncan and Donald, who rode from his residence at Dunfermline to welcome the royal refugees to Scotland. What he found was that Princess Margaret was not a gangly 13-year-old but a beautiful, flaxen-haired, young woman in her early twenties and he instantly fell in love with her.

There was no doubt that Edgar would readily agree. With his new army plus support from the Scots and the Danes, it meant that Edgar was free to invade northern England.

Usually slow to anger, they had William's attention now and his patience finally snapped. Systematically, he devastated everything in his path as he headed towards Scotland.

With the war in the north all but lost, Edgar finally and reluctantly accepted defeat and stopped fighting.

The Normans were there for good and life would certainly be different.

PART II

THE NORMANS

WILLIAM THE CONQUEROR

Born 1028
Reign 1066 - 1087

One bright summer's morning, while birds dived playfully through dappled light filtering through the trees, Robert Duke of Normandy was riding towards his capital, Falaise, when he saw Herleve, daughter of a tanner, washing linen in a stream and he fell in love instantly. He forgot all about his wife sitting at home waiting for him and he forgot his vows to always love and support her, and only her. Instead, he carried Herleve off to his castle and lived with her for the rest of his life. Such a romantic story, and out of that love came William the Conqueror, hailed as one of the greatest and ferocious warriors of all time.

But despite this dreamy story, the little boy, adored by both his parents, would have to live with the stigma of being illegitimate for the rest of his life. As a child, his life was in constant danger from kinsmen who thought they had a more legitimate right to rule Normandy. But William's father had other ideas. When he died, he left everything to his illegitimate son, despite what the relatives thought. On that day, the little 7-year-old boy became William Duke of Normandy. He was knighted at 15 years of age by King

Henry I of France and was successfully dealing with threats of rebellion and invasion from the age of 19.

Against the wishes of Pope Leo IX (because they were distant cousins), William, at 24, then married Matilda of Flanders, aged 22, and together they produced four sons and six daughters. But despite this fairytale story, there was no hint that he had finally found peace. Perhaps he realised that his victory at Hastings was the result of a very large fluke aided by the invasion of the Norwegian army at the same time, thinking they would try their luck as well. Perhaps, it had been a bit too close for comfort.

On Christmas Day 1066, the coronation must have seemed like part of the battle. As William stood in Westminster Abbey, the crowds roared with anger and rebels burned surrounding buildings as a sign that this was not to be the end. As he stood at the altar, he must have been more than a little nervous as he listened to the heated shouting outside the abbey. What he didn't know was that this disturbance was just a prelude of what was to come.

In medieval times, society was separated into three distinct classes: those who worked, those who fought and those who prayed. Workers were not leaders of rebellions, not until the 14th century anyway. But clergy, that was different. They were powerful men and more often than not, it was a career move rather than a vocational one. They were always in the background, stirring the pot. But most rebels were landed nobility and these powerful men resorted to muscle flexing to further their own ambitions.

Immediately, William had to face constant plotting and fighting from everywhere. Harold's sons were raiding the southwest coast of England, Wales, Devon and Cornwall. Edgar the Outlaw had supporters and they huffed and puffed in Exeter while noblemen in Northumbria began to grumble as well. If William thought Hastings would be the end of his problems, he was to find out it was just the beginning. He was forced to appoint earls in all parts of the kingdom just to guard his threatened frontiers.

What annoyed William most about the English was the way they fought. Always a man of action, he was perturbed by their methods of attacking and then melting away into the forests and bogs to hide. His way was to bash it out with a conventional military force. And that's just what he did.

Not about to let his new kingdom be taken away from him so early on in the piece, William took up the challenge with zest. History tells us of a

'Harrying of the North' where every town and every village in Northumbria was destroyed while thousands were either murdered or left to starve. This devastation included setting fire to the vegetation, houses and even tools used to work the fields. For more than a hundred years afterwards, the land would struggle to recover. And it was only the beginning.

To add to his resume, in as little as four years, William eliminated the English aristocracy. As he'd promised his supporters in Normandy, anyone who fought with him would be generously rewarded. And he kept his promises. Most English estates and titles of nobility were taken from them and handed over to the Norman noblemen who had supported him before the Battle of Hastings. He was smart enough to know that by handing out English parcels of land, it would ensure nobody would conspire against him if they wanted to keep their rewards. In the turmoil, many aristocrats simply fled to Flanders or Scotland leaving everything they possessed behind. The unlucky ones who were not so quick in leaving were captured and sold into slavery overseas while others escaped to join the Byzantine Empire's Varangian Guard and went to fight the Normans in Sicily.

Although William initially allowed English lords to keep their lands if they offered submission, by 1070 the indigenous nobility had ceased to be an integral part of the English society. By 1086, they maintained control of just 8% of their original land-holdings.

There was one more challenge William knew he had and that was Scotland. For years, Malcolm had been hiding Edgar the Outlaw in seclusion but with William breathing down his neck, time was running out. Malcolm could do nothing but reluctantly agree to a ceasefire by signing a peace treaty and as with many agreements, there always seems to be one side that emerges worse than the other. The Treaty of Abernethy was no different from many others. Malcolm was already reluctant to sign so to add to his unwillingness, he found there were also conditions. Firstly, he was to hand over both Edgar and his own eldest son Duncan as hostages and both were to be sent to William's court in Normandy. Secondly, he would have to hand over all his property and only be left with estates in Cumbria.

As you can imagine, it was a grudging and uneasy peace with tempers simmering for many years. But there was nothing Malcolm could do. The deal was done and the prisoners were duly handed over.

William took on none of the English customs. The only culture as far as he was concerned was French and for the next 300 years, French was to become the main language in the English court. The smart surviving Saxon barons sent their sons to monasteries in France for education where all would be taught French and things slowly began to calm down, as much as they could anyway. Compared to previous rulers, some version of peace began to settle among the English people and William was able to return to Normandy and leave the running of England to his Norman supporters.

But while a type of amity existed between William and the English people, it was not so in William's private household. William had his hands full with outright rivalry between his three sons, Robert, William and Henry and the three boys bickered continuously.

William's eldest son Robert (nicknamed Robert Curthose because he was so short) was reported to have been courageous and skilful in military manoeuvres. He was, however, also prone to laziness and many discontented nobles, as well as the King of France, used this weakness of character to stir up arguments with his father. Robert was very dissatisfied with the share of power allotted to him and he quarrelled fiercely with his father and brothers. To appease him, William made him the Count of Maine in view of his engagement to Margaret of Maine. But this still wasn't enough for Robert. He wanted more. Much, much more.

It took eleven years after William seized the English throne for his son Robert to instigate his first rebellion against his father and it was all because of a harmless prank played on him by his younger brothers, William Rufus and Henry. They had dumped a full chamber pot over his head and he was furious enough to start an all-out brawl that was only stopped by the intervention of their father. Feeling that his dignity was wounded, Robert was further enraged when his father failed to punish his brothers.

In defiance the next day, Robert and his followers attempted, and failed, to seize the castle of Rouen. That was the final straw for William who'd had enough of his son's tantrums and he ordered their arrest. In the nick of time, Robert and his companions took refuge with Hugh of Chateauneuf-en-Thymerais but were forced to flee again when William attacked their base at Rémalard.

With his father hot on his tail, Robert fled to Flanders to the court of his uncle Robert I, Count of Flanders but got a little side-tracked along the way and raided the county of the Vexin. Things came to a nasty head at a fierce battle when Robert unhorsed and wounded his father in combat, only stopping his attack when he recognised his father's voice. Humiliated, William cursed his son and declared he would remove him from his will before returning to Rouen.

William's relations with his family worsened even more, if that was at all possible, when William discovered that his wife Matilda was secretly sending their son money. As you can imagine, he exploded.

It was only when Matilda stepped in that everyone calmed down. She reminded William that as their second son Richard had died six years ago, Robert was one of only three sons left to him and in the violent medieval times they were living in, that could change at any moment. Reluctantly, William saw her point and restored Robert in his will.

But this appeasement only lasted for a short time. Two years later, Matilda was dead and with no one to stop him and talk sense to him, William became more tyrannical than ever.

Always itching for a fight, it seems that Robert Curthose had other pursuits in mind rather than fighting with his father. The war against the Saracens who were controlling the island of Sicily had begun and Robert and Edgar the Outlaw wanted to be a part of this crusade. Robert persuaded his father to allow him and Edgar to leave Normandy and sail for Sicily and it must have been with some relief that William willingly handed over 200 knights and enough money from the English treasury to feed and pay them for the whole expedition while he continued with his own battles. This relative peace with his son only lasted for a year until Robert suddenly turned up again in Normandy, leaving Edgar to continue the crusade alone in Sicily. Almost at once, the arguing picked up where it left off between William and Robert.

Even at the age of 59, William the Conqueror had not been able to find peace. The year was 1087 and William was still fighting. He'd just seized Nantes near Paris and was in the process of burning it to the ground when he fell off his horse and suffered abdominal injuries. Through the heat of summer, he lay in agony fighting his injuries. As death drew near, his sons William Rufus and Henry came to him. Robert did not even bother.

As William's injury worsened, he drew up a will. His third son, William Rufus, had one main virtue, his filial fidelity and it was this virtue that made him William's favourite. He saw Rufus as the one who would succeed him to the throne in England as William II and despite his reluctance to include his reckless and spendthrift son Robert, who hadn't even bothered to come and see him, he left the Duchy of Normandy to him to rule as Robert I. William's youngest son Henry would receive 5,000 silver pounds.

No portrait of William has been found although he was depicted as a man of around 5 feet 10 inches tall (around 2 inches taller than the average for the 11th century) with strong arms and a ferocious expression. Nevertheless, his noticeable podginess in later life eventually increased so much that French King Philip I commented that William looked *"like a pregnant woman"*. He is depicted in the Bayeux Tapestry as being clean-shaven as opposed to Harold and the English lords who wore moustaches.

Splitting the kingdom was not a recipe for peace and neither Robert nor William Rufus thought they had inherited as much as they should have. After all, Henry had been left all the money and none of the responsibilities. While Henry seemed quite happy with the arrangements, his brothers saw it as an insufferable insult and fresh rivalry sparked anew as they squabbled ceaselessly before William had even been buried.

Finally, all funeral plans were made for the burial in a church in Abbye-aux-Hommes in Normandy. But there was one snag. On the day of the funeral, the original owner of the land on which the church was built claimed that he had not been paid and demanded 60 shillings before he would allow the burial to take place.

Many days passed in the sweltering summer heat while the bickering continued over who was going to pay the money. Finally, realising they had to bury their father quickly, it was Henry who gave in and paid the full amount since he was the only one flush with cash.

By then, William's rotund body would not fit in the stone sarcophagus as his body had bloated so much due to the warm weather and length of time that had passed since his death. A group of bishops applied pressure on the William's abdomen to force the body downward but the abdominal wall burst and drenched the coffin, releasing putrefaction gases into the church.

Watching as the bishops worked, William Rufus stood clenching and unclenching his fists, eager for his chance to sit on the throne.

Standing by his side, slyly watching his brother and equally as eager, stood his youngest brother Henry.

WILLIAM II (WILLIAM RUFUS)

Born 1057
Reign 1087 - 1100

William Rufus had a florid complexion, red hair and almost always seemed to have a pleased expression on his face. His different coloured eyes varied depending on his emotions and although he was not very tall, he had astonishing strength, despite his protruding belly, much like his father. He earned the nickname Rufus either because of his red hair or his propensity for anger, but probably because of both.

As the third of four sons of William the Conqueror, Rufus was never regarded as a future king until the death of his elder brother Richard. That moved him up the ladder by one on the family tree. Then when his father died and his brother Robert became the Duke of Normandy, he found himself elevated even further to King of England.

The division of William the Conqueror's lands into two parts presented both hostility and dilemma for those nobles who held land on both sides of the Channel. Since William Rufus and his brother Robert were natural rivals, these same nobles worried that they could not hope to please both men at the same time. That meant they ran the risk of losing the favour of either one ruler or the other, perhaps both. The only solution, as they saw it, was to unite England and Normandy under one ruler. That meant they had to mutiny against William Rufus in favour of Robert with their uncle, the powerful Bishop Odo of Bayeux, half-brother of William the Conqueror, supporting them.

For some reason, perhaps the laziness gene again, Robert failed to even appear in England to rally his supporters and William won the crown hands down with promises of money and a better government to secure his safe passage to throne.

Almost overnight, William Rufus changed. Instead of keeping his fervent promises, the once loving, devoted son of William the Conqueror spent much of his time plotting against his elder brother in Normandy and using all his power to secure his own personal wealth. He manipulated feudal law to increase the royal treasury by levying heavy fines on shires, introducing exorbitant inheritance taxes and confiscating lands that belonged to the church. He bolstered the royal revenue by leaving clerical positions vacant and then diverting the money paid for these positions into his own personal funds. To him, the Church was nothing more than a rich corporation deserving of heavy taxing at a time when it was gaining too much influence.

But all of this added income and power wasn't enough. What he really wanted was Normandy. There was only one minor problem with that: Normandy belonged to Robert.

By then, Robert was restless again. He desperately wanted to re-join the First Crusade with Edgar but he needed money. The only way to get that money was to pledge his Duchy of Normandy to William Rufus in return for a payment of 10,000 marks—a sum equalling about a quarter of William's annual revenue in England.

This was a dream come true for William Rufus. With the prospect of ruling all of Normandy as regent in Robert's absence, William was more than willing to help with the funding for his crusade and in a display of the effectiveness of English taxation, William Rufus raised the money by levying a special, heavy, and much-resented tax, upon the whole of England.

Northumbria didn't like what they were hearing about Normandy and they liked the increased taxation even less. Twice they rebelled, the second time when Robert de Mowbray Earl of Northumbria and a handful of supporters conspired to put Robert back in charge of Normandy instead of

William Rufus. That was quickly squashed with De Mowbray sent off to prison indefinitely. Another noble was blinded and castrated and the third whipped in every church in Salisbury, before being hanged. No wonder Rufus did not face any more rebellions during his reign.

As regent for his brother Robert, William Rufus fought battles in France from 1097 to 1099 and secured northern Maine. He was even considering an invasion of Aquitaine in south-western France when fate stepped in on a beautiful August summer's day in 1100.

The sun shone brightly and a warm breeze rustled softly through the trees as William Rufus organised a hunting trip in the New Forest. As the hunting party spread out to chase their prey, an arrow, perhaps grazing a stag first, lodged in the breast of the king who fell forward, driving it through his lung. He died on the spot.

According to some chroniclers, William's death was not murder, but then again... The story tells like this. Walter Tyrell Lord of Poix and William had been hunting together when Walter let loose a wild shot, but instead of hitting the stag he aimed for, the arrow struck William Rufus in the chest. Walter apparently tried to help him, but there was nothing he could do. Fearing that he would be charged with murder, Walter panicked. He left William's body lying at the exact place where it fell and leapt onto his horse and fled. Other nobles in the hunting party, perhaps with a little insight on what could happen to them as well, followed suit and fled, possibly with the thought of securing their personal estates before the news circulated.

Other chroniclers point out that Walter was renowned as a keen bowman, and it would have been highly unlikely that he fired such a reckless shot. Another point to consider is that William Rufus's brother, Henry, who he fought incessantly with, was among the hunting party as well that day and was a devout friend of Walter. Henry, of course, would benefit directly from his brother's death.

How long Henry crouched over William's body will never be known. What *is* known is that Henry made straight for the royal treasury at Winchester with lightning speed and gained possession of it after a loud argument with the custodians, ensuring Robert would miss out completely.

Abbott Suger, a chronicler, who was Tyrell's friend and who sheltered him in his French exile, said later:

"It was laid to the charge of a certain noble, Walter Tyrell, that he had shot the king with an arrow; but I have often heard him, when he had nothing to fear nor to hope, solemnly swear that on the day in question he was not in the part of the forest where the king was hunting, nor ever saw him in the forest at all."

This leaves the question open: "Where was Henry?""And if Henry was not guilty of the murder of his brother, he certainly wasted no time mourning him either. The inscription on the Rufus Stone indicates that the king's body was left to a local charcoal-burner named Purkis to take to Winchester Cathedral on his cart. By then, Henry was fully funded and crowned in London before the archbishop had even arrived.

William Rufus ruled for thirteen years, never married and had no offspring. With his elder brother Robert away on a crusade with Edgar the Outlaw, the way was open for Henry to step forward and become the next King of England.

One year after Henry declared himself the king, his brother Robert had heard the news and would return in a fury.

All hell would break loose.

HENRY I

Born 1068
Reign 1100 - 1135

Henry was born around 1068 in Yorkshire and his mother, Matilda of Flanders, named the infant prince Henry, after her uncle Henry I of France. As the youngest of four sons, he was almost certainly expected to become a bishop and given the appropriate extensive education that was usual for a boy with his future mapped out.

With his brother William Rufus dead and the royal treasury plus the throne of England in his possession, Henry waited in trepidation for his brother Robert's reaction. While he waited, knowing his position was shaky, Henry married Edgar's niece Matilda (the daughter of Malcolm III of Scotland and Edgar's sister Margaret). The marriage gave him a Scottish army at his disposal and with it, he was ready to face his elder brother whenever he should return.

He only had to wait one year. As frost lay heavily on the ground and clung to leaves in droplets, Robert and Edgar arrived back from the crusades on a cold day in October. Robert's anger was always close to the surface, but this time, he had good reason to be angry. As he stood before his brother, there was a hard light in his eyes as his anger seethed.

Immediately the familiar aggressiveness began and Henry saw the only way out of the volatile situation was to negotiate a settlement that would suit them both. Robert wanted the territories back, plus the money they provided, and Henry wanted the throne of England. To Henry, it seemed like a fair trade since Robert had very little money left and the offer saved Robert from a sticky situation. The juicy carrot was in front of his nose and Robert reluctantly agreed to the deal.

But the animosity was always there between the brothers. For six years, Henry and Robert squabbled incessantly until one day in 1106, Henry finally snapped. He decided to take matters into his own hands and cross the channel to finally have it out with his brother. Henry was to be the first post-Conqueror king to realise promises made to rebels did not have to be kept.

On the cool morning in September, exactly forty years after William the Conqueror had landed in England, his two surviving sons, Robert Curthose and Henry Beauclerc accidentally met at the crossroads at Tinchebray in Normandy. Henry was marching south from Barfleur and Robert, together with Edgar the Outlaw, was marching from Falaise on their way to Mortain. The meeting was totally unexpected and both Robert and Edgar were very unprepared. They hadn't even known that Henry was on his way.

What happened is very typical of brutal medieval battles. Fighting continued throughout the day until far into the evening, leaving Robert and Edgar both exhausted. They could see they were not going to win the battle so in their haste they tried to escape. All to no avail. Henry was fully prepared and waiting for them.

Henry wanted to gloat. He had two rabbits in his hat and he wanted everyone to see how victorious he had been on the battlefield. Without thinking too far ahead, he took his brother back to England and placed him in the Tower. It was only then that he realised that this was perhaps not the best idea since Robert's supporters were around every corner waiting for the right moment to release him, Henry hurriedly changed his mind and sent his brother off to prison in Cardiff instead. With Robert out of the way, Henry seized the Duchy of Normandy as a possession of England and took control. With the new possession, his power covered both sides of the Channel and both countries knuckled down under his rule.

Edgar was more fortunate, thanks to his sister, who was married to

Malcolm of Scotland. Her daughter Matilda was now married to Henry and she begged for her brother's safety. Feeling magnanimous, Henry allowed Edgar to retire to his estate near Berkhamsted in Hertfordshire. At his death, and with no children of his own, the end of the male line of Wessex died as well.

To everyone, Henry looked like he had the Midas touch. He owned Normandy. He was the King of England. He had an heir, William Aetherling aged 16, his indisputable successor, as well as a daughter. There was nothing more that Henry could want.

And then the winter of 1120 arrived.

William Aetherling was a privileged youth pandered to on both sides of the channel and nothing was deprived him from richly embroidered silk garments stitched in gold to attendants and titles. William was to be the next king in a brilliantly planned peace.

Henry's son had been in Normandy for a celebration marking the end of his childhood and beginning of his manhood. William Aetherling was now the crowned Duke of Normandy and heir to the English throne and the world was his oyster.

Along with 200 young members of the Anglo-Saxon nobility elite, friends and cousins, Prince William boarded a ship called the White Ship to journey home. On board as well, were his half-brothers and half-sisters, all illegitimate from a brood of twenty-two children fathered by his father to various mothers. Together this group were the golden generation of the nobility and they only ever travelled in style.

William Aetherling had chosen this ship because the reputation was that it was the fastest and most luxurious ship there was. It was packed to the rafters with happy, inebriated teenagers hell-bent on celebrating. And William had good reason to celebrate along with his friends, family and crew.

In hindsight, a well-lubricated crew was probably not the best choice to bring the young prince back to England and it was the apology of an upset stomach that was to excuse his cousin, Stephen of Blois, from the festivities to wait it out for the next ship bound for England the following day.

The White Ship may have been fast but she didn't even make it out of the Benfleur harbour. Whether it was a simple navigational error or a result of over indulging, no one will ever know. Within minutes of leaving the shore, the White Ship crashed on sharp rocks and a hole was punched in the prow of the ship. Freezing water flooded in.

A vision of terrified passengers, screaming as they were hurled into the water, comes to mind and the heavy brocaded clothes would have soon become heavy, making it impossible to swim or even tread water.

The immediate priority was to save the prince. A lifeboat was found for William and he was already on his way to safety when he heard the cries from one of his half-sisters. It was to be a fatal decision to turn back and rescue her.

His sister wasn't alone and as the boat approached her, other passengers in the water scrambled to clamber aboard William's boat to safety as well. The result was the boat capsized and sank. She had not been rescued and neither had William.

There was only one survivor. He was a butcher from Rouen who had boarded at Benfleur to collect money owed him and he was accidentally carried away when the White Ship sailed. He had clung to the wreckage during the night and then managed to find shore in the morning along with the bodies washed in with the tide.

The news was slow to reach England. Another ship, crewed by a sober captain this time, had sailed and reached England unscathed while the king and his household were preparing for Christmas.

Henry received the news in horror and as grief overwhelmed him, he must have felt like he couldn't breathe. He was dumbstruck and devastated. Historians remark *"he never smiled again."* William's planned marriage to a young French princess had meant peace with Anjou and the future of the whole realm had rested with him. Without him, it was all gone.

For all of Henry's triumphs during his reign, he failed in one vital task: to secure the future of the Norman dynasty. With William, the consolidation of Henry's life work was gone and a disputed succession to the throne glared upon England once more as every nobleman took bets on who would succeed to the throne.

Henry tried hard to father another legitimate son to whom he could pass on his title. His remaining illegitimate children would become significant political assets in subsequent years and his bastard daughters cemented alliances with a flock of lords whose lands bordered Henry's. But there was no one to take the title of King.

In 1118, Henry's wife died and in an effort to father more children, he married a virile teenager, Adeliza of Louvion two years later. Surprisingly, with so many illegitimate children, he could not impregnate her.

Henry only had one surviving child, Matilda, but in those days the aristocracy did not take kindly to the idea of a woman ruling. Against Matilda stood Henry's nephew Stephen Count of Blois, who owned great estates in England. And both were grandchildren of William the Conqueror.

You should remember that Stephen was the same young man who had chosen, rather miraculously by the way, to return from Normandy to England on another ship instead of the White Ship, full of happy revellers, willing women, good food and expensive wine. By making that fateful decision, he had put himself in the position of becoming the rightful heir to the throne and I'm sure he would have been very aware of the impact if the young prince died.

More than anything, Henry wanted his daughter to have his legacy as ruler of England and on her, he hung all his hopes. On several occasions in the past, he even made his barons swear to stand by his daughter.

At the age of 8, Matilda (or Maud as she preferred to be called) had been married to Henry V of Germany, the Holy Roman Emperor. She had grown up in utmost splendour and her power spanned from Germany to Tuscany. Five years after the White Ship sank, her husband was dead and she was a 22-year-old widow and one of the most powerful women in Europe. Henry brought her straight back to England for her new role as future Queen of England. It was asking a lot of England to accept her and Henry knew it. But he had no other choice.

In later years, there would be queens to serve her country but not at this time in history. A queen was simply not allowed and there was deep division as quarrels erupted and everyone took sides, even though many had already sworn allegiance to Henry's daughter.

Clearly, Maud needed a new husband to boost her claim and again Henry turned to Anjou. On 17th June 1128, Maud now 26 years old, married Geoffrey, Count of Anjou, aged 15.

Geoffrey was an energetic, tall, conceited, ginger-haired teenager with fair skin and good looks. Despite all of this, Maud was very underwhelmed by him. Not only was he from Anjou but he was 11 years younger. In her opinion, Angevites were barbarians with shocking table manners. And didn't he come from a line of plunderers and rapists? Rumour even had it that his great grandfather had burned his wife in her wedding dress when she had been discovered in a compromising situation with a goat herder.

It turned out the dislike was mutual. Neither of them cared for each other and they argued incessantly, even to the point of separating for the first couple of years of their marriage. This settled down when Henry reminded his daughter of her duty to provide her country with a son and heir.

In March 1133, she did just that and she delivered a son, which she named Henry. With a grandson as his heir, Henry seemed pleased with life once more.

The castle and the forest surrounding Lyons-la-Foret was a regular destination planned every year at the same date for two centuries by the Norman dukes and in November 1135, Henry arrived with the full intention of living it up. Even at 68, he still felt strong enough to enjoy the hunt. He arrived the night before with those very thoughts. But during the night he began feeling sick and by the end of the week, he was seriously ill. An Archbishop was called in and Henry confessed his sins. Three days later, Henry was dead of suspected food poisoning and although he had eaten the same food as everyone else, he had been the only one affected.

Are bells clanging madly in your head?

We have heard of gruesome stories of burials and William the Conqueror's comes to mind instantly. Henry's burial was no different, though perhaps a little excessive. Even though Henry had confessed his sins, it has been written that his body was '*brought to Rouen and there his entrails, brain and eyes were buried together. Then, the body was cut all over with knives and copiously sprinkled with salt and wrapped in oxhides to stop the strong pervasive stench which was already causing the deaths of those who watched over it. It even killed the man who had been hired for a great fee to cut off the head with an axe and extract the stinking brain, although he had wrapped his face in linen cloths....*'

It was certainly not the burial that Henry would have had in mind for himself and there was none of the splendour expected for a king. But with no direct male heir, the fallout from his death was far worse. In the past three years, Henry had asked his barons to swear that they would be loyal to Maud but from the moment he died, they forgot their promises.

With something almost like premonition, Stephen of Blois had already left his wife's country of Boulogne and was crossing the channel on his way to England. Despite his promise to Henry to honour Maud's succession, he went straight to London and proclaimed himself king. On the 22nd December, he then went to Winchester and seized the royal treasury and had himself anointed by the Bishop. He had moved incredibly quickly and in the confusion, Maud, Geoffrey Plantagenet and her son were suddenly disinherited.

By all accounts, Maud was remarkable. She was said to *"have the nature of a man in the frame of a woman"*. Fierce, proud, hard and cynical, her love of politics overshadowed all other passions. But Maud was with her husband in Anjou when Henry died and Stephen was first on the spot. Stephen also had an advantage – his brother was Bishop of Winchester, with a great voice in council and with this backup, the barons stood by him.

The speed with which the aristocracy accepted Stephen was mind boggling and speaks volumes about the rules regarding female queens in the 12th century. The prospect was not a promising one for Maud. There was also the question of who had the most power, and in England at this time in history, succession was still not fully decided by blood alone. If that had been the case, Henry would never have been king in the first place. Henry had snatched the throne from William Rufus, and then stolen the throne from right under his elder brother's nose while Robert was crusading in Sicily.

It seems that history was repeating itself because Stephen had no real claim to the throne since there was an elder brother, Theobald of Blois, whose blood claim was stronger. But Stephen was wealthy, powerful and charming and his wife's country of Boulogne was important to the English. The 40-year-old man was simply at the right place at the right time and with the strength of his wife's army behind him, he was fully able to defend England and Normandy against any danger, especially if that danger was a woman.

Maud was not so lucky. She was pregnant with her third child and was much further away from England and unable to move as fast as her cousin Stephen had. Even with a more impressive royal bloodline than Stephen, there was no chance that a toddler would be proclaimed king purely by his birth. Well, not in this century anyway. And so, Maud and Geoffrey were elbowed aside.

The nobles may have pushed to put Stephen on the throne but not everyone agreed with them. A bastard son of Henry I, Robert of Gloucester, a distinguished soldier and a powerful man in the West Country, who was not rated high enough to compete with either of the legitimate heirs, loyally supported his half-sister Maud and became one of Stephen's most determined opponents. And Maud was going to need every bit support she could muster.

The struggle between Maud, and Stephen would result in a long civil war known as *'The Anarchy'*. Stephen's snapping-up-the-throne efficiency was not a good sign of things to come.

STEPHEN

Born 1096
Reign 1135 - 1154

A succession established on such disputable and questionable grounds could only be maintained with great skill and in the early years of his reign, it became apparent that Stephen lacked quite a few of those necessary fundamentals. He did not find the job of being a king as easy as it had been to acquire it in the first place. He lacked the ruthlessness and intelligence that Henry I had possessed and began relying on advice from some of his of his baronial friends while ignoring others who ought to have been his greatest supporters. He was lavish with Henry's accumulated treasure to friends but he was not even-handed with it.

Fearing that they were about to change sides, Stephen arrested the Bishop of Salisbury who was the head of the royal administration, the Bishop of Lincoln and the Bishop of Ely. He demanded their castles be given back to him and he asked them to show how they were entitled to own castles in the first place as bishops of the clergy.

Many nobles, seeing their own futures laid out in the same fashion, were angered that Stephen had dishonoured the clergy in such a way. The baronage, all except those formed by Stephen, began to believe that it was the time for them to show solidarity and express their strength. Most of them were having second thoughts about their hasty decision to put Stephen on the throne. One by one, linked together with royal family ties, possessing knowledge and education and trained in English administration, they began to stand apart from Stephen in support of Maud.

All of a sudden, Stephen found himself surrounded by enemies and facing attacks from everywhere. In Normandy, Geoffrey Plantagenet had taken up the fight for his son Henry, soon to be named the Duke of Normandy, and began waging war on Stephen. Almost at the same time, Maud's uncle King David I of Scotland crossed the border and advanced to Northumbria in support of his niece.

Maud watched all of this delightedly from Normandy. She had not believed that her uncle would back her so strenuously. She must have been wondering if perhaps there was a chance after all. In 1139, she finally took action. She appealed her cause to Rome and set up her headquarters in Bristol, ready to invade England with her half-brother Robert of Gloucester. War had begun.

When she returned to England, she was to find it a very different place from when she had left. There was a three-way split in England. There were those who supported Stephen, those who supported her and those who supported themselves and no one else. Under Henry I, England had been strong and wealthy, well governed and all boundaries were secure. Now David of Scotland ruled in the north and a patchwork of barons exercised their power in England. General violence had escalated and the air was filled with smoke from burning crops and the cries of suffering people. Stephen's army had tortured and killed a vast majority and then taken any possessions they could find while many thousands were left dying of starvation. He had imposed taxes on villages and called it *'Tenserie'* and when the people had no more to give, he burned the villages to the ground.

Maud's presence immediately made things worse. Seeing the prospect of their personal property disappearing, the barons began taking sides knowing that she was nowhere near powerful enough to take the throne on her own. Everyone could see years of war looming in front of them.

Then while Stephen was attempting to take over Lincoln castle, Robert of Gloucester marched his troops into Lincoln and attacked. In the heat of the battle, Stephen was captured.

This should have been Maud's moment. With her cousin captured, she had secured England for herself and her son. She even went as far as organising a date for her coronation, preparing to call herself Queen of the English. She had support from many barons as well as Stephen's brother, Henry the Bishop of Winchester, and with newfound confidence, she began to settle down to the business of ruling.

It was not to be as easy as she had thought.

Although many supported her, there were many who did not. She was to find that the barons weren't interested in a unified England. What they wanted was a weak ruler to strengthen their own personal monopolies. Months later, Stephen's wife rallied support for her husband among the barons and things went from bad to worse for Maud when the Bishop of Winchester swapped sides yet again.

Maud had only been on the throne for eight short months. She was only just settling in when the barons gathered their forces together to fight her once and for all. In the battle Robert of Gloucester was captured and Maud was given a final ultimatum. They would only release Robert if she freed Stephen and restored him to the throne. Her choice.

Maud wasn't stupid. She knew if she did what the barons demanded, she and her three sons would spend the rest of their lives in exile. And once Stephen was back on the throne, all their lives would be in danger as well.

Fleeing was the only option available to her and she barely escaped with her life. She managed to lower herself on a rope from the walls of Oxford Castle where she was being held and in the thick snow, she escaped. Dressing in ghostly white as camouflage was the only thing that saved her in the better cold as she rode across the eight miles of snow to Wallingford Castle held by her staunchest supporter, Brian FitzCount. The throbbing on the ground had panicked her horse as the earth fairly shook. Even then, she had managed to clutch the reins tightly in the driving snow. In the distance, she heard the soldiers' frenzied shouts and she imagined their mighty swords glistening threateningly in the weak sun.

From Wallingford Castle, she was able to secretly flee back to France to join her three sons, Henry, Geoffrey and William. Tired, exhausted and disheartened, she knew she was finished.

It wasn't that she felt that she had abandoned England. It was more that they had abandoned her. After only eight months of trying, she had no energy left to fight. They had made it more than abundantly clear that they didn't want her. So be it. She didn't want them. And she didn't want to live another day with her brutish husband. She had produced three children as her father had demanded so she had fulfilled her purpose. It was *her* time now. She would live out the rest of her life in comfort at the priory of Notre-Dame-Du-Pre, where across the Seine she could see Rouen. She would sit back and enjoy the view from her room and leave it to her eldest son Henry to take up the fight for the throne if he wanted it.

Henry had listened to his mother intently and watched her attempts to reclaim the throne for him. At fifteen, he was arrogant enough to make his first attempt at an invasion.

The wild teenager who understood the English language but couldn't speak it terrified England. He was a strange looking young man with a ruddy complexion and a large round head with eyes that grew bloodshot in anger. His mood could change from good-humoured to fierce anger at a switch.

Of course, Henry failed at his first attempt. He was young, inexperienced and ill prepared. But it was early days and he would try many more times.

Stephen's reaction to Henry's first invasion was amusement as Henry could barely pay his troops. Half of them had even abandoned him in the early weeks. Stephen arrogantly paid the soldiers off and sent them back home with their tails between their legs.

Then on a freezing January morning in 1153, it was a very different figure who was blown ashore. Twenty-year-old Henry felt the blood of William the Conqueror and his grandfather, Henry I, flowing in his veins as he kissed the ground.

The people of Malmesbury could only watch in terror as this fiery warrior landed with an army of 140 knights and 3000 infantry hell-bent on taking England at all cost. Torrential rains fell and mud clung to everyone as his solders shivered in the dawn and the blustery wind blew through the trees.

Stephen had known an attack was coming. He just hadn't imagined it would be in Malmesbury. Belatedly, he gathered his massive army together and headed off to meet Henry despite the bitter winds and freezing rain.

By the time Stephen's army arrived, it wasn't just that they were tired, hungry, cold and drenched. It was worse than that. By then, they had lost faith in his leadership. Even before the battle had started, they had watched as he'd fallen off his horse three times. There wasn't even a promise of a reward for any of them at the end of the battle.

In the end, they simply refused to fight. Realising that Stephen had a mutiny on his hands, the barons turned tail and left to stand by Henry's side. All Stephen could do was run and try to rebuild his shattered army before facing Henry again.

As Stephen hid, he watched and waited and finally in July, he met Henry at Wallingford. By then, Stephen's small army had endured a lot over the past two decades and once again, they refused to fight.

Henry knew the end of war was near. He could feel it in his blood. With scarcely any soldiers supporting him, all Stephen could do was call a truce and agree to talk with Henry to discuss a peace settlement.

Then, in the middle of discussing terms, Stephen received the devastating news that his eldest son Eustace, heir to his throne, had taken ill and died.

At 61, Stephen was heartbroken. With the terrible news, all enthusiasm went out of the discussions. Stephen still had another son, William, but the 16-year-old young man had made it perfectly clear that he did not want to challenge Henry for the throne. He was more than happy to be given the title of Ist Count of Boulogne and settle down with a wife in peace. A wise decision, I would say, for one so young.

Stephen was now in the position that Henry I had found himself in. He did not have a suitable heir to pass on his realm. Distraught, Stephen lost all interest. He named Henry Plantagenet, the scruffy redheaded 20-year-old, as his successor and Henry waited in limbo for his new role to begin.

He didn't have to wait long. One year later, in October of 1154, Stephen died and the brilliant, energetic, but quick-tempered young man came into good fortune as Henry II.

Henry Plantagenet, at the age of 22, was Count of Anjou, Count of Maine, Duke of Normandy, Duke of Aquitaine, Duke of Gascony, Count of Nantes, Lord of Ireland and King of England.

The Plantagenets had arrived and England was in for a wild ride.

PART III

THE PLANTAGENETS

THE PLANTAGENETS

The Plantagenet's were powerful. They were rough masters and the temper of the time was violent. From Henry II to Richard III, they ruled for more than two centuries with boundaries that had already been established by the Normans. Heroes were born but so were villains, names that would echo through history. Famous battles were fought in an age where victory meant seizing whatever you could at any cost. During this period in time, battles were commonplace and the English were the scourge of Europe.

Early Plantagenet years were full of savagery and cruelty but by the end of the dynasty, they had transformed England into a sophisticated and revered kingdom. It hadn't been easy and it was all because of the Plantagenet struggle for power.

This incredible and exciting era began with the death of Stephen and promised to be more sensational than any era before it. It was the era of Thomas Beckett, Richard the Lionheart and his brother John of Lackland. It covers Henry III and his brother-in-law Simon de Montfort as well as Edward Longshanks and the butchery that William Wallace endured. There were heroic warriors and kings with questionable sexual preferences. There were also plagues that devastated the kingdom.

This dynasty did not invent England but they made it more significant than it had ever been before.

The next part of the story begins with Henry II after coming through a paralysing war. It was a time that England would never forget.

HENRY II

Born 1133
Reign 1154 - 1189

The Plantagenets were rough masters and the temper of the time was violent. England had great soldier-kings but there was no man with instincts like Henry II.

At the time of his father's death, Louis VII was King in France and Henry Plantagenet was a bachelor on the prowl.

Louis VII of France was regarded as the French equivalent of Edward the Confessor in every regard, practicing his devotion by day and doing penance at night. However, his hot-blooded 30-year-old wife, Eleanor of Aquitaine, a reigning princess in her own right, had warmth in her veins and complained that she had married a monk and not a king.

Eleanor was famous for her beauty and sexuality. At the age of 13, she had been an orphan and the sole heir to one of the greatest inheritances of Europe and Louis VII of France had no hesitation in taking her for his bride. She was undoubtedly a catch.

But her life in the French court was not what she had expected. While she embraced the splendour, her husband dressed and ate like most of the monks she had seen. From the very beginning, the marriage had been doomed. Her scandalous reputation followed her wherever she went and though she gave Louis two daughters, the marriage was in serious trouble. With no male heir, she was aware that she could be replaced at any time with a newer version that suited Louis better.

When Henry Plantagenet arrived at court, he was a square-shouldered, sprightly 19-year-old brimming with confidence and overflowing with energy, if you know what I mean. He was impulsive and ambitious and needed little sleep and Eleanor did not waste time coming to a decision. She petitioned Louis for a divorce on the nominal grounds that they were related by birth and two months later, she generously awarded Louis custody of their daughters on the condition that her lands were restored to her. Two months after that, she married Henry. With the marriage to Eleanor, half of France passed out of royal control right into Henry's hands. For an ambitious youth, there could not have been a more valuable bride.

The marriage was one of the most brilliant political strokes of the age. Henry, later admitting his designs, accepted the admiration of Europe for his audacity. Everywhere men shook their heads at Henry's nerve and the love intrigue that was unfolding.

But with the marriage, Henry found himself threatened from all sides. While England had been struggling to strengthen their ties with France, this marriage did the opposite. King Louis, who had recently married Constance of Castile, felt slighted, and he certainly had grounds for complaint, as did Stephen who had disputed Henry's title of Duke of Normandy in the first place. Then there was the Count of Champagne, the Count of Perche and Henry's own brother, Geoffrey. All of them became spontaneously angry. To add to Louis' anger, within another two months, news reached him that Eleanor was pregnant.

As everyone fumed, Henry turned his abundant energy towards England. He couldn't have cared less what anyone thought.

Through the next few years, Henry certainly had disastrous failures during early invasion attempts on England. Eventually it was the death of King Stephen's son Eustace that had taken the wind out of Stephen's sails. He had fought long and hard to keep the throne for his family but it had all come to nothing.

As we know, Henry waited patiently. He only had to wait until October 1154 when Stephen died.

Henry took his time to claim the throne and arrived with two toddlers and a heavily pregnant wife by his side on 19th December 1154 promising stability and peace. With two boys under two and another child on the way, Henry needed a home quickly and they set up house at a palace in London. After a hundred years of invading armies and quarrelling descendants, Henry was confident that England would become a stable kingdom under his guidance. As for England, they found the new ruler well educated even though he only spoke Latin and French.

Even in a royal family in the Middle Ages, child mortality was high and after the death of their first son, William, aged three, they rejoiced months later when their daughter Matilda was born. In rapid succession, two more boys, Richard and Geoffrey, were born. By 1155, Henry had four healthy children below the age of four with more on the way.

His first job was to mop up the mess of the English civil war. Rebellion hadn't died with Stephen. Henry was still challenged by powerful nobles who were 'testing the water' as they tried to set limits on his power although Henry's no-nonsense attitude soon put an end to that before it could develop into a more widespread conflict.

When it looked like trouble in the north, Henry's response was quick. He marched into York in person to confront the earls who were responsible for the tiff.

Like his grandfather, Henry I, this Henry had an outstanding knowledge of the law and he sat on councils whenever possible. He dressed casually and laughed easily although when opposed, his temper had no boundaries.

No episode opens up to us a more vivid picture of Henry's temper than his quarrel with his former friend, Thomas Beckett, Archbishop of Canterbury.

In feudal times, the Church was powerful, enriched continually by donations from barons who were anxious about their life beyond the grave. In this atmosphere, a great personality stood at the summit of the religious hierarchy: Thomas Beckett.

Henry first met Beckett when he was a clerk in service to Theobald, the Archbishop. Henry befriended him and promoted him as the face of England and Beckett more than rose to the task. He excelled. He became Henry's closest friend and trusted adviser as he took the day-to-day drudgery off Henry's shoulders. Secretly however, Beckett accumulated a great deal of wealth and kept a luxurious household in London eating exotic food served on gold and silver platters.

Despite the skimming, Thomas Becket served Henry well. He helped to implement a tax that would eventually bring the feudal system to its knees and Henry was sure he had found a faithful comrade and colleague in Becket. He even trusted him with a far greater task – the betrothal of his three-year-old son to Louis VII's daughter, Margaret, from the marriage to Constance of Castile.

In private, Becket wore a hair shirt and scourged himself, but he knew how to put on a real show. With Henry's approval and an open cheque book, Becket swept into Paris with gifts and an entourage of servants.

A chronicle from William FitzStephen who accompanied him says:

"IN HIS COMPANY he had some two hundred horsemen, knights, clerks, stewards and men in waiting, men at arms and squires of noble family all in ordered rank...All these and their followers wore bright new festal garments. He also took twenty-four suit...silk cloaks to leave behind as present....furs, hangings and carpet...Hounds and hawks were in the train...and eight five-horse chariots.....Two carts carried nothing but beer for the French who are not familiar with the bre...He had twelve sumpter horses and eight chests of table places gold and silver...Every horse had a groom in smart turn-out...every horse had a fierce great mastiff on a leash standing with the car or walking behind it, and every sumpter beast had a long-tailed monkey on its back....

Then there were 250 men marking six or ten abreast, singing as they went in the English fashion...then the men at arms, with the shields and chargers of the knights, then the other men at arms and the boys and men carrying hawks...Last of all came the chancellor and some of his friends...."

FOR A LAYMAN OF THE CLERGY, he certainly knew how to throw a party. But in the end, he did what he was required to do and the betrothal took place.

By 1156, while things were still settling down in England, Henry was forced to leave England for Anjou to settle a rebellion by his younger brother, Geoffrey. The feisty youth thought that since Henry was King of England, then Anjou, Maine and Touraine should be his.

Henry had no intention of giving up any of his lands, even to his head-strong brother who had attacked Henry's property in Normandy five years before. He knew that giving anything to his brother was simply asking for trouble.

A peacekeeping attempt was made with their mother present, but it all came to nothing. Then suddenly, almost as a Godsend, Nantes and Brittany elected Geoffrey as their Count and everything settled down.

Henry was more than happy with this new situation as it expanded the Plantagenet enterprises further down to the Loire Valley to a place they had never controlled before and for a year, all seemed well. Until one day when Geoffrey was returning home from a royal meeting. He suddenly developed a fever, collapsed on the couch and died.

Geoffrey's death had an impact on Henry. It wasn't that he mourned his brother. It was more that he didn't want to lose the French territories his brother had governed. Instantly, Henry stepped in to tidy up the frayed ends with the largest army he could raise.

It was the summer of 1159 when Henry crossed southern France on his way to Toulouse. The sun beat down mercilessly as his army marched and people quaked in terror at the sound of the soldiers thudding footsteps. Trumpets and drums blared as they marched, and they destroyed everything in their path. Crops were burned and properties were ruined.

There was no doubt what Henry was doing. He had come in conquest and he was expanding his territories and boundaries from Scotland to the Pyrenees. Alongside him were lords and barons as well as Malcolm IV of Scotland whom he had recently reconciled with. In the middle rode Thomas Beckett.

For all Henry's efforts, Toulouse proved hard to break and when autumn came, he was caught completely unawares by Louis VII who was not about to sit by and let Henry conquer a land he had already tried to conquer himself. Not surprisingly, in light of the size of the French army, Henry decided to give up the fight and head home despite the huge amount of money he had wasted on the conquest already.

But as it turned out, his campaign in Toulouse was not to be a total financial disaster after all. On his way back to England, Stephen's last remaining son William died.

It was a chance too good for Henry to resist. He never left a stone unturned if there was the faintest glimmer of hope that he could increase his personal wealth, especially if that wealth meant claiming French territories. He saw an opportunity and stepped in, promptly taking all William's widespread estates and reverting them to himself. What had been an expensive summer for Henry had ended up by being quite profitable after all.

The death of the Archbishop of Canterbury was the turning point for Beckett. Although ill-educated and disliked, Henry saw his friend Beckett as the ideal candidate for the job, even though the monks at Canterbury were outraged. Everyone complained that Beckett only had a second-rate education and he was not even a lawyer. And he certainly was not a theologian. Even Henry's own mother wrote to discourage him.

But nothing could change Henry's mind. The advantages of having a friend in such a high position far outweighed the whining of the monks. On 2nd June 1162, Beckett was ordained a priest and the next day, a bishop.

Beckett knew full well his inadequacies, but he had a desperate need to prove himself worthy of this new position. From the moment he became Archbishop, something like a transformation happened in Beckett. He took his new job very seriously and this change in attitude changed his relationship with Henry. Almost overnight he became an adversary of Henry.

Throughout the ages, all English kings thought of themselves as appointed by God not only to rule the State but also to protect and guide the Church. Rome was making claims, which were hardly compatible with these traditional notions, stating that the King was a mere layman whose one religious function was obedience to the church alone. By Henry's reign, bishops were not only spiritual officers; they were great landowners and the secular equal of earls. Henry's questions were: *"Who appoints the bishop? And when one is appointed, to whom did he owe his duty, Pope or King? And if the King agreed upon a law contrary to the law of the Church, to which authority was obedience due?"*

It was a sore point for Henry and he resented the Church for interfering in his personal business. He had hoped that by appointing his trusted servant Beckett to be Archbishop, he would have a loyal friend on his side. But Henry had missed ominous signs of the change in Beckett's attitude.

What he actually had done was unwittingly provide the Church with a leader of unequalled strength and obstinacy and Beckett defended the church vigorously in every aspect.

And so the quarrel began. As Beckett's actions became increasingly provocative, it seemed like he was 'asking for it'. It was as if he had declared war on Henry. In a fit of rage, Henry demanded that Beckett return all the castles granted to him at his consecration and then in October of that year, still in a vindictive mood, Henry accused Beckett of embezzlement.

Beckett panicked. In a state of fright, he fled on a small boat to Flanders to beg Louis in France to intervene on his behalf. When a new man was appointed as Archbishop of Canterbury, his panic turned to rage.

The whole ruling class in England were shaken by this terrible dispute between the two men who not so long ago had been inseparable friends. As if he had wiped his hands of the incident, Henry turned himself to the conquest of Brittany.

While Beckett seethed in France, Henry was determined to secure the peaceful accession of his son, the young Henry, to the throne. It meant crowning his son while Henry was still alive instead of at his death but that seemed insignificant in Henry's eyes. The Archbishop of York performed the lavish ceremony, meant to establish an undisputed heir and when Beckett heard, it was like waving a red flag to a bull. He sent word to the Archbishop of his anger, demanding that anyone who had participated in the ceremony be excommunicated. The Archbishop then told Henry what Beckett had written.

Give Henry his due, he made an attempt to let bygones be bygones. He allowed Beckett a safe return home and even returned all the possessions back to him. Everyone saw it as a giant step forward in the breach of their friendship. Beckett didn't see it that way. He had more important things on his mind.

The welcome home after the years of exile was astonishing for Beckett. The unsuspecting Canterbury monks received him as an angel of God as he made a triumphal progress through London, scattering handouts to the beseeching people. No one saw the look in Beckett's eyes and no one suspected that his next intention was to renew his demand to excommunicate all the clergy who had taken part in the crowning of young Henry.

No one is above a tattle or two, especially the doomed monks. They hotfooted it to Henry telling a tale of revolt and usurpation where Beckett was ready *"... to tear the crown from the young King's head"*.

Of course, Henry was livid. He bellowed *"What miserable drones and traitors have I nurtured and promoted in my household who let their lord be treated with such shameful contempt by a low-born clerk!"*

Those fateful words will go down in the annals of time. Four knights had been close enough to hear Henry's furious words and eager to please their king, they called for horses and rode at full speed to Canterbury intending to dispense with the niceties.

When they arrived at the cathedral, the heavily armed knights found the doors bolted. They then smashed their way with axes through a side-door where an unarmed Becket was waiting for them. When he resisted arrest, they hacked the top off his head and trampled his brains on the floor of the cathedral with their boots and then took it in turns to slash him with their swords. It was a technical knockout and Beckett never had a chance.

England was horrified and outraged that the murder had been committed on sacred grounds and when Henry heard the news, he was prostrate with grief and fear. He had never dreamed that such a deed would be done even though they were his own hot words spoken. To make it even worse, Pope Alexander was ready to excommunicate Henry. If nothing else, Beckett had proved that a challenge to the king's authority did not need an army to make it work, just willing subjects.

Henry never fully recovered from the humiliation. It was as if his wheel of fortune had suddenly turned downwards at Beckett's death and the position he had so carefully built suddenly shattered because of those few words spoken in anger. He spent many years on anniversaries of the death, stripped to the waist and kneeling humbly, submitted to being scourged by the triumphant monks.

Eighteen years of life lay ahead for Henry after Beckett's death. At the age of 43, Eleanor had given birth to her last surviving son John, bringing the number of children to seven – four boys and three girls. In those years, all of Europe desired Henry's kingdom and he knew his position was shaky.

Henry should have been looking at his own family closely instead of watching Europe. From out of nowhere his four sons rose up against him, all with axes of their own to grind and urged on by their mother, Eleanor.

All of them felt they deserved titles of their own and the power that went with them.

At 39 years of age, Henry worked hard to mollify his boys with gifts. For the three eldest, he provided titles. Henry would have Normandy, Maine and Anjou. Richard was given Aquitaine as he was his mother's favourite and it was her family's home, and to Geoffrey went Brittany. John was only four and too young to have anything yet, Henry stated.

Henry treated his children with generosity but he had no illusions of what they were capable of. Prince Henry was tall, blond, good-looking, gracious, affable, courteous and the soul of generosity, which made him the only one of his family who was popular. Unfortunately he was also shallow, vain, careless, incompetent and irresponsible and he did not appear to be very interested in the day-to-day business of government. He showed no evidence of political astuteness, military skill, or even ordinary intelligence. And he was always in need of money. His reputation, however, was by no means negative and if he lacked political weight, he had an almost celebrity status throughout Western Europe in the tournament culture.

Things went terribly wrong for Henry in 1173 after a falling out over arrangements that had been made for the 6-year-old John's future marriage. As a wedding gift, Henry gave John three castles: Chinon, Mirebeau and Loudon, all strategically important and all lying between Anjou and Maine. Regarding Anjou as his own rightful inheritance, Prince Henry demanded that he be allowed to reign independently over at least part of the territory his father had promised him.

Even as Henry was making the arrangements for John, he knew there would be the inevitable fallout. Still he refused to give in to his eldest son. Within days, Prince Henry left for the French court looking for an ally in Louis VII. With an army and support from Louis, he knew he would be a serious threat to his father.

What Henry hadn't expected was that Richard (who was only 15 at the time) and Geoffrey (who was only 14) would rebel as well, all fuelled on by Eleanor.

Why Eleanor turned against her husband is something of a mystery and is regarded as revenge for Henry's dalliance with his mistress Rosamund Clifford. What is probably more to the point was that Henry had begun to dispose of parts of Eleanor's inheritance of Aquitaine when he saw fit. He gave Gascony to one daughter when she married the King of Castile and Eleanor felt that she was being deprived of her own power. Gascony was a part of Aquitaine and the land was hers to give away, not Henry's. Besides, she stated, Aquitaine was to be left to her favourite son, Richard.

Together, the three brothers made an oath at the French court that they would not make terms with their father without the consent of Louis first. Immediately after the oath, Richard left to raise an army in Aquitaine.

Henry had a very expansive army of his own consisting of over 20,000 mercenaries with which to face any rebellion. And he knew what his son was up to. Fully prepared and with all his ducks in a row, Henry marched on Vermeil and sent Louis packing back to Paris. He then moved on to recapture Brittany.

It was only a matter of time before Henry found out that Eleanor had been a part of the plot. As you can imagine, he was furious and out for revenge at any cost, despite being the mother of his children.

While her boys were with the French king, she rode across the French countryside dressed as a man towards the castle of Faye-la-Vineuse for safety. She never arrived. She was 50 years old and easily recognised. When Henry's men saw her, she was arrested immediately and taken to Chinon.

Knowing Prince Henry was still with Louis, Henry sent word to Paris demanding his boys end their foolishness and give up the fight. When Louis asked who had sent him the message, the reply was *"The King of England."* Looking at Prince Henry, he replied, *"The King of England is already here."* It was only then that Henry decided to return home with his prisoners, including Eleanor and his sons' wives and fiancées.

For the rest of his life, Henry never trusted his children again. One day, while viewing a painting in the royal chamber at Westminster Abbey of four eaglets preying upon the parent bird while the fourth one poised at the parent's neck, Henry is reported to have said *"the four eaglets are my four sons, who persecute me even unto death. The youngest of them, whom I now embrace with so much affection, will some time in the end certainly insult me more grievously and more dangerously than any of the others."* In hindsight, it was almost a premonition.

For Henry, gaining more wealth and power made him feel alive. The year 1173 brought fresh violence as every castle occupied without his approval was taken back and replaced with his own loyal men in charge. The clear message was: all castles came from one source – the king.

The one he loved more than any other was Dover Castle, overlooking magnificent white cliffs and a sea sparkling like diamonds that rippled towards France. The castle, originally built by William the Conqueror, needed major repair but that was only a minor technicality. After twelve years and immense cost, the jewel was completed.

As Henry's 50th birthday approached, he was feeling old and his busy life had taken its toll on his body. His legs were bowed from years in a saddle and a fractured femur from years earlier had never really healed properly. These injuries slowed him down as he limped around his territories during bouts of incapacitating illness.

With his father weakening, Prince Henry saw it as perfect timing to step in ahead of his brothers and demand some territory where he and his wife could live. After all, he was the heir to the throne. The implication was that he wanted Normandy and of course, Henry still refused.

The 28-year-old flew into a rage. Once again, he went to Louis for help, knowing full well that including the French in any matter would spark a reaction from his father.

It just wasn't the reaction he expected.

Throughout his life, Henry thought he had been fair with his boys. He'd given them titles and a certain amount of responsibility. The rest he believed they could wait for until he died. Rightfully furious, he called a meeting of his sons.

It was Le Mans and it was Henry's birthday and he had things to say to them. What he wanted left them speechless. He demanded an oath that their allegiance was to him the King of England, their father, and not to the King of France. He would not accept any other alternative.

Without a second thought, Richard refused. He could not remember having spoken any words to his father that weren't in anger so any sort of allegiance to him was laughable. He'd spent almost a decade on military manoeuvres in France, not England, and he felt he should only be responsible to the King of France. His title after all was Duke of Aquitaine. Not only that, he had no desire to be a part of anything that his vain brothers were involved in. He stormed out without a backwards glance and returned to Aquitaine.

His brother Henry was the first to react violently to the insult and his behaviour was atrocious. He attacked diplomatic ambassadors and robbed churches throughout Aquitaine leaving Richard scrambling from town to town trying to repair the situation. Richard had no idea how to control his elder brother. In the end, it was fate that finished it. Three days into the attack, during an assault on a church, his brother Henry contracted dysentery and died.

Despite the recent heartache his son had caused, Henry was distraught. His heir had just died and he was feeling old and feeble himself. A decision had to be made. Clearly he had to nominate who was to be his heir.

Henry recovered slowly from his grief then called his remaining sons together for another meeting. The last time they'd all been together had gone rather badly and he wasn't expecting it to be much better this time. He told Richard that he had to give Aquitaine to his younger brother John and prepare to be the King of England.

It wasn't a pretty scene. Richard had already voiced his opinion regarding England and the death of his brother hadn't changed anything. With his eyes blazing with anger, he once again refused. Aquitaine was *his* and he was definitely not handing it over to anyone else, especially not his little brother.

With his plans in chaos, the only other option for Henry was to declare Geoffrey as his heir and leave Richard to fend for himself.

Apparently Richard didn't like that decision either. He gathered an army together and attacked Geoffrey.

Henry finally snapped. His famous last words to his son that day were spoken in bitterness. *"God grant that I may not die until I have my revenge on you".*

Sometimes when things don't look like they can get any worse, fate steps in with a cruel blow to prove everyone wrong. Henry would never forget July 1186. He was about to receive another terrible blow. While in a tournament in Paris with King Philip II of France, Geoffrey was badly injured and by August, he was dead from his wounds. It was said that Phillip was so distraught that he attempted to throw himself into Geoffrey's grave.

Henry was now desperate. As a fever for the crusades gripped Richard, Henry grew more anxious and Richard firmly believed his father would disinherit him from succession to his kingdom. In November 1188, Richard demanded to know outright if he was to succeed or if it would be his younger brother John.

Henry said nothing. It was to be a final break between the two.

It was seven months later when Richard joined up with King Philip and together they launched a surprise attack on Henry in Le Mans. Henry was totally unprepared for the attack and all he could do was watch as the whole town was set ablaze. By then, Henry was desperately ill and it was only his ailing health that made him do what he had never done before. He simply gave up.

For the next fortnight, he lay in bed gradually becoming weaker and weaker. On a hot day that threatened a late thunderstorm, Henry dragged himself out of bed to attend court with Louis. Sick in mind and body, he quietly agreed to everything the French king asked. By then, he was too weak to stand.

While an angry sky erupted in a summer storm, he was carried home. Barely able to stand, he asked for a list of supporters who had left him and gone over to Richard. When he saw that the first name on the list was his favourite son John, his grief was too much for him and he collapsed.

A clever man might look back and see how much had changed in the 35 years that he'd been on the English throne. What had started out as a bright and shining future for the handsome king and his beautiful wife had ended with all of his children fighting like scavengers for morsels of his kingdom. Everyone he had loved, his wife and every one of his sons, had betrayed him.

It was in the midst of this personal grief that Henry died. In his sorrow, he made no attempt to suggest the succession. As the eldest son, Richard would naturally take the throne. Henry had ceased to care.

As expected, Richard showed little grief for the man whom he had been fighting regularly throughout his whole life. He stood silently and looked down at the sarcophagus holding the body of his dead father, showing no emotion. In the dimness of the church, his eyes seemed to glow. His eyes travelled up and down the body of the man he knew so well, dressed in the finest armour money could buy. Apart from his lips pressed tightly together, Richard's face was blank. He stood for no longer than it would have taken to recite the Lord's Prayer before turning around and walking out, ready to commence the duties of his realm. It is said that Henry's corpse bled from the nose in Richard's presence.

In the back of the church, his brother John silently glared. At his father's death, Richard had become King of England, Duke of Aquitaine and Count of Poitiers, Anjou, Maine and Nantes. John had to make do with a few paltry counties in England and live forever off Richard's throw-offs. His anger threatened to consume him.

As John watched maliciously, Richard walked past him without even a glance.

During Henry's reign, the crusades had begun in earnest and Saladin had become Vizier of Egypt in 1169, declaring himself Sultan shortly afterwards. By origin, he was a Kurd and soon his power was stretching out into Syria, taking Damascus in 1174 and Aleppo in 1183. By 1186, Saladin had proclaimed a Holy War. By 1187, Jerusalem had surrendered followed by Palestine and Syria.

The shock of these events was felt throughout Europe and together England, France and Germany responded to the call. The Holy Crusades were in full swing and Richard was eager to begin preparations to join them.

And so the legend of Richard the Lionheart, one of history's most famous figures, began.

RICHARD I (THE LIONHEART)

Born 1157
Reign 1189 - 1199

Richard was never expected to ascend to the throne and many believe he never really wanted it. It was more to spite his father that made him insistent. He was a warrior and a soldier and he loved war, not for the sake of glory or political ends, but for the excitement of the struggle and the glory of victory. This formed his whole personality. But the Richard you will read about in my story is perhaps a different one from the heroic crusader we know from Hollywood.

This extremely handsome man was born in Oxford but could not speak English. He didn't even want to. He was above average height at 6 feet 5 inches tall with strawberry-blond hair and a pale complexion. His magnetic eyes burned with passion and he was a man on a mission. All he wanted was an adventure that would cause the musicians to immortalise his name, as well as guaranteeing him a place in heaven. Crusading appealed to every need of his nature and seemed made for him.

When news reached France that Jerusalem had fallen to Saladin, he began making plans. He had heard of atrocities committed, such as the brutal slaying of holy knights whose heads had been removed by Saladin's own sword. He had also heard of the defeat at the Battle of Hattin where thousands of soldiers were burned alive in blazing forests while archers finished them off. He'd heard of Christians being sold into slavery in Africa and he'd heard that Saladin had taken the holy relic, the True Cross. This new crusade appealed to Richard in every way as a soldier of Christ and a Plantagenet king. His departure had been delayed for two years because of his quarrels with his father but he would not wait any longer.

But first, he had to settle the issue of his new inheritance as well as his relationship with King Philip of France.

On 13th September 1189, Westminster was packed to the rafters with bishops, abbots, barons, knights and officers of the realm. There had been a riot of colour as the clergy were dressed in purple and white robes and Richard's favourite knights raised golden swords high above their heads. As the sickly smell of incense filled the cathedral, the procession moved into the inner chamber amid the flickering of candles while hymns echoed off every wall.

Pride swelled in Eleanor of Aquitaine's heart as her favourite son took his three oaths. He swore he would uphold peace and reverence to God and the Church. He would administer justice and he would abolish bad laws and replace them with good ones. As he held the sceptre, he was anointed with holy oil on his head, shoulders and sword-bearing right arm as golden spurs from the treasury were strapped to his feet. Impatiently, Richard waited as his crowning ceremony progressed agonising slow. Gripped in the crusading fever, he was eager to begin his preparations to leave. Outside, there was no glory.

There is a story that historians know all too well but don't often tell. On the day of Richard's coronation, and like every other European leader, Jewish leaders arrived to present gifts to the king. Instead of the expected welcome, they found themselves barred from the ceremony. They were the lucky ones. The ones who were admitted earlier were stripped and flogged by Richard's courtiers before being thrown out of court empty-handed. It was only the beginning for the Jews.

Rumours soon spread throughout London of what had happened at the coronation and very soon, things began to get out of hand. It was as if permission had been given. Jews were beaten to death, robbed and burned alive. Some had their homes destroyed and only a few managed to escape with only the possessions they could carry. Crusader fever had arrived in earnest and none were more ardent than Richard.

In his first year as king, Richard spent £14,000, (a huge amount in those times), stockpiling goods for his crusade. He ordered 14,000 pig carcasses, 60,000 horseshoes, countless wheels of cheese and thousands of arrows. Before Henry II's death, the old king had fully stocked his treasury by raising the enormous sum of £100,000, issuing threats of excommunication and imposing taxes to all and sundry. This treasure trove was only the beginning for Richard. As England buzzed with activity, Richard sold everything he could: lordships, earldoms, castles, towns, land ... everything. He even joked that he would sell London if he could find a buyer.

The biggest problem for Richard was what to do with his younger 22-year-old brother John who did not want to take up the cross with him. Grudgingly, Richard had honoured his father's will and given all the land and titles promised to his brother including Cornwall, Devon, Somerset, Dorset, Nottingham and Derby. But with this wealth and power under his belt, John had become a serious threat to Richard overnight. Richard had never fully trusted any of his brothers, much less John, and the last thing he needed was conflict with his younger sibling while he was away on a crusade.

As the King of England, Richard considered banning John from entering England but his mother intervened on her youngest son's behalf and Richard relented. There was no easy way to solve his problem except to leave John with his inheritance and hope his mother's advice had been wise.

And then there was King Philip of France to contend with. Fearing the French might seize his territories in France, which he was more concerned about than his reign in England, Richard tried to persuade Philip to join him on the crusade. The juicy carrot he offered to convince Philip was his promise that he would honour his betrothal to Philip's sister Alys.

Philip didn't need too much convincing. He was young and excited to be a part of the wonderful adventure Richard had promised and he willingly agreed. Both gave their crusader oaths on the same day and declared that they would equally share whatever plunder they gained.

After repositioning a part of his army to guard his French possessions while he was away, Richard had only one thing left to do. With his huge fleet ready to set sail to meet Philip in Marseille at the end of July 1190, Richard appointed Hugh, Bishop of Durham, and his chancellor, William Longchamp, as his regents. Then he promptly left for the crusades.

As you can imagine, John was at first surprised by the choice, but his anger became pretty obvious in a very short time. *He* was the one who owned titles and lands in England. *He* was Richard's brother. Shouldn't *he* be the obvious choice to be regent in Richard's absence? Richard did not know perhaps that the best means of keeping the throne safe was for the king to be a resident.

Richard's first stop was in Lisbon where he allowed his massive army the luxury of expressing their zeal by raping, pillaging and plundering the city before moving on to Sicily. By this time, Philip and Richard were on very good terms.

Unbeknownst to Philip, in the middle of winter that year, Richard's mother Eleanor was putting the finishing touches to a plan she and her son had devised several years before. Despite Richard's ardent betrothal to Philip's sister Alys, Eleanor's job was to pick up an 18-year-old girl, Berengaria of Navarre, and take her to meet Richard in Sicily so that they could be married.

It had taken a lot of persuasion for her father Sancho VI to allow his young daughter to endure the dangerous journey through difficult and treacherous terrain and head for the world's most dangerous battle zone. He knew that Eleanor and his daughter would only be safe if they slept in monasteries and picked their way slowly and carefully through the countryside. It could be weeks before they reached their destination.

Eleanor found the young girl intelligent and beautiful and worthy of her son in every way, but she was also aware that the marriage would cause major concerns for Richard. He was, after all, still engaged to Philip's sister and had been since they were children.

But if Berengaria was nervous about the arrangements made for travelling through dangerous countryside with an ageing widow, she was to find that she was in the company of someone who had endured far worse and Eleanor's age had not slowed her down one single bit.

They met up with Richard in Sicily in March 1191, six months after his arrival. Eleanor had been looking forward eagerly to the visit as her daughter, Joan, lived in Sicily as well and she had not seen her for years.

Eleanor arrived to find a furious Philip.

At first, she thought it was because Richard had conquered Messina and flown the English flag high above the city, ignoring their pact to spit the spoils evenly. If Philip was angry at Richard for breaking their first agreement, he would be apoplectic when he learned about Berengaria of Navarre.

But Eleanor needn't have worried. Philip was angry because Richard had told him that the wedding was off, claiming that his father had already slept with Alys and had fathered a bastard child. Stunned and with no way to prove whether it was the truth or not, Philip had no choice but to reluctantly agree, angry that Richard had strung him along for years.

Part of Alys's dowry, the territory of the Vexin, in northwestern France, had already been given over to Richard during their engagement and by rights, this should have reverted back to Philip at the end of the betrothal. But Richard stood firm. Vexin was his. It had not been *his* fault that the wedding was called off. It had been his father Henry who was to blame.

Finally, Richard made an offer. The territory would remain in Richard's hands and would be inherited only by his male descendants. The territory would revert back to Philip if Richard were to die without an heir.

In rage and humiliation, Philip knew that there was no way of taking back the territory without a major battle. He agreed to the meagre compensation that Richard offered and left Sicily in a huff.

Back home in England, John was fast becoming a problem. He was certainly making it known that he was not happy and with all sorts of bad news filtering back to her, Eleanor's visit with Richard only lasted for three days. She left Berengaria to be chaperoned by her daughter Joan and she left to return home as Richard prepared to leave for the Holy Land.

Richard's plans changed as a gale blew up at sea and half of his fleet, containing his sister and Berengaria, were blown off course towards Limassol in Cyprus. Everyone on board was captured and when Richard heard the news, he stormed ashore and battled fiercely to capture the town. To celebrate his victory, he married Berengaria.

For three weeks, he continued his conquest of the island amid screams of terror as his soldiers, bearing the white cross of England, raided towns and castles. His next plan was to move on to Acre in the Holy Land, which lay tantalisingly close by.

When Richard arrived, he saw a city filled with the dust of war and bloated bodies bobbing in the water. There were rotting corpses and the stink of disease, as well as dead horses and soldiers with their bodies riddled with arrows. Women had been raped and trench diggers worked until they were exhausted, gagging as they dug in the hot fetid air to bury the bodies before the starving people ate them. Philip had beaten him to the prize and had already been there for months.

Within a week of setting up camp Richard became seriously ill with a scurvy-like disease. His teeth and fingernails began to loosen and his hair began to fall out in huge clumps. Thinking his death was near, he named his nephew Arthur, the son of his elder dead brother Geoffrey, to be the heir to his English throne. Arthur was only four years old at the time.

Though very serious, Richard's illness only slowed him down. In July, he was carried on a litter to the battlefield, covered in a silk quilt and carrying a crossbow. He came from the north as Philip came from the east and it was surprising that he was able to hold Philip's soldiers back for as long as he did. By the time Acre fell, Richard's brilliance as a warrior was the talk of Europe.

What let him down were his paralysing quarrels with allies. Guy of Lusignan, the exiled King of Jerusalem, was disputing with Conrad of Montferrat for the crown and as expected, Richard took one side and Philip took the other. Even though a compromise was finally reached, Philip, driven by jealousy, humiliation, homesickness and anger, announced he was finished for good and was going home.

In England, problems loomed as well. William Longchamp, Bishop of Ely, was enjoying the splendour of being a monarch, moving around the country with pomp and spending the crown's money like there was no tomorrow. Unfortunately, this did not endear him to the nobles, or to John. Even though John held many shires and the sheriffs were responsible to him alone, he wanted more, much more, and he saw the Bishop as an obstacle that needed to be removed.

John had also heard the news that Arthur was named as the heir to Richard's throne and he reacted as you would expect. Violently.

Beside himself with anger, he began to make fresh plans. With Longchamp becoming increasingly unpopular because of his lavish spending as well as unsavoury rumours circulating, John leapt at the opportunity to set his plans into motion. He accused Longchamp of every atrocity he could imagine. But when he called him a pervert and a paedophile, people sat up and began to listen.

A triumphant John hauled Longchamp before the council to stand trial and there was no doubt what the outcome would be. Longchamp was stripped of his office and forced to hand over his castles. He was ruined. And it was exactly what Richard had been trying to avoid.

John was proving to be a medieval bogeyman and it was during Richard's absence that accounts of a fictional rebellion led by a famous, and more than likely non-existent, rebel appears in English history.

The first mention of Robin Hood is in 14th century in a poem called 'Piers Plowman' where it is joked that he was better known than the Lord's Prayer. Robin Hood was depicted as a highly skilled archer and swordsman known for 'robbing from the rich and giving to the poor'. He was assisted by a group of fellow outlaws known as his 'merry men' famous for 'riding through the glen' and wearing Lincoln-green long johns. The early ballads link Robin Hood to identifiable real places and many are convinced that he was a real person, more or less accurately portrayed.

It is not until 1521 that a Scottish writer, John Major, dated Robin Hood and his activities to the time when Richard was away on crusade.

If there is any truth of the legend of Robin Hood, and there are many people who state such an outlaw did actually exist, it would be in this period of history. Robin of Loxley's legend was important, although decidedly odd, because it emphasises his support of the true king while taking and redistributing the king's wealth at the same time.

There was however a character called William FitzOsbert, (his name has nowhere near the same romantic appeal as the name Robin Hood) who took up the role of 'the advocate of the poor'. William had a university education and had been with Richard on one crusade but had returned to England while Richard stayed. It is said that William held gatherings and gave stirring speeches, travelled throughout England surrounded by mobs of the poor for protection, and started, according to one source, "... a powerful conspiracy, inspired by the zeal of the poor against the insolence of the rich". He had gathered over 52,000 supporters, stocks of weapons cached for the purpose of breaking into the houses of the rich citizens of London.

His brief moment in history ended with a public hanging and a type of cult was formed. His rope was said to cure fevers and the soil under his place of execution was even dug up as a relic. His hairiness was also intriguing. William FitzOsbert was a Norman name, high bred, and even in the Bayeux Tapestry, Normans were depicted as short haired and clean-shaven. It was the Anglo-Saxons who had the long hair, moustaches and beards and William had that wild 'native' look about him – a significant sign of rebellion that we all recognise today.

Unlike Robin Hood, William FitzOsbert, is remembered by almost nobody.

Sorry – back to Richard.

Richard was receiving alarming news constantly about John in England but when the worst news of all came that John was plotting with Philip of France against him, it put paid to Richard's plans of crusading any further. If John and Philip were successful in ousting Richard from the English throne, he would lose his English cash cow and that he could never allow. His position in Jerusalem was deteriorating anyway by October 1192, so Richard set sail for Europe as a stop before heading back to England. He was going to sort his brother out once and for all. He had no idea what he would find when he arrived back in England but for all he knew, John may already have usurped the throne.

When he arrived in Europe, it was to find that he had become a very unpopular man. He had gone back on his betrothal to marry Philip's sister. He had deposed the ruler in Cyprus and it was widely thought that he had sponsored the murder of a Count while on his crusade. His enemies knew he was coming and they were gathering with the intention of blocking all his sea routes back to England. Every path back to England was now through enemy territory.

In rough seas, Richard and a handful of men headed north but as fate would have it; his ship was wrecked in the Adriatic. Shaken a little, he realised it meant a long walk lay ahead of him so he began making his way carefully through Germany disguised as a peasant. Three days into the journey, the Duke of Austria was soon on his track. Richard was arrested and taken prisoner and promptly sold to Emperor Henry VI of Germany as a hostage. And with Henry he stayed.

By early 1193 in England, things were at a crucial point for John. At any time, he was expecting his brother to walk in the door and take the throne back from him and then where would he be? It was critical to his plans that

Philip and his allies in Europe waylaid Richard before he set foot back in England. They had to stop him at any cost.

It was right at this time that news reached John. Richard had been taken prisoner 'somewhere in Germany'.

John was in heaven. It was exactly what he had wanted and without hesitating, he dressed in his full armour and stood before all of England. Richard was dead, John stated, and he, as the only surviving brother, was claiming the throne. William Longchamp had controlled Richard's kingdom for far too many years, but with William now disgraced, no one would hold him back any longer.

The Church, the Bishop of Rouen and Eleanor could do nothing as John took over.

Now bear with me for a second. There are always two sides to a story. On one side we have Richard who had the throne of England in his hands, but who abused the position incredibly from the very beginning. To him, England was just a source of money to fund his crusades. On the other side, we have John who was sitting in England with the economy going down the drain because his spendthrift brother went off with all the money to Sicily leaving his greedy counsellor William Longchamp in charge.

Without condoning anything that John did, perhaps in his own way, he was doing the best he could in a very difficult situation while trying to stop the English economy from going belly up. He may have gone about it rather badly by throwing tantrums and taxing everyone to the max and he certainly had an escalating cruel streak, but maybe this escalation began for a very good reason. He had an unreliable brother who was taking every bit of spare cash he could find out of the country leaving John frustrated and scrambling around trying to make ends meet. To me, it seems to have been the catalyst that started John on his downward spiral into absolute cunning, cruelty and deviousness. But then again, he was a Plantagenet.

Despite John's success in gaining the throne, his control was only brief. Four months later, news arrived that Richard was alive and well but on trial in Germany. England could have him back, they said, but his release would be very expensive.

The Emperor was demanding a ransom of 150,000 marks, twice the annual revenue of the English Crown and Richard's council quickly agreed to the ransom even though the treasury had been almost drained to fund his crusades. To make up the shortfall, the nobles were told they would have to contribute.

John promptly turned to Philip for help. Something had to be done, and quickly. The two of them put their heads together and secretly made two offers to the Emperor. He could either have 80,000 marks to keep Richard under lock and key or he could have 100,000 marks to deliver him into their hands ... personally. You didn't need to be genius to know where *that* would leave Richard.

To their anger, the Emperor refused both offers. His word had been given and he was standing by it. Besides, their offer was a shortfall anyway. All that remained for England to do was to somehow collect the ransom and deliver it to him. Only then would they get Richard back.

Archbishop Rouen, Eleanor and the church faced their duty resolutely but the consequences staggered the kingdom. All laymen had to give a quarter of their crop while the Church gave plates and treasures and three of the monastic orders gave money to the value of a year's wool crop. John, in a reluctant show of support, set an example by collecting these taxes person-ally throughout his shires. When England and Normandy, taxed to the limit, could not scrape together the whole sum, the Emperor, satisfied he had all he could get and no more, decided to set Richard free anyway. On 4th February 1194 Richard was released and Philip sent John an infamous message: *"Look to yourself – the Devil is unloosed."*

We can be sure that Richard picked his way very carefully throughout Europe and he would have especially avoided the French territories. He certainly did not want to be captured in *that* country with John and Philip firm buddies.

John was not a stupid man. Ambitious and cruel, yes, but not stupid. He knew what his brother was capable of and he was smart enough to high-tail it to France before Richard arrived back in England in full splendour. And he only just made it. Richard arrived back in London a month later with the full weight of his army ready to bear down on John.

Amid the embers of his brother's final revolt, Richard was re-crowned king.

You would think that Richard would have been grateful and humbled to find the impoverished English people rejoicing his return, considering he'd never supported them in the first place. Instead, his first move was to try and raise more money to fund his return back to France so he could defend his personal French possessions against John.

On 12th May 1194, Richard sailed from Portsmouth for Barfleur. He would never set foot in England again.

By then, Richard was openly at war with Philip and his enemy was strong. While he had been away, Richard had drained England of every morsel he could while Philip had significantly increased his personal wealth and power. Now joined by John and several lords whose lands bordered Normandy, Philip had overwhelming power and the tables had turned for him.

For five years, Philip and Richard battled against each other – first one of them winning a battle and then the other. That is until 1196, when Philip came upon Arthur.

As we know, Richard had named Arthur as his heir to the English throne. Arthur was also the only legitimate grandson of Henry II and, aside from John; he was the only alternative heir to the Plantagenet possessions if Richard died childless. This seemed highly likely since Richard's wife was living with his sister in Sicily and he hadn't seen her for years.

Finding Arthur was Philip's trump card. He knew the advantages and he encouraged the friendship between his own son Louis and Arthur, both the same age, and as fortunes seesawed, Arthur returned to his mother in Brittany.

In April 1199, when the difficulty of raising revenue in England was at its very worst, a golden treasure was found near a castle in Chaluz on the lands of one of Richard's vassals. The Lord of Chaluz certainly tried to resist Richard taking it away from him but it seemed inevitable that Richard would win against the small and weak castle with only forty men and women inside. This greed was to be Richard's downfall.

Richard bought with him his usual entourage: men with swords and crossbows who burned everything in their path. For three days, the terrified people inside the castle walls resisted. On the third night of the siege, Richard left his tent armed with only a crossbow, a helmet and a shield and rode arrogantly close to the ramparts of the castle.

As Richard stood looking up, he saw a man reach over the top of the rampart carrying a crossbow in one hand and a frying pan from the kitchens as a shield in the other. It is said that Richard took the time to applaud as the kitchen hand fired a lone shot.

Richard ducked a fraction too slowly. The arrow struck him in the left shoulder near the neck. He tried to pull it out but the arrow snapped, leaving the barb buried inside his body. By the light of a fire, a surgeon would try to take out the shard of metal but as he dug, the wound widened.

As we can all imagine, surgery on a battlefield in medieval times was disastrous. The wound swiftly turned gangrenous.

Richard knew the end was near and began to set his affairs in order once more. He sent word to his mother and he divided his personal belongings among his friends. As Richard had no legitimate children, he relented and declared John to be his heir.

At the age of 42, ten days after his injury, Richard died in the arms of his mother who had ridden hard to be at her favourite son's side as he passed away. It was ironically 10th April, the day before Palm Sunday and the celebration of Jesus's triumphant entry into Jerusalem.

Historian, Jean Flori has analysed the work of contemporary historians and reported that they quite generally accept that Richard was homosexual. But not all agree. There is mention of one illegitimate son, Philip of Cognac but Flori concludes that Richard was more than likely bisexual.

While future Kings of England continued to make claims to territories on the continent, they would never again command the territories Richard I had inherited... and lost.

It was with immense happiness that John took the English throne that he had been plotting and scheming to gain for years.

JOHN

Born 1167
Reign 1199 - 1216

The character of the man who ascended the throne is well known. Richard's virtues were likened to a lion after which he was named, but there was no animal in nature that combines the conflicting qualities of John. He was a hardened warrior with the subtlety and cunning of a Machiavellian and from time to time during his furious rages, his cruelties were executed with cold, inhumane intelligence. Monks at the time emphasised his violence, greed, malice, treachery and lust and a French writer went as far as to write of his *"madness"*.

As the shocking news of Richard's death travelled through Europe, John found himself in the middle of many disputes. Did the son of a king's older brother, namely Arthur, beat the claim of the king's youngest brother, namely John? No one could agree. Richard had declared John to be his heir, but there were still two distinct views to this succession. His older brother Geoffrey had left behind a son, Arthur of Brittany, and a daughter Eleanor, which meant both of them had a better right to claim the throne than John, the youngest son of Henry II. Of course, John disregarded all of this and simply took over.

England reluctantly accepted John, but it was not a smooth accession and he did not inspire confidence in anyone. No one could forget his appalling behaviour while Richard was absent nor could they forget his vicious temper.

Philip now owned Anjou, Maine and Touraine thanks to Richard, and the two men had been to war, beside and against each other, for a long time. But as John's strength lay only in Aquitaine and Normandy, Philip never regarded him as his equal, despite being the King of England. What John *did* have was an eligible 12-year-old niece Blanche, the daughter of his sister Eleanor and King Alfonso VIII of Castille. And what Philip had was an equally eligible 12-year-old son, Louis. A match made in heaven.

One year later, a treaty was signed and the very next day, the wedding was celebrated in Paris although consummation was banned due to their youth.

From the very beginning of his reign, John feared Arthur. When Richard died, John had been in Brittany at Arthur's Court but he made a hasty exit out of the dangerous zone before quickly claiming the throne for himself with the support of his mother Eleanor. Like Emma of Normandy, she had been the wife of two kings and she would make sure that she was the mother of two kings as well.

There was little time for a crowning ceremony and it was regarded as a formality anyway. Within two weeks, John was on his way back to Europe.

As the 13th century dawned, there was relative peace for John. But one year later, war was on the horizon again when John set sight on the fiery, blue-eyed blonde Isabella of Angouleme. Overnight everything changed because John decided he was going to marry her.

Many historians say he was infatuated with the young girl, already renowned for her beauty, while others say it was a strategic move to gain key lands between Poitou and Gascony, which significantly strengthened his grip on Aquitaine. It was possibly a bit of both.

There were however a couple of problems. Her tender age of twelve was of no importance as many girls married at a young age. The first real problem he had was that to marry her he had to rid himself of his wife, Isabel, Countess of Gloucester whom he'd been married to for ten years.

After thinking long and hard about the situation, he came up with a very good reason. He declared that the marriage was illegal because both he and Isabel were related to Henry I (Isabel was the great-granddaughter of Henry I's illegitimate son, Robert of Gloucester, and John was Henry's great-grandson through Maud). This made them both second cousins, even though removed quite a few times. Several bishops in Normandy reluctantly approved his request, (and by the way who in their right minds would cross John?) and the marriage was quickly annulled. John however got to keep her lands after the annulment.

The other problem was that unfortunately, Isabella of Angouleme was already engaged at the time to Hugh IX le Brun, Count of Lusignan, an important member of the Poitou noble family and brother of Raoul, the Count of Eu. Just as John stood to benefit from this marriage, so the marriage threatened the interests of the Lusignan family. Although John was Count of Poitou, the Lusignans could legitimately appeal John's actions to Philip in France and the one thing John could be certain of was that Philip of France would suddenly become his enemy.

They appealed to Philip and the two men became vehement enemies.

Philip did not need much to anger him regarding the English monarchs. Philip, as John's overlord in respect to these territories, sent a summons to John to attend a court to answer charges made against him. John replied that he would not attend. Philip declared he must. A to and fro began with both parties sure that they were in the right and when all legal manoeuvres were exhausted, John, who was not even guaranteed safe-conduct, flatly refused to attend.

So, up on his high horse and armed with this legal right, Philip invaded Normandy in the summer of 1202 having sentenced John to be deprived of all the lands he held in France and given the disrespectful title of 'John Softsword'. And of course, Philip undoubtedly supported Arthur.

Philip was met with barely any resistance when he knighted Arthur. He gave Arthur all of John's French territories but allowed John to keep Normandy and Guienne. Once that was done, Philip betrothed Arthur to his own daughter Mary. Arthur was 16 at the time.

When we remember that the French provinces counted just as much with the Plantagenet kings as the whole of England, it is understandable that John was furious. While John fumed in England, Arthur felt confident enough to begin his own plans since he had the support of Philip behind him. When Arthur heard that his grandmother, Eleanor, was in a castle in

Mirabeau in Poitou, he decided to storm the castle and seize custody of the old Queen. She would make a fine prize in the war against his uncle John.

In July 1202, 250 knights rode noisily to Mirabeau castle. As she gazed down at the source of the noise, she would surely have been able to see her grandson looking back up at her.

Eleanor escaped through the countryside in the nick of time, (the second time in her life she had ridden to escape danger) and sent an urgent plea to John for help. She knew he was at Le Mans at the time and he had ample forces.

John covered the eighty miles in forty-eight hours and surprised Arthur at dawn.

Arthur had no chance whatsoever.

All of John's captives found his prisons bleak but in medieval times, the well-bred could expect more lenient conditions than their poor counterparts. Arthur was to be the exception and he soon found that he would be not be given preferential treatment at all.

Arthur's imprisonment was to become notorious. He was a high-grade prisoner and he rivalled John for the throne of England so John was expected to give Arthur a certain amount of freedom and leniency. Knowing his own value, Arthur would have been certain that no serious harm would come to him. He may be in prison, but Philip would buy his freedom from John eventually. Surely.

Arthur waited and waited and waited.

As more people learned of Arthur's situation, grumblings could be heard that John was not playing fair. One by one, his allies deserted him and piece-by-piece, he lost Anjou until only a few castles remained. Aquitaine was the last to fall. And the more friends he lost, the crueller he became.

What happened to Arthur from then on is unknown. The horrid crime of murder has been suggested but a cone of silence descends on the tragedy. That he was murdered by John's orders was never disputed at the time or afterwards, but there is a story that tells of a commander who was transferring Arthur from Falaise to Rouen. Agents of John who had been sent to intercept the party met him. Their instructions were to capture and castrate Arthur.

But another story tells that on 3rd April 1203, the Thursday before Easter, John was drunk and he was in the mood to lash out. He was surrounded by enemies and could not trust anyone. After dinner and some more wine, he became possessed with a fury worse than ever before. He would have certainly looked fearsome as he made his drunken way down to Arthur's cell. It is highly likely that John entered the cell and killed Arthur himself before throwing his lifeless body into the Seine where it was later found by a fisherman. That John always saw his 16-year-old nephew as a threat was widely known and the fact remains, Arthur was never seen again.

Although Arthur had been removed, John failed to profit from the crime. It turned out that Arthur had merely been Philip's tool and his disappearance did not alter Philip's resolve. In all future negotiations, Philip always said, *"No peace until you first produce Arthur."* John would never be able to do that.

By 1204 it was official. John was the most despised man in Europe. He spent much of that year securing England against potential French invasions supported by a small team of leading barons.

That same year also marked the cruellest winter in England's history. The Thames filled with ice so thick that people could walk from one side to the other. There were no crops and what vegetables there were, people dug up to eat when they were just seedlings. Prices soared as the suffering and starvation increased and superstition had it that God was punishing them for the wrongs that their king had committed. Even John could not fail to see the hardship of the people. And then, a rumour began that they were to be invaded from France and everyone panicked.

John knew Philip well and he knew to take this threat seriously. As Philip took Normandy, John ordered every man over 12 years of age to take up arms and protect their country. It was clear that John was making a stand and with the country's fear escalating, he planned his attack. He intended to set sail from Dartmouth with his 45 ships, together with any others he could seize that were able to be converted to warships, and head off to Normandy. It was the biggest navy since Richard had taken off to the crusades.

But when John arrived in Portsmouth ready to leave, he found the barons refusing to come with him. With his eyes bulging in disbelief, he screamed at them that this was mass mutiny. Still, they refused. Across the channel, Philip went happily on his merry way taking more of John's territories. Normandy was soon gone.

As John seethed, he silently promised that England would pay dearly for what it had done and he set about filling his coffers funded with new taxes. In his rage, he abused every avenue he could.

England was just beginning to come back from the terrible winter and John was determined to tap into that wealth. He set taxes on everything he could think of: shipping, forests and even judicial courts. He declared he could auction off an aristocratic widow or heiress to the highest bidder or they could simply pay him a fee if they did not want to remarry. If a child inherited before the age of 21, they could not take control of the inheritance; the king would do that for them. The king could even sell the right of control to anyone who paid for that right. And then there was inheritance tax, an amount set at the king's discretion.

In his anger at losing Normandy, he found great joy in plundering his own country. This was their new king whether they liked it or not, born out of their mutiny, and as England suffered more and more, his confidence grew.

At the height of his cruelty, men and women watched as the moon turned *"first a blood red colour and afterward of a dingy nature"*. It was a lunar eclipse and it had a powerful effect on the simple people in an age of superstition. They saw it as a prediction of evil and within five weeks, they were proven right.

Not only had John lost Normandy but his mother Eleanor died and almost immediately, Archbishop Hubert Walter, John's chief administrator and the only statesman he trusted and respected, died as well. This left the question open again of who would be elected as the Archbishop of England.

At the time, the Papal throne was occupied by Innocent III, one of the greatest and most influential medieval Popes in history. Innocent III seized the opportunity to elevate the power of the Church in England. Setting aside the candidates chosen by both the clergy and John, he announced a third and successful candidate, Stephen Langton, who was an English cardinal with great appeal in Rome.

John was understandably angry at the Pope stepping in and telling him what he should and shouldn't do. To retaliate, he set about seizing Church lands and Innocent III reacted by laying an embargo on all of England. The church bells would be silent, he declared, the doors of the churches would be closed and the dead would be buried in unconsecrated ground until John relented.

The decision from the Pope only made John angrier and his reaction outdid everything he had ever done up till then. He cursed the Pope and declared he would pluck out the eyes of every priest. He redoubled the attacks on the Church's property and as bishops escaped overseas, more and more abbeys fell vacant. The treasury overflowed and John enjoyed every minute of it.

And then he turned his attention to the Jews. The Jews had a monopoly on money lending and although they were a small community, they were incredibly rich. John took an exception to this and he ordered Jews to be imprisoned and tortured, resorting to taking out their teeth one at a time on a daily basis, until they handed over their wealth to him.

Even by the standards of Richard's coronation, this was brutal. Finally, in 1209, Innocent III excommunicated him.

John could not have cared less. Instead of putting the fear of God into John, it aggravated him to the point of absolute insanity. He was now fully funded for an attack to regain Normandy and that was all he cared about. He had made allies with his nephew, Emperor Otto IV and the Counts of Toulouse and Flanders, and he planned his attack meticulously. But with his insecurity at home overshadowing him, together with the strength of Philip and the Pope's armies gathering, John had to devise a new plan of attack.

It was actually a stroke of cunning and it was enough to be called political genius.

At all lengths, he had to close the circle of his enemies. And greed was the true and trusted way. To start with, he offered to the Pope the lure of making England a fief of the Papacy, and as John suspected, Innocent III leapt at the offer. The offer would have added to the Pope's worldly dignities and while forgiving John, he would take the sovereignty from John only to then return it back to him as his feudal lord.

This totally turned the tables on John's enemies. Philip, who had gathered his armies ready to invade England, was angered by this new turn of events as the Pope immediately turned on Philip, telling him to cancel all plans of invasion. The situation had dissolved without his help.

John, who had lain low at Dover while calculating his plan, would have been laughing while he pulled all these strings and threw his enemies into confusion. But he still had one final move left.

Encouraged by the Pope, he took the vows of a Crusader and invoked a sentence of excommunication upon his opponents. No one could deny him this right and the barons, who had thought to be activists against John, were now under the ban themselves. John was ecstatic.

While all this was going on, many nobles had voiced their displeasure at John's treatment of Arthur and among them was the Briouze family. Hindsight is a wonderful thing and I'm sure, given the choice, they would have kept silent if they'd known the consequences because John began terrorising them. Firstly, he took all of their possessions, then he called in all of their debts. He had William Briouze's position taken from him and in terror, the family fled to Ireland for protection.

With his recent successes under his belt, John gathered an army together and followed the Briouze family to Ireland, ransacking his way through Wales, castle after castle. He was really getting into the swing of things and in less than two months, he had destroyed everything in his path. William Briouze could only send his wife and sons to Scotland for safety. And John followed them there as well.

When he finally captured them, they were to suffer much same punishment that Arthur had. In less than a year they were dead having starved to death in their prison. When their bodies were found, it was told that they were huddled together and there were teeth marks on the body of the youngest son as his mother had tried to eat him.

For John, the year 1214 should have been his best year ever. But he should never have set foot in Scotland. As ruthless and powerful as he was, this one act was the beginning of the end for him.

On a cold December morning in 1214 in Scotland, King William of Scotland died leaving his 16-year-old son, Alexander, to become Alexander II, King of the Scots.

For the past 200 years, English kings had declared that the land of the Scots belonged to them. The early Canmores since Constantine had played the game and recognised English authority but subservience was not Alexander's style. As far as he was concerned, he was every bit as good as any English king. Better in fact. Maybe he was brash and arrogant, but he was on a mission to take his kingship back from the English overlords once and for all and that's all that mattered to him.

Northumbria, Cumberland and Westmoreland were lands to which the King of England and the King of Scotland had both considered their own.

To settle the argument, Alexander's father had given England both money and two of his daughters. Alexander was determined to take back what was rightfully his.

Alexander wasn't the only one with a grudge against John. There was a long line of English barons with grievances as well. Their biggest gripe was John's constant request for money to fund his war in France. So Alexander allied himself with the English barons.

In 1215, the barons grouped together with one fundamental principle, that Government would be more than the arbitrary rule of one man and the law must stand even above the King. They drew up a short document on parchment and with a handful of resolute men they set off to present it to the king.

On 15th June 1215, they dismounted without ceremony at Runnymede and met with John. The Archbishop of Canterbury and several bishops handed over their suggestions. The *'Articles of the Barons'* was read and to their amazement, agreed upon immediately by John. On this document were 60 articles for John to consider and at the bottom, Item 59, was Alexander's claim to the northern territories – *'I promise to do right by Alexander King of Scots'*. John duly signed. The most famous document in our history, the Magna Carta, was signed in one quiet, short scene.

Not that John had any intention to stand by his word and uphold the document. John soon disregarded it as utter foolishness and continued on regardless. He had thrown down the gauntlet.

The nobles made their first move by seizing Rochester Castle, owned by Stephen Langton and which had been left unguarded. But John was well prepared. He had stock-piled money and gathered his own men, his most trusted advisers being William Marshal, Earl of Pembroke and Ranulf of Chester. His plan was to isolate the rebels, protect his supply of mercenaries in Flanders, prevent the French from landing in the southeast and win the war through slow but deliberate destruction. For William Marshall's support, John betrothed his newborn daughter Eleanor to William's son who was then aged twenty-five. An impressive effort at multi-tasking.

His campaign started well. He took back Rochester castle, named as one of the greatest siege operations in England up to that time. Then everybody who had signed the Magna Carta had their hands chopped off first and then they were beheaded. John then split his forces, sending William Longespée,

John's illegitimate half-brother, to take the north side of London while he headed north to the estates of the northern barons.

For Alexander, this was too good to miss. He had the opportunity to reclaim the borderlines and take back what he saw as rightfully his. With Newcastle in his sights, he headed south into Northern England. First he burned Newcastle to the ground then took Carlyle. He meant business.

While Alexander tightened his grip in the north, the barons turned to the French for help. Philip's son Louis, the dauphin of France, was the husband of John's niece Blanche, who was also the granddaughter of Henry I, and as such Louis had the right to claim the English throne for himself through his marriage. He was the ideal person to lead the challenge and Louis wholeheartedly agreed

When John heard, he was furious. Again. This presented a huge problem for him and he was forced to turn south to deal with this fresh oncoming invasion.

It wasn't just the barons who had reached out to the French. Alexander had the exact same thought and he struck a deal with the French prince Louis as well. The deal was Alexander would support the French if, in return, they recognised the disputed territories in the north as Scottish territories. Louis was in a great position no matter which way you looked at it.

In one stroke, John had been swept aside and Alexander began marching into England with little resistance to meet up with the French army in Dover.

The plan was for Louis to wait in London while Alexander and Louis's army, together with the barons, advanced. With enemies on all sides, John had no choice but to retreat. As he withdrew, he watched angrily as many of his military men deserted to the Scots, including his half-brother William Longespée.

What happened next is something that has been rubbed out of the history of English monarchy.

At the request of the barons and with enthusiastic public support, Louis was proclaimed King of England at a mass in Saint Paul's Cathedral. Louis did not have a coronation since John had already excommunicated all the bishops, so he was merely *proclaimed* king by affirmation only. The coronation could come later, they assured him.

But as far as Louis was concerned, he had the throne to himself and he was in. Almost immediately, and prematurely, he began to appoint his friends in France into high English positions.

The barons had looked at everything from all sides, but they had not seen that one coming. Although they all spoke French, they were beginning to *feel* English and with the arrival of more and more of Louis's French friends, they panicked. They had expected to be given more control once they were rid of John but instead; control had merely passed from John to Louis. Worse than that, it had passed on to the French.

They began thinking. John had a 9-year-old son, Henry, didn't he? Of course, no 9-year-old had ever been a king, but there's always a first for everything, right? And if the young child was to become the king, then one of the barons would have to be the regent and then they really *would* be in charge of everything. But Louis had control of London and the child was at Corfe Castle in Dorset with his mother. They would have to get the child to the nearest abbey in Gloucester and crown him quickly. Of course, they didn't really have a crown - Louis had that - so they would have to use his mother's gold neckband. And actually, they didn't even have an archbishop to perform the coronation either. Never mind, the bishop of Winchester was available and he had the keys to the treasury as well. Perfect!

The next thing Louis knew, the 'affirmation' was withdrawn and he was stupefied. How could they withdraw the offer? he asked. Everything was finally coming to a head, he stated. His armies had gained territories in the southeast of England as well as parts of the north. John was on the defensive after marching from the Cotswolds to Cambridge and had finally arrived in Lincoln. Alexander was invading from northern England and marching south and was set to meet John in battle. In the five months that he had been in the country, he had gained more and more support and was just about to deliver the final blow. He listed all his achievements one by one. At the end of the list, he stated that he was certainly not about to give the crown back to them after everything he had done, not to mention that he was married to John's niece Blanche.

While Louis and the barons argued, the battle between Alexander and John at Lincoln was in full swing. For six hours, the terrible sounds of clashing swords, the screams of men as limbs were either crushed or severed and the cries of dying horses as they were butchered echoed through the city. The streets were said to have flowed with heads, blood and human entrails.

In the end, John was successful. Both the French army and the Scots had been defeated and Alexander returned to Scotland, dejected and destroyed.

But as always, fate stepped in and put an end to the dilemma of having three kings on the throne at the same time. Negotiations stopped as news arrived that John had contracted dysentery. Even though he determinately continued west to Wales, losing a significant part of his baggage and belongings including the Crown Jewels sucked up by quicksand in the bogs, his illness grew worse. On 18th October 1216, John died.

From Dover, Louis was energised when he heard the news and he began a fresh campaign for the throne. He packed up and headed on to London.

But Louis was in for a shock. He arrived fully expecting to be greeted by the same cheers he had received only five months ago. To his astonishment, the English were now showering him with arrows and lime to blind him. All of a sudden, everyone was patriotic and for the first time since the Norman Conquest, the French were being described as foreigners who were looting the English. It was enough to stop Louis in his tracks and with no more than a backwards snarl, he headed back home to France. He'd had enough of the fickleness of the English.

As we know, Louis did not become the king of England and this insult would be well remembered by both Louis and future generations.

John's 9-year-old son became Henry III and a new terrifying chapter in English history was about to begin.

HENRY III

Born 1207
Reign 1216 - 1272

As far as kings go, Henry III could not have been less like his father in the usual Plantagenet mould either in character or build. He was petulant, weak and ineffectual. But then again, he was only 9 years old while his little brother Richard was just 7 years old.

The government, which had not supported his father, now flocked to young Henry's side in droves. As far as they were concerned, Alexander II of Scotland had outgrown his usefulness and the 9-year-old child of King John could be swayed a lot easier than a moody Frenchman or an ambitious Scotsman.

The first nine years of Henry's reign were amazing. But as he made an almost sluggish progress into adulthood, an awful lot happened.

At the insistence of his advisers, Henry reissued the Magna Carta removing all references, not even a footnote, regarding Alexander's claim of Scotland. To soften the blow, negotiations began for his 10-year-old sister Joan to marry 23-year-old Alexander. Within two years Henry's 9-year-old sister Eleanor, betrothed at birth by their father John (who she had never met by the way), was married to 34-year-old William Marshall, 2nd Earl of

Pembroke. By then, Louis had become King Louis VIII of France in 1223 and then died of dysentery three years later, leaving his 12-year-old son Louis IX to rule under the regency of his mother Blanche. To top it off, Henry had been victorious in a battle against the French to regain Gascony and his younger brother Richard, then 16-years-old, fought valiantly beside him. The victory had given England a valuable and lucrative wine trade and as a reward, Henry gave his little brother the title of Earl of Cornwall as a birthday gift at the beginning of the next year.

All in all, everyone agreed it was a terrific start to Henry's reign.

Passions had gradually cooled over the years so it was not until Henry was 19 years old that he took over the reins of his own government.

As an adult, Henry was a good deal less than average height and like his father, inclined to be plump. He had a drooping left eyelid that covered half of the eye, which rendered him a rather sinister appearance and from his earliest years, seemed almost vague. But if he hadn't inherited his ancestor's strengths, he certainly inherited the Plantagenet temper and pig-headedness and often flew into rages hurling abuse, even objects, at his ministers. Despite the intensity of his attacks, he rarely stayed angry for long and he soon lapsed back into a type of lethargy.

It was not until the year 1230 that Henry met Eleanor of Provence. Eleanor was the second daughter of Raymond Berenger, Count of Provence and Beatrice of Savoy. Eleanor's elder sister, Margaret, had married Louis IX of France so the match had many benefits ranging from allegiance to economy.

Like her mother, grandmother and sisters, Eleanor was renowned for her beauty and though no indication of Eleanor' height exists, since her son, Edward I, would be well over six feet tall and handsome and her husband was ... uh ... not, it can safely be assumed that she was a very striking woman.

At this stage, neither of them had met and Henry had no idea that she was a dark-haired brunette with beautiful eyes and a strong will. After Margaret's desirable marriage to Louis IX, her uncle William of Savoy corresponded with Henry to set up a match of equal importance between Henry and his niece.

Henry's attention had been drawn to her by a poem she addressed to his younger brother, Richard, and although Henry was touching 29 years of age, he decided that he wanted the 12-year-old beauty for himself. The wedding plans began in earnest.

Their wedding was like something out of a Walt Disney fairy tale. She was dressed in a shimmering golden gown that was tightly fitted at her waist that flared out in pleats around her feet. The sleeves were long and lined with ermine. Her almost black hair seemed to glow as she walked with her head respectfully lowered down the aisle towards Henry. Her lovely eyes glanced up from time to time almost shyly through long eyelashes towards the entire nobility who were in full attendance. The couple had never met and she had never set foot in England prior to the wedding but from the very beginning, she had Henry wrapped around her little finger. It was lucky she did because in her entourage she brought a large number of uncles and cousins, crudely called *"the Savoyards"*.

Almost immediately, her relatives began to arrive en masse and began taking notable positions in England. As her influence over Henry increased, so did her unpopularity with the English barons, creating a terrible conflict for Henry. As they had suspected, her family were an ill-mannered, arrogant bunch and even though society was regularly disrupted by violence, her family's outlandish behaviour attracted quite a bit of attention. For this, the Londoners hated Eleanor with a passion and she returned it fervently.

Through the years, Henry had many confrontations with Hubert De Burgh, his chief minister beginning when Henry was 24-years-old. He accused De Burgh of a confusing number of crimes including poisoning both the Earl of Salisbury and his sister Eleanor's husband, William Marshall, both of whom had recently died without De Burgh's assistance. De Burgh was tried and sentenced to life-long imprisonment in Devizes castle and a new adviser, Bishop Des Roches, stepped up to replace him. Instantly, Des Roches rid the court of any opponents and unbeknownst to Henry, helped himself to valuable royal offices, lands and castles. With Des Roches's assistance, Henry exiled nobles and barons without a trial of their peers, burning their villages and houses, cutting down their woods and orchards, and destroying their forests.

Hostility at Henry's rule was by this time rife amongst the nobles as he shook himself into action although he still foolishly continued to shower titles on Eleanor's foreign family. Her maternal uncle, Peter of Savoy, was granted the honour of 1st Earl of Richmond and his brother, Boniface, was made Archbishop of Canterbury. The situation was further inflamed by Henry's support of his French relatives, the Lusignans, who were arriving by the shipload as well. Upon the death of his sister Eleanor's husband, William Marshall Earl of Pembroke, Henry gave the title to his half-brother, William de Valence, the son from his mother's second marriage to Hugh of Lusignan. Another half-brother was made Bishop-elect of Winchester and to add more fuel to the fire, large sums of money meant for Eleanor's mother was actually funding a war for her brother-in-law, the Duke of Anjou. With every title given over the years, the barons glowered more.

After the death of her husband, Henry's sister Eleanor had pledged to the church that she would be celibate for the rest of her life. After seven years of widowhood, she was still a young woman of 23 and had probably been thinking she had made a rather hasty decision. When she met Simon de Montfort and fell head over heels in love with him, she knew for certain she'd made a mistake. The charismatic 30-year-old was a distant French cousin of Henry who wore a hair shirt, which appealed to Henry who was beginning to see himself as the next Edward the Confessor. They became good friends and Henry looked up to him in a type of childish admiration. He soon became a favourite in Henry's inner circle.

This was the last straw for the English nobles. No sister of a king should be allowed to marry a man of modest rank, and especially not to a French-man. Everyone protested passionately but Henry stood firm. The marriage would go ahead.

It was Henry's younger brother Richard who surprised Henry by rebelling against him when he learned of his sister's marriage. Richard pointed out that this meant the manor of Sutton Valence in Kent would be in De Montfort's possession after the marriage and it was only after Henry mollified Richard by offering him 6,000 marks that peace was grudgingly restored. When Simon and Eleanor's first son was born in November 1238 (despite rumours that it had been short of nine months since the wedding), there was nothing the barons could do. He was baptised Henry in honour of his Royal uncle and in February 1239 De Montfort was finally invested with the Earldom of Leicester.

Despite their disapproval of Henry's past actions, everything was forgiven when news came that Henry's wife Eleanor had given birth to a baby boy. Almost immediately, people began choosing a name for their future king. Another Henry? Perhaps Richard? Maybe even William?

When Henry told them the boy would be named Edward after his beloved Confessor, they were more than a little surprised. Edward the Confessor had not even been a Plantagenet. The name even sounded old-fashioned to their well-bred ears. But Edward it remained and one year later, a daughter Margaret was born and then another son.

Soon after De Montfort's phenomenal elevation in position, a rift began to show between Henry and his brother-in-law. De Montfort owed a great deal of money to Eleanor's uncle and he had named Henry as security for his repayment. Henry was furious he'd used his name without being asked first and after confronting De Montfort; Henry threatened to have him thrown in the Tower.

For the first time, Henry began to see De Montfort's arrogance and he took exception to what he thought was abuse of his generosity. He seethed at the political cost the marriage had cost him and even though his sister now had two children under two, his resolve to rid himself of De Montfort began to consume him. In the end, he banished them all from England.

After the birth of De Montfort's first child with Eleanor, he had announced his intention to go on crusade with Henry's brother Richard. This seemed like as good a time as any so he raised funds and set off to the Holy Land, leaving his wife and two children behind. Eleanor pleaded with her brother to allow her to stay in England but he was adamant: she had to leave. Sobbing, she fled with her children to Sicily where she lived with her sister Isabel and her brother-in-law, Frederick II.

Two years later, Simon de Montfort and Richard returned from the crusades to find Henry in a much better frame of mind after promising to join Henry's campaign against Louis IX of France and for a while, all was forgiven.

The year 1244 was a crisis year for Henry. As money slipped through Henry's fingers, a baronial commission was appointed to fix the terms of money given to him. Somehow, they had to put a hold on his spending. The only way council could see that happening was to elect the Treasurer and certain judges, as well as the clergy, to take control. Henry, angered that the church would not, and could not, help him with finances anymore, found himself forced to sell jewels and gold plates and give new grants to those who would buy them. Meanwhile, he discovered himself with greater continental obligations as well.

The death of the Holy Roman Emperor Frederick in 1250 revived Rome in trying to unite Sicily. As usual, with no idea how to handle money, Henry agreed to pay the Pope the breathtaking amount of £90,000 (the equivalent today would be around £4.7 billion) for the Sicilian crown to be offered to his youngest son Edmund, then 5 years old. The Pope, of course, agreed but on one condition: if he didn't pay up, he would be excommunicated. Almost at the same time, negotiations began for the marriage of his eldest son Edward to Eleanor of Castile and as if all of that wasn't enough, at the Imperial election in 1257, Henry's brother Richard offered himself as Emperor, which meant Henry had to spend lavishly to secure his election as well.

When the council heard, they exploded. At a time when Henry was short of cash, it was a crazy thing to do and of course, both the Great Council and the clergy refused to give Henry the money.

It was a terrible time for Henry, not just politically but domestically. During the span of two years, Henry and Eleanor lost five of their children, all still young children under the age of seven. Both Henry and Eleanor were inconsolable but Henry shook off his grief resolutely and sent his 15-year-old son Edward to Castile in Spain for his arranged marriage to 9-year-old, Eleanor. As a wedding present, Henry gave Edward a package, which included parts of Ireland, the Channel Islands and the King's lands in Wales to provide an income for him. *This* son's life, Henry decided, would be glorious.

Henry's governing council can be forgiven for their next decision. As his foolish spending increased and mental instability became more apparent, they were forced to take steps to help him manage the country. It was a fair decision to elect fifteen nobles to help govern but in hindsight, allowing Henry's own brother-in-law, Simon de Montfort, to take the lead was probably their biggest mistake.

As De Montfort took the lead with utmost relish, Henry and his 23 year-old-son Edward were told in no uncertain terms what was expected of them. He also told William Valence, Henry's half-brother and a member of the Lusignan family, *"Know for certain and make no mistake about it, you will either give up the castles which you hold of the king, or you will lose your head."*

Horrified, the Lusignans fled and were formally expelled a year later from the country.

Henry had never been a jolly man but he was feeling more and more defeated and depressed. From what had been a great Plantagenet dynasty, all was now in ruins as Henry became, in most ways, irrelevant to the running of this own kingdom. At 52 years old, he felt old and humiliated.

As for his son who stood close by, Edward seethed at the treatment his father was receiving from De Montfort. He had watched as his father cowered for long enough and one month short of his 25th birthday, he exploded, as any true Plantagenet would do. He declared all-out war.

Shortly after dawn on 14th May 1264, an army stood silently outside the town of Lewes in Sussex. There were 1,000 knights and thousands of infantrymen, all in foul moods and all hell-bent on vengeance against De Montfort. Edward and his army had refused offers to negotiate with the rebels and they looked forward to ridding themselves of the rebels once and for all.

56-year-old De Montfort led his own small rebel army, wheeled out to battle on a cart because of a broken leg. Since the turn of the year, his army had coped well in a series of sieges across the country but it was clear that the day of reckoning had arrived as both armies faced each other across the Downs.

Edward took command of the army near Lewes castle where he had been staying while his uncle Richard was at the head of the army. Henry was on the left flank closest to the priory. Together they faced the rebel band. To Edward, the rebels were unpardonable and as a roar went up, he charged with an aggression that he would be famous for the rest of his life. The strength of the attack was so great that he drove the small band over the bank, across the valley and on to the banks of the river Ouse, chasing them and killing everyone they could reach.

When Edward's army regrouped victoriously back at the battlefield, it was past midday. He had expected to see the rest of the rebels slaughtered but instead, what he saw was devastation. While he had left the lines to chase away the rebel's left flank, he had left the rest of the army vulnerable. Henry's division had been attacked by another band of rebels who had been hiding behind the priory while his uncle had pushed his division on to high ground but had then found himself surrounded. Edward returned to hear laughter and jeers as the rebels hurled insults at his father and uncle. The Battle of Lewes had been lost and Henry, Edward and Richard were all placed under house arrest and told that if they did not agree to come peacefully, they would all be short a head. Queen Eleanor, however, could return to France.

It was the lowest point in Plantagenet history. After the victory, De Montfort assumed control of the government and along with a council of nine nobles, he began ruling in the name of the king as a Parliament. It was the first time the word 'Parliament' was used in history and De Montfort was smart enough to realise the need to obtain the support of the strengthening middle classes. He summoned knights from each shire in addition to the high churchmen and nobility and invited burgesses from selected towns to attend. De Montfort was now in every respect the ruler of England and if he had been as brutal as those before him and proceeded with wholesale slaughter as they had, his grip as a ruler might have lasted a while longer.

What is surprising, and probably stupid, after having fought so hard to be at the top, De Montfort began dividing the spoils of these wars unfairly. He gave himself and his sons territories and castles that had been plundered but forgot to reward supporters who had stood by him loyally. This included property owned by Edward and by doing so, many barons who had initially supported him now started to take a better look at him. All too soon, De Montfort's many enemies began scheming night and day to overthrow him.

Henry lived docilely in De Montfort's care and was treated at all times with a respect not shown to Arthur by his father. Edward was allowed a level of freedom, which could only have been founded on his word not to escape. However, one day in May 1265, Edward left to go out hunting in a buoyant mood with a few friends and simply forgot to return as he had promised. With him, Edward took De Montfort's ally, Thomas de Clare and his battalion. Together they became active in organising the total destruction of De Montfort.

This time, Edward vowed he would not lose.

On 1st August, Edward's group attacked De Montfort's young son Simon at Kenilworth and when De Montfort heard of the attack, he was stunned. He had been staying at a nearby priory and had been totally unprepared for the confrontation. Though boosted by Welsh infantry, De Montfort's forces were severely exhausted and there was a desperate scramble as De Montfort finally found a place to cross the River Severn with his army. Two days later, he made it to Evesham.

As the skies darkened with rain, De Montfort waited in the gloom, intending to rendezvous and join up with his son. Three hours after dawn, he saw his son's banners flying high and his spirits rose in hope. With the two armies joined, they had a fighting chance to retain England.

But then a cry suddenly called out from the tower. It was Edward, not his son, leading the army carrying De Montfort's stolen banners. When De Montfort realised that his son had been ambushed, probably killed, he said *"May God have mercy on our souls because our bodies are theirs."*

Escape was impossible. His army was trapped in a horseshoe bend of the river and the only exit was via a bridge, and that had been blocked. De Montfort watched silently as Edward and his 8,000-strong army approached. He did not have to watch for long. As the storm broke above them, Edward's men attacked.

De Montfort is said to have fought bravely but his last moments were filled with scenes of his men being dragged from their horses and stabbed to death while the smell of blood hung heavily in the air. One son, Henry, was killed and another one, Guy, was captured. The battle was a total massacre.

It would be Roger Mortimer who would sever De Montfort's head from his body. His feet were cut off, then his genitals, and the last were stuck in his mouth. Lying dead in the summer rain were highborn men and those who had not been killed, were wounded or captured. The battle has been described by some as the *'Murder of Evesham'*.

Many of De Montfort's supporters wished they had been killed alongside him. Puffing his ample chest out, Henry declared that all supporters of De Montfort were to be disinherited and all their property to be distributed to the king's supporters. On that day, at the stroke of a pen, 300 men were ruined. Many lost everything they owned and found themselves living in the forest much like the stories of Robin Hood.

In the last years of his life with De Montfort dead and his son Edward away on a crusade, Henry retreated into himself and enjoyed comparative peace, oblivious to everything else around him. Half a century had passed since he gained the throne at 9 years of age when England had been in the middle of a civil war. Six years after Evesham, at the age of 56, Henry died.

Eleanor and Henry had nine children, five of whom died while still children. Eventually, it was his eldest son Edward who would become King of England but it would be years before he returned from his crusade in Sicily to claim the throne.

Through the years, England watched in trepidation as the Scots and the Welsh became more and more disgruntled and vocal.

But no one could have predicted what was about to happen. Very soon, Edward would return from the crusades and the legend of Edward Longshanks would begin.

EDWARD I (LONGSHANKS)

Born 1239
Reign 1272 - 1307

At 33 years of age, Edward was an experienced leader and a skilful general who had learned the art of war well. He had also learned patience. When at any time in the closing years of his father's life he could have taken control, maybe even should have, he preferred to patiently wait, unlike many of his impatient ancestors.

As a child, he was seriously ill on several occasions but in adulthood, he was an intimidating 6 feet 2 inches tall, a head and shoulders above the ordinary man. His hair, always abundant, changed from blonde in childhood to black in manhood and snow white in old age. The only things that marred his features were a drooping eyelid, which had been characteristic of his father, and a lisp. But neither of these impediments affected Edward in the slightest. He could be very persuasive when he put his mind to it.

Even at an early age, Edward showed that he had a taste for violence. He revelled in war, tournaments, hawking and hunting and when he chased a quarry, he galloped at breakneck speed to cut the beast down. At one time, Edward attacked a man, cut off his ear and gouged out an eye. People began asking themselves if this was what a young boy could do, what would he be like when he became king?

However, in his private life, the marriage between Eleanor of Castile and Edward was a huge success. As you can imagine, arranged royal marriages were rarely happy, but this couple was devoted to each other. They were rarely apart, and he is one of the few medieval English kings not to have fathered children out of wedlock.

Edward and Eleanor were second cousins once removed as Edward's grandfather King John and Eleanor's great grandmother Eleanor were the son and daughter of King Henry II and Eleanor of Aquitaine. I know ... a lot of Eleanors. When they married, he was fifteen and she was thirteen.

After three short-lived daughters, she finally gave birth to a son, John, who was followed by a second boy, Henry a year later, and in 1269, another healthy daughter they called Eleanor.

After Evesham, and before his father's death, Edward was restless. He had found an eagerness for war and the timidity of hawking and tournaments had lost their appeal for him. With the crusades still in full swing, it seemed like the perfect chance for him to indulge himself. He scraped together enough cash for a small army, and with his wife Eleanor determined to come along with her husband, they left their three children behind in the care of Edward's uncle, Richard of Cornwall and headed off to the middle east.

From the beginning, it was clear that the crusade was not going to amount to much. The days of great triumphs had passed and Edward found there was no war left to join. He stayed for a year during which an attack by a Saracen left him with a nasty wound to his hip. Thankfully for Edward, there were better surgeons available than when Richard the Lionheart had suffered his shoulder wound and after a lengthy recovery, which involved cutting the rotting flesh off his hip on a daily basis, Edward heard that his father had died.

He left immediately, together with his wife and their new daughter Joan, but took his time carefully zigzagging through Europe for almost two years. He'd heard the stories of Richard the Lionheart's capture and ransom at the end of his crusade and had no want for the same thing to happen to him and his family. At his coronation, Eleanor was in the early stages of her 10th pregnancy with Margaret.

Edward had always shown disinterestedness in political matters but with accession to the throne, he undertook a ceaseless process of administrative reorganisation, travelling continually about his kingdom, holding inquiries into abuse of all kinds and correcting them forcefully. In every way he could, he tried to correct the management of his realm and he was remarkable among medieval kings for the seriousness that he regarded his work. He had a copy of the Magna Carta posted in every cathedral and every church and all who violated the charter was threatened by excommunication.

The Welsh had always been a problem for the Plantagenets and every king since the Norman invasion had come across them at some point in their reign. The mountains of Wales nursed a subdued race and Edward, as his father's lieutenant, had first-hand experience with the Welsh.

Edward grew up in a time when the tales of Arthur and the Knights of the Round Table were a truth not a romantic story, as we know today, and Edward had a fixation with the story. In the story, Arthur was depicted as a Welsh warrior who defeated the English. Edward was going to do the opposite. He was going to be the warrior who defeated the Welsh.

Five years into his reign, he gathered up any army of 1500 men, supplies, horses and weapons and headed off to Wales. When he had planned his crusade to the Holy Land, he had been unable to gather more than a handful of knights. Now he found that everyone wanted to go to war with him against the Welsh.

It was at this time in history when the Welsh introduced a new type of weaponry. Not clubs, swords or hand-flung missiles but improved archery called a 'longbow' and this new art of warfare made an astonishing entrance on the military scene. For the first time in history, infantry possessed a weapon that could penetrate armour and was superior to any method used before or again until the coming of the rifle.

For Edward, it was a war of conquest but for the Welsh, it was their national identity they were protecting and they fought back with a vengeance. But despite their undying passion after several years of persistent warfare, Edward coldly and fiercely broke them. He marched deep into Wales through the heat of summer and blocked them from their only escape route to Ireland. It was a huge success and almost immediately, he commenced building castles everywhere he went.

For the seven months of every year during the warmest months of the year, his building went into full swing. Forests were levelled, stones collected and dragged to the dirty, smelly sites on the beginnings of roads and endless carts brought huge logs and timber as the furnaces roared. A new innovation was devised that they called the arrow-slit. It would be very difficult for the Welsh to shoot an arrow into the castle through the slit but it would be very easy to fire a crossbow bolt out. Work abounded with labourers, carpenters and stonemasons as the buildings grew.

As these magnificent buildings grew through the summer months, towns popped up around them. And so did the rubbish and filth. With the building progressing at breakneck speed, sanitation became a huge problem and with it came diseases. Government was directed to step in but it was a problem that no one could solve, not in this time in history anyway. To top it off, Edward was badly in need of money to fund the vast number of castles that he was building so everything else, including sanitation, was put on hold. And with sanitation on hold, child mortality rose as disease increased.

It was during the spring of 1284, while building Caernarfon Castle that Eleanor was brought to town in labour for the sixteenth time. At least eight children, including Henry and John, had died in infancy and of their six remaining children, all were girls except for Alfonso named for Eleanor's grandfather. All fingers were crossed for another boy.

Finally, in April, Eleanor delivered the long sort-after boy and they named him Edward of Caernarfon after his father. But while the couple were still rejoicing over the birth of a second boy in the family, there came a terrible tragedy. In August of that year, their 10-year-old son Alfonso fell ill and died, leaving Edward, now only four months old, as the only male heir to the kingdom of Britain and the first Prince of Wales. I can't help but think it is a great shame that the English were deprived of a King Alfonso.

By the time he returned to England from Wales, he found he owed bankers more than £116,000 and the financial atmosphere was tense. There were allegations that some officials and judges were corrupt and many nobles were complaining about the amount of financial assistance Edward needed with building still continuing in Wales.

Desperate for money, Edward enthusiastically turned to a long-employed tactic by the Plantagenets of getting rid of the Jews. As with many of his ancestors, there was intense pressure for him to cripple them financially.

By early 1290, it had become increasingly difficult for Jews to live in England. They had endured the synagogues being burned down, they had watched as friends were hanged and they were forced to wear yellow badges on their coats to distinguish them from Christians. Many realised that their only way of surviving was to leave England and the Jewish population dwindled to 2,000 people.

Their departure gave Edward some capital and income from their confiscated property but he needed more. By July 1290, a law was passed at Westminster Abbey and read aloud in synagogues. All Jews were to leave England by 1st November on pain of death.

They began to leave during the summer months but some were less fortunate than others. As they left for an equally unwelcoming Europe, many were butchered along the way and Edward's revenue increased at an even faster pace. And he helped it along with further taxes imposed.

The people groaned and the Jews cried but Edward wasn't listening. He had raised £100,000 and the Plantagenet realm looked promising once more. It was opportune that he had saved some money in his bank because he was about to be plunged into another expensive war and the bloodiest of all.

The greatest quarrel of Edward's reign was Scotland. For many years, England and Scotland had dwelt in friendship but in the years between 1275 and 1284, Alexander III of Scotland's life turned into a tragedy. In the space of nine years, he had lost two sons and one daughter in quick succession followed by his wife, Edward's sister Margaret. As Alexander grieved, Edward watched as the Canmore dynasty was withering on the vine. As befitting the brother of Alexander's wife, Edward sent condolences and there seemed a genuine friendship and sorrow between the two kings. After all, Edward knew what it was like to bury children. By then, he'd already buried ten of his own sixteen children.

Then in March 1286, two years later, Edward heard of another death. Alexander himself was dead. Alexander had finished his business in Edinburgh but wanted desperately to travel the 25 odd kilometres and return to his palace where his new young bride awaited him. His advisers begged him not to go as it was a foul night but Alexander ignored them. In the darkness, he rode his horse over a cliff and was found the next day with his neck broken. He left as his heir, 3-year-old Margaret Maid of Norway, a granddaughter by his deceased daughter Margaret who had married King Eric II of Norway.

The country was in a state of utter confusion and distress.

Edward was said to have mourned his brother-in-law's death but some said they were crocodile tears. After all, he wasn't related by blood to the Scottish king and at that moment, the dynasty was hanging by a single thread. An infant female thread at that.

An idea began to form in Edward's head and the logic was simple. A marriage pact between Margaret the Maid and Edward's 1-year-old son would unite the royal families. If they could do that one simple thing, the antagonism between Scotland and England would cease. Let's not forget that medieval women were regarded as property and whatever Margaret owned would instantly belong to Edward's son as soon as they were married. It was a great plan and one Edward wholeheartedly endorsed.

In any case, it turned out to be just a dream.

In the autumn of 1290 when Margaret was 7 years old, she embarked on the trip from Norway upon stormy seas bound for Scotland. The security and future of Scotland rested on her tiny shoulders.

The trip was not a particularly dangerous one as Norway and Scotland were geographically close and Vikings had made the trip many times success-fully in past centuries in less sturdy boats. By early September, she was at sea and by the third week she had landed in Orkney on her last leg to Scotland. Then in the last days of September, news reached Edward that Margaret had died on the island after a week's illness, having eaten rotten food while at sea. Scotland was again without a ruler.

Almost at the same time, Edward's wife of thirty-six years began suffering from a recurrence of a persistent fever. Eleanor had travelled to Lincoln to meet Edward and upon arrival, had taken to her bed with a temperature. Edward was by her side night and day, but she never recovered and for the next six months, Edward grieved publicly for his dead wife.

For two years after the death of Margaret the Maid, guardians of Scot-land dithered endlessly over who would be the next ruler. For the Scottish nobility, there was a clear choice of only two men: John Balliol and Robert the Bruce. Both were from powerful families and both had enough military muscle to back their claim. But by 1292, still no choice had been made and it became very clear that the guardians needed help in making a decision.

Perhaps a friendly arbitrator could help, the nobles thought. Someone with experience who commanded respect. Who else but the King of England, someone suggested. After all, Edward *was* family. There was no reason to doubt him. Was there?

Edward took great interest in the proceedings. For him, this was divine providence and he called for a parliament to decide the matter. But under the condition: it had to be held on English soil.

And of course, the Scots smelled a rat.

It didn't take Edward long to reveal his true colours or his true intention. He sent word to the Scots that the parliament would not start until the claimants acknowledged his position as superior overlord of Scotland.

The Scots were stunned. Sixty years of peace and now this? To top it off, Edward then produced eleven more claimants from prominent families and declared if they didn't acknowledge his overlordship, they would be eliminated from the contest altogether. If they wanted the throne of Scotland, they had no choice but to agree to his terms. He had them exactly where he wanted them and one by one, the claimants swore allegiance to him.

From Edward's point of view, it didn't matter who was actually chosen. He had all the claimants in the bag anyway and he had it all stitched up without a single drop of blood being shed. He could choose whoever he wanted.

John Balliol was the perfect man for the job. He was the great, great grandson of King David I of Scotland, which put him one step ahead of his rival Robert the Bruce. And John had inherited lands from his father but no money for the upkeep. Better still, he was married to Isabella, daughter of John de Warenne, Earl of Surrey and Alice de Lusignan, who was related to King John's widow, Isabella and a cousin of Edward's late wife Eleanor. Balliol was like a lamb among the wolves and the choice for Edward was easy.

There was never any doubt that John Balliol would inevitably become Edward's puppet. Everyone knew that John would have very little actual power and Edward would personally gain from the arrangement. It was a clever move and a win/win situation for Edward.

As always, relations with the French were still tense so when King Philip III of France died and his 17-year-old son Philip IV came to the throne, Edward saw it as the ideal time to begin efforts to try and appease the strained relations. He was to find that even at this young age, Philip's conniving abilities exceeded his own.

The world was entering a time when France was once again becoming a notable power and the Plantagenets were still too small a family in Europe to be taken seriously. And Philip knew it. If Edward wanted peace, Philip stated, he should hand Gascony back, the French territory that Richard the Lionheart had kept when he refused to marry Alys. And if he was *really* serious, Edward was to marry Philip's 15-year-old sister into the bargain.

It was an insufferable humiliation that Edward could not swallow. He promptly began preparing an army.

It was the age-old plan of assembling allies and demanding that Scottish troops help him in his war against France and in his haste to exert his power, he went one step too far. He insisted, without any choice of refusal, that John Balliol himself stand behind him and together, their combined armies would head off into battle.

It was a glaring mistake for Edward not to realise that bullying Scotland would only result in their defiance.

But as Edward was preparing for war with France, a fresh wave of rebellion side-tracked him in Wales costing him time and money during a winter of heavy floods. Although it resulted in a victory for Edward, it gave Scotland valuable time to put things in order.

Scotland could see what was happening and without a doubt, it was time for action. With the slighted Bruces defiantly refusing to accept Balliol as the new king, a Scottish council of twelve began making plans of their own.

Knowing that France was Edward's sworn enemy, a delegation left Stirling to negotiate a treaty with the French king. The treaty was simple. Should Edward attack France, the Scots would wage war on England. In return, the French promised to wage war on England if Scotland were attacked. And as promised, as Edward's army marched into France, the Scots duly, and willingly, marched into England sending raiding parties into Cumberland and destroying towns around Carlisle.

Edward's short fuse was lit.

Scotland waited for Edward's response but they didn't have to wait long. With the biggest army ever to be sent north, Edward's army marched into

Scotland on 30th March 1296. He'd had enough and he was going to show them that he was not a man to do things by half.

He must have looked like a giant as he stared down from the hill overlooking Berwick. As trumpets blared and drums pounded, the blustery wind would have been blowing his beard strewn with silvery grey whiskers wildly and his long hair would have whipped around his face. His handsome, twisted mouth would have been smiling but it would have been the smile of a man who wonders which bug to squash first. As the two armies clashed below, they would have seen him high above them, a clear blue sky behind him, his hair blowing, mail gleaming and that evil smile on his battle-weathered face. He would have been thinking that vengeance was best taken piece by piece.

What occurred was the beginning of one of the most terrible massacres in medieval history. Berwick would never be the same and it was to be a bleak day for Scotland as thousands of corpses were thrown like garbage down wells and into the sea.

For two days, blood flowed from the slain and in his rage, Edward ordered 7,500 of both sexes to be massacred. The local clergy begged for pity but Edward was just warming up. He advanced into the heartland of Scotland and all resistance buckled. Then he turned his attention to John Balliol. Balliol had a lot of explaining to do and Edward was angry and out for a show.

Balliol had no chance whatsoever of escape. He was captured and sent to the Tower of London for a spell during which time Edward took full advantage of his victory and stripped Scotland of their crown jewels. Worse still, he stripped them of all their symbols of independence.

The Scots loved their country and they loved their independence. They were nothing if not totally patriotic and it was this final act that tipped the Scots over the edge.

From his refuge in the Scottish Highlands, a knight by the name of William Wallace had been watching and seething. He'd been holding back his raggedy army of men who had been itching for a fight and he wasn't about to hold them back another day. Wallace had behind him the spirit of a race as set and resolute as any man and what they lacked in experience they made up for in cold-bloodedness and determination. He was about to show

Edward what it was like to face a race of people who were fierce in their patriotism and who would never give up without a fight.

Edward should have left his grievance with France behind him. Instead, he returned to France and left John Warenne, Earl of Surrey as his commander in the north and on 11th September 1297, Warenne found himself face to face with Wallace on one side of Stirling Bridge and his own troops on the other side.

In hindsight, Warenne should have listened to his knights. Only one hour before, he'd watched as Wallace and his band of brigands glared at him from the other side of the bridge. He'd listened in silence as his officers urgently tried to convince him of the dangers of deploying across that bridge, especially with Wallace waiting and watching. They argued that it would take eleven hours to move their entire army across to the other side. In that time, they would be open to attack and totally vulnerable. And what if Wallace met them halfway and attacked before the passage was complete?

Warenne was a battle-hardened commander but he made a fateful mistake that day. He refused to listen to his officers and he ordered his troops to cross the bridge anyway.

As predicted, Wallace watched eagerly as the accumulation of the English troops marched slowly cross the bridge. He had no experience as a leader but he did what any good commander would have done. He waited for the exact right moment and then he hurled his full force at them.

The English were dumbfounded. Harder for them to believe was that their mighty English army had been defeated by a band of peasants, and Scottish amateur peasants at that. In the chaos, 5,000 Englishmen were slaughtered.

It was beyond Edward's resources to stay in France and struggle with the Scots at the same time. With bad news after bad news filtering back to him, all Edward could do was to enter into a long series of desperate negotiations with France.

It certainly wasn't the truce he'd imagined. After five years, Philip was still demanding that 60-year-old Edward marry Philip's 20-year-old sister Margaret, as well as making a betrothal between Edward's son, Edward of Caernarfon, and Philip's youngest daughter Isabella. To soften the deal Philip agreed to hand over a handsome dowry for each girl and with little money in his pocket, Edward began to listen.

Edward knew that in England, time was running out for him. Wallace was proving to be his equal in every way. He was ruthless, brutal and he played dirty. Edward had released the monster and Wallace was the result.

Without too much further ado, the marriage took place and very quickly, Margaret declared that she was pregnant.

When Edward returned to England, he found Wallace was the new ruler of Scotland. Before he had been angry. Now, with everything he had been forced to give up in France, he wanted absolute revenge. There would be no truce with Scotland and there would certainly be no mercy. Edward hastened with his whole army, as well as the Welsh army, to Scotland where Wallace waited for him.

The Battle of Falkirk was a sharp contrast to Stirling Bridge. This time, Wallace's army was battle-weary and hungry and Wallace was forced to take a defensive position. His only strength lay in his spearman, but he knew he had few cavalry and even fewer archers.

Edward wasn't about to let a repeat of Stirling Bridge happen. This time he was fully prepared. He had his full cavalry and his Welsh archers and they relentlessly rained arrows into the Scottish lines, sending them fleeing into the hills. The battle was lost for the Scots almost as soon as the first arrows began to fall, sending them fleeing into the hills.

This was Edward's victory and he relished it. Confident that he would soon be told where Wallace was hiding, he went on an orgy of executions.

Wallace evaded capture, but only until 5th August 1305. On that day, is was John de Menteith, a Scottish knight loyal to Edward, who turned Wallace over to English soldiers near Glasgow. Wallace was transported to London, taken to Westminster Hall and tried for treason.

As an outlaw, Wallace was already a condemned man. There would be no jury, no witnesses and no defence. His only response was, *"I could not be a traitor to Edward, for I was never his subject."*

On 23rd August 1305, Wallace was taken from the hall, stripped naked and dragged backwards through the city at the heels of a horse to the Elms at Smithfield. He was strangled by hanging but released while he was still alive. He was then castrated, eviscerated and his bowels burned before him. After that, he was beheaded. His body was then cut into four parts while his preserved head (dipped in tar) was placed on a pike atop London Bridge. His limbs were displayed, separately, in Newcastle, Berwick, Stirling and Aberdeen.

As far as Edward was concerned, Scotland was dead. But as far as the Scots were concerned, they had only just started. They were sick of having Balliol as a useless king when Robert the Bruce was more than willing to stand up to Edward and Robert the Bruce had already presented himself in an English court to push his point.

But as well as Robert the Bruce, there was another man who had his eye on the Scottish throne. John Comyn was a blood relative of John Balliol and he wanted his name remembered in history as well. At any cost.

Unbeknownst to Bruce, in a secret agreement with Edward, John Comyn agreed to forfeit his claim to the Scottish throne if the Bruce lands were handed over to him. With the agreement hot in his hands, Edward planned to arrest Bruce while he was still at English court.

Fortunately for Bruce, a friend heard of Edward's deal with Comyn and warned him in the nick of time. Bruce barely escaped the English court in the dark of night, making his way quickly to Scotland. He was on his way to the Church of Greyfriars at Dumfries and he was going to have it out with Comyn once and for all.

Both were ambitious men and they certainly did not get on. In the heat of the argument, Bruce accused Comyn of treachery. Swords clashed and blows were exchanged but in the end, it was Bruce who fatally stabbed Comyn while he was standing before the high altar of the monastery.

Barely seven weeks later, Robert the Bruce was crowned King of Scots with an alliance of land owners standing firmly behind him. It was no more than he felt was right. After all, he was a true descendent of the House of Wessex, not a usurper like the Plantagenets or the Normans who had invaded in 1066.

But word of Comyn's death had reached Edward and he responded with brutality. Bruce knew what was about to happen. He sent his wife, two sisters and his daughter north for safety along with his supporter, the Countess of Buchan, who had crowned him King of Scotland but along the way, they were captured by a Balliol supporter and handed over to the English as Bruce was forced to flee.

For four years, as Bruce gathered his army together once more, his wife, one of his sisters and his daughter suffered solitary confinement with daily public humiliation. Another sister was hung in a wooden cage outside of Roxburgh while the Countess of Buchan was hung outside of Berwick Castle. His youngest brother was hung, drawn and quartered.

If Bruce had wanted Edward dead in the past, he was desperate now. Bruce had learned a hard lesson delivered by Edward four years ago and he would never allow himself to be trapped again. He knew his greatest weapon was his knowledge of the Scottish countryside and he planned to use it to his advantage. He also knew that with his small ill-equipped army, he could never expect to defeat the English in an open battle.

At 68, Edward was far from well. He was physically shattered from years of warfare and his health was beginning to fail him. By 1306, he was being carried around in a litter. Beside him was his young bride who wanted for nothing and close behind was their two young boys and a daughter sleeping in beautiful cradles and dressed in finery.

Although cosseted, they were not the most important children in Edward's life. That was reserved for his son, Edward of Caernarfon Prince of Wales from his beloved Eleanor. At 16 years old, Edward Prince of Wales believed he was more than ready to take over from his ailing father.

But this young Edward was not the soldier his father had been and he had not inherited his father's love of war. There were also rumours in the court that he was far too friendly with his companion, Piers Gaveston, much to his father's intense anger.

As Edward struggled with his health while bringing Robert the Bruce to justice, he raged at his son over the dalliance with Gaveston.

There was one more remaining battle left for Edward, and that was to try and capture Bruce. But Loudoun Hill would be his downfall. Just outside of the Scottish border, Edward developed dysentery and died.

Edward, the bold warrior who had struck down Simon de Montfort, reduced the Welsh to obedience, hammered the Scots and laid the foundation of Parliament, died while his son was enjoying the sun in southeast England with his friend, Piers Gaveston.

England was going to regret the day the old king died.

EDWARD II

Born 1284
Reign 1307 - 1327

It seems to have been a Plantagenet characteristic because as with Richard the Lionheart, Edward could not remember having spoken any words to his father that weren't in anger. His father's voice was as sharp as glass and always full of derision.

Edward's father had spent years trying to train his son in the art of warfare but Edward continually disappointed him. It wasn't as if Edward wasn't as physically impressive as his father, because he was. He had all of his father's good points and none of the bad ones. That is, except for their Plantagenet tempers. That little personality trait they definitely shared and they continually clashed.

But instead of learning to hold a sword and lead an army, his father watched irritably as his son rowed, swam and dined late into the night with his friends. He lacked the drive and the ambition for war and his father never let Edward forget it.

Edward took over the throne at a very favourable time and should have taken full advantage of it. Instead, it seemed he went out of his way to annoy everyone. He had a reputation for making friends with inappropriate people who flattered him endlessly and from the beginning; Edward was regarded with suspicion and contempt. The nobles had seen this sort of behaviour before in the past and it never turned out well.

One friendship in particular was with a handsome, intelligent and wily young man by the name of Piers Gaveston. His father had hired Piers as a suitable companion for his son but this had backfired spectacularly towards the end of his reign when the two young men became ... er ... close. Piers was banished from England because of their strong attachment to each other but one of the first things Edward did when he took over the throne was to bring Piers back to England from exile. First mistake.

To say Edward was homosexual is perhaps not true. A weak young man, perhaps bisexual, led along by an ambitious, arrogant man like Piers was probably more to the point. In any case, their relationship was regarded as unhealthy, beyond friendship and decency, and the friendship soon became intolerable for barons and scandalised his subjects.

Then Edward made his second big mistake. He gave Piers the earldom of Cornwall along with permission to marry his niece, Margaret de Clare, daughter of his sister Joan.

Cornwall was a famous Plantagenet title and had traditionally been held by his great-uncle Richard the Lionheart. This royal title bought with it land in the south east of England as well as Yorkshire and a sizeable income. Everyone was outraged in particular his stepmother, Margaret of France, who had been led to believe by Edward I that the title would go to one of their children, either Thomas of Brereton or Edmund of Woodstock. Flatly refusing to listen to their gripes, Edward left for France to marry Philip IV's daughter, Isabella, as arranged and made his third big mistake. He left Piers as regent in his absence.

Outside Edward's select group, angry barons prowled and seethed. But if they were angry before, they hadn't seen anything yet. Edward's coronation was about to unfold.

The nobility from both France and England attended the grand ceremony and Edward's 12-year-old bride of one month accompanied him. Westminster Abbey throbbed with excitement and the streets were packed with onlookers dressed from rags to cloths of gold pushing and shoving to see the new king and his queen.

Coronation ceremonies were strict and niggling arguments could always be expected as variations occurred in the protocol and order of procession. As expected, Edward entered barefoot wearing a green robe and black hose alongside his young bride as they walked amongst flowers scattered on the carpet. The earls of Lancaster were next carrying great swords and the king's cousin Henry of Lancaster entered carrying the royal sceptre. Four barons then followed with the heavy coronation robes.

But among these great men walked Piers in pride of place, directly behind Edward and Isabella, decked out in royal purple silk studded with pearls. In his hand he carried the crown worn by Edward the Confessor. He even assisted in fixing the left spur to the king's boot after the anointing ceremony, a duty always reserved for the Earl of Pembroke. To top it off, Edward spoke his vows in French. And then, when you would think it couldn't get any worse, Piers led the outward procession carrying the royal sword that should have been carried by the Earl of Lancaster.

In a society where straying from royal protocol could have grave consequences, no one could believe their eyes and many nobles could not stop themselves from protesting loudly as he passed by.

And then came the wedding banquet, which Piers had organised, by the way. As people pushed aside the inedible food, Edward ignored Isabella and spent the entire banquet laughing and talking to Piers instead. It's not surprising that Isabella felt justified in complaining to her father, King Philip, of her ill-treatment. For a new queen's family to be so blatantly sidelined was deeply offensive but later, she would also find out that the best of her jewels and wedding presents had been given to Piers as well.

So many big mistakes. To Edward and Piers, it was a game that had been carefully planned for months in advance. It was entertainment. To the barons, it was a vile insult and within days, their anger peaked. It was the spark that ignited a political crisis.

Scotland and France were always either flaring or smouldering but when Parliament convened shortly after the coronation, virtually every baron, except for Hugh Dispenser the Elder, directed their first angry statement at Edward's elevation of Piers Gaveston's position. They barely tolerated the weak rule of Edward but they would definitely not tolerate Gaveston's pretensions.

There was no mistaking the fact that there was a lot of resentment directed towards Gaveston. He had risen through the ranks in remarkably short time through dubious means and as a result, the majority saw him as a serious threat. Obviously, Gaveston had to go, one way or another.

Everything his father had taught him should have told Edward that he was going about this the wrong way. Always a sensitive bunch, the barons would jump at the first opportunity to take a grip of the government if they thought the king was not doing the job properly.

There wasn't a lot Edward could do except to get Gaveston out of harm's way and Ireland seemed like the best option at the time. So with his title of Earl of Cornwall still intact, plus the added bonus of some castles and manors in both England and Gascony, Edward sent Gaveston off with the utmost dignity as the King's Lieutenant in Ireland while he tried to fathom out how to have his friend returned in the shortest possible time.

While Edward fumed at Gaveston's situation, news filtered in that Robert the Bruce had moved further south into England from Scotland. As Bruce advanced, he was claiming back more and more of the land that Edward I had taken from Scotland during his reign. And it looked like he was a long way from finished.

At that, Edward declared he needed Gaveston back in England as a reward for a job well done in Ireland and to help him hold back the Scots.

Immediately, with Gaveston back, tension grew again. The barons accused Edward of breaking his coronation oath and threatened that they would have him removed as their king if he didn't grant them their demands. They also accused him of losing Scotland by his negligence.

With those words ringing in his head, by the end of 1310, Edward left for Scotland to try and remedy the situation. But by the end of 1311, Robert the Bruce was still advancing and Edward had not made any progress at all. In the back of his mind, he must have been wishing he'd paid more attention to his father's advice.

Dejected, Edward decided to head back home. It was only when he returned that he became aware of another family member firmly establishing himself.

Edward's cousin Thomas was Earl of both Leicester and Lancaster and was married to Alice, the daughter of Earl of Lincoln. On her father's death, Thomas also added this new title to his already substantial list. When he inherited the Lincoln estates, he became the most formidable man in England with no exception. His lands increased and his income increased and that gave him the ability to raise private armies at will. It made him powerful and it made the barons sit up and take notice of him.

As Simon de Montfort had antagonised Henry III, so Thomas Earl of Lancaster terrorised Edward. And Gaveston was always the number one topic on the agenda. For the third time, it looked like Gaveston would be exiled. But not just from England this time, from the whole of the British Isles and to a land far, far away, never to return.

On 3rd November, Gaveston left Dover for Flanders. He was only gone for two months but he returned yet again with Edward's blessing in time for the birth of his first own child and was fully restored as Earl of Richmond by January the next year.

It was then that Gaveston truly stepped over the line and made a fateful error. Feeling safe and secure, he had begun a petty name-calling habit and the barons' aristocratic pride took a dangerous turn. It's where things started to go terribly wrong for him.

By May, the barons had Gaveston on the run and a manhunt was underway. When news came that he was hiding in Scarborough Castle, Oxfordshire was turned upside down in the attempt to capture him. The barons were about to put the finishing touches to their plan.

It was a warm night in June, at the height of the siege, when the Earl of Pembroke, the main instigator of the manhunt, suddenly announced that he would be leaving to visit his wife. As he bid farewell, he gave permission for the castle to be held under light guard, then he headed off into the darkness.

All was quiet when the Earl of Warwick, in the company of friends, silently entered a gate to the castle hours later. They bypassed the guard, who it seemed was looking the other way at the time, and captured Gaveston in the early hours of the morning.

To say the townspeople were overjoyed is perhaps an understatement. To the sound of cheers, Warwick marched Gaveston to Warwick castle and had him thrown in prison. Within a week, Warwick's friends, the Earls of Lancaster, Arundel and Hereford, arrived and at a makeshift trial, Gaveston was tried for breaching the terms of his exile. He was standing before them so clearly, he was guilty. He was sentenced to death then immediately marched to the top of the hill in Oxfordshire and passed on to two Welshmen. One ran him through with a sword and the other chopped off his head.

Gaveston's death was the beginning of the deepest hatred between the Earl of Lancaster and Edward and it nearly tore England apart. For all his crimes, Edward regarded Gaveston's trial as a serious breach of justice and whether the earls liked it or not, Edward regarded it as murder. It was something he would never forgive or forget.

The year 1314 is remembered for many reasons. It was the year that Robert the Bruce advanced his army to Stirling after a skirmish started between Bruce and Henry de Bohun, Earl of Hereford's nephew. It was the year that Bruce cleaved Henry de Bohun's head clean in two with his sword and it was the year that Bruce's army was camped half a mile away by a stream called the Bannockburn that was notorious for flooding and boggy conditions. It was also the year that Edward put his total army of 25,000 men into the field to face Robert the Bruce in battle. The Battle of Bannockburn was about to begin and it was the most wretched and memorable battle in Scottish history.

Edward made a serious mistake by thinking that his superior numbers alone would be an advantage to defeat the Scots. He forgot that 25,000 men took a lot to feed, and his ill-disciplined men had seen little success in eight years of campaigns. Still, he insisted they march and ride towards Scotland to defeat his old enemy, the Scots. Towards the end of June, they left under Edward's nominal and baffling command, sure in the fact that Robert the Bruce would now face the full vengeance of England.

But not only had Bruce been given prior warning from his spy network, he knew the actual day that Edward would come north and fight. It gave him time to think about his strategy.

Scotland's army was composed of around 10,000 men consisting of infantry spearman who feared nothing. Robert the Bruce thought long and hard about the impotence of his spearman, however fearless and fast they were, against the English archers. With foresight and skill, he took three precautions.

First, he chose a position where he was surrounded by impenetrable woods on one side and the bend of a river on the other. It was an area that covered barely 700 metres and it was a hard spot for the invading army to see. Secondly, his army dug potholes along the side of the road. His plan was that his army would wait in the potholes that had been covered and concealed with bracken, for the attack on the unsuspecting English army.

Thirdly, his knights would be waiting at the rear to stop any English soldiers from retreating.

With these plans in place, Bruce waited for three days until 24th June.

There was no way to quieten the incredible noise made from Edward's army of steel-clad horsemen. Bruce could hear them coming from miles away, giving him plenty of time to have his men in place. Unaware of anything except attacking and killing the Scots, Edward thundered down the slope towards Bannockburn.

When they were almost upon them, the Scottish spearmen sprang out of the potholes in an almighty crash just as Bruce had meticulously intended. Edward's plan had been for his archers to shoot arrows into the air as William the Conqueror had done at Hastings but in the mayhem, they soon saw that if they did, they would hit more of their own men than the Scottish infantry. With the English army in terrible disarray, Bruce increased the pressure and sent reinforcements thundering towards them.

From Edward's vantage point, he could see Bruce's army high on the hills roaring towards him and he knew he was in serious trouble. As the Scottish hurled themselves down the slope, Edward gave the order to retreat before the bulk of the army could recross Bannockburn. And of course, Bruce's men were waiting for him to do exactly that.

Edward barely escaped with his life. As the English army fled over the border, Edward's men managed to drag him from the battlefield after his horse was killed beneath him. In their panic, they left behind precious military equipment, expensive armour and gold plate that Bruce made full use of.

It was the worst defeat sustained by the English since the Battle of Hastings in 1066 and Bruce kept the pressure up by advancing further into English territory and further on to Ireland.

Edward limped his way back to London in humiliating defeat to find a very different England to the one he had left. England was suffering the harshest winter they could ever remember. Floods had swept villages away and massive lakes had formed in low-lying parts. The rain had ruined crops and had plunged England into a horrendous famine. People were starving and had begun to eat anything they could find. They resorted to eating pets, rotten corn and on occasion, the bodies of their dead. Disease was even spreading through their precious sheep and cattle. People were close to insanity.

He also found that his cousin Thomas Earl of Lancaster had become one of the most influential men in England and Edward knew he desperately needed help.

With Lancaster at the head of a fresh rebellion, it seemed no one could stop the civil war from happening. Huge armies belonging to barons such as Earl of Hereford, Roger de Mortimer and many others, calling themselves Marchers, plundered and murdered their way through Wales and western England stealing cattle, sheep, horses, wagons and they smashed their way into manors taking anything of value they could find.

Help for Edward came in 1318 with Hugh Despenser, 1st Earl of Winchester and his son Hugh the younger.

It was a dilemma for the barons. Sure they disliked Edward, but they despised Lancaster even more and Edward was in mild shock to find the barons supporting him this time, especially after the disaster of Bannockburn. It seemed relatively easy for Edward to gather supporters together and slowly they took back castle after castle. Edward was beside himself with joy.

Finally, Edward met Lancaster at Boroughbridge but this time it was a different story. He had enough men to at his disposal to defeat Lancaster's tiring army, and while some saw the writing on the wall and ran, escaping to France, Lancaster was captured and taken prisoner along with many of his loyal supporters.

Edward had a long memory. He knew it was Lancaster who had murdered his friend Piers Gaveston without a trial and he wasn't about to forget it. Lancaster had not allowed Gaveston a defence and Edward was going to give Lancaster the same treatment. He was not allowed to speak in his own defence during his trial nor was he allowed to have anyone to speak for him.

One thing held Edward back. Lancaster had royal blood and as such, was entitled to leniency. The traditional sentence for treason was to be hung, drawn, quartered and beheaded and so after being convicted of treason, Edward generously declared he would commute Lancaster's sentence. He would be merely beheaded. The smile on Edward's face was enough for Lancaster to know there would not be any waiting period in the Tower while supporters plotted his escape. He was taken away and executed immediately near Pontefract Castle along with thirty of his followers. And more executions soon followed.

The horror of Edward's revenge shocked the country. Bodies of executed men hung on the outskirts of town, left decaying in the sun as a reminder of what would happen if you crossed Edward the king. The Tower of London buzzed with prisoners who had been condemned to death but who'd had their sentences commuted to life imprisonment. Roger de Mortimer was one of these men, but luckily, he escaped.

The story of Mortimer's escape from the tower is all very romantic and daring. In the dead of night while snow fell softly over the hushed city, Mortimer legged it over the walls and jumped into the freezing river in his attempt to reach France before daylight. And he had to be quick because Edward was out for revenge. Very soon, Edward would fervently wish he had finished him off when he had the chance in the first place.

In France, Charles IV, Isabella's brother, was taking advantage of the unrest in England. He marched into Gascony and seized it and after several bungled attempts to regain the territory, Edward decided to send his wife back home on his behalf to negotiate terms with her brother.

By then, Isabella's marriage to Edward was seriously faltering and she could hardly believe her luck. The thought of escaping the Despensers and her husband at the same time to the safe haven of her brother's castle was simply too good to be true. Before Edward could change his mind, she left for France on the next ship.

Springtime in Paris is magical but for Isabella, it was more than she had dreamed possible. After taking the time to visit family, she and her brother put their heads together. The plan was for Isabella to tell Edward that she had convinced her brother to make a truce. But first, as a sign of respect to his Uncle Charles, their 13-year-old son, Edward, would have to go to France on a visit. A heartfelt promise was made that she and her son would both return to England by the summer when her brother's ruffled feathers were smooth and after a slight hesitation, Edward reluctantly agreed and sent his eldest son to meet his mother in France. His youngest son, John, would however remain with him in England.

Isabella must have had her fingers crossed behind her back when the promise was made because once her son arrived in France, there was no way she was leaving. By the end of summer, Edward began to send urgent messages to the Pope and to Charles IV, expressing his concern about his son and wife's absence. All to no avail. By then, she had met Roger de Mortimer and they hit it off straight away.

Isabella was reintroduced to Mortimer in Paris by her cousin, Joan Countess of Hainault, who appears to have approached Isabella suggesting a marital alliance between their two families, marrying Prince Edward to Joan's daughter, Philippa. Within months, Isabella and Mortimer were lovers.

It was a huge risk for Isabella to take. Female infidelity was a very serious offence in medieval Europe and both of Isabella's former French sisters-in-law had died by 1326 as a result of their imprisonment for exactly this offence.

Very soon, a surprised Edward heard news that Isabella had started dressing in black, claiming that Hugh Despenser had destroyed her marriage to Edward and warning bells began to sound in his head. Then he heard the rumour that Isabella had begun a relationship with the English exile Roger de Mortimer and he was stupefied.

While Edward panicked in England, Isabella was thoroughly enjoying her stay in the French court and as part of her promise to her cousin Joan, Isabella and Mortimer took young Edward with them and travelled north to visit William I, Count of Hainaut. The plan was to betroth Edward to Philippa, as Joan had suggested, in exchange for a substantial dowry. This money, plus an earlier loan from her brother Charles, would be used to raise an army.

On 22nd September, Isabella, Mortimer and their modest force set sail for England.

When Edward saw them coming, he was amazed at the small number of soldiers. Feeling confident, he made plans of his own to gather an army to crush them. That's when it all began to fall apart for Edward.

Henry of Lancaster was still angry at how his brother Thomas had been executed and he was making plans of his own. He seized a cache of Despenser treasure and marched south to join Mortimer, taking the most able-bodied men he could find with him. With Lancaster's army joining with his, Mortimer was unbeatable.

When Edward found out, he high-tailed it to Wales with the younger Despenser, now a firm friend.

Isabella and Mortimer's victory was swift and paybacks against Edward's allies began immediately. As always, beheading was the favoured punishment and many barons were executed in this fashion. Hugh Despenser, however, suffered a far worse punishment and was hung, drawn and quartered, much the same as William Wallace and as Isabella and Mortimer dealt out justice indiscriminately, Henry of Lancaster was sent to Wales to bring Edward back.

With people more than willing to hand Edward over, Lancaster was back in London within weeks and the king was safely tucked away in the tower.

Isabella and Mortimer were now faced with the problem of what to do with him. The simplest solution was execution but that would require the king to be convicted of treason and while they doubtfully reasoned that he had failed in his duty to his country, Edward could not be legally executed on those grounds. Then they had a brilliant idea.

On 20th January 1327, Edward was informed of his new charges. He was found guilty of incompetence, not listening to good advice and pursuing occupations unbecoming to a monarch. He was also accused of losing lands in Scotland and Gascony, allowing nobles to be killed, failing to show fair justice and thereby losing the faith and trust of his people. He had two choices: abdicate in favour of his son or relinquish the throne to someone who had barely a drop of royal blood in his veins that had trickled down from King John's daughter i.e. Roger Mortimer.

Although Edward was shocked at this judgement and even wept while listening, he must have seen this coming for a long time. It was as if he had walked into this with his eyes wide open.

Four days later, Edward abdicated and the following day, his 14-year-old son Edward was proclaimed King of England, under the control of Isabella and Mortimer. Edward was then imprisoned and 'encouraged' to die as soon as possible.

Stories abound about Edward's final days. Some reports say that while he was in Berkeley Castle, he was suffocated, some say strangled, then thrown into a pit of rotting corpses. The popular story is that an agent of Isabella and Mortimer murdered him on 11th October 1327 by having a red-hot poker thrust into his anus and his screams, as his bowels were burned, could be heard outside the prison walls.

In English history, disembowelling by a red-hot poker is an embarrassingly popular method of getting rid of someone you don't like and was probably intended to reflect Edward's early decadence regarding Piers Gaveston. True or not, the fact remains that Isabella and Mortimer's patience was exhausted and Mortimer ordered the king to be murdered in his prison cell. Edward was to become the first English king to be murdered since his namesake Edward the Martyr but whereas the Martyr had only been a boy, Edward had merely acted like one.

At the beginning of Isabella and Mortimer's reign in 1327, a state of truce existed between England and Scotland but it was clear it was not going to last. All hell was about to break loose.

EDWARD III

Born 1312
Reign 1327 - 1377

It seemed that the tough blood of Edward I had slept soundly while his son Edward II reigned, but in Edward III, England again found a strong leader. The entire attitude of the new king was to restore the glories of his grandfather, Edward I, and the most interesting, intriguing and complicated era in English history was about to begin.

The four-year reign of Isabella and Mortimer was based on the murder of a king and the guilty couple paid their way by abandoning English interests in both Scotland and France. One treaty signed in France by Isabella and Mortimer condemned England to pay a war remuneration and restricted their French possessions to a commune in Gascony. But another treaty signed in Scotland the next year would mark them infamously in history forever.

The Treaty of Northampton, written in French, signed in Edinburgh by Robert the Bruce, King of Scotland on 17th March 1328 and co-signed by the English Parliament, was a cry out for cash. The terms of the treaty agreed upon was that, in exchange for £20,000, the English Crown would accept:

- The Kingdom of Scotland as a fully independent nation
- Robert the Bruce, and his heirs and successors, as the rightful rulers
- The border between Scotland and England as recognised under the reign of Alexander III
- Princess Joanna, Edward's 6-year-old sister was to be promised in marriage to 4-year-old David, son of Robert the Bruce

Isabella and Mortimer signed the treaty readily in the name of King Edward III. There were two copies of the Treaty on one single sheet of parchment and after the English and Scottish ambassadors verified that the copies were the same; it was cut in half across the middle with a wavy line so that the two copies could be matched together if ever questioned. The kings then affixed their seals to straps that hung from the bottom of the document. Four months later, on 17th July, the marriage took place and David was declared the heir apparent of Scotland.

Barely a year later, Robert the Bruce was dead and 6-year-old David and 8-year-old Joanna were crowned King and Queen of Scotland in Scone at almost the same time as Edward was crowned King of England in London as Edward III.

Westminster Abbey was once again filled to capacity with barons as they watched the crown of Edward the Confessor being placed, with extra padding of course, on the 15-year-old head of Edward. As he stood in front of the throne draped in gold cloth, he swore the same oath his father had made as the banquet hall began to fill with luxuries not to be seen for another 50 years.

Isabella had one more task to complete before she could fully relax. Her son had been promised in marriage to Philippa of Hainault and that's what she intended would happen. Edward was then married to his 14-year-old bride in an opulent ceremony designed to show that English power was definitely not on the decline.

Everyone was smiling and everyone seemed happy.

But Edward's mind was calculating, even at that young age. He watched silently as Mortimer dragged men into court who had been loyal to his father. Among them was his half uncle, the Earl of Kent, accused of treason.

Letters were produced and the Earl was duly found guilty and sentenced to death, while his wife and children were sent to prison for life.

It was a savage decision, even for Mortimer, and for a while there was no one to perform the execution. Eventually, another prisoner whose job it was to clean the latrines was offered his freedom to lop the top off this uncle's head. Edmund, another son of Edward I, suffered much the same fate. As heads toppled, the questions on everyone's lips were: Were Isabella and Mortimer any better than Edward II? Where they perhaps worse?

Edward watched what was happening in silence as he grew into manhood. He had not forgotten the fate of his father or his kin nor had he forgotten how his mother and her lover had treated him as a child. By 17, he was ready for revenge.

Bad news and gossip travel fast and Mortimer had heard rumours that some friends of Edward were plotting to kill him. Of course, at court, Edward's friends all strenuously denied it but they knew that the time had come to act with Mortimer watching their every move. Everyone knew what he was capable of and they had begun to fear for Edward's life as well.

One night as the castle was settling down for the night, Edward, and at least fifteen armed friends including young Henry of Lancaster, moved stealthily through the dark passages deep in Nottingham Castle. Edward's physician had provided him with an alibi for his absence during the evening meal and had helped by unlocking the door leading from the hidden passage to the castle keep. From deep within, they climbed the steps to the royal quarters, now known as Mortimer's Hole. Inside their quarters, Isabella, Mortimer and his two sons, Geoffrey and Edward, as well as three bishops, were discussing what to do regarding the very men who were slowly advancing towards their room.

Suddenly, Edward's men burst into the room with their swords drawn. Amid the confusion, tables were overturned and two guards were killed while one bishop attempted to escape by throwing himself down the lavatory shaft into the squalid waste below. Mortimer ran for his sword but he was far too slow. He barely made it across the room before he was captured along with his sons and the entire family was sent to their new home, the Tower.

Isabella waited silently in the dark room for her son to return. Knowing her son's mood, it must have been the longest wait of her life.

For a young man out for revenge, simply sending Mortimer to the Tower of London was never going to be enough for Edward. Not by a long shot. He had watched his father's humiliation and he wanted Mortimer to suffer as much as his father had suffered. Bound and gagged in Westminster Abbey, Mortimer was accused of usurping royal power along with thirteen other crimes including the murder of his father.

It was the first time that murder had been spoken out loud and it was enough for Mortimer to be sentenced to death. Everyone knew he was guilty. He was hung, his lands and titles removed from his family and his body was left on the gallows for two days and nights in full view of the public. Isabella got off lightly. She was simply sent into exile for the next thirty years of her life.

This was to be the age of tournaments and Edward was a willing participant, energetic and athletic. People flocked to see this handsome young man with his slender nose, thick wavy hair and deep-set eyes and a taste for fine clothes. Edward and his wife Philippa travelled every month to a new venue and the people loved it. His court rang with singing minstrels, beating drums and in the middle of it all was the king's laughter. England forgave the young man for spending thousands of pounds on entertainment for himself and his friends as he began to absorb himself in the job of being king. And his first task was to tackle the Treaty of Northampton.

Many regarded it as humiliating and Edward fully agreed with them. Even though it was his young sister Joanna sitting on the Scottish throne with King David II, Edward overturned the Treaty, which you can imagine started fresh tempers erupting in Scotland. Barely five years after the signing and a semblance of peace, the quarrel with Scotland had resumed all over again with a vengeance. As he worked, Philippa produced child after child.

It had been 120 years since any king had set foot in Ireland and Edward wanted to be *that* king. He had fire in his veins, money in his treasury and he was more than ready for a fight. Troops were gathered and he was days away from invasion when news arrived that Scotland had regrouped and were preparing to fight. When he heard, all plans were immediately put on hold. He told parliament there was a change of venue and Ireland could wait. He was going to invade Scotland instead.

Throughout the summer of 1333, battle after battle was fought.

Berwick was taken and then he moved on to Halidon Hill. By his side was his new friend, Edward Balliol, the son of the deposed king, John Balliol.

With an army that seemed like half the size of Scotland, Edward took up a defensive position in the centre as the Scots advanced down Halidon Hill. Edward Balliol sat on his horse to his left, his uncle Earl of Norfolk was to his right and beside him was his younger brother, John of Exeter. All men watched intently as Edward's archers shot a vicious hail of arrows on the approaching Scots and by the time it became hand-to-hand combat the Scots were retreating and Edward had won.

The English victory at Halidon Hill meant that David and Joanna had to flee from Scotland to escape Edward, who was closing in fast, burning, looting and killing with no purpose in mind apart from exercising his power over his Scottish enemies. In the nick of time, they reached the safety of Boulogne and were greeted with open arms by Edward and Joanna's cousin, Philip VI of France.

But England wasn't the only unsettled kingdom. There were issues brewing in the French monarchy as well.

Six years earlier in 1328, Philip's first cousin Charles IV had died without a direct heir and it opened up a serious problem for France. Philip was one of the two chief claimants to the throne. The other was Edward III through his mother Isabella of France.

The question on everyone's lips was whether the crown could, or should, be passed on to Isabella's son Edward when she had not possessed the crown herself. French nobles faced a choice: who would give them more power and independence in their own country – a French King in Paris or a distant English King ruling mostly from London?

Ultimately, as Philip was the eldest grandson of the late king through the *male* line, he was crowned king instead of Edward. But Edward had other ideas.

He did not have to wring support from Parliament for an expedition to France. They were all urging him to act. To add fuel to the fire, Edward's sister Eleanor had been betrothed to Philip's son, John, but Philip had reneged and decided his son should marry Bonne of Bohemia instead.

Threats were sent backwards and forwards and Edward steadfastly declared that the French crown was his as the only living male descendant of his deceased maternal grandfather Philip IV, while Philip was just as determined to maintain his rights and the crown.

In the end, the only solution was to throw England into a war. And so began The Hundred Years' War.

With Scotland fuming in the north and France raging over the channel, Edward needed supporters and resources to help him fight both of them at the same time. Many of his supporters were given either knighthoods or titles as rewards and alongside this new nobility was Edward's eldest son, 6-year-old Edward of Woodstock. In later years, he would be called Edward The Black Prince not just for his black armour but also because of his diabolical reputation. When he was given the title of Duke of Cornwall, he was marked as the heir to the throne.

As always, for an expedition of this size, Edward needed money. Taxes were raised yet again and in their exhaustion, labourers were lucky to reach forty years of age. If they did, their lives were a constant war of plummeting wages, higher taxes and endless famine. In the coming years, Edward would put up the crown and jewels as collateral against loans that were at 40% interest, but after only three years of fighting, he was floundering badly and almost bankrupt.

For Edward, it seemed no matter what he did, it always turned out to cost him more money. Without taking any personal responsibility, he became obsessed with the idea that this state of affairs was due, not to his bad management, but the corruption in his government and he set out on a shocking vendetta to dismiss leading officials from the top down.

First to go was the treasurer, then senior judges, a constable of the Tower was next, followed by leading merchants. The exchequer was fired and it was decreed that all taxes were to be paid straight into Edward's own treasury. He replaced sheriffs and even fired his own brother Robert who was Bishop of Chichester. Then he turned on the Archbishop of Canterbury accusing him of treason. He vowed never to appoint a clergyman as one of his minsters again nor anyone he could not hang, draw or behead if he failed in his service to his king. No one was safe and no one was spared.

It was a grand speech that shifted the blame of the disaster in France from himself to his government and while he ranted, Philippa gave birth to another son, Edmund. While she nursed her new baby, Edward decided to stage a major attack on France.

He sailed for Normandy with a force of 15,000 men and quickly defeated Caen. From there, he continued marching across northern France. While he marched, David of Scotland, now 21-years old, and his wife Joan hastily returned home. His supporters had obtained the upper hand in Scotland and David finally took the reins of government into his own hands and waited for Edward to return to England.

It was fortunate they did leave Europe because while war was holding Edward's attention, a far deadlier enemy was marching across the continents. History has no catastrophe equal to the Black Death.

The summer of 1348 was wet. The royal family was maturing and multiplying and even though Edward was only 35 and Philippa was 33, they already had nine children ranging from Edward the Black Prince, who was 18, down to the baby William of Windsor, who was only a few months old. It was the year when their daughter Joan boarded a ship and set sail to marry the man of her dreams, the King of Castile.

When the ship stopped in Bordeaux on the way, the mayor rushed to the docks and told them it was not safe to disembark. A deadly plague had arrived. It had ripped through Cyprus and Italy and had reached Marseille.

For two years Joan had waited for the moment when she would finally meet her new husband. She'd lived over and over the first embrace and she imagined being swept off her feet and taken to his castle nestling quietly by the sea. She was 13 years old, buzzing with excitement, and there was nothing in the world that would stop her from reaching her destination. The mayor's words of warning were pushed aside.

The character of the epidemic was appalling. The disease itself, with its frightful symptoms, was swift. At the onset, appeared the blotches, then the hardening of the glands under the armpit and the groin, followed by the horde of virulent pustules. After that the victim developed a hacking cough that would develop and produce blood followed by vomiting. Breath, sweat and excrement stank. Delirium and insanity completed the suffering.

It seemed no one was safe from the disease. No one knew how the disease spread and no one knew of the different methods of cross contamination. In an attempt to protect themselves, doctors filled a 'beak' containing herbs and placed it over their noses but of course, eventually everyone knew that method of protection was basically useless. Seeing a doctor with this strange contraption on his face would have sent dread into the hearts of the already terrified people. All that could be done was place a red cross on the doors of infected houses to inform others that the inhabitants had developed symptoms of the Black Death.

Joan never wore her wedding dress made from thick imported silk embroidered with rich strands of gold. She never wore the suit of red velvet with two sets of twenty-four buttons made of silver gilt and enamel nor the five corsets woven with gold patterns of stars, crescents and diamonds. And she never reached her future husband waiting for her in Castile. Joan died horrifically at the same time as her baby brother, William of Windsor, died in agony in England.

The plague entered Europe through Crimea and in the course of twenty years killed at least one-third of its entire population as well as two other daughters of Edward and Philippa. We hear of monasteries where half the residents perished, of dioceses where the surviving clergy could scarcely perform the last offices for their flocks, of Goldsmith's Company who had four Masters in one year and of lawsuits where all parties died before the cases could be heard in court. A whole generation was obliterated as blank spaces appeared on all sides of society and destroyed life. This disease, along with all the other severities of the Middle Ages, was almost more than the human spirit could endure.

At length, the plague abated and recoveries became more frequent as the more resistant revived. But the calamity had only reduced numbers without reducing their quarrels. The war between England and France still continued, although in a broken fashion, and Edward's first-born son, Edward the Black Prince, his heir apparent, became a land-based buccaneer. There had been reasons for Edward's invasion of France, but the character of the Black Prince in Aquitaine had no such excuse.

Edward the Black Prince advanced northward from Gascony and Aquitaine towards the Loire Valley. His younger brother, John of Gaunt, advanced from Brittany.

Together, the new King of France, King John II, his son the dauphin and the king's brother, Duke of Orleans, were determined to finish the prolonged war with one quick stroke and while some advisers suggested caution, others urged the king to fight. Being a hothead, John chose to attack. For ten years the French had brooded over a past battle at Crecy where they remembered that horses could not face an arrow storm and win.

Edward I had won that battle with an army entirely dismounted and, in the confusion, the charging line of horses collapsed as they were driven back with pain. It had been a total disaster for the French and John was not going to let that happen again. He was sure that all his men must attack on foot this time and he had the overwhelming numbers. He could almost *feel* the victory.

They met outside Poitiers. As the two forces prepared to strike, the Black Prince found himself with a force reduced to about 4,000 men, of whom nearly half were archers, compared to the French army of 20,000. The haggard group of English marauders who had pillaged and burned their way through French country were looking at defeat in the eye.

It would have been smart to retreat, and I'm sure the thought crossed his mind as the mass of mail-clad footmen advanced towards him in overwhelming numbers. As he watched, he would have known that they would not be stopped with horses and archery alone. No matter how good the target, that was not going to save him. He had to counter-manoeuvre.

What he did was the opposite of what military opinion would have considered correct. As the French left their horses at the rear, the Black Prince ordered all his knights to mount. The French, overloaded by their chainmail, plodded ponderously forward through vineyards and scrub as arrows whizzed through the air.

At some stage, the Black Prince must have seen that arrows were making very little impression on the heavily armoured men so the order to his mounted knights to ride around the French left flank and strike with axes and swords made a lot of sense. It was this decision that turned the battle. As swords sliced through mail, the screams of French men echoed through the vineyards.

After two hours of hard fighting, John ordered his son to leave the battlefield so as not to put him at risk. The Duke chose to leave as well. By then two-thirds of the French army had decided to join them and the king was left to fight with the remainder of his dwindling army.

As soon as the French soldiers turned to flee for their lives, they made themselves easy targets. The result was a wholesale slaughter larger than Crecy and with worse consequences. Many of the nobility were slain and left to rot in the fields while around 3,000 Frenchman were captured, including

King John. The Black Prince duly brought him back to England and presented him proudly to his father.

You can imagine Edward's reaction to his son's victory. At first, he was stunned. Then as realisation sunk in, he was absolutely ecstatic. This was not just a victory over the French, worth the death of each and every one of his soldiers; this could be a land grab as well.

The Treaty of Bretigny gave Edward nearly everything he asked for. The French gave back Gascony as well as the whole of Henry II's possessions in Aquitaine. They gave him back Edward I's inheritance of Pointieu and the famous port of Calais, which the French held for nearly 200 years. But what they refused to give Edward was his claim to the French throne. In place of this, they agreed to a ransom that was fixed at £500,000, eight times the annual revenue of the English Crown.

Edward was absolutely jubilant. In one day, he had wiped out his debts and beaten the French and to celebrate, he lavished his sons with new titles on his 50th birthday. Edward the Black Prince, now married to a notorious woman by the name of Joan of Kent who had been married twice before (heaven forbid), received a new home as well as the duchy of Aquitaine. John of Gaunt was given the title of Duke of Lancaster and Lionel of Antwerp was to be the given the dubious title of Duke of Clarence since Lionel had been in Ireland at the time. His youngest son Edmund was barely 10 years old and would have to wait until he came of age for a title.

When looking back at Edward's blessed reign, it is astonishing to watch the speed at which his good fortune came to a grinding halt.

Just a few years after the treaty was signed, The Black Death resurfaced and Edward's wife died a terrible death. He was in poor health himself. At the same time, his son Lionel was returning from Ireland after the death of his wife, declaring Ireland a lost cause. He soon remarried but two months later, he was dead as well. As well as that, Edward's eldest son, the Black Prince, was returning to England from Aquitaine a broken, ailing man who had fought too many battles. In his last battle, he had to be carried around on a litter. He had gradually lost his personal fortune and was returning home bankrupt, too ill of mind and body to contribute to either war or parliament. Within a month, he would be dead along with his own eldest son.

It was a terrible time for Edward. As he grieved, everyone seemed unhappy with him. His bishops were arguing constantly, the plague was raging, his government was corrupt and his mistress was prancing around in magnificent finery while she amassed jewels and land and the country collapsed in disorder.

In parliament, his son John of Gaunt could only listen to a parliament that condemned loyal supporters of his father. After the death of his own wife Blanche, John of Gaunt requested that his relationship with his mistress Katherine Swynford be recognised as a legal marriage and his children to her be legitimised. He kept quiet in parliament since he did not want this request jeopardised at this late stage. All he could do was watch silently as members of his father's household were dismissed, arrested and worse.

Worn down by war and silly pleasures, Edward subsided into senility at Sheen Lodge where he and his mistress made wild plans for when he would recover. By the time of his death, his muscles and skin were wasting away and his mistress had already taken the rings from his fingers and other movable property in the house and hastily departed.

It was a turbulent life and a magnificent long reign, but it was a sad ending for a man who had four strong sons, all of them waiting for him to die, so they could begin the rest of their lives.

On his death, the Black Prince's only remaining child, 10-year-old son Richard, became the King of England and his uncle John of Gaunt, became the head of the Council of Regency.

Through all that England had suffered, this would prove to be the worst.

RICHARD II

Born 1367
Reign 1377 - 1400

Both the impact and the shadow of the Black Death dominated Richard's reign but there was a general feeling of survival by the time he succeeded to the throne. The disease began to abate once more and vacant places began to fill as many men of all classes had unexpected promotions. The community had been largely reduced but individually they prospered in the aftermath of the plague. There was an undoubted feeling of wellbeing among the survivors. Generally, they felt invincible.

His coronation, organised by his uncle John of Gaunt, lasted for two days and was meant to show English magnificence. But for the 10-year-old, the ceremony was exhausting and at the end, the fragile boy who was already introverted and spoiled by his mother Joan of Kent, had to be carried on the shoulders of Sir Thomas Buly to the banquet.

Richard was never intended to be the king in the first place. He was the second son of the Black Prince and both his father and his elder brother had predeceased him. As a result, the Richard was pushed into an unexpected early reign and it was to be an unhappy start from the very beginning for him. Because of his youth, government was in the hands of a series of councils, which the community preferred rather than a 'regency' led by his uncle, John of Gaunt.

John of Gaunt was an influential and wealthy man in his own right. He had acres of land and castles in both England and France and he had skills in the military and diplomacy. He had been married to Blanche of Lancaster who had owned lands and titles in her own right, and all of them had naturally come to John at her death in 1368 making him even wealthier. As such, he was a natural and obvious choice to be the regent for his nephew. Together with his younger brother Thomas of Woodstock, Duke of Gloucester, they held a lot of influence in the government.

The only problem was that no one liked or trusted John of Gaunt. They were always suspicious that this powerful man, who was the third son of Edward III, would want the crown for himself. He was, after all, just one little boy away from being the king.

Also in the picture was Edmund of Langley, Duke of York. He was married to Isabella, the sister of John of Gaunt's second wife, Constance, making an even stronger bond between the brothers. There was not much Richard could do at this tender age against three strong and powerful men.

Richard matured into a tall, good-looking and intelligent young man with a face that was white, rounded and feminine although he had a tendency to stammer. He loved elegant clothes and wore coats with padded shoulders, high collars and tight two-toned hose with pointy shoes. I would guess that these costly outfits were for show rather than comfort. But for all his good looks and grandeur, there was something odd about the boy that no one could put a finger on.

In those early days, the Scots were still rebelling, taxes were still heavy and the French had been raiding up and down the coast, looting and burning. One captured Frenchman said, *"If the English had made the duke of Lancaster the king, they would not now be invaded by Frenchman as they are."*

If that wasn't enough, as a result of the Black Plague, there was a shortage of manpower giving villains and ruffians the upper hand and an advantage. In a world where the people were supposed to know their place, the old order of service began to waver. English peasants began ransacking their own counties with the flash points being in Kent and Essex. One of the two main issues that set the ball rolling was why the burden of taxes should fall so heavily on the very people who could least afford them. The second issue was whether a noble had a right to keep his servant as a slave with no privileges at all. It was a common enough practice, but was it right?

With discontent growing more heated, England finally erupted. As landowners began to join in, Richard, his mother and an adviser moved swiftly to the Tower of London for safety as peasants began to run through the streets of well-to-do areas murdering anyone they regarded as 'foreign'. The Savoy, John of Gaunt's main residence, was set fire to and almost destroyed. In frenzy, people charged through the building smashing and dragging whatever they could into the streets to fuel the bonfires. They saw John of Gaunt as the man responsible for the new Poll tax, or a 'per person' tax, and they knew he was the power behind the throne. He was also noticeably absent during the riots, busy in France.

The palace itself did not escape notice and was almost destroyed by barrels of gunpowder. Prisons were opened and violent criminals were released. Even Edward the Confessor's shrine in Westminster Abbey was violated and two members of the council, including the Archbishop of Canterbury, were dragged to the Tower of London and promptly beheaded. Five of Richard's friends were hung, drawn and quartered. Even his tutor was not spared. England was in total chaos.

At 14 years old, there wasn't much Richard could do but watch pale faced from a turret in the Tower as London burned. Even the breeze would not have been able to take away the stink of the city below. The smell would have been indescribable. During the heavy rain, filth had risen to the surface from the remains of the Roman sewers. On the streets, the slurry would have run past pots of urine and faeces and rushed over animal dung and slop trodden down by more horses and carriages. The English had hardened themselves to the smell but in everyone's heart and mind was the memory of a disease that could emerge again at any time.

While Richard watched in horror, tucked away in a closet for his own safety, sat his cousin, Henry Bolingbroke, John of Gaunt's son.

How much Richard understood, we will never know, but perhaps this vision of violence scarred him for life. What showed was Richard's streak of courage and an aptitude for leadership.

The end of the revolt was terribly dramatic. Some councillors were able to convince the rebels that Richard wanted to discuss their demands, which distracted the rebels from killing Richard's supporters hiding in the tower. It was agreed where they should meet and Richard rode through London with his half-brothers, plus his uncle Thomas of Woodstock, various earls and the mayor. Even his mother rode behind them.

Rebels shouted abuse at him as he rode but the royal party continued steadily through to Mile End to the designated spot where they were to meet. To their surprise, Richard granted them everything they asked for. There would be no return to serfdom, everyman could rent land for a maximum of 4 pence per acre and the commanders of the rebel army, Tyler and his men, would be free to hunt down all the traitors they desired and bring them to him for judgment.

Perhaps it wasn't just a change of personal circumstances the people were looking for. Perhaps it was purely that they were out of control and looking for vengeance because for all the planning the mayor and councillors had done, the plan didn't work. On hearing that all had been granted, an angry mob stormed the Tower and murdered a bishop, John of Gaunt's personal physician and eight others. The bishop's mitre was even nailed to his skull. A wooden chopping block was set up and the ground soon was soaked with congealing blood. In St-Martin's-in-the-Vintry, more than 100 merchants and traders were piled lifelessly in the streets. It was a miracle that Henry Bolingbroke managed to escape capture.

It appeared honeyed words were not enough and another plan was needed. Fast.

It's not known how much part Richard played in the next part of the plan but word was sent out that the king would meet them again, at Smithfield this time, outside the city. With the mayor close by his side, Richard arrived to meet Wat Tyler once again. Knowing what happened the last time, it would have been a very nervous time for the young king.

Tyler remained on his horse throwing a dagger threateningly from one hand to the other as Richard asked what was required to end the revolt. As Tyler told Richard his extraordinary demands, Richard listened silently. This time, the list of demands had grown and included the abolishment of religious titles and the confiscation of church land.

Once again Richard agreed and Tyler was told to go home. In hindsight, nothing Richard said or did was going to work because that was when Tyler did the most stupid thing. He demanded a flagon of wine then spat the wine at Richard's feet. A fight broke out and the mayor rushed forward and drove a dagger deep into Tyler's side, mortally wounding him.

In his dying moments, Tyler mounted his horse as best he could and rode towards his men, shouting *"Treason. Treason"*. As rebel archers drew back their arrows, Richard realised that something had to be done quickly. He spurred his horse straight towards the rebels, bellowing these famous words *"What are you doing? Surely you do not wish to fire on your own king? Do not fire on me and do not regret the death of that traitor ... for I will be your king, your captain and your leader"*.

It was astounding courage for one so young, and amazingly it worked. He had distracted the rebels long enough for the militia to arrive and surround them.

But the magic at Smithfield was not to last long and it is only after this revolt that Richard begins to emerge clearly. Not for the last time, they would find that Richard had no intention of keeping his word and within a fortnight, not surprisingly, Richard formally revoked all that he had agreed upon. He rounded up all the ringleaders and had them executed saying *"Villains you are, and villains you shall remain!"*

Of course, it hadn't entirely been Richard's decision to make. It was his government who had put the words in his mouth. Richard was only a 14-year-old boy but it is very likely that these events impressed on him the consequences of disobedience to royal authority. It would form his personality and later define his reign.

With Richard growing up, the all-important need for him to produce an heir emerged, which meant he needed a wife. After considering Caterina, one of the Duke of Milan's 38 children, 15-year-old Anne of Bohemia, daughter of the Holy Roman Emperor Charles IV, was chosen.

They were a strange, fragile couple. Anne was a wispy little thing and Richard was radiantly boyish with slightly protruding eyes and a mournful Plantagenet face.

Hopes were high that Richard would be a better ruler than his past family members but very soon it was obvious he was going to follow his own star. Despite a shy stammering speech, an inclination towards petulant tantrums was emerging and Richard would turn white with rage if opposed.

Frightful memories of Piers Gaveston came to everyone's mind as Richard began to appoint court favourites. Richard gave Michael de la Pole the title of Earl of Suffolk and Robert De Vere was made Earl of Oxford. With the appointments came rumours and without producing any hard evidence, it was believed that there was a degree of *'improper intimacy'* involved. Irritation festered bitterly in silence as De Vere was then elevated to the new title of Duke of Ireland as well. No one dare say anything against Richard's friends and risk another tantrum ... or worse.

As tension grew in England, conflicts were also growing in France where John of Gaunt was leading a large-scale campaign to protect English possessions. The relationship between Richard and his uncle John had been slowly deteriorating with more and more military failures and the rumour of a plot to kill Richard had begun to spread. With this, relations deteriorated even further and John of Gaunt must have seen which way the wind was blowing. Leaving Richard to calm down, he left England to pursue his claim to the throne of Castile in Spain, through his second marriage to Constance of Castile. By now it was obvious that Richard's reign was showing signs of unravelling.

Satisfied that he had solved the problem with his uncle, Richard turned his attention towards Scotland. He was to regret this absence from home because firstly the effort failed miserably, but secondly, and probably more importantly, because it left an opening for another crisis at home to happen, which proved to be a momentous disaster in many ways.

With John of Gaunt gone and Richard in the north, the unofficial leadership passed to his uncle, Thomas, Duke of Gloucester (who by then had been created Duke of Buckingham) together with Richard FitzAlan Earl of Arundel. Steadfastly, as leaders of a new parliament, the two men refused to pass any requests from Richard unless Michael de la Pole was removed.

Of course, Richard was going to do no such thing, especially when Michael de la Pole was concerned, and he stated he would not dismiss "... *even a scullion from my kitchen at the parliament's request."*

Now we know Richard had a serious temper, but it became pretty obvious that Gloucester and Arundel could out-yell him. In retaliation, they demanded an appeal of treason be brought against de la Pole and the conflict stepped up a notch when Henry Bolingbroke joined in the fight as well.

Once again, Richard found himself in the Tower of London looking out over an angry crowd. Once again, Henry Bolingbroke was in the tower with him. But this time, Bolingbroke was not hiding in a cupboard. He was telling Richard how unpopular his government had become. Arm in arm, the Earl of Warwick and Bolingbroke walked in and named themselves the 'Lords Appellant', daring Richard to try and remove them and stating that they would lead parliament when it opened session the next day.

Richard was 21 years old, but he was no match for this collection of nobility. Richard could only look on as they took over.

To give Henry Bolingbroke, the youngest of the three, the benefit of the doubt, he restrained himself as the older men went for the extreme punishment. Five of Richard's friends were hung, drawn and quartered and a number of his knights were beheaded. Michael de la Pole and Robert de Vere were lucky enough to escape from the country by the skin of their teeth but were sentenced to death *in absentia*. Even Richard's tutor did not escape death. The circle of favourites around the king had been removed and Richard had been humbled and humiliated. And so began what is famously called 'The Merciless Parliament'.

You just know Richard wasn't going to forget this.

He waited one full year, just before his 23rd birthday, to retaliate. For ten years he had done as he was told and for ten years he had agreed with everything parliament had advised. But he was not about to do it anymore.

You can only admire his patience. In all that time, people had directed him, people he thought he could trust, as they made decisions for the country and even disregarded him totally during parliamentary sessions. But this last cruel declaration must have left a lasting impression on his state of mind because he was beginning to show a streak of cunning that any past Plantagenet king would have been proud of. On 3rd May 1389, Richard took action that no one had foreseen.

Taking his seat at the Council, he asked blandly how old he was. Councillors must have looked at each other with smiles on their faces at the absurdity of the question. 23 years old, he was told, almost condescendingly.

It was the answer he'd been waiting for. He jumped up and declared that he had certainly come of age and would no longer submit to restrictions on his rights. He would manage the realm himself, thank you very much, and choose his own advisers. He would be king in every respect from that day onwards.

This speech had been prepared with uncanny cleverness, and Richard had set the trap brilliantly. He demanded the Great Seal be given to him and instantly began replacing old members of parliament with new ones. It wasn't until October 1389 when John of Gaunt returned from Spain that Richard had settled down and appeared to reconcile with John's son, Henry of Bolingbroke. As Richard busied himself assembling a loyal party, his uncle and cousin rallied to his side with helpful suggestions and advice. It was a smart move on their part, but Richard's generosity was just the lull before the storm.

We all know that Richard had a long memory for injuries and the patience and skill that he used to accomplish his revenge had always been incredible. For eight years, he tolerated Gloucester and Arundel who still held high positions even though there were moments of sudden outbursts where his anger flashed brightly. But he waited for just the right moment.

He waited until 1394. And it would be worth it.

His first step was to go to Ireland for the sole purpose of creating a large army dependent on him and him alone. An alliance with France was his second step. As a widower since his wife Anne had recently died, he was free to marry again. With superb calculation, he made an arrangement with Charles VI of France where he would marry the French king's 6-year-old daughter, Isabella, on the condition that if Richard was to be menaced by any of his subjects, France was to come to his aid. It was an old ploy used by the Scots during Edward I's reign, and it proved just as effective this time as it was then.

By January 1397, Richard was ready to strike for the third time. Gloucester and Arundel must have believed that they were safe from any consequences of what they had done in 1388. It had been nine years ago after all, and a lot had happened since then.

They were to be sadly mistaken.

Richard's temper was legendary and people were only beginning to realise that a lot was going on in his mind that they were unaware of. It would have been with trepidation that they saw Richard walk towards them with cold hatred in his fiery eyes. With the whole court watching in amazement, Richard declared that Arundel and some of his friends were traitors and as such, the punishment was decapitation. He would however be lenient with Arundel's brother, the Archbishop of Canterbury: he would instead be exiled to the Isle of Man. His uncle Thomas, Duke of Gloucester, could keep his head but he was to be sent into exile in Calais.

Thomas did not have to endure his punishment for long. Weeks later, a group of men led by Thomas de Mowbray 1st Duke of Norfolk, presumably on behalf of Richard, entered Thomas's cell and murdered him.

Watching everything unfold before their amazed eyes, there was nothing parliament wouldn't do for Richard. At his request, it suspended almost every right and privilege it had gained over the preceding century, and they did it eagerly. By doing this, it raised Richard to a more absolute position than even William the Conqueror had enjoyed. Everything the nation had won through the crimes of King John, all of which had been established by the great Edward I and the degeneracy of Edward II was surrendered up to Richard. The *'Tyranny of Richard II'* had begun.

Richard was enjoying himself immensely. Portraits were painted and a new form of address was introduced. Where kings had previously been addressed simply as *"highness"*, Richard insisted the title *"royal majesty"* or *"high majesty"* was required to be used. He would sit on his throne during solemn festivals in the royal hall for hours without speaking, and anyone on whom his eyes fell were required to bow on his knees to him. And no one was to turn their back on Richard either. They had to step slowly backwards away from him, bowing all the way.

But it was the existence of his cousin, Henry Bolingbroke, who consumed Richard's thoughts. The two cousins lived their lives in uneasy comradeship: one was the king and the other one was the eldest son of John of Gaunt and thus heir to the throne since Richard had no children at that time. As a result, Richard saw Henry as a constant threat. The House of Lancaster, represented by John of Gaunt and Henry Bolingbroke, not only possessed greater wealth than any other family in England, they were also of royal descent and, as such, were likely candidates to attempt to usurp the throne from him. It was a serious subject always on Richard's mind.

Then one day, at the perfect time for Richard, a quarrel between Boling-broke and Thomas of Mowbray, Duke of Norfolk, occurred. There are conflicting stories over the reason for the quarrel but that is of no consequence. What is important was the decree from Richard stated that a dual to the death appeared to be the only solution to the quarrel.

The country was buzzing with excitement. The famous scene was to take place at 9 am on 16th September 1398. Lines were drawn, the English were assembled and both parties had presented themselves. Henry rode out on his white horse decorated in green and blue velvet embroidered with gold swans and antelopes, accompanied by six attendants. He had a dagger, a sword and a shield with the red cross of St George painted on it. He swore his oaths, weapons were checked and he was given a small portion of wine and food to sustain him if the battle should continue throughout the day. Then he pulled down his visor, took his lance from an attendant, did the sign of the cross and rode towards the pavilion decorated with red roses representing the Lancasters. The time had come for battle.

Both men stood still, and then Henry advanced.

Suddenly, Richard stood up shouting, "Ho! Ho!"

Everyone stopped, shocked. Both men were sent back to their tents with their lances confiscated and for two hours they waited while Richard deliberated. Eventually, the king's verdict was announced. The trial was over. There would be no combat after all. Instead, cousin Henry was to be banished for six years and Mowbray banished for life.

Knowing now the little time Richard had left on the throne, we can see this as a fatal error on his part, but at the time it hadn't looked that way to him. He was young and at the height of his power. Both men, he stated, were to leave within a month and in one fell swoop, Richard was rid of his archenemy cousin Henry and the lands of Warwick, Gloucester, Arundel and Norfolk all reverted back to the crown: himself.

By now, not only the old nobility but all the gentry and merchant classes were aghast at Richard's paranoid rule and his theatrical actions. People lined the streets in sadness as they said their farewells to Henry. No one could know just how soon he would return.

Mowbray soon died but Henry seethed in France in the court of Charles VI.

Old John of Gaunt had been unwell for years. Some said his body was rotting away from syphilis, others said his heart had simply broken. John had not protested when Richard murdered Thomas of Woodstock, John's youngest brother, in his prison cell in Calais and John had been forced to stand by and watch as his son and heir was exiled in the exact same fashion. He fully expected Henry to be murdered in France as well by Richard's men. Richard's temper was legendary. So was his patience for vengeance.

John of Gaunt never expected to see his son again and six months after Henry left England for France, John went to bed and died. He simply gave up. On his father's death, Bolingbroke became the Earl of Lancaster and a powerful, wealthy man who now had lands in Lancashire and the North, with scattered territories all over England.

The extent of Henry's wealth and power terrified Richard. He'd already built up his own personal estate with the previous land grab but the Lancaster estates would make his cousin one of the wealthiest men in England. That Richard couldn't abide. It left him with one option: to disinherit Henry and take the Lancaster estates for himself.

This turn of events was hardly a surprise to Henry, as he had known Richard all his life. What *did* surprise him was the news that Richard was preparing a second invasion of Ireland and he would be taking his supporters with him. This meant the country would be unguarded for months. Well, not unguarded exactly. Richard left behind a government headed by Edmund of Langley, Duke of York, Henry's favourite uncle.

It was too good to be true.

News of Richard's departure reached Henry. The moment had come, the coast was clear and he didn't hesitate. He was now fully determined to take the throne and he justified his actions by saying that Richard, through his tyranny and misgovernment, had rendered himself unworthy of being a king.

In reality, Henry was not really the next in line to the throne. The heir presumptive was Edmund Mortimer, Earl of March, whose mother descended from Edward III's *second* son, Lionel of Antwerp. Henry's father had been Edward's *third* son.

Nonetheless, Henry argued the point by emphasising his descent in a direct *male* line solved the problem, whereas Mortimer's descent was through his *grandmother*. But it was the same old story of might over right and Henry had the might behind him.

Richard was in the depths of Ireland when Henry landed in Yorkshire, kissing the ground as he landed, surrounded by supporters and declaring he had come to claim his rights as heir to his father's estate.

It took some time for the news to reach Richard but battling stormy seas, he made a three-week march through North Wales in the attempt to gather forces. What he saw convinced him that his reign was over. The whole structure of his power, so patiently built, had vanished.

Henry and Richard met face to face at Flint but it was obvious from the start that Richard had lost. He rode through London as a captive and was imprisoned in the Tower but later transferred to Pontefract Castle, a popular choice it seems. After barely four months in prison, probably on St Valentine's day, he was dead having starved to death. His death was inevitable.

In 1386, he overcame his tyrannies. In 1389, he was victorious. In 1398, he was supreme. In 1399, at 33 years of age, he was destroyed.

The character of Richard II remains an enigma. Though probably not insane, he suffered from certain personality disorders especially towards the end of his reign and some historians suggest he suffered from schizophrenia. That he possessed high qualities of design and action was evident and we know that he was capable of cunning, atrocious behaviour and incredible patience. We also know he was capable of foolishness that even a simpleton would have thought twice about. The injuries he suffered at the hands of his uncle Thomas, Duke of Gloucester, certainly would have affected him.

After 246 years of unstable rule, the Plantagenet's had transformed England. They had changed a broken realm and shaped it into one of the most powerful realms in Europe.

In September of 1399, Henry ascended the throne as Henry IV and opened a new chapter of history destined to be fatal to medieval England. Although Henry's lineage from the House of Lancaster had good grounds to claim the throne of England, a higher right in blood was to descend through both the House of Mortimer and the House of York.

It was a family conflict that would never be forgotten.

WAR OF THE ROSES

THE COUSINS' WAR

The War of the Roses was basically a terrible family squabble between royal cousins greedy to snatch the crown and the throne of England for themselves away from other family members. These two royal houses, the symbolic red rose of the Lancasters and the equally symbolic white rose of the Yorks, were each making a claim for the throne and it would end up being a long and bloody battle. Both were powerful families, and both could trace their lineage back to the sons of Edward III.

There were sporadic periods of extreme violence and bloodshed and an unprecedented number of attempts to usurp the throne, dethrone the current royal, murders, betrayals, plots and the savage elimination of the direct descendants of the Plantagenets. It was a dangerous period full of unfathomable brutality and cruelty and shifting alliances. It also reflects the genius of the Tudors for self-mythology.

It is also a story of vain aristocrats attempting to take over the throne for their own personal gain and it is a story of a mighty realm that descended into civil war worse than any previous times in the middle ages.

The conflict came after the dreadful reign of Richard and it is truly understandable why people were glad to see the last of him. But whether Henry was any better than Richard and whether people who lived in those times knew the tragedy that was about to unfold is anyone's guess.

To imagine what the Middle Ages looked like at this time in history, you need to start with a massive woody forest in your mind. There would have been scrubland and marshes interspersed with open grasslands and fields of crops. There would have been animals everywhere such as boars, deer, rabbits, foxes and wolves, even some cattle and lots and lots of sheep. Upwards of 10 million sheep as the wool trade was the basis of England's wealth and income.

There would have been hundreds of towns and villages and road systems remaining from Roman times. The population in these towns would have varied from a couple of hundred to about 13,000 in York and 100,000 in London.

People needed to be self-sufficient and whatever was surplus was sold in the markets. Serfdom was on the decline and people earned money for their services from their employers, which in turn gave them the freedom to better themselves. In time, they could farm their own land.

Their diet would have been boring, consisting of roots and vegetables but in another 50 years, meat and fish would appear regularly. Wheat could have been purchased to make bread, milk could be bought to make cheese while ale was the only beverage that most people drank. Looking at the state of the rivers with human waste bobbing around, it's no wonder.

Clothes were rough but soon people who had a little spare money would have imitated their superiors by wearing brighter colours, sometimes jewellery. For all this, the basic home would have been little more than a slum surrounded by a yard where vegetables were grown. Infant mortality was high and men were lucky to reach 50 while women barely lived into their 30s. It could explain why Heaven seemed a welcome place compared to the life they were living. Churches overflowed and clergymen grew richer.

The king believed he had supreme authority from God to rule, and to help him he had powerful men from the church and nobility. Directly beneath the king came the dukes and earls who were wealthy landowners and who were cautious of marriages that did not give them some sort of advantage over their peers. Under these were knights. All knights were landowners but not all landowners were knights. A knight needed to kit himself and his squires with horses, armour, swords and lances so it was a costly exercise that some knights would not afford. These knights offered their services to the king in exchange for room and board and were some-times the only men the king could rely on in times of emergency and war.

The king had a parliament who raised taxes and passed laws and it was becoming more and more powerful as time went by.

By then, English had become the native tongue but French was still spoken and Latin was understood. Illiteracy was becoming a thing of the past and books and chronicles were being written, which is why we have so much literature from these times and so little before. Architecture flourished and Westminster Abbey became a glorious jewel in the crown.

There was still tension with France and Scotland, with skirmishes popping up in varying levels in both countries, while Irish and Welsh kings were gradually losing their power. Powerful men like Richard Plantagenet, Duke of York and his son, the future Edward IV, as well as the Earl of Warwick and Richard of Gloucester, would soon emerge to lead uprisings that overlapped but didn't always relate.

These uprisings were dramatic and the dubious logic of revenge worked well for all sides. In actual fact, it was a power struggle between family members that comes across as blue-blooded gangsterism with the prime antagonists being members of the landed gentry. Many of them controlled huge estates with powerful alliances, all trying to improve their political position and their own personal lot in life.

We can probably blame Edward III for all of this. He and his wife had thirteen children, including five strong-minded boys who all reached maturity. He arranged solid marriages for all of them with English heiresses and created the first ever Dukedoms of Cornwall, Clarence, Lancaster, York and Gloucester. Their descendants were the ones fighting each other fiercely for the throne.

Like most families, differences and intrigue slowly emerged and it wasn't until 1455 with the first Battle at St Albans that anyone even knew there *were* two sides.

This period in time seems to have been an experiment in monarchy as king after king came and went in very quick succession. But as with most rebellions, it left both sides vulnerable since it usually meant that battles were fought 'to the bitter end', leaving fewer contenders alive after every battle.

As cracks opened in Henry's inefficient rule, the first battle of the War of the Roses took place.

Let the War begin.

PART IV

THE LANCASTERS

HENRY IV

Born 1366
Reign 1399 - 1413

If Henry Bolingbroke thought that his violent take-over would end the squabble, he was sadly mistaken. His rule was definitely not to be a quiet one and his vicious invasion set a more dangerous pattern into motion than he could ever have imagined. But to point Henry as a brutal king in a long line of brutal kings is misleading. Henry was violent and cruel even to members of his own family, but such were the times.

When Henry came to the throne, anyone who had run the risk to put him there now rushed to cement their position in his shaky court. As expected, France regarded Henry as a usurper and they certainly were never going to accept him as the king. He was after all the son of the *third* son of Edward III and there were more rightful claims to the throne than his. There was Edmund Mortimer. With the Black Prince and his line gone, the proper heir to the throne should have been through Edward's *second* son, Lionel of Antwerp. From Lionel's daughter, there was an 8-year-old boy, Edmund Mortimer, and he was alive and well in Ireland.

But Henry was a big man with a big army and he was sitting right there in England, not in Ireland, and he was not an 8-year-old boy.

That's when things began to go tail up for Henry.

Without a doubt, Henry was young, charming, brave and a great leader in battle. But without validity, his claim was shabby. Henry was clinging to power by his fingernails and he knew it.

But there were few people who were brave enough to voice their opinions. Anyone who doubted that Henry should be king could look forward to being part hanged and then have their intestines pulled out. To prove it, the air hung heavy with the smell of smoke as bodies were burned. Because of his insecurity, Henry ruled by fear and the most frightened person in England was Henry himself.

At his coronation, he promised to rule fairly with parliament's assistance and he promised to live off his own income. All well and good but the problem with Henry was he had trouble living up to those promises. Within a year, he already had his hand out for money, despite his vast Lancastrian estates. Money seemed to just slip through his fingers.

This was a sticky point for the barons and Henry spent most of his time defending himself against plots, rebellions and assassination attempts because of it. After such an amazing start, within a year, his popularity was almost destroyed as trouble with the Welsh and Scots became continual and fierce.

As it turned out, Scotland was having serious problems of their own with rulers. At the time, there were three main families in Scotland, all brawling with each other and all chest beating. All were rich and all had powerful men pushing and shoving each other – the McDonalds, the Black Douglas and the Stuarts. After Robert III died along with his two eldest sons, Robert's youngest son, James, was to be Scotland's ruler at 8 years old with his uncle acting as regent.

By the time James was 12 years old, things were not going well. To keep him out of harm's way, he was sent to France for safekeeping until he was old enough to rule on his own. Coincidentally, (and once again, I've never been a big believer of coincidence) on the way to France, 'pirates' off the English coast captured his ship and he was delivered to Henry IV. For the next eighteen years, James was held in an English prison as a type of 'security' against invasions from the north.

After six years on the throne, Henry's almost amiable nature was beginning to wear thin as a debilitating skin condition began to surface. It started simply as just a nasty looking rash but sometimes he would stay behind doors for days, only to resurface rejuvenated enough to tackle the next problem.

During this time, Henry's most serious conflict, which lasted three years, was with Henry Percy, Earl of Northumbria. Percy's fiery son Henry Hotspur was married to Edmund Mortimer's sister Elizabeth, so you can see the problem instantly.

The Percy's were the lords of the Northern marshes and they were an important family in North Wales who had played a subdued part in helping to place Henry on the throne. The Percys had been holding their own in the north against the Scots at their own expense but they could no longer carry this financial burden. They demanded their account be settled. The old Earl presented the bill of £60,000 to Henry to be paid but the best Henry could offer was £40,000, stating he was in abject poverty. Take it or leave it.

Henry Hotspur decided to leave it. Always a fierce man, hence the name, Hotspur, Henry felt he had no other choice but to raise a revolt.

He didn't live long enough to regret his impulsive nature. At Shrewsbury in 1403, Hotspur was killed after a small but fierce battle. During the fight, Henry's 16-year-old son, Henry of Monmouth, was stuck in his face by an arrow and almost killed. Henry was horrified to see his son in so much pain and in those days, most men would have died from such a wound. But the young prince had the benefit of the best possible care. The broken arrow shaft was removed without doing any further damage and treated with honey but it left terrible and permanent scars.

Two years later, old Percy rebelled again but this time he brought with him Thomas de Mowbray, Earl of Norfolk (the son of the man who had been banished with Henry years before by Richard II) and Richard Scrope, Archbishop of York. The Archbishop also had a gripe of his own regarding a clerical tax imposed by Henry. Together they combined all of their armies, making up 8,000 landed gentry, and marched to confront Henry. Instead of Henry, it was his half-sister Joan Beaufort's husband Ralph Neville who confronted them to discuss negotiations. Perhaps seeing so many men in front of him, Ralph Neville agreed to all of the demands and guaranteed Scrope's personal safety back home.

Of course, he lied.

Once the army was disbanded, Scrope and Mowbray were arrested and taken to Pontefract Castle to await Henry. The old earl had managed to melt away into Scotland but Scrope was doomed from the start. Without a trial, Henry watched as the Earl of Arundel and his half-brother Sir Thomas Beaufort condemned them both to death for treason. They were to be beheaded immediately. Together the men were taken to a field belonging to a nearby nunnery beside the walls of York and it has been told that Scrope asked the axeman to deal him five blows in remembrance of the five wounds of Christ. A painful way to die.

Henry should have remembered the consequences of Thomas Becket's murder. Sure enough, miracles began happening around the archbishop's tomb. In fact, Henry had made Scrope more important in death than in life and it marked the beginning of the fault line between supporters of the Lancasters and supporters of the Yorks.

It is surprising that Henry was so merciless when previously he had shown a certain degree of humanity, but perhaps it was because his health was deteriorating rapidly. By 1410, he was in a sorry state and unable to even ride his horse. He had tumours on his face and was described as having *"a rotting of the flesh, drying up of the eyes and a rupture of the intestine"*. The French believed his toes had dropped off while the Scots were adamant that he had shrunk to the size of a child.

Today it is believed that he had leprosy, which can be cured, but in those days, there was nothing to be done and his condition would have tested the strongest stomach.

No one could ignore his condition anymore and Parliament took full advantage of Henry's ill health by taking over all his duties, even suggesting mildly that he step back in favour of his eldest son. It was a sensitive point for Henry but a valid one and young Henry was eager to sit down in the empty throne. And his two other sons, John and Humphrey were more than willing to help their eldest brother.

By 1412, Henry was gripping the reins of power convulsively. When he could no longer walk, his council discouraged him from attempting to send troops to Aquitaine. He lingered through winter but in March 1413, while praying in Westminster Abbey, he was helped along by the Grim Reaper with a prolonged fit.

On Henry IV's death, Henry V, at 27 years old, succeeded his father the next day and was crowned in April of the same year.

Unfortunately, he was to find that where his father had been one of the wealthiest men in England with his vast Lancastrian estates, there was virtually nothing left in the treasury when he assumed the throne.

His father had been practically bankrupt at his death.

HENRY V

It snowed at Henry V's coronation, a sure sign everyone said that good times were ahead, but he still knew that he had to watch his back. After all, he had other family members waiting in an impatient queue to take his place on the throne, namely the Yorks and the Mortimers. And both families had thousands of supporters. But by now, England was tiring of senseless feuds and brawls and Henry was more than ready to wind up the endless squabbling.

He didn't have to wait long for his family to make their presence felt. The Mortimers and the Yorks were breathing down his neck.

The Southampton Plot of 1415 was a conspiracy aimed at replacing Henry with Edmund Mortimer, Earl of March, a direct descendent from Edward III's second son Lionel of Antwerp. The three alleged ringleaders were Richard Earl of Cambridge, (a grandson of Edward III who was also married to Mortimer's sister Anne), Henry Scrope, 3rd Baron Scrope of Masham (whose uncle Richard le Scrope had been executed for his part in a 1405 revolt also supporting Mortimer's right) and Sir Thomas Grey of

Heaton, a direct descendant of Edward I through his mother and who was betrothed to Richard Earl of Cambridge's only daughter, Isabel.

There's no doubt about it: together the three families were a formidable enemy. They had weight on their side and they certainly meant business. But what they were doing was risky. They were plainly sticking their necks right out and everyone knew that Henry would not hesitate for a heartbeat to relieve them of their heads. What they were doing was treason and if it all went wrong, well, they were history. Literally.

On Henry's side were his brothers John of Lancaster and Humphrey of Gloucester. John was a Knight of the Garter and had been given the forfeited lands from the Percys so he was a wealthy man in his own right. He was Constable of England, Warden of the East March, Earl of Kendal, Earl of Richmond and his brother Henry had recently made him Duke of Bedford. Humphrey of Gloucester who, without the lengthy titles, carried just as much weight as his brother and together the two brothers were ready to stand side and fight.

But Henry had another amazing and confusing advantage. The person who informed Henry of the plot was Edmund Mortimer himself. Mortimer was entirely loyal to Henry and had never made a claim for the throne, despite being senior in descent than his cousin. He was happy in his role as trusted counsellor and while Henry was busy making invasion plans, he was present at a meeting and was informed of the plot. Days later, on 31st July 1415, he told Henry and all hell broke loose. Henry rounded up all three ringleaders and had them arrested then put on trial at the site now occupied by the Red Lion pub in London. As lead official at the trial, Edmund Mortimer did not disappoint Henry. All three men were sentenced to death.

The executions were carried out according to class: Richard Earl of Cambridge and Sir Thomas Grey were beheaded, while Henry Scrope of Masham (whose involvement was always dubious and considered unfounded by many) was dragged across Southampton from the Watergate to the north gate and hung, drawn and quartered two days later. His head was then sent to York to be put on a spike on Micklegate Bar. This special treatment was reserved for him because he had been one of Henry's favourites at court.

But throughout the trial, even while sentences were being passed, it was obvious that Henry's mind was elsewhere. Henry was planning a war against

France to reclaim his right to rule France through his great grandfather Edward III and he was putting all his ducks in a row. Weapons were being stockpiled including battering rams and artillery, ships were built or hired and his soldiers were at the ready. Even James Stuart of Scotland, still imprisoned in the Tower, was given free rein to move around at will. Henry needed a new ally to help him fight an old enemy.

The trials of the three traitors were just an annoying hindrance for Henry when he had more important things on his mind. Satisfied that justice had been served and all three traitors had got what they deserved, Henry got down to more important business and sailed for France on August 11th.

Henry's army of 12,000 men landed in northern France on 13th August 1415 and immediately took the port of Barfleur. In the summer heat, there were millions of flies and mosquitoes and after a month of fighting, up to 5,000 men died of either starvation or dysentery before the town finally surrendered. Instead of returning home in the cold winter months with only one rather expensive victory under his belt, Henry pressed on with his army, now only 7,000, through Normandy to Calais and then on to Agincourt.

On 25th October, there would be a battle that would be remembered as the bloodiest battle in medieval history.

On an obscure slope near Agincourt, Henry's depleted army of foot soldiers and archers stood watching 20,000 French soldiers and knights march towards them. The land had been recently ploughed and was hemmed in by dense woodlands that the English loved. The French army had to wade through thick mud from a previous night of heavy rain to reach them and the terrain was arguably a significant factor in the outcome.

It wasn't just the French who were exhausted. Henry's own army was weary and hungry from marching and he was forced to make a momentous decision and a calculated risk that would mark history forever. Instead of retreating, Henry moved his army further forward to start the battle.

The French seemed to be caught off guard by the English advance and as their own crossbowmen came within shooting distance, thousands of English archers unleashed their own fury and the sky darkened with the shadow of arrows. With heavy casualties, the French fled backwards leaving their cavalry to take over. Horses soon became bogged in the thick mud and the knights were forced to proceed on foot, confident that their plate armour would be enough protection. But as frenzied horses plodded back across the fields, they collided with men. And the arrows kept coming. Wearing armour weighing around 50 – 60 pounds, the French knights pressed headlong to almost point-blank range, forced to step over the dead and mutilated bodies of their fallen comrades.

The impact of thousands of arrows, combined with the slog in heavy armour through the mud, the heat and lack of oxygen in plate armour with the visor down, meant the French soldiers could scarcely lift their weapons when they finally engaged the English line. The exhausted French were knocked to the ground by the English and were just unable to get back up again. Many suffocated in their armour but most were simply hacked to death while completely stuck in the deep mud. The survivors would find that Henry was not taking prisoners.

Due to a lack of reliable sources it is impossible to give a precise figure for the French and English casualties. However, it is clear that because the English were outnumbered, their losses were far lower than those of the French. The French sources all give 4,000–10,000 French dead, including three dukes, eight counts, a viscount and an archbishop, along with the fathers, sons and relatives of nine major French towns, with up to 1,600 Englishmen, who died as well.

How so much death and abject misery can be called a success is beyond me but it has been termed as a glittering victory for the English.

But in the heady days after Agincourt and through the miserable decade that followed, a black shadow cast itself over Henry's triumphs as a fierce religious group called the Lollards, set upon him.

Lollards believed that Christianity should be closely based on the Bible and that everyone should have access to a vernacular Bible. Everyone should also be allowed to interpret its meaning for themselves. Not such a bad idea you would think but this posed a threat to the Church because they had the sole authority on the translation of the Bible, and it was the Church's sole interpretation of the Bible that they wanted society to read. The Lollards main concern was that the clergy had become so caught up in secular affairs that they had forgotten their spiritual obligations. The way they saw it, the clergy should live off alms and their own labour. You can imagine how *that* went down.

All this seems pretty fair and logical but the Lollards went one step too far. All hatred was turned on them when they announced that their main belief was the denial of the transformation of the Eucharistic bread and wine into the body and blood of Christ.

To the English people, it seemed frightful beyond words that they should declare that the Host lifted in Mass was a dead thing *"less than a toad or a spider"*. There was a horrible scene when Henry, then aged 24, was present at the execution of a tailor by the name of John Badby, who was also a Lollard. Henry offered him a pardon if he recanted, and when he refused, the fires were lit under him. John Badby was not the only one to be burned at the stake. Many more followed.

Henry's problem, like so many of his ancestors before him, was that he couldn't stop himself from warring with France. Two years after Agincourt, he set out for another battle to Rouen but this time on a much grander scale. But unlike Agincourt, this siege would cast another shadow on Henry's reputation.

Rouen, starving and unable to support their people during the worst winter in their history, forced their women and children through the gates believing that Henry would allow them to pass through his army unmolested. But Henry was still dreaming of a glittering victory. The success of Agincourt was still very clear in his mind and there was no way he was going to let anything, much less sentimentality, stand in his way. He refused to let them through and the women and children were left to starve and freeze to death in the ditches surrounding the town.

Rouen fell in January 1419 and by August, Henry and his army had advanced to just outside the walls of Paris. With the city in a terrible panic, the French court threw themselves at Henry's feet.

The current King of France was Charles VI and over the past ten years, Charles had been showing definite signs of mental instability. His hair and nails had fallen out and he had occasional bouts of fever when he behaved incoherently. Sometimes he ran from room to room until he collapsed from exhaustion and eventually he was kept in closed shuttered apartments while his voice could be heard wailing and screaming through the walls of the castle. On a journey one day, a page dropped the king's lance with an almighty clang causing the king to draw his sword and swing it around wildly shouting *"Treason!"* He killed five men before he could be stopped. On many occasions, he forgot who he was and at times refused to wash or change his clothes, which resulted in a nasty skin complaint and lice. One time, he insisted he was made of glass and would break if anyone approached him.

His physicians blamed Charles's mental abnormality on his mother Jeanne de Bourbon who had suffered a complete nervous breakdown following the birth of her seventh child. Whatever the diagnosis, Charles's condition was catastrophic.

After six months of negotiation with Henry, Charles VI, in a period of supposed lucidity, signed the Treaty of Troyes. He would disinherit his own son in favour of Henry as the heir and regent of France: on one condition. Henry was to marry Charles's youngest daughter, Catherine of Valois, *without* a dowry. Catherine's elder sister, by the way, had been Isabella of Valois, who had been Richard II's 6-year-old bride.

There was no doubt about it, at 18 years old, Catherine was a slim beauty with delicate features, a small prim mouth and round eyes above high cheekbones. Compared to Catherine, Henry was battle-hardened and coarse. He had dark protruding eyes that stared out of a face showing scars including a deep one that dated back to when an arrowhead had lodged deep in his cheek and had to be cut out by a battlefield surgeon when he was 16.

The carrot Charles was dangling was a delicious one. Kings of England had been fighting their French cousins for centuries in battles for territories with rare success, and not even the mighty Edward III had managed to come this tantalisingly close to victory. Even the marriage between Edward II and Isabella of France had not been enough to prevent the Hundred Years' War. Catherine and Henry's marriage, therefore, was momentous for both families.

The marriage took place in an elegant church in Troyes while a large band of musicians played a glorious tune. But perhaps Henry should have looked a little closer at Catherine's father's 'instability'. Through Catherine, a gene would be passed on and it would affect British monarchs for many generations in the future.

Fate could not let Henry go on for much longer. A return to France one year later would be Henry's undoing. By August, in full stride after conquering Dreux and Meaux, Henry contracted dysentery in the battlefield.

It was a miserable six months for both sides during a cruel winter where the garrison slowly starved and the townspeople suffered the ravages of winter stranded from their homes. It was an ugly way to fight a war and Henry suffered the consequences.

His condition was fatal and he knew it. He was an experienced soldier who had seen many men suffer the same fate so he knew to make a detailed will outlining his wishes. His eldest brother John Duke of Bedford would take over affairs in France. His youngest brother Humphrey Duke of Gloucester would be 'protector' and take responsibility for his son's education and upbringing.

This was interpreted that Gloucester would have full regency powers, accountable only to the king himself, and many approved because Gloucester was held in high esteem. He promoted artists, wrote and collected books and he was a veteran of Agincourt. This however would lapse when his elder brother John of Bedford visited England.

Henry did not live to be crowned King of France as he had hoped after signing the Treaty of Troyes, because ironically the crazy, sickly Charles VI, to whom Henry had been named heir, survived him by two months.

Henry died in the royal castle at Vincennes on 31st August, two weeks short of his 36th birthday, and a baby of nine months was to be the future King of France and the youngest person ever to become the King of England. For Catherine, there would be no fairy tale ending. She would presently leave for Windsor and a frightening new chapter would soon open up for England in the future.

If England thought things had been bad before, they were in for a terrible shock.

HENRY VI

Born 1422
Reign 1422 - 1461
Reign 1471 - 1471

Medieval times were pretty crazy but they reached the pinnacle of madness with a king who was barely nine months old. It left the ruling of the kingdom wide open for his uncles John Duke of Bedford, and Humphrey Duke of Gloucester to step in with agendas of their own. Two months later on the death of his grandfather Charles VI of France, Henry also took on the title of King of France as well as King of England and the madness went up another notch.

It appeared the only thing his uncles could agree on was the order for 'reasonable chastisement' to the carefully chosen nurses and teachers. Not that it was really needed. The child was extremely mild and gentle, almost simple. It seemed that through his father he had inherited the physical weaknesses of the House of Lancaster but through his mother, it was looking like he may have inherited the mental difficulties of mad King Charles VI.

Despite Henry's gentleness, the Scotsmen still had an enduring hatred for the English and their rage was uncontainable. After eighteen years, James Stuart was still in prison and they wanted him back home in Scotland.

Considering the amount of money being spent on James, Bedford and Gloucester couldn't see too many benefits in keeping him in England anyway. The original idea of a hostage was to keep Scotland in line but nothing of any value had come out of it. If anything, James was having a pretty good time while in captivity. He'd been given a good education and Henry V had made sure he understood how the English ran things. He'd even struck up a love interest with Joan Beaufort, Henry's half-cousin.

Then an idea struck the two men. Instead of throwing good money after bad, they could cash in their chips and ransom James back to Scotland for £40,000 and as a bonus, they would throw in Joan as James's bride before sending him back to Scotland. They could make money and create an allegiance with Scotland and at the same time, get a few hostages back from Scotland to England as well. Before too long, Scotland had agreed and James headed back to Scotland with his new bride.

Unfortunately for James, his return was not to be as joyous as it could have been. After so many years under English supervision, some saw James as a stranger, possibly even an English spy, and he faced many attempts on his life through the coming years. After thirteen years of quarrelling, a conspiracy was finally hatched by a group of nobles to remove James permanently from the throne and place the Earl of Atholl in his place. It came to fruition in February 1437 when the plotters surprised James at the lodgings he kept at a Dominican nunnery in Perth. Forced at short notice to find a hiding place, the powerfully built king ran to a forgotten privy, tore up a plank from the wooden floor, and concealed himself and a loyal lady he had been 'visiting' at the time in the overflowing cesspit below.

The privy, we are told, drained into an adjacent tennis court often used by James, and he was fed up with continually losing balls in the sewer. So shortly before this incident, James had the drain bricked up. It's one of the great 'if onlys' of history. If only he'd left it as it was he would have found it a simple matter to escape through the privy-hole instead of being trapped in the stinking prison below. His only hope was that his would-be assassins would not discover him. But once they had gained access to the privy (using saws, levers and axes to get in), the lose plank in the floor was quickly noticed and lifted, revealing James hiding in the muck below. In the darkness and the filth, they descended on him and submerged him before stabbing him sixteen times ... just to make sure he was dead.

While all this brewed in Scotland, England had its own troubles. The Dauphin of France wanted his kingdom back and everything the English had done, ravaging their country and destroying stability, had created a passionate nationalism. To the French there seemed no way to deal with the rugged, violent islanders with their archery, tactics and audacity.

When a young girl called Joan miraculously appeared on the scene, it was entirely natural for the people to believe that an angel sent from God had appeared.

In a poor village of Domremy, this young girl served at an inn and rode the horses of weary travellers bareback to water. She would become the most splendid of France's heroes and the most beloved of all their saints. The French believed that she was on a divine mission to drive the English out of France and give them back their rightful king. The girl was the ever glorious, Joan of Arc.

The story goes that one day while walking through the forest at Vosges, Saint Michael appeared to her to command the armies of liberation. She shrank initially but when he returned with Saint Margaret and Saint Catherine, she obeyed. She was to find the most stubborn obstacle in her own family. Her father was appalled that she would cut her hair and ride among rough soldiers in male attire. And how was she supposed to buy horses and armour? How was she supposed to gain access to the Dauphin?

Perhaps the saints really were watching over her, or maybe the French were just clutching at straws, because she managed to convince the governor of the neighbouring town of her visions. She made the perilous journey across France to see the Dauphin in what remained of the city of Chinon. When the people saw her on horseback and in armour, crouching with her lance, the spectators went wild with delight. There amongst the crowd, she picked out the Dauphin, who had dressed as a peasant to fool her. She said, *"I am Joan the Maid, sent on the art of God to aid you and the kingdom, and by His order, I announce that you will be crowned in the city of Rheims."*

At the time, Orleans lay under siege by a few thousand English who were slowly destroying the city. Joan led a convoy to the rescue at the head of the troops with a simple plan. She would march straight into Orleans between the strongest of English soldiers. The reports of a vigilante sent by God to save France clouded the minds of the English and froze them with a sense of awe and fear. Fearlessly, she called for an immediate onslaught on the English and led the army forward to charge, only to be wounded by an arrow, which she plucked out before returning to the charge. One by one the English forts fell and soldiers were slain. Orleans was to be only the first victory.

Previously, she had told Charles he must march on Rheims if he wanted to be crowned upon the throne of his ancestors and as she had predicted, every town opened their gates before them. By his side stood Joan, with her banner flying, as he was crowned King Charles VII with the crowds cheering.

England reacted instantly by crowning Henry the King of England. Henry was now 7 years old.

We all know Joan's plight. She had fought almost twenty victories but now her 'voices' were silent. She wanted to go home but was convinced to make one more attack on Paris. In doing so, she had condemned herself to death.

On the insistence from the Duke of Bedford, the governor pulled up the drawbridge in her face and left her to face the English on her own. She was charged with heresy and for a whole year her fate hung in the balance while she was questioned endlessly in a tribunal overseen by the Duke of Bedford and the Earl of Warwick. The ungrateful Charles did not even lift a finger to save her.

There was never any hope for her. She was condemned and sentenced to die. In the immense open square of Rouen, she was tied to a pillar and the kindling was lit. Below her, the flames rose and the smoke curled. At the end, she raised a cross made of firewood above her head. Her last word was *"Jesus!"* History has recorded the comment of an English soldier who witnessed the scene. *"We are lost"*, he said. *"We have burned a saint."* After she died, the English raked back the coals to expose her charred body so no one could claim she had escaped. Then they burned it twice more to reduce it to ashes so that there would be no collection of relics. Her ashes were then cast into the Seine.

While Joan burned, 9-year-old Henry was crowned King of France in Paris, amidst a chilly crowd.

Henry had an almost crushing burden of expectation on his young shoulders. He stood at 5 feet 9 inches tall with a round boyish face, a high brow over curved eyebrows and large widespread eyes. His nose was long and his mouth was a delicate pout, much like his mother's. He always had a faint look of surprise on his face.

At 17, Edward III had led an army against his mother and Mortimer. At 14, Richard II had faced a Peasant's Revolt. At 16, Henry's own grandfather had led troops at the Battle of Shrewsbury. At 14, Henry VI was a work in progress.

Vague hope was held for this Henry, especially when his uncle John of Bedford died in Rouen at only 46 years of age. He was the only one holding the peace together between his brother Humphrey Duke of Gloucester and his uncle Cardinal Beaufort of Winchester so at his death, things began to unravel a little.

The combination of Bedford's death and Henry's inability to step up to the task of ruling left a vacuum and William de la Pole, Earl of Suffolk, was happy to fill it. As Suffolk amassed power and wealth, he was quietly ruling an almost sluggish king and playing with fire by stealthily manipulating Henry.

As Henry grew up, his soundness of mind became a serious question. At 18, there were some accounts of limited intelligence matched by accounts of his being incapable of even distinguishing between right and wrong. If the royal lineage wasn't complicated before, it becomes even more complicated now as Richard, Duke of York became an important element in the future of the British monarchy.

Richard could trace his own ancestry back to Edward III in two strong lines. Firstly, he was the grandson of Edmund of Langley, Duke of York, the third son of Edward III through his father Richard Earl of Cambridge. And secondly, he was the great grandson of Lionel of Antwerp, the second son of Edward III through his mother Anne Mortimer. To complicate things even more, Richard had married Cecily Neville whose great-grandfather was John of Gaunt, through Joan Beaufort, his legitimised daughter by Katherine Swynford. Again, back to Edward III.

It was impressive lineage, and terribly complicated, but it effectively meant that if Henry did not produce an heir, Richard Duke of York and his children, were certainly the top contenders for the throne. And Richard Duke of York wanted it ever so badly.

Finally, it was decided that at 23, it was high time that Henry produced an heir to put an end to the squabbles and Richard's claim, once and for all.

But to do that, he needed a wife. Some of the Lancastrians were eager to provide him with a queen and they bickered ceaselessly about who should be the heir apparent until Henry produced a son.

Something had to be done and it had to be done quickly.

Henry's cousins Edmund Beaufort and his close ally William de la Pole had had enough of the squabbles and convinced Henry to look to France. Ideally a marriage to one of Charles VII's many daughters would soothe ruffled French feathers, they said, and in one swoop, strained relations with Charles VII could be appeased and a truce could be arranged. But then someone else mentioned the close family link. Any daughter of Charles would have been Henry's cousin and as they knew, mental issues were already poking through the thin veneer. England already had enough problems in *that* respect without introducing more.

That's when they began looking closer and found Margaret of Anjou, the niece of Charles VII's wife. This rare beauty owned an intellect and a dauntless spirit already likened to Joan of Arc. A perfect union, they thought, for their feeble-minded king. Henry would have someone strong by his side to secure a certain future for England.

Henry wholeheartedly agreed, especially when he heard reports of Margaret's stunning beauty, and Suffolk was sent to negotiate with Charles. Charles, knowing his full worth and knowing England's desperation for an heir, agreed on the condition that he would not have to provide the customary dowry. Not only that but he would receive the lands of Maine and Anjou back from the English with the promise of a 20-year truce that would come into effect *after* marriage.

The unspoken truth that was being conscientiously avoided was that all English people living in Maine and Anjou would have to evacuate their homes immediately after the marriage. Those territories would now belong to the French.

For someone who supposedly had 'the crazy gene', Charles had come up with a pretty good idea in a moment of lucidity. To me, it sounds more than a little dubious but all was reluctantly agreed upon.

Almost immediately, problems began.

When the French stated that they expected the marriage to take place in Tours, doubts surfaced regarding Henry's safety. Tours was in French territory with French soldiers. Surely they couldn't just let Henry leave the safety of England and expose himself to certain danger? It was like dangling a mouse in front of a cat. Once he was there, the French would never let him out of their clutches.

As an alternative, Calais was suggested as the venue. But as with the English, there was no way the French were going to allow their king to be surrounded by an English army.

No one would budge an inch.

And then Suffolk had an idea. They could go ahead and say that Henry would marry the princess in Tours as the French had requested but at the very last minute, on the day even, they could say that Henry was too ill to attend. A proxy marriage would take place with Henry safe and sound in England. Later, when Margaret travelled to England, a real ceremony would be performed. It would be touch and go, but they were confident that the French desperately wanted the two territories back just as much as England wanted a bride for their king.

The plan went into full swing and the date was set for one month before Margaret's 15th birthday in 1445.

When hearing of the plan, Richard Duke of York was shocked. Everything Henry V had fought for with English blood would be gone. Did they realise that it would all revert straight back to the French? And what of the people who had trusted the crown and set up their lives in France, sure in their hearts that England would protect them?

Suffolk stood firm. Henry wanted a truce between the French and the English, he said, and this was the only way.

Like a bad omen, York predicted that the people in both territories would absolutely resist. They would not give up their homes without a fight, truce or not. And he didn't blame them.

The day of the wedding dawned magnificent. The eastern sky gradually lightened long before the sun rose over a clear horizon with a promise of a gloriously warm day. Charles and the French nobles had assembled at the church in Tours and Margaret had already arrived. That was when Suffolk broke the news of Henry's illness.

Margaret looked shocked. With a strength she would show in the future, she accepted the new plans in silence but with trepidation. It certainly wasn't the ideal way to start a marriage. As for Charles, as long as he was still given the two territories, he was happy. The wedding was to proceed.

As soon as Margaret had finished saying her vows in halting English, all the assembled soldiers turned their horses towards Main and Anjou to fulfil King Charles's orders. The English could find somewhere else to live. Maine and Anjou belonged to France, as of now.

Of course, it was inevitable that the French would find resistance in Maine and Anjou, just as York had predicted. Every farmer and noble, who in the past would not have given the time of day to each other, joined forces to fight and protect the land they had worked on for decades. With resistance, came anger. And with that anger came France's declaration. The truce was over and war was back on.

As the fighting began in earnest, Margaret left Calais, on her way to England to meet her new husband, whom she had never set eyes on, while French troops moved further into Maine.

All Margaret knew of Henry was what she'd heard. Henry was young, handsome, gentle and had a sweet nature. With all the terrible marriage possibilities that had been considered for her, (after all, there were a lot of rich old men looking for a virginal bride), she couldn't wait to meet her young husband. In her dreams, she imagined the handsome king sweeping her off her feet and into his arms after having gallantly ridden through the night to greet her. He would seat her in front of him on his white horse and together they would ride off to their castle.

She was sadly mistaken. Instead, she disembarked alone after a terrible bout of seasickness and looked around desperately for Henry on the shore. As the wind buffeted her dress and her hair whipped madly around her face, she realised Henry had not come to greet her at all. Within minutes, she was whisked away secretly and it would be weeks before she was to meet him.

It was a nervous crowd that stood on the grassy slopes of the Thames watching 15-year-old Margaret as she stood beside the happy Henry, waving to the crowds. The sky was the bluest they could remember as the daughter of the impoverished Duke Rene of Anjou came into their sights. Her father had spent most of her life locked up in enemies' jails, beaten in wars, but he was the brother of the Queen of France, so all was forgiven.

The city did not quite look its best. The wooden steeple of St Paul's had been set alight during a winter lightning strike and the gates were in need of repair. Still, gutters had been cleaned, roofs straightened to support clambering onlookers and tavern signs were made more secure so they didn't fall on the heads bobbing below.

After the rather shaky start, it seemed Henry and Margaret were perfect together although rumours had popped up around the court that she had found a 'special' friend in Edmund Beaufort.

Then one year after the marriage, Henry did a strange thing. Urged on by Suffolk and Edmund Beaufort, Henry summoned his uncle Humphrey Duke of Gloucester. Since the wedding, Gloucester had become a bystander, openly mocked by Suffolk, and rumours had been circulating that there was a plot to kill the king. When Gloucester was ceremoniously summoned to court, he must have realised the danger. And he had a right to be nervous. The charge read to him was treason.

The bewildered and anguished Duke of Gloucester was dragged to the Tower to await his sentence but he soon died, cold and alone in the Tower. Although supposedly of a stroke, rumours of poisoning began to circulate. The Duke of York, Henry's heir presumptive until a child was born, was then sent packing in rage to govern Ireland as a Lieutenant, while Suffolk and Edmund Beaufort were both promoted to Dukes and Suffolk was given the dubious honour of fighting for England in France. Things were definitely heating up.

While England reeled over the death of Gloucester, Charles's huge army continued their march through Maine and Anjou. Suffolk sent appeals to Henry for more soldiers to help him fight the French army who had begun to cross the border into Normandy but his requests fell on deaf ears. All Henry's soldiers were fully occupied trying to enforce peace in England without sending them to help in France.

Refugees were returning home from France in the thousands with stories of fear and terror as the French raped English women and slaughtered families not quick enough to escape. As the stories circulated, riots began popping up everywhere in England and angry, indignant citizens, led by a brutal man by the name of Jack Cade, began marching to London, gathering supporters as he went. With him were returning troops who had often not been paid. Everyone was insisting on justice from their king and they weren't about to leave without it.

Suffolk was told he had to wait and make do with what he had.

By 1450, the English were losing badly in France and the French had taken provinces back that had been so hard to win in the first place by Henry V. It was a total disaster just as Richard of York had predicted. And someone had to be the scapegoat.

Parliament was very good at the pointing fingers and they all pointed them at Suffolk. With his recommendation for Henry to marry Margaret and set up a truce, Suffolk had made himself some very powerful enemies, in particular the Duke of York. Being the next in line for the throne, the last thing York wanted was for Henry to produce an heir.

When Maine and Anjou were finally taken by the French, closely followed by Normandy, Suffolk was ordered to return to England. He arrived expecting a welcoming crowd to greet him and with the full intention of begging Henry for more soldiers. What he saw was angry people lining the streets waving their fists in the air. As he marched towards London, the mood grew uglier by the minute. Even some stones were thrown.

Suffolk was in a state of shock. He knew they would be upset by his losses but he had also expected them to know why. He needed men to help, but that help had been refused, as had the money to pay them. His men had been slaughtered and defeat at French hands had been the outcome. Resolutely, he kept marching to London and was promptly arrested.

Although Suffolk defended himself vigorously and reminded them of his past loyalty to the king, within four days he was charged with treason as well as *"corrupt practices at the king's expense"*.

Of course, all the charges were utterly ridiculous, as there was no evidence that he had conspired with the French, or anyone else for that matter, nor had he plotted to kill Henry. But in the group presenting the charges were the Duke of York and the Neville clan, both angry that Suffolk had arranged for the marriage that could supply England with a new heir.

While the trial continued, Cade was collecting more supporters on his march towards London and England was slowly going up in flames.

Henry was never been a mentally strong man. He had always depended on someone else to make decisions for him and this time was no different. He had no idea what to do. It meant either admit the charges against Suffolk were false or admit that he had made a dreadful mistake in signing the treaty with France in the first place. That admission could cause a civil war with people outraged that their king was the one who had actually authorised their homes be taken away and given to the French. It would also give York ammunition to depose Henry for incompetence and snatch the throne for himself. It put Henry in a very difficult situation, and he was faced with an impossible choice of either killing his lifelong friend or exiling him.

Henry chose the exile option. But Suffolk could return to England after five years, he stated.

As the sentence was passed, Cade was outside the gates of London waiting to hear Suffolk's fate. The decision sent London into a fury, angry at Henry's weakness towards his favourite adviser, and Suffolk was lucky to get out of the capital alive.

Within a few weeks, Suffolk arrived at Ipswich ready to depart on the first leg of his exile to Burgundy. People pushed and shoved to come close enough so they could hiss and spit at him.

As he stood sadly on the deck watching the white cliffs of Dover fade to a dim line on the horizon, the air must have felt clean with a hint of spring warmth after the stench of London. It would have felt like a new beginning for him. No more wars and no more fighting.

Then, out of the salt spray, a warship appeared. Orders were given to head as fast as possible for Calais and as Suffolk watched the warship approaching fast, a glimpse of the French coast came tantalisingly into view. The sail fluttered wildly but still the warship leapt closer. As time crept on, Calais grew closer as thunderclouds grew angrier and the cold salt water misted in the air. Still the warship advanced through the first drops of heavy rain. And then the first of the arrows thumped around them.

Suffolk's fate was sealed on that day. His grisly corpse was found days later on a Dover beach. His head had been mangled off and stuck on a pole in the sand.

As Suffolk was being murdered, Cade's army had reached the edge of London, ready to tear it apart. As he approached, men spilled out of their homes to join him while their women blew kisses to him as he passed. It almost seemed that if he got to Westminster, he could take the throne for himself with the support of the city behind him. In one hand, they held crackling torches and in the other, any weapon they could find. As they reached the heart of the city, Cade struck the ground with his sword and listened as the ringing sound echoed through the streets. He held his shield in one hand as his sword glittered in the torch-light, high above his head. And the crowd roared their approval.

As drops of rain began to fall in the fading twilight, men surged forward and their torches sizzled. Everyone was roaring for the king to be removed and be put on trial. No one cared what the charges would be. They just wanted him gone.

Henry and his soldiers watched wide-eyed as the rioters advanced across London Bridge. That night, the bridge shone brightly in the wash from the bowls of flaming oil lit all along its length and the Thames glittered like diamonds as the rain began to fall heavily. As the rebels reached halfway, the first bolts from crossbows hit them. Screams of shock and pain filled the air as men fell with arrows bristling out of them. Their only hope was to continue their struggle across the bridge to the other side as fast as they could. The rebels swung savagely with their axes as they lurched on slippery ground. Finally, groups of men managed to cross to the dark streets of London.

As the streets filled, men began to peel off from the main group to enter taverns they came across along the way. Before long, they were just drunken looters, carrying away anything they could carry. What had driven them before had been overridden by the desire to loot, rape and murder.

But the main group had a lot more than loot on their minds. They were out for blood and the brutal fighting continued until dawn. Among the dead were the Archbishop of Canterbury and Henry's treasurer, Sir James Fiennes, whose heads were chopped off and placed on poles. In the early morning light, frost-covered bodies lay strewn with their bodies ripped apart and blood running through the mud and filth.

If Cade's army thought that the people of London would treat them like heroes, they were sadly mistaken. As his army slept, angry crowds emerged from their homes ready to slit the throats of the men who had destroyed their city during the night. By then, those who were not dead or lying on the ground in a drunken stupor were marching away from the city carrying their spoils.

If there was anything Henry's advisers knew it was that London could not stand another night like the last. After the battle on London Bridge, Archbishop Kemp (Lord Chancellor) persuaded Cade to call off his followers in order to stop a repetition. In the king's name, Kemp offered a truce to Cade. He assured Cade that his demands would be met and he and his men would be given a royal pardon if the fighting ceased.

Cade's army, so brave the night before, had seen the destruction they'd caused and they lined up in the streets to get their pardon. Henry's clerk set up a desk and each name was written down. The bishop blessed each and every one, made the sign of the cross above their heads and told them to go home in peace. Once the pardon was in their hands, they melted away, happy to get off scot-free. After being so filled with hope for a better world just one night ago, they would be going back to a life where they couldn't pay their taxes and couldn't feed their family. Just as they had before. Even Cade lined up for his piece of paper.

What Cade hadn't realised was that shortly after the pardons were offered, and while people were even queuing up for them, Henry was in the process of revoking them. Henry's name was on the paper and the bishop had blessed them all but the pardon wasn't worth the paper it was written on and the signature of the king was worthless.

Cade was pursued relentlessly and finally captured. Mortally wounded, he died on his way back to London where his corpse was hung, drawn and quartered and his head placed on a pole on London Bridge while carrion birds pulled the flesh from his body.

From Ireland, York heard the news. First there was the death of Gloucester, then there was Suffolk's death. Then unbelievably, London had barely survived the Jack Cade riots. During that time, Henry sat in Westminster wringing his hands while his cousin, Edmund Beaufort, 'befriended' Margaret and took over. York had had enough. Incensed, he gathered men together and left Dublin for London.

York's ships landed in northern Wales and headed through Ludlow then across the midlands. As York travelled, he gathered followers, all tired of Henry's inefficient rule. On 27th September, he arrived in London with almost 5,000 men, marching through the streets to Westminster.

The panic his arrival caused is easy to understand. Cade's uprising had caused a summer of chaos that had followed Gloucester's death and Suffolk's murder. And York saw himself as the saviour of both the crown and the country since his royal blood gave him privileges in the government. When he arrived in London, his first shock was to find his cousin Edmund

Beaufort appointed to more or less the position York saw as his and immediately, the two dukes collided.

York was a smart man. He knew his rank and position as one of the greatest men in the realm and he wasn't about to be sidelined. He sent letters to most towns demanding they join up with him in London and remove Beaufort in the name of good government.

Now we all know that Henry was sensitive. He had his advisers and he had men telling him what to do at any given time of the day and they were the ones who made all decisions for him. So it's understandable that while at a hunting lodge near Salisbury, when Henry heard the news that York had arrived in London with an army, his mind suddenly snapped.

This was to be the first time that Henry slipped into a mental breakdown and became completely unaware of everything that was going on around him.

Henry sat for days without moving or speaking. He was fed by spoon and had to be lifted from his bed to a chair and a commode. He lost his memory, he lost control of his body and he lost the ability to speak or to understand what was being said to him.

Since nobody knew what was wrong, nobody knew what to do. They beat his feet, shouted and threatened him and if he'd been awake, his tender heart would have broken. They slapped him until his cheeks were red. They bled him, fed him scalding drinks and spicy soups. They made him sleep under thick furs with a hot brick at his feet until he was sweating and crying softly in his sleep. They purged him with enemas, made him vomit and put poultices of fiery mustard seeds on his back until it was raw. Nothing stirred him. He lay inert as they moved from one torture to another. Not even Margaret could rouse him when she told him she was pregnant with their first child.

York had had enough. He stormed into parliament demanding to take over the regency and be named Protectorate of the country since his cousin Henry was obviously unfit. Almost immediately, York and his wife's nephew, Richard Neville Earl of Salisbury, a man who was possibly richer than York himself, placed Edward Beaufort in the Tower and Margaret was told to stay confined to her rooms.

If the illness had been permanent, York would have naturally become the next ruler as Richard III. What he hadn't counted on was Margaret's pregnancy. Like everyone else, York was doing the math when six months later she delivered a baby boy and named him Edward. Even so, no one could prove whether the baby was Henry's or Somerset's and certainly, Margaret wasn't about to open that Pandora's box. With the birth, everything became complicated again. And York was furious ... again.

For more than a year, Henry slept. Then on Christmas Day, for no reason whatsoever, Henry miraculously regained his senses. He greeted his wife and was delighted when Margaret took the 14-month-old boy to see his father. When Henry asked his name and was told 'Edward', he held up his hands in joy.

The same could not be said for York. Henry's recovery not only meant the end of his protectorate but a reversal of everything he'd been working towards. By January, Beaufort was out of prison, at Margaret's insistence of course, and all charges were drooped. After that, Henry began dismissing York and all the ministers, including Salisbury, who had served with him. As Edmund Beaufort stood firmly behind Henry, and Margaret sat snuggly beside him, the squabbling became more intense between the Yorks and Lancasters.

During this lucid period, Henry was to hear an extraordinary story regarding some unknown relatives. The story told to Henry by the Abbess of Barking, Katherine de la Pole, was that after the death of Henry's father, his mother, Catherine of Valois, moved house to Windsor Castle. It was there she employed a Welsh wardrobe man by the name of Owen Tudor and she and the servant had an affair. It was not known if she actually married him but together, they had raised two boys. Edmund was the eldest son and Jasper was the next youngest and the two boys had been in her care for many years.

Katherine de la Pole was the sister of William de la Pole, Duke of Suffolk, and she had every right to be happy. The abbey she ruled was elegant and richly furnished and most likely the wealthiest nunnery in England. Wealthy daughters and widows from the titled autocracy came to Barking to retire from the world and it was with this money that she controlled thirteen manors and lands in various counties.

Katherine was used to taking care of children. Privileged offspring had been placed in the abbey for their education since the 8th century and she was not expected to spare any expense. In 1437, Katherine welcomed two young visitors, 7-year-old Edmund and 5-year-old Jaspar Tudor, sons of the late queen. Katherine's task was to shelter them, which she had done for five years, and it is probable that her brother was paying the fees. But Suffolk had recently died and the money had stopped.

Katherine stood before Henry and told him the story and with no other brothers, Henry was delighted. At this stage, the name Tudor did not send shivers of panic and fear into English hearts. Henry immediately had the priests bring his two half-brothers to him so that they could grow up and be educated in his court as befitting someone of royal blood.

While Henry was processing this amazing story, Beaufort heard that York and Salisbury, together with Salisbury's son Richard Earl of Warwick, had combined forces again and were marching south. Knowing that they were not coming for a royal tea party, Beaufort gathered troops and together with Henry, they went to meet them. They met at St Albans and the mood turned ugly.

The first battle of St Albans was just a short scuffle in a street. It lasted for an hour and the number of slain and wounded was small. No more than 120 people died, possibly as few as sixty and of the forty-eight bodies buried, only twenty-five were those of unknown common soldiers. The others were lords, knights and squires. There was no massacre of fugitives or prisoners and the victors contented themselves with relieving their captives of their valuables.

What was unfortunate for Henry was his main supporter, Edmund Beaufort, was hacked to death and while men screamed and arrows whizzed around him, Henry's thin clear voice was heard laughing and singing as he sat under a tree.

But as disastrous as this battle was, it was the second significant battle at St Albans that was Margaret's undoing. As the battle raged, Henry was wounded in the neck and captured.

Everyone was jubilant and wild with relief at the short ride back to London with York, Salisbury and Warwick escorting Henry as their prisoner. People who had lined the streets and watched a confident Henry leave could not believe what they were seeing when he returned. He looked like he had collapsed in on himself. His head was down and a dirty bandage covered the wound in his neck as he stumbled, one foot after the other.

Flush with success, York truly took over. This time, he vowed, he would not make the same mistakes. This time he would exclude Margaret completely from any input but he would allow Margaret to take Henry and her son to her castle in Staffordshire. What he didn't know was she had arranged for her staff to take artillery pieces from the Tower of London to Wales with her as well.

At 34, Henry was quick to tire and physically weak. Not so Margaret. At 26, she was mature and confident with a large circle of supporters. And she was in possession of Prince Edward, the heir to the throne. In Anjou, she had seen her mother and grandmother take control of her father's territories during his long periods of imprisonment so she couldn't see why she couldn't do the same in England, either through her husband or her son. Added to this was the fact she hated York with every fibre of her being and was committed to undermine him whenever she could. As far as she was concerned, York had got as close to the throne as he was ever going to get.

No one thought Margaret could do much on her own from her castle in the Midlands, so for four years, Margaret surrounded herself with more and more Lancastrians. As she waited patiently, tension grew and a burning resentment bubbled underneath everyday life. Finally, the time was right and Henry was once more lucid.

York hadn't realised that Margaret was so determined to win back the throne on behalf of her husband and her son so things came to a sudden and nasty head in May 1459. Three thousand bows and countless sheaves of arrows suddenly went missing from the Tower and it became obvious that the Lancastrians were moving preparations up another notch once more.

But while Margaret was making preparations, so was York. He had assembled his two sons, Edward and Edmund, and they were given their orders. Edmund was to come with him and Salisbury to meet the Lancastrians while Edward was sent to Wales to gather more forces. York's wife Cecily was to take their youngest sons, Richard and George to safety. She had seen enough battles during her marriage to now she was in terrible danger and needed to protect her youngest children.

The two forces clashed on a freezing cold December morning in Wakefield with York leading his army and Henry leading his. Both men would have known that this was to be to the death. The wind would have gusted and filled their chests with icy particles and their mouths would have stung from the cold. As they clutched their swords tightly in the howling wind, their hands would have been numb as the cold crept into their bones. They would have been well aware that there was always the chance their men could desert and as the valley yawned open before them, most would have considered it a painting that resembled hell.

What happened is all too typical of those times. The final gasping moments of life came down to men rushing at each other with a sword or a club until no one could stand. To the sound of jiggling harnesses and horses snorting, thousands of men carrying axes, swords and bows pounded the earth, swords flashed through skin and maces hammered armour into great dents to the sound of breaking bones beneath.

Ordinary foot soldiers were spared but not so the nobility. York was dragged from his horse and killed alongside his 17-year-old son Edmund, who had been running away at the time. Salisbury would be captured the next day and beheaded. All three heads were then placed on spikes and displayed over Micklegate Bar, the south-western gate through the York city walls. Jammed on York's bloodied head sat a paper crown.

It was common to display the dead enemy in such a fashion but this time, it was a bad move for the Lancastrians to disgrace York so humiliatingly. York's 18-year-old son Edward had been in Wales during the slaughter and as such had survived. And he was furious. He had his sword, a father and a brother to avenge and England was the ultimate prize. With anger bubbling over, Edward formed a pact with Warwick, by now nicknamed The Kingmaker, and intrigue would indeed go up one more level again. Together with Warwick, Edward drew his army together but this time he did not hold back.

The Battle of Mortimer's Cross is famous for a number of reasons. It was the first major battle of the War of the Roses between the Yorks and the Lancasters fought by the future Edward IV, but it was also the first known appearance of a meteorological phenomenon known as the 'Sun Dogs' or 'Parhelion'.

Parhelion is an atmospheric phenomenon that consists when a pair of bright spots appears on either horizontal side of the sun. These red 'sun dogs' are created when light interacts with ice crystals in the atmosphere during very cold weather and two subtly coloured patches of light appear when the Sun is close to the horizon, giving the appearance of three suns rising. They can be seen anywhere in the world during any season but they are not always obvious or bright. As dawn broke on 3rd February 1461, the phenomenon appeared over the Welsh skies.

Medieval troops had never seen the phenomenon before and as you can imagine, they were terrified. Edward on the other hand was jubilant. He saw it as a sign from God and the Holy Trinity. Edward was one of three remaining sons of the Duke of York and three 'suns' rising in the sky just as the battle was to begin, symbolised that he and his two brothers would rise up to defeat the enemy. As Edward held his frozen breath, he was sure it was a sign from God and that He was on his side.

For two hours, arrows hammered them from above while blinding snow turned into red slush beneath their feet. Maddened by a killing rage, men stabbed, clubbed, kicked and stomped on each other in the blinding snow. Some saw the writing on the wall and started to run, stumbling and falling in their heavy armour only to have a mace take their heads off from a chain-mailed rider behind them. As they scrambled, their bodies fell bleeding over their fallen comrades. All that could be heard was the thumps of arrows on wood, metal and bodies, amid chocked screams of confusion.

Nothing had prepared them for this savagery. All day both armies fought, pushing and stabbing each other in the pointless nightmare. It was only as it grew dark in the eerie twilight that the true evidence of the carnage was seen. Four thousand Lancastrians were killed that day on the frozen York heartlands and among the dead was Owen Tudor who did not believe that he would be beheaded until the collar of his red doublet was ripped off. He never even saw the axe coming his way.

The victorious Yorkists had one thing in mind: to claim London. Edward headed off to London with the bulk of the army while Warwick marched south with poor Henry, a prisoner again.

As it turned out, it was lucky that Edward had made that decision. What Warwick hadn't counted on was Margaret waylaying him and she took him totally by surprise. In the mayhem, half his men were slaughtered, while Warwick himself barely managed to escape. With every ounce of energy, he headed off to London to warn Edward.

The next morning, with Henry propped up against a tree, Margaret put to death captains and commanders, in particular two knights who had been ordered to protect Henry. When the knights were led to her, Margaret produced her 7-year-old son and asked him *"Fair son, with what death shall these two knights die whom you see here?"* The quick reply in a thin piping voice was: *"Their heads should be cut off".*

She could not deny her son anything, so she willingly obliged.

Margaret and the Lancastrians now had Henry back safely with them and the plan was to take him on to London to reclaim the throne. Flush with victory, Margaret was all ready to leave when she found that her Scottish mercenaries had deserted her. Most of them were already jogging home with all the spoils they could carry.

The Scottish departure was the turning point in Margaret's struggle. It meant a delay she could not afford knowing Edward was on his way to London nine days ahead of her.

York was marching day and night and as expected, he reached London well ahead of Margaret. The way he saw it, his father had been killed and he was going the claim the throne for himself as the eldest surviving son. He declared himself king, stating that anyone who disagreed would be guilty of treason, then he took off with Warwick to sort the out the problem with Henry, once and for all.

Margaret had already heard the news that Edward had reached London and was on his way back with Warwick to face her. There was nothing she could do but wait at Towton near York for them to arrive. She had everything to lose, as well as nothing to lose, by waiting patiently. Behind her was the full force of the Lancastrian army and on March 28th, they clashed once more. On that day, 100,000 men filled the fields: 40,000 were Yorkists and 60,000 were Lancastrians.

Once again, the battle began in a blinding snowstorm and once again, the snow drove into the faces of the Lancastrians as the Yorkists spearman advanced up the frozen slopes. Regardless of the falling snow, at 9 am both armies, trembling and cold, shuffled into position, ready to fight. The blizzard swirled around them making the battlefield a blinding nightmare.

In the lashing wind, the Lancastrian arrows fell short as they fired into the driving snow. The Yorks had the wind behind them and they never missed their targets.

The decision made by the Lancastrians was an easy one. Advance down the slopes to meet their enemy and stab and hack at anyone they could and for six hours, that's exactly what they did. The two sides fought furiously as arrows plunged into men and horses and at the height of the battle, Warwick is said to have dismounted and slain his horse to prove to his men he would not quit and leave them. And still the arrows continued to fall. By late in the afternoon, the battle hung in the balance. In the nick of time, the Duke of Norfolk's men arrived upon the exposed flanks of the Lancastrians and drove them across the bridge over the river Cock.

It was a terrible sight. Thousands of heavily armoured men, wielding heavy swords sitting on metal-clad horses, plunged into the swollen river, struggling to reach the other side where York's men waited with axes, swords and pikes. The lucky ones fell from their frightened horses and died quickly as hooves trampled and crushed them as they struggled to rise. Many men drowned, weighed down by their heavy breastplates as horses screamed and scrambled in the churning waters. As they died, Edward's men danced up and down in the driving snow on the far bank of the river eager to finish them off by thrusting a knife into a belly or slashing a throat. Some York men didn't wait. Some impatiently plunged into the icy river swinging their axes in the bloody water. In the frenzy, faces were split to the bone, heads were cut in half, holes were punched through foreheads, ears were ripped off and fingers were cut off to remove any rings.

But in the mayhem of horses and corpses, a bridge formed and some managed to escape by climbing and scrambling over dead bodies. Gathering Henry and her son together, Margaret fled as fast as she could with a cluster of men to the Scottish border.

In the aftermath, Edward did not take any prisoners. When he reached the town of York, his first thought was to remove the heads of his father and brother from the pikes, along with any others that Margaret had killed, and replace them with those of his own captives.

Once again, England's world turned upside down. Poor Henry was forced to take refuge anywhere he could while Margaret escaped with her son to France where King Louis XI had succeeded his father Charles VII.

When Louis came to the throne, he inherited a country that was almost a desert. Fields were untilled and villages were just clusters of ruined hovels. The people were reduced to scavenging among the ruins for food and all as a result of the English wars. England would find that the French hated them just as much as the Scots did.

In England, the bewildered Henry's run didn't last long. He was soon tracked down, captured and paraded through the streets like a trophy his feet tied to the stirrups and a straw hat placed on his head. His home for the next five years would be the Tower.

Three months later on June 28th, Edward was officially crowned at Westminster Abbey in his purple robe. He sat on the throne with the sceptre of Edward the Confessor in his hand as he took his oath and as he was crowned King Edward IV. Standing tall at 6 feet 4 inches, he must have presented a magnificent picture. By November, parliament passed an Act of Attainder where a hundred and thirty-three estates were taken from the Lancasters and handed over to the new king.

While Henry sat in the Tower, the years were full of battles, intrigue and confusion over who was ruling and who was not. Yorkist men were making the country their own by imposing massive fines on lords they now called traitors. Everywhere there was a need for revenge and not many came out of it unscathed. Alliances were made and men swapped sides when they saw the advantages and then swapped back again when all was not going as well as expected.

In France, Margaret was plotting and scheming. When she had first taken her vows to Henry in faulting English years ago, she had believed that the responsibility to protect the country was not hers. Over the years, her opinion had changed. Her husband was overly merciful to his enemies and so tender-hearted that many people said he would let thieves and murderers live. He was like a helpless puppet presiding over a progressively decaying English society, hovering bewildered on the outskirts of battles, three times taken prisoner on the field and afflicted from time to time by total or partial idiocy. Yet for all his failures and incapability, the English people recognised his goodness of heart and they never lost their love for him.

Things had changed dramatically for Margaret since Henry's capture. By herself, there was little she could do but wait for the right time.

And that's exactly what she did. She waited for ten years.

The next part is Edward's story.

PART V

THE YORKS

EDWARD IV

Born 1422
Reign 1461 - 1470

Edward's reign began in a bloodbath. He was in the Welsh marshlands when his father died at Wakefield but instead of mourning, he was energised enough to cross into Herefordshire to fight the Lancastrian army in revenge for his father's death. His triumph sent him floating on a cloud of confidence only eclipsed on 4th March when he was crowned King of England, fifteen days after a final battle at St Albans. But if he thought he'd put any question of who was going to be the king to rest, he was to find that instead of stopping the Lancastrians in their tracks, it made them even angrier. By then, after decades of fighting, everyone was just so accustomed to warfare, danger and cruelty; the only logical thing for them to do was to fight.

Even at 19 years of age, Edward had remarkable military knowhow and an outstanding physique. His height is estimated at 6 feet 4 inches making him one of the tallest among English, Scottish and British monarchs to date. In war, nothing daunted him or wearied him and as things worsened, the better he became. But for all of his wonderful qualities, what he lacked was any serious enthusiasm for ruling. And that strength was the single thing that England desperately needed.

Luckily for Edward he had his cousins, Richard, Earl of Warwick and Henry Percy, 4th Earl of Northumberland, who were more than willing to step up to the mark and help him out. They believed they had fought hard to put him on the throne and they meant to keep him there. And Edward had no objection whatsoever. He could continue his pursuit of women, no obstacle for him, combined with hunting, feasting and drinking to his heart's content.

The years slipped by and while he gripped the reins of authority from time to time, much of his life was spent in relative ease. But always close by were Warwick and Northumberland, continually reminding him that all the fun had to stop sometime and it was his duty to produce an heir. A *legitimate* heir, that is.

Not that finding a bride for Edward would have been a problem. With his good looks, everyone knew he was a real catch. Warwick proposed Mary of Guelders, James II of Scotland's widow, but Mary's sudden death in 1463 put paid to that idea. Another option was 12-year-old Princess Isabella of Castile. Warwick used good arguments involving a bond of peace between the two countries but Edward seemed strangely hesitant to make a commitment. While he dithered, Isabella's father became impatient and she ended up married to Ferdinand of Aragon instead. Next Warwick suggested the beautiful Bona of Savoy, Louis XI's sister-in-law, and it finally looked like the deal was done.

It wasn't until negotiations were being finalised that Edward astonished everyone suddenly by confessing the truth. He was already married. He'd met Elizabeth Woodville as she stood standing beside an oak tree and he was instantly smitten. They had been married secretly for five months and the marriage had been consummated.

There was no doubt in anyone's mind that Elizabeth was a true beauty with her willowy figure, white skin, auburn hair and dark eyes. She could certainly turn heads and it is easy to see why Edward fell for her, hook, line and sinker.

But his news caused an uproar for so many reasons. It wasn't that she didn't have royal blood, because she did. Elizabeth's mother, Jacquetta of Luxembourg, had been a princess in her own right before her marriage to

John Duke of Bedford, Henry's uncle, at the age of 15. As was the custom, Jacquetta was not given a choice in her first marriage but four years later, after Bedford's death, she remedied the situation by marrying the man of her choice, her deceased husband's squire, Sir Richard Woodville. The marriage to Woodville had not been the wisest or most beneficial of choices she could have made since it relegated her and any subsequent children to the status of a 'commoner'. But she had been in love and nothing else mattered to her. Together they had produced fourteen children: the eldest child being Elizabeth.

And it wasn't just the fact that Elizabeth was five years older than Edward and already the widow of Sir John Grey of Groby, a staunch Lancastrian who had been killed in the second battle of St Albans fighting on the losing side at Towton. Even her two children from her previous marriage wasn't the big issue although her large family were noted for their ambitious and obvious desire to advance themselves.

What had really stung Warwick was the fact that Edward had made him look like a complete fool in front of the French king over the ruined plans for a marriage alliance with Bona of Savoy. Add that to the fact that Edward had also overlooked Warwick's eldest daughter Isabella and you have Warwick seeing it all as a personal insult. As far as Warwick was concerned, a king had never made his own matches before and any such matches would certainly never include the marriage to a commoner. And most definitely, not in secret. Even the word *sorcery*, in the form of incantations, spells and charms was tossed around. Wasn't her mother rumoured to be a witch from Luxembourg?

Elizabeth was expected to be fertile and she didn't disappoint. A mere five months later, (sending all tongues wagging), she gave birth to a daughter they named Elizabeth as well. The birth helped to ease the tension between the child's grandmothers (although Edward's mother, Cecily Neville, was doubly annoyed when the daughter was christened to flatter his wife and not his own mother). In the next five years, she produced daughter after daughter, but not the all-important son and as each daughter arrived, resentment grew.

Warwick hated Elizabeth Woodville with every fibre of his being but he wasn't the only one: she was also making herself very unpopular at court. Not only was she the first common Englishwoman to marry a king in more than two centuries but she was also bringing with her a whole flock of greedy relatives eager to snap up valuable and powerful positions that nobles felt were not their right to have. Elizabeth had five brothers, seven sisters, and two sons and by royal decree, Edward either raised them to a desirable high rank or married them off into the greatest English nobility he could find. He even arranged the marriage of Elizabeth's fourth brother, at the age 20, to the Dowager Duchess of Norfolk, who was at the time, aged 80. Eight new peerages came into existence and were given to Elizabeth's father, five brothers-in-law, her son, and her brother Anthony. To top it off, Edward then arranged the marriage of his own sister Margaret to Charles, Duke of Burgundy.

Edward had totally underestimated Warwick. Warwick watched in horrified angry silence as the Woodville's power increased and his own slipped backwards at an alarming rate. Warwick had suffered personal slights and material losses by the creation of the new nobility for the Woodville clan, but the marriage arrangement that linked Burgundy to England was something else entirely. What was Edward thinking? What possible help would Burgundy give England if France joined with the house of Lancaster and invaded England? As Warwick angrily watched, he began making plans and those plans were truly brilliant.

He knew that in York veins, blood mixed with greed and envy and Edward's brother George Duke of Clarence was no exception. By whispering to George about the upstart Woodvilles who might succeed Edward as king if Elizabeth Woodville had her way, he put the idea into George's head that since Edward only had daughters at this stage it should be George himself who should be named as the heir apparent since he was the next male in a direct line. And Warwick offered a promise of undying support to put him there: under one condition. George had to marry Warwick's daughter Isabella.

It was quite a clever plan really. It effectively made Isabella a princess but it also meant that Isabella could one day be the Queen of England. A definite bonus for the Warwick family. As for George: he could almost see himself sitting on the throne of England with the world at his feet. And he rather liked the whole idea. But to do that he needed help, Warwick's help, and it became all rather easy to convince George to leave his brother's team and join Warwick's.

When all was ready, Warwick struck.

The rebellion began in Yorkshire with thousands of men and Edward was forced to go north to fight. The problem was, except for his bodyguards, Edward had no troops of his own. Knowing full well his predicament, he called upon his new family members, Pembroke and Devon, before marching north to meet Warwick. It ended up as one big disaster.

As well as Edward being captured, 168 knights, squires and gentlemen of the king either died in the carnage or were executed afterwards, including both Pembroke and Devon who were both beheaded. To make Warwick's lesson to Edward even plainer, Elizabeth's father and her brother were both arrested and executed without any trial and Edward was placed under house arrest in Warwick's castle at Middleham.

Warwick had struck quickly and suddenly before anyone realised what had happened and the nobility viewed all this with stunned astonishment. At this stage, Warwick actually had two rival kings in his prison – Henry VI was in the Tower of London and Edward IV was at Middleham. A remarkable achievement for anyone.

Staggered by George's treachery, there seemed no easy solution to the rather tricky problem for Edward. Except escape somehow. The only way out of the scrape as he saw it was by declaring that, of course, Warwick and George were right. He promised he would mend his ways and he signed pardons for all who had fought against him, even declaring that all was forgiven and Warwick and George could return to their posts. To juice it up, he said he would send his wife, Elizabeth the 'Woodville Witch', and his daughter, young Elizabeth, away to the Tower. With his assurances of fidelity, Edward was released.

Who could blame the heavily pregnant Elizabeth from quickly making her way up the Thames to sanctuary at Westminster Abbey instead of the Tower? It was here that she would deliver her first son, named Edward after his father.

What Warwick hadn't seen coming was that Edward could not be trusted.

While Warwick and George basked in the glow of their triumph, Edward raised a huge army and attacked. Astounded that their own methods had been used against them, Warwick and George high-tailed it to Calais where they found, not surprisingly, a not-so-friendly welcome because of Warwick's strong objection to Margaret's marriage to the Duke of Burgundy.

As Edward finally settled himself comfortably back on the throne again, Warwick and George's only recourse was to tuck their tails between their legs and turn to the King of France, Louis XI, for help.

Louis must have been rubbing his hands together in glee at the turn of events. Two years earlier, both Edward and the Duke of Burgundy, together with Warwick, had threatened war on France and now, here Warwick was in his very court.

With gusto, Louis XI set about combining his own resources. He gathered Warwick and George together and ordered them to join him and Margaret and her son Prince Edward, now a fine young man of 17, for a little meeting. At Angers, he told them his conditions. If they wanted his help, they all had to work together to help him overthrow England.

Of course, at first, all parties recoiled visibly. And no wonder. All that they had fought hard for during those cruel years was to be eliminated by this alliance. Margaret and Warwick had slain each other's dearest friends and family members. She had helped in the decision to behead Warwick's father, and his uncle the Duke of York as well as a cousin or two along the way. For his part, Warwick had butchered her father and brother and many of her supporters. The multitude of common people along the way was uncounted. Margaret had declared Warwick an outlaw and he had branded her a witch and her son a bastard. The bad feelings between them were certainly mutual.

This is probably when the potential for revenge suddenly hit Warwick. If he was the man who could make a king, then he was also the man who could *unmake* one. After all, he and Margaret had one thing in common, they both hated Edward.

Reluctantly, and with more than a little suspicion I should imagine, they decided to put the past behind them and forgive and forget. To seal the merger, Margaret's son, Edward Prince of Wales was to marry Warwick's younger daughter, Anne. With Isabella married to George and Anne married to Prince Edward, there was no doubt that at least one of them would be married to the next King of England. I guess that's called 'hedging your bets'.

But what Warwick had overlooked was the effect this wedding would have on George. As George considered the fact that the birth of a child from Anne and Prince Edward's marriage would eventually beat his chance of claiming the throne on any given day, he became a dangerous man. He had no public role or power as such but he still had ambitions to remedy that little detail.

In England, Edward was alarmed at the turn of events in France as told to him by his brother-in-law, Charles of Burgundy. Before he knew it, Warwick, George and Prince Edward had landed in Kent, (minus Margaret and Anne due to bad weather) and were marching towards London with a major part of his kingdom who had turned against him. He also learned that while the northern rebels were moving south towards him, and while Warwick was moving north, Warwick's brother, the Marquis of Montagu, up to then faithful to Edward, had also changed sides and had gone over to Warwick and George in support of Henry VI.

With enemies on every side closing in, Edward's only ally it seemed was his brother, Richard of Gloucester. The only smart thing for Edward to do was to flee to Burgundy. Hurriedly, Charles of Burgundy gave Edward 12,000 soldiers all waiting on the island of Walcheren, along with ships and money, to help him in his escape.

When Margaret and Anne arrived from France, they found the battle was already over. True to his word, when Warwick arrived in London, he had taken Henry from the Tower and placed him back on the throne with the crown on his head and a sceptre in his hand.

However, by this time, years in hiding followed by years of captivity had taken their toll on Henry and it is hard to say if Henry really understood what was happening to him. He had always been simple-minded but now he was unresponsive and seemed confused at what was taking place around him. Bewilderingly, he signed statutes that reversed all previous disinheritances and exiled nobles from Edward's reign were returned from poverty and expulsion and reinstated to their rightful seats.

War was only days away now and Henry had no idea what he was doing. He was putty in Warwick's hands. But through all these violent transformations, almost the whole of the population believed that finally, the war between the Red Rose of Lancaster and the White Rose of York was finally ending.

They were terribly wrong.

Henry's return to the throne lasted less than six months. In March 1471, Edward had regrouped yet again and had landed in Yorkshire. He hadn't expected the city of York to shut their gates on him but, thinking quickly on his feet, he insisted he had only come back to claim his previous estates and he told his troops to declare themselves loyal to Henry. When fighting for his life and manipulating people, Edward was at his very best.

Accepted and nourished, he set forth to march to London as Montagu, with four times Edward's number of men, began plans to intercept him. But as Edward marched, the number of his troops swelled as he gathered more and more men to join him. By the time he reached the town of Warwick, he was ready for anything. He had the numbers, the strength and the inclination to declare himself king once again. And this time, he meant to keep the title.

What surprised Edward was an unexpected ally. With resentment towards Warwick building, his brother George had once again swapped sides and left his father-in-law to join back with Edward once more.

By April, the battle was on.

In Barnet, while their breath misted around them in the early morning fog, Edward and his Yorkist army faced the house of Neville and the new Duke of Somerset, the second son of Edmund Beaufort. In the pre-dawn darkness, both armies clashed as Edward rode out of the mist like the devil himself.

In the vile conditions, it is understandable how so many of their own men were killed by mistake. Three hours into the battle, Warwick knew he'd lost. His own banner had been mistaken for Edward's banner by his own troops and his own archers had let loose on him.

Warwick made for the horses in an attempt to retreat but the Yorkist soldiers pulled him down from his horse. They pried open his visor, smashed his face to a pulp then stabbed him through the neck just to make sure.

If only Edward's soldiers hadn't gotten to Warwick first. Edward had decided that Warwick was more valuable alive than dead and he sent an order to his guards to bring him back alive. Maybe he thought Warwick would be an ally against the Lancastrians or maybe he just wanted to capture Warwick for a public execution. Regardless of Edward's intent, his guards found Warwick's corpse, mutilated and stripped of his beautiful gilded armour.

Only Margaret and her supporters remained now. Having landed in England, her only hope was to reach the Welsh border. And Edward knew that. At Tewkesbury, he intercepted her and the last of the Lancastrians were annihilated. Going by the number of beheadings, Edward was angry. Very angry.

Of the many nobles who were captured and decapitated, Henry's only son, Edward Prince of Wales was killed as well. A devastated Margaret was captured and moved from place to place, before being ransomed back to King Louis XI. She never recovered. Eleven years later, she would die in poverty in Anjou.

With her husband Prince Edward dead and her mother-in-law back in France, Anne Neville was not only a widow; she was a very wealthy widow. She had money from her husband and she had money left to her from her father. But at 15 years of age, she was far too young, and wealthy, to be left to her own devices. And her elder sister Isabella could not agree more. She was now a loyal supporter of the house of York with her newly turned husband George, and she had her eye on the family fortune. She scooped Anne up and took her into 'safekeeping'. It would turn out to be nothing short of house arrest.

You'd think after all this the war would be finished. But it would seem that the cousins had not had enough of the slaughter. There is so much more to come.

Richard of Gloucester was Edward's youngest brother and his most loyal supporter. He'd stood by Edward's side from the beginning and he knew what had to be done now that the battle was over and Henry's son Edward was dead. While the young prince had been alive, Henry had been safe. But after the young man's death, Henry's fate was sealed. He had to die, too.

On 21st May, Richard hastened to London Tower and with Edward's permission, he supervised Henry's murder. Edward would no longer have to keep looking over his shoulder to see what Warwick was doing and the Lancastrians were now virtually extinct.

For some reason, Henry's body was exhumed in 1910. According to an architectural historian present, some hair was still attached to the skull. The hair was brown in colour, save in one place where it was much darker and apparently matted with blood. The substance was not confirmed as blood but Dr A. Macalister, a professor of anatomy who was also present at the exhumation, supplied a report about the condition of the remains. He made no mention of the hair or the blood but did state however, *"The bones of the head were unfortunately much broken."*

The winning side always gets to write history as part of the spoils of war and Margaret of Anjou has been portrayed as a cold calculating woman. She was not the first mother and she would not be the last one to be aggressive as far as her son's succession was concerned. But a weak husband had also hindered her so she would have been forced to show some level of resilience in order to survive in that brutal male-dominated world.

With the threat of war once more on France after Louis XI's implication in the invasion, Louis backed down completely and offered Edward the lump sum of 75,000 crowns and a further yearly tribute of 50,000 not to invade France. This was almost enough to make Edward totally independent of Parliament and balance the royal budget.

For seven successive years, Edward pocketed this substantial payment for not harrying France and at the same time pocketed most of the money that Parliament was offering him to do the exact opposite. As a result, in this second reigning period, Edward was not a shrinking violet when it came to spending. He lavished out on clothes made of satin, velvet, ermine and sable as well as jewellery and his circle of supporters were well rewarded.

Amongst them was his brother Richard whose loyalty had never wavered unlike his brother George whose head must have been spinning from changing sides so often depending on who had the most advantage at the time. For his devotion, Richard received the main Neville strongholds followed soon by posts previously held by Warwick. As the youngest brother, he previously had very little in the way of titles and power, but with this little windfall, he quickly became one of the wealthiest men in England. The following year, he cemented that hold by marrying his cousin Anne Neville, who had run away from her sister's house and who had inherited the remaining Warwick properties. Richard was now a very, very rich man.

And George was furious. As he saw it, he was the next eldest brother and his position was being outrageously undermined. One thing led to another until both Richard and George were openly bickering.

This sibling rivalry must have been a huge headache for Edward and no amount of intervening did anything to help. In the end, Edward chose the easiest option and simply divided the estate evenly between the two of them while leaving nothing for Warwick's widow who was left penniless and forced to live with Richard and Anne.

Edward had prevented a serious conflict that had been spinning out of control, but he had overridden everything that was legal to do it. In the process, both brothers looked petty and greedy with George faring far worse. No one came out with dignity. But while Edward was pouring oil on troubled waters, nothing could burn from his mind the fact that George had been a traitor who had betrayed his family time and time again. George was simply devious and untrustworthy.

George for his part must have known the wound had only scabbed over and not healed properly and Edward's solution to the squabble did not settle him down at all. It probably made things worse. As an act of defiance, George began disobeying Edward defiantly and started executing people who offended him with trumped up allegations. His final undoing was stupidity.

George had discovered a secret. It seems that in Edward's youth, he had betrothed himself to a young girl by the name of Eleanor Butler. Because of this betrothal, Edward's marriage to Elizabeth Woodville, George declared, was invalid and all their children were bastards. This, naturally, would make him, George Duke of Clarence, as the next eldest son of the Duke of York, the rightful king on the throne of England. Hurrah!

Bad move George.

Edward's patience was finally exhausted. George had gone one step too far and Parliament was called for the express purpose of dealing with George. Despite George being Edward's brother, he had stepped over the line for the very last time.

George was doomed before his trial even started because sitting quietly in the background of all this upheaval was the one person who held sway with Edward. The one person who could whisper in Edward's ear and persuade him to do almost anything. The one person who had the most to lose and the one person who hated George more than anyone else. That person was Elizabeth Woodville.

Edward formulated a string of crimes all amounting to treason. Parliament, as can be expected, agreed with Edward eagerly. They weren't buying George's story at all.

Their reasoning was terribly complicated. If a pre-contract between Edward and Eleanor Butler had existed, it would not affect his two young sons, both born after 1470 because Eleanor Butler had died in 1468. So, if Edward indeed had made a binding promise to Eleanor prior to marrying Elizabeth Woodville on May 1st 1464, allegedly then making himself a bigamist, he was no longer a bigamist after 1468, following Eleanor's death. By the time Edward's two sons had been born, Eleanor was no longer alive: she had been dead for years. Therefore, only Elizabeth of York, (born in 1466), and Mary of York, (born in 1467), would be affected. The remainder of Edward and Elizabeth Woodville's children were born after Eleanor's death.

Another point was that when Edward publicly announced his marriage to Elizabeth Woodville in September 1464, Eleanor could have, and definitely would have, found plenty of people who would have loved to hear her story. Most importantly, Richard Neville, Earl of Warwick. Warwick had reason to hate the marriage between Edward and Elizabeth, which had been done behind his back while he was in France negotiating a marriage between Edward and the French princess. But Warwick had said nothing, which was pretty conclusive he had been unaware of the betrothal.

Parliament took everything into account and George was proclaimed worthy of death and sent to the Tower.

How he died is not definite. Some say Edward gave him a choice of deaths. Certainly Edward did not want a grizzly public spectacle. The most common legend is he was drowned in a barrel of Malmsey wine. Worse ways to go, I guess.

Over the years, Elizabeth Woodville put up with many of Edward's indiscretions with mistresses and had produced not only five daughters but also two fine healthy boys, who were growing up. In 1483, one was twelve and one was nine. The succession to the throne was plain and secure, wouldn't you say? The king himself was only 40 years old and in another ten years, the Yorkist triumph would be permanent.

But sometimes, life takes a strange turn, as it did for Edward. Around Easter 1483, Edward began feeling unwell and his condition quickly worsened as he complained of an increasing number of strange ailments ranging from pneumonia to suspected poisoning.

Through all of this, his brother Richard was very supportive and concerned. The best doctors were called and nothing was too good for his brother the king.

But still Edward's condition deteriorated. Edward lingered long enough to add some codicils to his will: the most important was his naming of his loyal brother, Richard Duke of Gloucester as the Protector of the realm until his eldest son, Edward, came of age.

At 41 years of age, there was no reason why a man in his prime should die so suddenly when he had always been in the best of health. Over indulgence in food and wine leading to a stroke was considered and it was true, he *did* have a tendency to overindulge. Melancholia over losing more French territories was another consideration offered but that excuse had already been used before when trying to explain Henry VI's death. Malaria was another option from when Edward was in France in 1475. But in the end, no one really knew. By all accounts, he was overweight and increasingly self-indulgent and probably took little exercise, which could explain his unfitness and lethargy. But can you die so suddenly from a lack of exercise? I certainly hope not, for my own sake.

The one thing that was missing from Edward's reign was an easy succession and all too typically, it led to a blood bath. At his death, the rift between his brother Richard and the Woodvilles was still flaring up and once again, battle lines were drawn and rival camps began building up their strength.

But the Woodvilles held the trump cards with young Edward and Richard safely in their hands.

Or did they?

EDWARD V

Born 1470
Reign 1483 - 1483

When Edward IV died, the old nobility gathered confusingly around Richard, Duke of Gloucester. There was no doubt that despite a slight deformity in his back, Richard was renowned in war, competent in administration and enriched by Warwick's inheritance and many other great estates. But could he look after the country? That was the big question. One thing they were sure of was that Elizabeth's lowborn relations should no longer have the power they had enjoyed when Edward was alive. On the other hand, her family *did* have possession of her son, and he was the new king.

Possibly because of the suddenness of Edward's death, Elizabeth was given very little attention in Edward's will. To make matters worse, the one ally she thought she might be able to count on, Edward's steadfastly loyal, but frequently absent brother Richard, was again away from London at the time of his death, although he had sent Elizabeth some very gentle, thoughtful letters of condolences.

On the surface, there was a degree of normality in London. Plans for the coronation were in progress and Richard had confirmed his new position as regent of the young king.

It is difficult to place a date on when Richard had a change of heart. And why. Certainly he wanted to be king, who wouldn't, but it is not known if he had made any plans *before* he reached London in May. His loyalty was always taken for granted and for that whole month of April he went about his business as if all was fine and dandy.

But something had definitely changed somehow and no one could actually put a finger on it.

For three weeks everyone eyed one another suspiciously until it was agreed that in April, the young king would be crowned and that he should come to London, attended by 2,000 horsemen, and proceed to the Tower for protection. All very normal, you might think. Yet in this normalcy, something was not quite right. Had Richard decided that he preferred to be the king and not just the regent?

Edward's party, headed by his uncle Lord Rivers, rode through Shrewsbury and Northampton until they reached Stony Stratford where they learned that Richard and his ally, Humphrey Stafford the Duke of Buckingham, (another cousin), were coming to London from Yorkshire and were only ten miles behind. They left the prince with the commanders of the 2,000 men and turned back to Northampton to greet the two Dukes. Richard received them amicably and they all dined together in friendship. By morning, things had changed for the worse.

When Rivers awoke, he found the doors to the inn locked and when he asked why, he was met with scowling gazes from Richard and Buckingham who then accused him of *"trying to set distance"* between the young king and them. Stunned, Rivers and his nephew were immediately held prisoner by Buckingham while Richard rode off to Stony Stratford to arrest the commanders of the horsemen. Forcing his way in to young Edward, Richard embraced him and then told him of a plan devised by Lord Rivers and others to seize the government from him. On this declaration, the 12-year-old Edward wept. As well he might. Richard then dismissed the 2,000 horsemen to their homes, as their services were no longer needed. He then proceeded to ride to London with young Edward.

It seems Elizabeth Woodville, who was already in London, had been informed of the arrests and was under no illusion about what was happening. Together with her other children, she made a hole through the wall between Westminster Abbey and the palace to transport as many personal belongings as she could. The Abbey would be her sanctuary.

The report that the young king was under Richard's guard caused a ripple of apprehension and commotion but Lord Hastings, who was the Lord Chamberlain and married to the sister of the deceased Duke of Warwick, reassured the Council that all was well and that any disturbance would only delay the coronation on which all peace of the realm depended. Even the Archbishop of York tried to reassure Elizabeth by giving her the Great Seal as a sort of guarantee. Later, it was declared that he was not in on the plot but only an old fool playing for safety first and foremost. Later, frightened by what he had done, he managed to get the Great Seal back.

Originally, Edward was to be sent to the Bishop of London's palace but Richard, as Protector, felt that it was hardly becoming that the young king should be the guest of an ecclesiastic. Elizabeth's friends suggested the Hospital of the Knights of St John but Richard argued that it would be more fitting to the royal dignity to dwell in one of his own castles – for example the Tower of London.

The young king arrived in London on 4th May for the coronation, which had been fixed for that very date. Unfortunately, Richard declared, it would have to be postponed, temporarily of course, until Edward had settled in to his new home.

With the postponement, apprehension grew.

Even moving the young Edward to the Tower hadn't been threatening. In those days, it was a safe haven and royal residence after all. The lords of the Council agreed and with much ceremony and protestations of devotion, the 12-year-old child was conducted to the Tower, and the gates closed firmly behind him. All above board, right?

But something wasn't right and Londoner's gazed at each other in doubt and fear.

The next step in the terrible tragedy involved Lord Hastings who played a leading role in the closing years of Edward IV's reign. After Edward's death, he had been strongly against the Woodvilles but was the first to detach himself from Richard's proceedings. It did not suit him that all power should so rapidly be falling into Richard's hands. Absolute power corrupts absolutely, they say. Although Richard was married to his wife's niece, he had become friendly with Elizabeth who was still in Westminster Abbey.

At 9 o'clock on Friday 13th June, another 'Black Friday', Richard arrived in a good mood at council and proceeded with business as usual. Very soon, Richard asked to be excused for a while but when he returned between 10 and 11 o'clock, his whole manner had changed. He frowned and glared and at the same time clusters of armed men gathered at the door.

"What punishment do they deserve who conspire against the life of one so closely related to the King as myself?" he demanded of the council. Hastings said at length that such people deserved the punishment of traitors. Richard cried, *"That sorceress, my brother's wife, and others with her – see how they have wasted my body with sorcery and witchcraft."* He is supposed to have bared his arm and showed it to the council, shrunk and withered as legend says it was. It has been noted in history that Richard was physically disabled with a crookback and a withered arm. Later in recent times, it would be diagnosed as Scoliosis of his spine, which gradually deteriorated from when he had reached his early teens.

Hastings was taken aback, and replied, *"Certainly if they have done so heinously they are worthy of a heinous punishment."*

"What?" cried Richard. *"Dost thou serve me with 'ifs' and 'ands'? I tell thee they have done it, and that I will make good upon thy body, traitor!"* As he struck the council table with his good fist, armed men ran in, crying *"Treason!"* Richard then demanded that Hastings be prepared for instant death.

There wasn't even enough time to find a priest. On a log of wood that was lying close by per chance, Hastings was forced to lay his head down and he was instantly decapitated in front of everyone. Screeches of terror rang out as blood gushed and sprouted over the floor.

Hastings's brutal murder had required a good deal of planning and was not done on impulse as Richard had pretended. What council did not know was that days before, Richard had already ordered Buckingham to regroup his army of 2,000 men in the North and come to London, bringing Lord Rivers, Vaughan and Grey with them. A few days after Hastings lost his head, these three men were to lose theirs as well.

By the end of the month, Richard turned his attention to Elizabeth and he began to persuade her to leave her sanctuary at Westminster Abbey and bring her youngest son Richard with her to the Tower to join his brother. When she refused, persuasion turned to insistence as Richard quietly, but firmly, demanded. Turning to the stunned council, he instructed them to have Elizabeth give the young boy up immediately.

England held its breath.

The council contemplated what would happen in the event of their refusal. Considering what had happened to Lord Hastings, they, and Elizabeth, had no choice. Reluctantly Elizabeth submitted and the little 9-year-old prince was handed over to Richard. While council watched in silence, he embraced his nephew affectionately and escorted him to the Tower to join his brother.

Neither of the boys was ever seen again.

Meanwhile, Richard's army was fast approaching London in huge numbers to join him and he must have felt strong enough to take his next step.

Parliament was due to meet on June 25th 1483, and on the day, Richard and Buckingham appeared together. As parliament convened, Buckingham stood up and declared that the late king's marriage with Elizabeth Woodville was no marriage at all and that the children were bastards. He stated that Edward IV's marriage to Elizabeth Woodville had included sorcery and that their marriage had not been performed on consecrated grounds and had been carried out without witnesses. As Buckingham spoke, Richard sat quietly and watched the astonished faces.

Parliament knew full well that this little bombshell meant that Edward IV's children were illegitimate and that the crown rightly belonged on Richard's head after all. It was even suggested that Edward V himself was not even his father's son.

In front of the council, Buckingham asked that Richard assume the Crown, but Richard refused. On bended knee Buckingham begged, and Richard answered his call to public duty with a humble nod and finally accepted.

The council stood as if turned to stone. After everything that had happened, all one can suggest is that parliament was just too scared by then to oppose him.

The next day, Richard was enthroned and the coronation date was set for July 6th to an uneasy public. The question on everyone's lips was *"But where are the boys?"*

RICHARD III

Born 1452
Reign 1483 - 1485

On 6th July, Richard was dressed in blue and gold trimmed with ermine. His wife Anne Neville accompanied him with five ladies-in-waiting led by Lady Margaret Beaufort and watched by Elizabeth Woodville who was hiding in the shadows in fear of her life. These three women all lived in a world full of treachery, and full of ruthless men. They had started off as allies but they had become calculating adversaries. As the violence escalated, they had found themselves in the middle of it all.

The crowning ceremony was celebrated with all possible splendour as the crowns were placed on the heads of Richard and his queen, Anne. They were anointed with oil and they received the Blessed Sacrament in the presence of the assembly and finally left for Westminster Hall. Richard had his title acknowledged and confirmed by Parliament, based on the theory of the bastardry of Edward's children as well as the lineal successor in his blood and his whole design was accomplished. Neither prince was present during the ceremony.

To anyone watching it was a beautiful ceremony but the three women had their own agendas: the new Queen Anne Neville, the former Queen

Elizabeth Woodville and the outsider, Lady Margaret Beaufort, who was the great granddaughter of John of Gaunt, the person who vowed she would see her son Henry Tudor, the last of the Lancastrians, crowned King of England.

At this extraordinary ceremony, Anne was transformed into the leading woman in the realm as Richard's wife but as Warwick's daughter, she was already destined for greatness from birth. She was born in Warwick Castle and her childhood was full of opulence and privilege beyond anyone's dreams. She was the youngest daughter of Richard Neville, Earl of Warwick, who had been the greatest and wealthiest noble in England with enormous influence over the realm. But for Anne, there was a price to be paid for her luxuries and she was extremely valuable in aristocratic alliances. Her father had wanted her to be as close as she could to the throne and he had pulled it off. As her father's status rose as 'Kingmaker', so did Anne's status and she became caught up in the throne war, although it has never been told how much influence she actually had on Richard and the choices he made.

Holding Anne's train at the ceremony was Margaret Beaufort. Thirty years before in Wales, her cousin Henry VI (both Margaret's grandfather and Henry's grandfather were half-brothers) had given her to Edmund Tudor to marry and the fragile 12-year-old was sent to face a new life married to a man twice her age that she barely knew.

It is true Margaret Beaufort had a terrible childhood. In a time when women did not count for much except to breed, she was a desirous commodity. But she was also the sole heiress to the valuable Beaufort family fortune after the death of her father, John Beaufort, whose grandfather was John of Gaunt. She would have had no control of her life and she would have known at a young age that she would have no choice of her husband. Marriages were made to forge alliances, not for love, and it was certainly in Henry VI's best interest to hide her away in a remote castle in Wales. She was after all the *legitimised* Lancaster heir from John of Gaunt and if Henry didn't produce an heir, any children she may have would be one of the contenders queuing for the throne along with the Yorks and Mortimers.

Henry VI sealed her fate when he gave her to his 24-year-old half-brother, Edmund Tudor, and though she was small and undeveloped for her age and still a little girl, her husband had definite ideas. He wanted a son and an heir for his properties and titles and he wasn't about to wait for her to grow up. Two months after the wedding, she was pregnant. Even in those times, it was a selfish and brutal act but he was determined to have an heir and as such, he risked both her life and her unborn child's. But for Margaret, life would take a menacing turn.

During one of the prominent battles of the War of the Roses, the Yorkist army captured Edmund and placed him in prison where months later, he contracted the plague and died. Margaret was only 13 years old: a widow, seven months pregnant and a long way from home.

In those days, one in ten women died in childbirth and it would have been a frightening experience for young women. Living with Edmund's younger brother Jasper, Margaret almost lost her life during the difficult birth because of her youth and tiny size and as a result, she was never able to have any more children.

One year later, Margaret was again married off to Sir Henry Stafford, 1st Duke of Buckingham, her second cousin, while her young son stayed with his uncle Jasper to be raised. By 1471, she was a widow again, but still influential in her dead husband's family, more importantly his nephew, 2nd Duke of Buckingham, who would soon become the High Constable and Richard's most staunch supporter. He was also the man left to take charge of prisoners who were in the Tower. Something to put aside and remember for later on.

And then, in the shadows and in fear of her life, was Elizabeth Woodville. From a young age Elizabeth had been a prominent lady in waiting to Queen Margaret, Henry VI's wife, and being a beautiful woman, she had attracted many suitors. She married John Grey, a very wealthy heir and military commander under Queen Margaret, and she was promoted as one of the ladies of the Queen's bedchamber. She was also a mother of two sons, Thomas and Richard. When her husband John died in 1460 at the Second Battle of St Albans, things had looked bleak for her. Her two sons would be deprived of their inheritance and Elizabeth had been grief-stricken for two long years. But then she met Edward.

The story is that Elizabeth heard Edward was in the neighbourhood near her castle at Grafton, so she waited for him beneath a tree now known as 'the queen's oak,' in Northamptonshire, with her two sons. When Edward arrived, she begged him to restore their lands and he was immediately love-struck. Of course, Edward, the playboy that he was, did not actually want to *marry* Elizabeth and she did not want to settle for anything less. Playing hard to get however only increased Edward's fervour and he fell hard for her. He eventually offered her his hand and they were married secretly on May 1ˢᵗ 1464. In those days, she had a valuable tool in her beauty and she used it to its full advantage. It had been a dangerous plan to hatch but it had worked beautifully for her.

Richard's story is not too different. It's perhaps a story of ambition gone awry and the damage it leaves in its wake. But on the other hand, perhaps it's the story of a man who was deliberately fooled by a close friend with stories of conspiracy and scheming.

Richard was the twelfth of thirteen children of Richard Plantagenet, 3ʳᵈ Duke of York (a strong claimant to the throne of Henry VI himself) and Cecily Neville (who was a direct descendant of John of Gaunt). As a child, Richard showed no sign of the crippling deformity that would mark him later in his life. Richard was to suffer from scoliosis, a deformity of the spine that was not congenital but only became apparent when he was between 10 and 13 years old, during his puberty before he had finished growing. This was to affect his height as well, leaving him at 5 feet 7 inches at maturity, slight in body and weak in strength with a quite feminine physique.

Now we come to the crime associated with Richard III. His interest in the throne was plain and his character has been described as ruthless. We are led to believe that the young princes were held captive in the Tower, never to be seen again, presumably murdered. But nobody is sure of who did the killing. In the future reign of King Charles II, during the restoration of a staircase in 1674, two small skeletons were found buried under a mass of rubble. They were examined and declared the remains of the two princes.

That the princes were murdered is certain. But by who? And when?

Suspect Number 1. There have been a few names pulled out of the hat and the first one, for sure, is Richard III. He had the most to gain from their death. He had also been implicated in the death of Warwick as well as the suspicious death of his brother Edward, which is something we should not forget as Richard gained dramatically because of that. But hadn't he always been a loyal supporter of his brother? Hadn't he vowed to uphold his brother's wish to be his nephews' protector? Did he have a change of heart or had he simply placed his nephews in the Tower to protect them from their mother's family and their schemes? Remember, the Woodville family's greed was legendary and no one in England trusted them.

Let's move on to Suspect Number 2. No man had done more to place Richard on the throne than the Henry Stafford, 2nd Duke of Buckingham. Yet strangely and suddenly, during the first three months of Richard's reign, Buckingham's allegiance suddenly did a complete turnabout and he became Richard's mortal enemy. Why did he do that? Was it perhaps his dislike at being an accomplice in what was seen as the usurpation of the throne and the murder of two young children? Ah, but then we ask … wasn't he of royal blood as well, being a descendant firstly through John Beaufort, son of John of Gaunt, and secondly, through the bloodline of Thomas of Woodstock, Edward III's fifth son? Was he the one who whispered in Richard's ear that Lord Hastings was a traitor? Had he deliberately coerced Richard into believing that his brother's marriage was illegal, thus making the children illegitimate, simply because if anything happened to Richard's son, Buckingham's bloodline could be strong enough for him to claim the throne?

Buckingham *did* change sides dramatically very soon after the coronation, and no one knows why. Was his previous allegiance just a clever plan? Had Richard simply fallen into Buckingham's trap? Someone had been whispering stories into Richard's ears. What we do know is that his job was one of responsibility and he was in charge of the safekeeping of the boys between June and July. Add that to the fact that he had a lot to gain by their deaths and we have room for doubt about Richard's involvement. As there were no physical injuries on the small bodies in 1674, suffocation was probably the method of killing them, especially when you consider their youth and frailty, and it was a tried and true means of getting rid of someone you didn't want around. Was Buckingham in fact the villain? Or was it someone else again?

Enter Suspect Number 3. In the background was Lady Margaret Beaufort, mother of Henry Tudor. No other mother in history seems to have been as dedicated as she was to have her son sit on the throne. But again, she would not have done it herself. There would have been a third party involved.

In 1472 after the death of her second husband, Margaret did the unthinkable and arranged for her own marriage to a prominent widower, Thomas Stanley, 1st Earl of Derby who was in good standing with Edward

IV. By all accounts, the marriage was one of pure convenience. This marriage enabled her to return to the court of Edward and Elizabeth Woodville and she was chosen by Elizabeth to be her daughter's godmother. After Edward's death and Elizabeth's rush to sanctuary in Westminster Abbey, Margaret became Anne Neville's lady-in-waiting carrying the train at her coronation. Richard had already stripped Margaret of her titles and estates and had given them all to her husband, Lord Stanley, which was a meaningless gesture as he would already have had the rights to her property as her new husband anyway. During all of this (and she must have been absolutely furious), she was actively plotting with Elizabeth Woodville and had betrothed her beloved son Henry to Elizabeth's daughter, young Elizabeth of York. She has been called a formidable opponent of Richard III, habitual conspirator and dedicated promoter of her son's cause.

Within a couple of months of Richard's coronation, Margaret's nephew, Buckingham from her previous marriage, (yes it is complicated), raised a rebellion against his friend Richard in favour of Henry Tudor and you can bet she used every bit of her influence on him to encourage the rebellion. She would have promised him anything for his support. I guess my question right now is: why did Buckingham raise the rebellion in favour of Henry and not for the princes since nobody apparently knew they were already dead? Unless he actually *did* know they were dead and he was the one who gave the orders to kill them. In view of that, and the fact that Buckingham had no immediate motive to move against Richard except that he had a very distant claim to the throne himself, what could he hope to gain by attacking the king in such a wild and reckless rebellion after having sworn his loyalty one month previously? My guess is Margaret Beaufort had a hand in it. As a consequence of the failed rebellion, Margaret's current husband, Lord Stanley, was promoted to the position of High Constable in charge of **all** prisoners in the Tower. Mmmmm

All Margaret wanted was for her son Henry Tudor to sit on the throne at any cost. At the beginning of Buckingham's rebellion, she sent word to Henry who was living in abject poverty in France with his uncle Jasper Tudor and told him to gather forces and hurry home. To me, it seems she was pulling the strings and had everything planned and under control.

And here is something else to think about – if Henry Tudor defeated Richard III in battle, Henry would not necessarily become king, as the throne would theoretically be restored to young Edward V who *might have been* in the tower. However, the princes' removal would leave her son Henry as the prime candidate for the throne. Another mmmmm.

Suspect Number 4. Henry Tudor had a great need to be king and he was the plausible alternative ... but only if the two princes weren't around. Henry was a Welshman, whose grandfather, Owen Tudor had been a page in the court of Henry V and as we know, Owen is reported to have secretly married Henry V's widow, Catherine of Valois. One of their sons was Edmund Tudor, who in turn married Margaret Beaufort.

Perhaps at this stage, I should remind you that Henry Tudor's grandmother Catherine of Valois was the sister of Charles VI of France who had sadly inherited a 'crazy' gene and we saw this gene pop its nasty head up during Henry VI's reign. Although Henry Tudor's claim to the throne was through his mother and the House of Beaufort as far back as John of Gaunt and Edward III, this gene from his paternal French grandmother should not, perhaps, be forgotten regarding future generations and their actions.

It has been suggested by some historians that Richard had stashed the princes in the Tower of London for safe keeping while he ruled in peace. It has also been suggested that it was in fact Henry Tudor, when he was King Henry VII, who had the princes executed between June and July of 1486 when his stepfather was High Constable of the Tower. That was two years later, and Richard was long gone by then. It was only after this date that orders went out to circulate the story that Richard had killed the princes. This could easily have been to cover up Henry's own involvement in their murder. It has also been suggested that Elizabeth Woodville knew that this story was false, and so Henry had to have her 'silenced' by confining her to a nunnery where she died six years later. All very plausible.

When you think about it, it seems impossible that no one knew what happened to the Princes after they entered the tower. Richard III, Henry VII and Elizabeth Woodville would have had their spies out and all of them would have known the boys' whereabouts and welfare. If both boys had died, the matter could have been discussed and the culprit would have been blamed openly. But neither Richard III nor Henry VII did so with the reason being that if the princes were alive, the boys' claim to the throne was better than either of theirs. The princes would simply have had to go in either case. It's something we will never know and it is history's best-kept secret.

Okay, back to the story and some things we *do* know.

From the very moment Richard came to the throne, there began a marked distrust and hostility of all classes towards him. The fact that the people rebelled against him so soon after the coronation can only prove how much he was loathed. No fact stands more unchallengeable than the fact that the majority of a nation was convinced that Richard had used his power as Protector to usurp the crown.

Meanwhile, Richard began a tour from Oxford and at every city he tried to make a good impression. Yet he could not escape the sense that behind all displays lay the unspoken doubt of his kingship. On everyone's lips was the demand that the princes should be released. Immediately after the cry for the princes' release came the rumour of their death. The news spread like wildfire and even though the English people were accustomed to long civil wars, this new horror was something they could not forget. The possible murder of two young boys by someone who was meant to protect them was atrocious. In September, Richard announced that his own son would be Prince of Wales. To England, they had confirmation of the terrible rumours.

The dubious facts that surround the deaths of the princes doesn't alter what happened next and at the time, Richard did not suspect his friend Buckingham's deception. He had already parted from Richard in Glouces-ter. Very soon, Buckingham became the centre of a conspiracy against the king possibly because he had reached decisions regarding the princes in the tower as well as his own claim to the throne. He had recently met his dead uncle's wife, Margaret Beaufort, and perhaps realised that he would never be on the throne as Margaret's son had a better claim to it.

Buckingham chose October to gather his own forces while Henry Tudor, with the help of the Duke of Brittany, landed in Wales with 5,000 men. Eager to be the first to strike the initial blow, the county of Kent began marching towards London.

But a series of misfortunes took place for Henry. Foul weather held him up, which made him turn around and go back to Brittany. The same terrible storm greeted Buckingham as well and Richard was the first one to use it to his advantage. He had his army ready and he marched them forward. Unfortunately, Buckingham was captured and within the hour, Richard relieved him of his head with the usual crop of beheadings that followed.

Richard must have felt a little more secure but he would still have been a worried man. He started wearing armour, he slept badly and he sometimes leapt out of bed at sudden sounds. After the failure of Buckingham's rebellion and his subsequent death, many nobles, perhaps seeing the writing on the wall, tiptoed backwards out of Richard's presence and made their way quickly to Henry Tudor.

And then, in April 1484, Richard's only son Prince Edward died at the age of ten and his wife, Anne Neville, who could not bear any more children, was devastated.

By then Richard had become very aware of his niece, Elizabeth of York, and rumours abounded of Richard's quiet, but insistent, attention to her. They walked together in the gardens, and spoke quietly to each other, their heads together, almost touching, in the morning frost. And he was always quick with his praise of her witty conversation and her gracefulness.

From her chambers high in the castle, Anne would have seen the two of them far below as they idly walked to the river. She would have noticed how they talked animatedly and she would have wondered what had made the tall golden-haired beauty laugh and stop to put her hand to her throat coquettishly. She would have seen her husband draw her closer and whisper in her ear and she would have seen him smile widely and make her take his arm to walk on. Both of them had the York charm and they had turned it fully on each other. Even the courtiers walked a little distance behind them so that the couple could imagine themselves alone. She would have wondered why they would do that if they did not think Richard and Elizabeth were lovers? Unless they thought Richard was a lecher who was seducing his niece. Unless they thought that Richard had forgotten his marriage vows to the bereaved mother of his dead son.

Anne would have seen it all but I doubt that she would have cared very much. In any case, it was a high-risk thing for Richard to do.

In France, Henry Tudor, who was betrothed to Elizabeth of York by both mothers, was gathering forces in Brittany while in England, Richard was supposedly seducing his bride-to-be and giving instructions to hold his mother, Margaret Beaufort, a virtual prisoner by her husband. Or maybe that's part of why Richard did it. To show Henry who actually *was* in charge.

Elizabeth became all but the first lady at court, dancing every night, her wrists bright with bracelets and her hair sparkling under a gold net. Anne must have felt extremely vulnerable. And Elizabeth Woodville seemed willing enough for the liaison with the stigma of bastardry apparently forgotten, along with the awful secret of her sons in the Tower. Every morning, gifts arrived for Elizabeth of York as she attended Anne and she would have shot guilty looks at Anne. Always with the gifts came a note that brought a smile to her face.

Anne would have remembered when Richard gave *her* a present every day but she would have remembered with indifference. The light had gone out of her life when her son died and her heart was permanently broken. Elizabeth's virginity and happiness would have been the last things that she cared about.

For everyone at court, the Christmas feast was an opportunity to get close to the royal family but that year, Richard had vowed that it would be the grandest that London had seen. He instructed Anne that Elizabeth was to join her at dress fittings and side-by-side, seamstresses pinned furs, silks and cloth of gold on them both. He openly gave Elizabeth jewels: on her head was a gold coronet, in her ears were diamonds and around her neck were sapphires. If Anne had looked in the mirror, she would have seen herself, tired and fading, while Elizabeth fairly glowed. The age difference was only ten years but it could have been thirty. The year before, Elizabeth had been called a bastard and acclaimed as the bride-to-be of a traitor. That year she was unstoppable.

Christmas was everything Richard had guaranteed. Everyone dressed in their best, musicians played and Elizabeth danced with Richard throughout the night. When she wasn't dancing, she was sitting beside Anne, who wore a forced smile on her weary face, as if she was tired of life.

Coincidentally, within two months of the Christmas feast and during an eclipse, Anne died. Have I mentioned, I don't believe in coincidences? England once more looked nervously at each other. The eclipse was a sure sign that Richard had fallen from heavenly grace.

By the beginning of summer, after months of gathering together substantial people who had all been tiring of Richard's reign, Henry was more than ready to launch his attack.

On 1st August 1485, Henry and 2,000 men left France and landed in Milford Haven in Wales where he fell to the ground and kissed it.

The prospect of one of their own on the throne had been a dream for ages and the Welsh gentry rallied together in support of Henry. His numbers quickly swelled a little as he moved through Shrewsbury and Stafford but he knew he was still greatly outnumbered by Richard's huge army. And Richard knew it as well.

It took five days before Richard heard of the landing and that Henry Tudor's little army was marching towards Watling Street, itching for a fight. He must have felt very secure as he gathered together his own army of 12,000 men and marched to meet his enemy at Bosworth Field. The odds didn't look good at all for Henry.

What Richard didn't know was that his staunch supporter Lord Stanley was planning to change allegiance at the very last minute. Richard would think the battle was his with the backing of Lord Stanley and his brother fighting beside him. They would actually enter the battle at the very end with their 5,000 men but in support of Henry Tudor and he would have the numbers to defeat Richard.

If Richard had thought about it, he would have seen it coming. Lord Stanley, though offering his undying allegiance, was the husband of Margaret Beaufort. And Margaret Beaufort was the mother of Henry Tudor. It wasn't the first time that someone had changed sides at a vitally important time. Warwick had done it to Edward as had his brother George, on many occasions. Even Lord Stanley had done it before. He was notorious for changing sides to support the person who was the most likely to benefit him the most. And why would he not support his wife and her son?

On 22nd August 1485, in a marshy field near the village of Sutton Cheney in Leicestershire, Richard led the last charge of knights in English history. With a circle of gold around his helmet, his banners flying, he threw his destiny into the hands of God in a battle that would be to the death.

As arranged, among the observers of this glittering array of horses and steel galloping towards them was Lord Stanley and his brother Thomas. From a nearby hill, both watched intently as Richard swept across their front and headed towards Henry Tudor, bent only on eliminating his rival.

Even at this late time, Richard must have been wondering why Lord Stanley was waiting.

As Richard battled his way through Henry's bodyguards killing Henry's standard-bearer with his own hand and coming within feet of Henry himself, William Stanley finally made his move. With his sword held high, he roared for his men to attack.

When Richard saw the sea of men thundering down the hill towards him, he cried *"Treason! Treason!"* followed with his famous last words *"I will die King of England. I will not budge a foot"*.

Lord Stanley dragged Richard off his horse and butchered him in the bloodstained mud of Bosworth Field. His crown, which Richard wore to the last, was picked out of a bush by Lord Stanley and then placed on the head of his stepson, Henry Tudor.

Included in the dead was the Duke of Norfolk while his son was taken prisoner. Many nobles were executed as they stood on the field but there was little of the usual bloodletting as Richard's men threw away their weapons when they saw their leader killed.

After only two hours, the Battle of Bosworth was over – not so much won by Henry nor lost by Richard but taken by Lord Stanley. Richard's body was thrown over the back of a horse and sent to Newark to be displayed for two days to prove he was indeed dead. Later, in 2015, his skeleton would be discovered in the carpark of Leicester Cathedral. Examination showed wounds from a large bladed weapon to his head and his feet had been chopped off.

The war between the Red Rose and the White Rose had truly come to an end and the ghosts of mangled generations were finally laid to rest. Neither the Lancaster dynasty nor the York dynasty had won and with Richard's death, the Plantagenet line had almost ended. Except for one little 10-year-old boy, Edward Plantagenet Earl of Warwick, the son of George Duke of Clarence, Richard III's brother.

For over three hundred years, this race of warriors had fought and survived. But on that day, the Plantagenets, a proud nobility, had torn themselves to pieces and the heads of most of the noble houses had been cut off as well.

If the elimination of rivals hadn't occurred, English history would have turned out differently. If Edward IV had lived longer or his sons had not died, there is no reason to suppose the House of Tudor would have come to the throne at all. Instead, Henry Tudor was crowned King Henry VII and he married Elizabeth of York, the elder sister of the young princes who were never seen again. At the coronation, his proud mother, Margaret Beaufort, wept tears of joy. Her lands and titles had already been returned to her.

A new age was to begin with Henry Tudor, and England began a new year with a wise, sad but careful monarch.

This is not the end but only the beginning. After years of bloodshed, a new king and a new dynasty would rise. The House of Tudor.

PART VI

THE TUDORS

THE HOUSE OF TUDOR

The five sovereigns of the Tudor dynasty are among the most well known in royal history. In this period, England would see men like Christopher Columbus, William Shakespeare and Sir Walter Raleigh. They would become heroes and William Shakespeare was not shy about writing all of the grisly details down on paper. Without doubt, the Tudors played a prominent part in the Renaissance that was taking place in Europe and art flourished. Theatre thrived and miniature painting reached its peak and with the wealth that Henry VII accumulated, they were to build country mansions and invest in expensive jewellery and clothes. But the Tudors would also see turbulence in religion, sometimes making that turbulence themselves.

Though called an 'enlightened era', it was not a time of great peace. Threats came from everywhere. There were threats from Scotland with the result of Elizabeth I imprisoning her cousin, Mary Queen of Scots, for nineteen years. There were also threats from Spain and France and much of Northern Ireland was rebelling. As a consequence, it was to be a time of severe economic depression and financial strain.

Theirs was a dynasty that seemed to have it all – powerful monarchs with powerful armies and wealth beyond our wildest dreams. But for all of this, they were to fizzle out as many dynasties before them had.

This is their story.

HENRY VII

Born 1457
Reign 1485 - 1509

Henry's reign almost fades into obscurity, overshadowed by the evil of Richard III and the future killing spree of Henry's son and granddaughters. And yet his story is possibly the most extraordinary of them all. His story is one of spies, intrigue, informers and extortion and the deeper you go, you find a manipulative king who created a terrifying and oppressive regime in English history as the first Tudor. His hunger for power and his determination to hold on to the throne at all costs turned him into a paranoid and infinitely suspicious man.

When you look at pictures of Henry you see a fine-boned man with his left eye slightly turned outwards. It is also a face emaciated by illness and stress and the face of a man who never knew the meaning of the word 'peace'.

Landing on the beach in Milford Haven with heavy cannons, artillery and horses and his raggedy bunch of mercenaries that he called an army was only his first battle. He chose that particular spot purposefully because he wanted to slip in to England undetected before facing Richard's army. He knew the odds were stacked against him and he knew that his army was greatly outnumbered and there's no doubt that he was feeling anxious. It literally had come down to either winning the throne of England or die trying.

By mid-morning on 22nd August 1485, it was all over and the man who had been a fugitive for half of his 28 years was the new King of England. Henry's army moved around the dead relieving them of valuables and piling their lifeless bodies onto carts to burn. But although he had won Bosworth, his fight was a long way from over. There were still the Plantagenets to think about, lurking around every corner and all of them with a better claim to the throne than Henry.

For over a century, no king had come to the throne without a fight and this man who was said to have *only a trickle of royal blood in his body'*, not exactly the ideal pedigree for a monarch, knew he would have to fight for the rest of his life to stay there. He had no training as a king but his time in exile had made him a sharp observer and he had learned to keep his emotions in check and never give anything away. For England, to believe he was the rightful king, he had to act like one. And that is exactly what he did.

Henry's first task was to marry Elizabeth of York, despite the rumours of her liaisons with Richard.

Elizabeth's importance in history is well known, but her life remains mysterious. She seems to have been sidelined, more as an appendage, rather than a leading member in the drama of Henry VII and his scheming mother, Margaret Beaufort.

Her life was a pendulum, frequently in sanctuary as her mother tried to hide her children from the York enemies. Other members of her family were slaughtered on the battlefield or murdered in cold blood. For Elizabeth, there was certainly always cause for concern. Let's not forget her two brothers who walked into the Tower of London and were never seen again.

But one thing that pops up every now and then is the question: was she smitten with her uncle, Richard III? Most historians agree she was, especially when you think back to her flirtatious behaviour at the Christmas party while his wife sat demurely beside him. And was this the final trigger that set Henry on his mission to invade England? If Richard put Anne Neville aside and married Elizabeth, such a union could produce a York son and end his claim to the throne.

Golden-haired and beautiful, Elizabeth was a good ten years younger than Henry and she was the darling of the English people, much like her charismatic father before her.

She must have been comparing Henry to Richard when she first met him. Perhaps she was expecting a giant of a man who had slaughtered Richard and his soldiers at Bosworth. She'd heard that Richard's body had been stripped of his armour and crown and his broken naked body had been thrown over the saddle of his horse. She'd also heard it was then dumped on the chancel steps of the church in Leicester with a thud for everyone to see that the House of York, along with Richard, was utterly dead.

The man she saw before her was tall but certainly not a giant. He was nearly thirty and slight of build with thinning reddish-brown hair. He had energy in his walk but every line on his face was evident of the strain he was under. His narrow eyes skittered everywhere, perhaps looking for an enemy to jump out and confront him. Her father had been unfailingly attractive and half the women in England were in love with him, but I don't think she was celebrating her good fortune when looking at her future husband.

Up until a few months before, she would have been praying for a Tudor defeat. But there she was, betrothed to marry the very same enemy who had killed the man she had apparently loved. She would have been far from happy.

Apart from her beauty, her sole purpose in life was to bear Henry's children to continue the Tudor dynasty. And she knew it. Henry and his mother were very upfront about it and being such an important female Plantagenet woman, there was no question in anyone's mind that this was intended to be a fertile marriage, vital to England's future.

Henry's second task was to secure his claim to the throne.

Parliament had been meeting at Westminster Abbey for over 800 years and Henry was determined to attend it the very next day and give them an idea of whom they were dealing with. He meant to rule with an iron hand and he was going to prove that he was a man to be reckoned with at any cost from the very beginning.

He'd thought long and hard about what he was going to do. With his head held high, he silently walked into Parliament and sat down. There's no doubt that he had an air of insolence about him as he gazed around and as silence finally settled, he calmly stated that Parliament's first task was to change the records of the first day he set foot on English soil from the 22nd of August to the 21st August.

What's in a day, you ask? A lot for Henry. By changing the date, it would be recorded that he was the conquering king as of the 21st and anyone who fought against him on 22nd could, and would, be charged with treason and executed as a traitor. Almost overnight, any surviving Plantagenet members were suddenly in fear of their lives.

As you can imagine, when the reality of his demand finally dawned on them, Parliament was shocked at the possible consequences. Men watched and waited to see who would be the first to lose his head and it was something like the sword of Damocles hanging over their heads for years to come. They didn't have to wait long.

Knowing full well that 10-year-old, Edward Plantagenet Earl of Warwick, the son of George Duke of Clarence who was Richard III's brother, could be the next potential claimant to the English throne, Henry had the young boy dragged from his schoolroom and deposited in the darkness of the Tower to ensure that didn't happen. What made it worse, if possible, was that poor little Edward Plantagenet was a little on the simple side and would never be 'King' material.

As the young boy screamed and pleaded, Henry was setting the genealogists straight. In order to strengthen his claim to the English throne, Henry instructed his personal genealogists to trace back his heritage to the Welsh king Cadwaladr. The royal historians were ordered to proclaim that Henry was related to King Arthur (if there ever was such a person), identifying his castle in Winchester as Camelot. Henry then declared that Elizabeth, now pregnant, would give birth to a son in Wales and he would bring a golden age back into England. His son's name would be Arthur in honour of his 'ancestor' and Henry moved the whole court to Winchester for the birth of his unborn child.

When a healthy boy was born, and indeed named Arthur, it was as if God was smiling down on Henry.

But Henry had good reason to feel his throne quiver beneath him. Within a year, the Yorkists led a rebellion led by an Oxford-trained priest who had noticed that a local 10-year-old boy by the name of Lambert Simnel looked an awful lot like Prince Richard of York, the youngest of the princes who had mysteriously disappeared into the Tower.

Medieval wives knew their place: they were to be loyal and obedient and Elizabeth of York was no different from the rest. But history tells us that she and her mother shared a secret.

Almost ten years before when Richard had taken Prince Edward and placed him in the Tower, he had also demanded that Elizabeth Woodville hand over her younger son Richard as well, to keep his brother company in the Tower, for their safety of course. And we know that she had no choice but to comply. But did she actually hand over the prince or did she hand over a young pageboy dressed to look like the prince? And did his mother bundle Richard up in warm clothes and send him away in the dead of night to the safety of her sister-in-law Margaret in Flanders? Elizabeth had seen what had happened to her eldest son Edward and she would have not wanted the same fate for her younger boy. To this day, the debate still continues and no one knows for sure.

You can't stop people from gossiping and rumblings were heard all over the country that Prince Richard was still alive and he wanted his throne back. But once again, God smiled down on Henry and it wasn't long before the Simnel supporters were defeated at Stoke Field and the 10-year-old boy was captured.

It was in Henry's best interests to be benevolent, the generous monarch, despite the challenges from the Yorks. He could afford to look kind-hearted and generous. He had the throne of England and he was married to Elizabeth of York, the daughter of a king and the mother of the future king. And he was pretty certain the 10-year-old boy could simply not have been young Richard of York. Richard of York would have been a couple of years older than the young boy before him since Richard had been nine at the time of his capture years ago.

Henry played it up though. He looked like he was debating how to punish the boy as the court looked on in horror. Everyone was aware that this was a hanging offence. Worse than that, he could be hung until he was almost dead then cut from his little genitals to his breastbone, his heart pulled out along with his lungs, set alight in front of him, then his arms and legs cut from his body.

No one in the House of York had ever dealt out punishment like that before and all of England held their breath to see if Henry, as the first Tudor monarch, would be a vindictive king. In the terrible silence, as Simnel stared up at Henry with pleading eyes, Henry turned from him and declared the boy would work in the kitchens of his court and everyone breathed a sigh of relief.

But Henry had learned a valuable lesson and he wasn't about to let that sort of thing happen again. With Simnel sorted, Henry looked for ways to strengthen his rule. One by one, other members of the Plantagenet family were sent to the Tower of London, their lands, their castles and their titles confiscated. And his wife's mother, Elizabeth Woodville, would spend the rest of her days in seclusion in Bermondsey Abbey.

York supporters paid a heavy price as well. The nobles were publicly beheaded while common men were hanged, gutted while still alive, their bellies and lungs dragged out and finally their rotting bodies chopped up and displayed on city gates to show that Henry's rule was not to be questioned. Then he took their money, titles and castles as well.

With the extra cash from the nobles in his pocket, Henry brought in the decorators to Westminster Abbey and had the Tudor rose positioned around the ceiling for everyone to see. He lavished money on his residence and even began minting money with his image on one side and the Tudor rose on the other. He was putting across the message that he was there to stay.

But aftershocks were happening. With Henry's Welsh blood, trouble in Wales weakened but not so in Ireland. Many of the Irish lords had Lancastrian blood coursing through their veins and several of them felt that they had more rights to the English throne than Henry. True rights, by the way.

It was a dangerous world, not only for the Lancasters and the Yorks but also for the Plantagenets. For years, they'd been living in the shadows and trying to be anonymous in the crowds; uncertain of whom they could trust. Some ghosts just never lie down.

Finally, by 1493, they'd had enough and Henry got wind of another plot. Exiles in Europe were raising an army headed by another man; a 19-year-old young man they were assured was the *true* Prince Richard. And he had unbelievable backing. He had Edward IV's sister, Margaret of Burgundy, the King of France, Maximilian the Holy Roman Emperor's son, James IV of Scotland, the Yorkist nobles in Ireland and Elizabeth of York's own grandmother, Cecily Neville. With Margaret's money, Flemish troops and Scottish sympathy, his cause looked very good. Incredibly good.

Henry was scared. The army he had brought with him to Bosworth had been a paid army of mercenaries and they had long gone. As well, if the rebels thought they had the true Prince, they would be absolutely relentless.

For want of a name, and for some unknown reason, Henry called this 'pretender' Perkin Warbeck and fabricated a childhood where his father was a drunken boatman and his mother was an idiot, both living in Flanders.

But this young man was different from Simnel and Henry was well aware of it. This handsome young man had the York golden hair and the York hazel eyes as well as Edward IV's easy smile and the York family charm. He carried himself like a prince, he spoke many languages and he was the right age. He was extremely convincing and the Irish and Scots believed him. And they were prepared to fight another battle like the one at Stoke Field to put him on the throne.

Henry knew from personal experience that if you wanted to usurp a throne, it took time and planning and you had to be ready for action at any given moment. It gave Henry well-needed time for his own preparation.

For seven years, Warbeck openly plotted and three times he unsuccessfully attempted to seize the throne with the help of Scotland and mercenaries from France.

The threat from Scotland played heavily on Henry's mind. If nothing else, Henry was shrewd and wise enough to know that he had to have allies if he wanted to win. His first idea was that he should try to unite England and Scotland just as he had united the House of York and the House of Tudor by marrying Elizabeth of York. Then he had a brilliant idea. Actually, two ideas. He had a daughter Margaret of marriageable age just as James IV had an available son. A marriage between the two would eliminate Scotland as an enemy. And then to gain Spain's support, he would betroth his son Arthur to their daughter, the Infanta Katherine of Aragon. With the two marriages, he would be guaranteed that there would be no rivals for the English throne.

Outwardly Henry was calm and inscrutable giving nothing away but if you looked closer, you would have seen he was beginning to have a savage look of intensity about him.

Finally, in 1497, the threat suddenly disappeared when Warbeck was finally captured and brought to Henry. Before him stood a young man who could very well have been Prince Richard of York who had somehow survived his ordeal in the Tower with his brother. This was the young man who had come to take his throne, and if that was the case, Henry was in serious trouble.

Then Henry did a strange thing. For seven years, Henry had struggled to capture Warbeck but when he finally had him, he gave him the freedom on his court. He was given an allowance, fine clothes, the best of food and he was allowed to ride his horse wherever he wanted and no one could understand why. Unless of course Henry, and indeed Elizabeth, believed that Warbeck was indeed Prince Richard.

But for all Henry's generosity, it was short lived. He'd promised the Spanish that there would be no rivals for the throne of England and there he was, sheltering that same threat in his very court. To keep his allies happy, he had to do something. Something that showed him to still be the benevolent monarch to his people, but more importantly, the injured benevolent monarch. The plan was to allow Warbeck to escape and a show of capturing him again was to be made. But this time, there would be no mercy. The prisoner must seem to be unworthy of trust.

Henry must have been laughing at the irony of placing Warbeck in the Garden Tower after his recapture. It was the same tower where the young Prince Richard was last seen, the same rooms from where he and his brother Edward had disappeared thirteen years ago. As people gathered on the green, the little boys had waved to the crowds and their little faces were seen smiling.

That same window only had one pale face looking out now and if people looked closely, they would see bruises on his face, a broken nose squashed mercilessly, an ear half torn off and a mouth with no teeth. No one would ever see his York charm again. One level below him, sat Edward Plantagenet, George Duke of Clarence's son, his emaciated body wasted after thirteen years in the Tower.

Henry's anxious mood had not lightened despite his two prisoners locked away. With two boys and two girls, Henry's growing brood should have made him feel confident that his dynasty was secure and long lasting. But every night, he would sit at his dining table with a hard look on his face. With pressure from the Spanish ambassador and new uprisings and rebellions brewing all over the country, Henry's food had lost its flavour and he barely tasted the dishes put before him.

Finally, Henry signed Warbeck's death sentence without waiting for a jury's decision. Henry found him guilty and sentenced Warbeck to death. There was no evidence supplied and his warrant did not even have a name on it. After having worked so hard to convince England that Warbeck was just the son of a drunken man, Henry did not even put the name on that one important document. He left it blank.

The scaffold was built high so that everyone could see it clearly and thousands pushed their way to watch the hanging. But where there would normally be catcalling and shouting, on that day there was stillness. Warbeck walked silently up the ladder and his gaolers put a noose around his neck. He looked around for a moment, perhaps hoping that there would be a reprieve, then he bent his head in prayer. They took the ladder away and he dropped.

It took an hour for him to die. No one was allowed to grab hold of his feet to break his neck and make it quicker. He hung quietly and then he was gone.

Three days later, it was Edward Plantagenet's turn. Edward, now a man of 24, had not felt the dewy grass beneath his feet for thirteen years or felt rain falling on his face. On that day, as seagulls screeched overhead and voices echoed from beyond the walls, Edward walked white-faced and unsteady in the mud through a fierce thunderstorm with a guard on either side of him across the drawbridge and up to Tower Hill. Shutters banged and lightning flashed as if Nature was raging at the cruelty. He placed his York head on the block, stretched out his arms and they beheaded him.

After the executions, Henry went into lockdown. He kept to his rooms and only his trusted servants were allowed to enter. People whispered that he had contracted the 'sweat' that he had brought with him when he landed at Milford Haven. But no one knew. The only one to enter his rooms was his mother for a couple of hours each evening.

Months later, he appeared again but it was a new Henry that materialised. This new Henry was obsessed with every part of his realm, especially his money. He began bringing spies into his household for his personal security and he kept his own record of accounts from wages, right down to cooks, barbers and gardeners. To Henry, money meant control. And control meant power.

By then Henry had been on the throne for fifteen years and he was as settled as Henry could ever be. He had come to love his wife and she had given him five healthy children. Of them, his eldest son Arthur was the jewel in his crown. The next child was his daughter Margaret, betrothed to James IV of Scotland, then came his effervescent son Henry. After him was another daughter, Mary, and last of all, was a newborn son Edmund.

Historians have told us how Henry survived all of the physical dangers associated with usurping a throne. But did he survive the psychological ones? Some have gone so far as to suggest that there was a curse on Henry's line after the judicial murder of Warbeck and Edward Plantagenet. A couple have even implied that Elizabeth Woodville, the *'Rivers witch'* as she was called, had put a curse on the person who had killed her sons in the Tower.

Looking back now, if it actually existed and knowing what happens in the future, it must have been a pretty powerful curse. If Richard had in fact killed the boys, the curse had already been fulfilled since his son had died young and his line had indeed died out. But what if the person who had killed the boys had been Henry? What if it was Henry who had firstly killed Prince Edward in the tower and then Prince Richard / Warbeck on the scaffold? If the Rivers' curse *was* a fact, you would wonder if Elizabeth Woodville had sat silently in her rooms in the Abbey with the knowledge that she had cursed her own grandchildren.

It all began seven months after the executions when Henry's young son Edmund, fit and healthy at 15 months old, died from unknown circumstances. But if that wasn't bad enough, there were worse things in store for Henry.

The Spanish ambassador was truly impressed with England and Henry's reign. England had become remarkably tranquil compared to the past rulers of England and as for Henry, Spain was a tremendous ally to have. It was at this time that they were supporters and funders of Christopher Columbus who successfully discovered the 'New World' in 1492.

The marriage of Henry's eldest son, Arthur, and Katherine of Aragon, daughter of Ferdinand of Aragon and Isabella of Castile (great granddaughter of John of Gaunt – doesn't that name keep popping up?) was fully approved. The dowry of 200,000 crowns was agreed upon and half the money was paid to Henry. The other half would be paid after the marriage.

15-year-old Arthur was already the Prince of Wales when Katherine arrived in November of 1501. Little is known about their first impressions of each other, but Arthur did write to his parents-in-law that he would be *"a true and loving husband"*.

Even so, Arthur was nervous. The only contact he'd had with his young bride were letters he'd written in stilted Latin to his bride-to-be. When they finally met, the couple found that they were unable to speak to each other since they had learned different pronunciations of Latin.

Despite the obvious difficulties of two rather shy teenagers, the celebrations were glorious and it was the ultimate PR event. Tailors, hatters and glove-makers were employed and a complete wardrobe of clothes was prepared for the young prince, as well as a suit for the wedding. The streets were alive with colour as Katherine and Arthur were carried through London. Following behind was the popular 10-year-old Henry who already loved the limelight.

On 14th November 1501, the couple were married and Katherine must have known she had become a part of something very special. Her future father-in-law smiled his rictus smile as he greeted guests at the wedding banquet, even Plantagenet kinsmen, with excessive affection.

Even at this early stage of her marriage, Katherine would have heard the rumours that Henry was at his most dangerous when he appeared at ease and laughing. She would have seen him strolling around the banquet hall, nodding and acknowledging guests, perhaps unaware that his spies were doing their work outside in the dark, narrow streets of London. At the end of the festive day came the bedding ceremony, and most of the court put the young couple to bed. Days later, the couple were sent off to Ludlow Castle in Wales to begin their new life together.

Henry must have begun to feel the Tudor line was secure. His eldest son looked very pleased with his new bride and she came from a fertile Spanish line.

However, it wasn't long before things went terribly wrong.

Late at night on 4th April 1502, a boat docked at the king's residence in Greenwich. Aboard was a messenger with terrible news. Arthur and Katherine had both became ill with the 'sweating sickness'.

Everything that could have been done was done for Arthur. Scalding plasters had been applied to his chest, leeches were put on his legs, his forehead had been sponged with icy water but still his fever had persisted and he had continued to sweat as if he was on fire. Eventually Arthur died and Katherine recovered to find herself a widow.

Arthur had been one of 10,000 who had died as a result of the sweating sickness. The sickness started with a merciless fever, accompanied by a foul smelling sweat. Sharp pains in the back and shoulders followed before moving to the liver. For some, the sleep of death was a release.

No one knew how it spread but people knew that it had followed Henry when he had marched into England with his mercenaries who had come from the gutters and prisons of Europe. Within the first few months after the battle, people were dying from the disease and everyone was calling it the *"King's disease"*. People were scared to let their children play in the streets, kiss someone on the cheek or even open their doors in case it let the germs into their house. But when you think of the times, their floors were covered in rushes and in the streets, sewers flowed with body refuse into the Thames. No wonder the disease spread quickly. Even Cardinal Wolsey carried an orange hollowed out and filled with vinegar pressed to his nose to block the stench.

The political impact of Arthur's death was immense. For every Plantagenet beheaded, another two seemed to appear and as the fertile Plantagenets and Yorks produced boy after boy, Henry realised he was left with only one son to carry on the Tudor name. After everything he and his mother had fought for, his dynasty hung by a single thread with his only surviving son, Prince Henry, nicknamed Harry.

Apart from this, Henry was devastated by the death of his beloved Arthur. No one could replace him. Arthur was his first son and he was his jewel. His treasure. Arthur had sparkled. And Harry had not been prepared, or even considered, for his new role. Of course, Henry loved his young son but even he knew Harry was spoiled. Henry had a lot of work in front of him if he was to guide Harry to be as good a king as Arthur would have been.

Apart from all that, Henry faced the challenge of avoiding the obligation to return Katherine's dowry to her father, half of which he had not yet been paid. To settle the matter, it was agreed that Katherine would marry Harry, even though Harry was five years younger. Due to his youth, it would mean that the marriage would be delayed until he was old enough.

Elizabeth was a bright woman. She knew everything her husband was thinking. Quietly and firmly, although grieving for Arthur herself, she assured Henry that she was still young enough to bear more children and sure enough, within months, she announced she was pregnant and the family moved to the Tower and prepared for the important birth. The future of the Tudor dynasty depended on this child and hopefully it would be a boy. But until she delivered, Harry was a rare and precious jewel that had to be protected.

While Elizabeth waited for the birth of her next child, she would have been making mental notes of things she had to teach Harry. He would have the best tutors, the best horsemen and his rooms would have been constantly cleaned so that there would be no sweating sickness. And he had to learn that being a king didn't mean that you had everything your own way. He had to be taught to be wise and just, a big task since he had always been indulged and spoilt.

Elizabeth's pregnancy was difficult. She carried low and was constantly sick and pale. Finally, after a traumatic and premature labour, she delivered a sickly, baby girl. As Elizabeth slipped in and out of consciousness with a raging temperature, Henry was beside himself with grief and called in specialists from all over the country. Nothing helped. On 11th February on her 37th birthday, both Elizabeth and her baby died.

Despite the unsteady start, their marriage had become one of genuine love and Henry was shattered by the loss, not to mention that their marriage had represented the unity of the Lancasters and the Yorks after a century of fighting. Many had only accepted Henry out of loyalty to Elizabeth's family but with her death, everything could tear apart again. With Elizabeth, the foundation for peace was gone.

London turned out for the burial of the York princess that they loved. As Elizabeth's coffin, draped with white York banners, was drawn through the streets of London by eight horses, the streets were ablaze with mourners holding torches all the way to Westminster Abbey as the church bells wailed. Two sets of thirty-seven virgins, dressed in white linen and carrying Tudor wreaths, silently lined the route carrying lighted candles and another thousand lights burned brightly on the hearse. The cathedral itself was draped in black and lit by 273 large tapers. She had not come with the diseased army when Henry had stumbled ashore at Milford Haven. She was their own born-and-bred princess with York blood and she would be sorely missed.

Henry physically collapsed at Elizabeth's death. Unable to function without her by his side, he retreated into his personal chambers at Richmond, leaving his mother to arrange for the funeral. He could not even bring himself to be present at the funeral as if he was denying the fact that she was gone. Without Elizabeth to help him, he had no idea who was his friend or who was his enemy.

Six weeks later, Henry emerged, still wearing black but with his mask back in place, although new lines of suffering were etched on his grey complexion. His skin sagged under his eyes and he walked slightly bent as if he was carrying a huge weight on his shoulders. But his drive was even more remorseless as old enemies began to resurface. He was a king driven by fear and ruled by greed and he would always be suspicious.

Although Elizabeth had been a York, it was hard times for her family members. Henry saw new enemies at every turn and it was as if he could sniff out any York or Plantagenet blood that was restless.

And Henry was right. The first threat came from a branch of Suffolk, who was raising an army in Europe. But this time, Henry had a stroke of good luck.

He received an unexpected guest at court, Prince Philip of Burgundy, who was the very man who was secretly sheltering the Duke of Suffolk. Seizing his opportunity, Henry welcomed the Prince with open arms and lavish hospitality, a smiling assassin if ever there was one.

From the beginning, it was obvious that Prince Phillip was trapped. Henry stated that he would only release him if he handed Suffolk over and Phillip really had no other choice. By mid-March, a ship docked and with a heavily armed committee Suffolk was escorted to the Tower.

He was to suffer the same fate as the two princes in the Tower. He never emerged again.

But all the fighting and plots had left its mark on Henry and his health was deteriorating fast. He became more and more intent on keeping his only son Harry safe and as a precaution, he began confining Harry to the household. He had lost two sons and he was not about to lose his last one.

As for Katherine, Henry was very unconcerned about her. Her father was still procrastinating over the payment of the remainder of her dowry and as such, she was being held a virtual prisoner at Durham House in

London. She had little money and she struggled to cope, supporting both herself and her ladies-in-waiting.

In 1509, it was obvious that Henry was seriously ill. He shut himself away for the last time and he never returned. His death was not announced until two days later and confirmed as tuberculosis.

From an isolated beach in Wales, he had fought and won his first battle. He had unified a kingdom and accrued immense wealth but his greatest legacy was his son, soon to be Henry VIII. For all the criticism of Henry's rule, he had achieved what he wanted. He had passed on his crown to a beloved son and everyone looked forward to the charismatic young prince sitting on the throne.

Lucky old England.

HENRY VIII

Born 1491
Reign 1509 - 1547

Some monarchs were more popular than others but the Tudors have scooped the pool when it comes to thwarted lives. Having said that, there were Tudors, and then there were *Tudors*.

Where do I begin with Henry VIII? So much happened just prior to his reign that shaped his life and could be seen as possible reasons for why he did so many terrible things during his reign. Everyone loves to hate Henry VIII and there's a very good reason why. Keeping this in mind, Henry's reign can't be rushed.

To give you an idea of the times Henry was growing up in, France was in a strong position due to the Hundred Years' War. King Louis XI was the head of both the Valois family and a united France, not just a group of feudal territories anymore, while the only territory that still belonged to the English from William the Conqueror's days was Calais. Even the smaller branch of the House of Burgundy had come to an end with the death of their ruler, Charles the Bold in 1477.

Louis XI had desperately wanted Burgundy for himself but the Burgundian inheritance passed to Charles' only child, Mary, who in turn had married the Holy Roman Emperor and ruler of the wealthy Hapsburg family in Austria, Maximillian I. That meant the inheritance all went to Maximillian and it gave the Hapsburgs a lot of control over counties, lordships, cities and fortunes. With her inheritance, Mary had become a wealthy heiress but together with the ruler of Austria, there was no greater house in Europe than the Austrian empire and Maximillian was using it to his full advantage. Their son, Archduke Philip, in turn married an even greater heiress than his mother, the mentally unstable Infanta Joanne, heir to Castile, Aragon, Sicily and Naples. It was Joanne's younger sister, Katherine of Aragon, who had accelerated the rise of the House of Tudor when she married Arthur.

Again, the Hapsburg and the Valois families were confronting each other on the northeast border of France and it was going to be a long struggle.

In this world of Austria's growing power, Henry could only move and act with far fewer resources than his neighbours. His people numbered only 3 million with no standing army and an almost non-existent navy. Yet by being so close to France and the Netherlands, he was forced to play an important part in European politics. As a result, Henry inherited a country that had become involved in wars, negotiations, shifts in alliances and changes of the balance of power, all of which he had very little experience. In this changing world, battles on the land were being decided by the invincible Spanish infantry of Cordova, occasionally the Swiss infantry or the terrible infantry of Gaston de Foix, a general of the French king.

For centuries, England had been forced to move warily, threatened with disaster if any shift of continental policies should leave them alone in the face of Spain or France. It was an even trickier time for this new England.

Until the death of Arthur, Henry as the second son had been intended for the Church and was brought up learning Latin, French, Italian, theology, music, jousting, tennis and hunting. He was a lovable little rogue, spoilt by doting women with good intentions and he had impressed one of the cleverest women of the age, Margaret of Austria, Regent of the Netherlands. She saw him as a young man who could be relied upon.

Henry was a handsome, strong man at over 6 feet tall and at many tournaments he would dress in outfits of velvet, satin with gold cloth dripping in pearls and jewels covered in a gilded armour. Margaret of Austria's ambassadors quoted her as saying,

"His Majesty is the handsomest potentate I have ever set eyes on; above the usual height, with an extremely fine calf to his leg; his complexion fair and bright, with auburn hair combed straight and short in the French fashion, and a round face so very beautiful that it would become a pretty woman; his throat rather long and thick...He speaks French, English, Latin and Italian, plays well on the lute and harpsichord, sings from a book at sight, draws the bow with greater strength than any man in England, and jousts marvellously. He is fond of hunting, and never takes his diversion without tiring eight or ten horses, which he causes to be stationed beforehand along the line of country he means to cover. He is extremely fond of tennis, at which game it is the prettiest thing in the world to see him play, his fair skin glowing through a shirt of the finest texture."

Wow! Where do I sign up?

His vigour and energy came from centuries of warfare on the Welsh marshes and his massive frame towered above the throng and his power and passion was almost tangible. Although Henry appeared as open, jovial and trustworthy with a good sense of humour to strangers, those who knew him well were aware that he seldom confided in anyone. Much like his father. He seemed like two men, one the merry monarch, patron of every kind of sport and the other, the cold acute observer at council, watching alertly, weighing up arguments, but refusing to speak his mind except under duress.

It was hard to predict Henry. He had bursts of restless energy and ferocity but then there were times of extraordinary patience. But as time passed, his wilfulness hardened and his temper worsened. His rages were terrible to watch and many heads were to fly during his thirty-eight years on the throne. Once he had a scheme in mind, he could seldom be turned from it and resistance only made him more stubborn. Although he prided himself on his tolerance of outspoken opinions, it was usually unwise to continue to oppose him after he had made up his mind.

Henry was crowned in the beautiful sunshine of Midsummer 1509 as a sign that England was coming out of a cold, bleak time and into a bright new beginning and London did not look like a city mourning the death of a king. People were roasting meat on the street corners, ale was being passed around and crowds were dancing in the streets. People in prisons who thought they would never see the light of day again were slowly emerging, blinking myopically into the sunshine. It was as if England's nightmare had ended and spring was here after a long hard winter. The old king had only just been buried and the new prince was not yet crowned yet the city was alive with revellers.

At his coronation, Henry's robes were stiff and heavy with diamonds, rubies, emeralds and pearls and the heavy gown would have glowed as he moved through Westminster Abbey. He radiated power and glory and beside him was his wife of thirteen days, Katharine of Aragon. She must have believed that all her Christmases had come at once.

Both of them would have been happy for this fresh start. Henry VII had been harsh and difficult in his last days. He'd been an overprotective parent towards the end and young Henry had been impatient to spread his wings and prove he was an adult. Up until his father's death, Henry had never been allowed to speak in public and he could only leave the palace under strict supervision through a private door. All that had changed at his father's death and Henry was eager to start his new life with his sizeable inheritance and his beautiful bride.

As he stood with the crown firmly planted on his head looking at Katherine, he must have felt invincible. Even the sight of his grandmother, Margaret Beaufort, dressed in deepest black and seated stiffly at the end of the room within a circle of silent ladies-in-waiting, could not dampen his mood. She was torn between grief for her dead son and fury at her grandson for marrying his brother's widow, but the black looks she sent to her grandson were conscientiously ignored. Henry was a portrait of magnificence as he strolled around the room, laughing amongst his friends with Katherine glowing by his side, like young lovers enchanted with each other.

For the commoners, it was a merciful release from their long hardship and for the nobility, it was a release from tyranny. But the Plantagenets, Lancastrians and Yorks were still very tentative. All of them had been waiting in fear for a knock on the door announcing they were to be taken to the Tower so they all started to emerge rather slowly.

As if to prove his benevolence towards his kinsmen, Henry's first act as king was two days after his coronation when he arrested his father's two most unpopular ministers and charged them with high treason. Days later, he had them executed. He restored lands and titles and released those who had been imprisoned unfairly. They were Henry's cousins, he declared, and they would share in his good fortune.

With this benevolence, a tide of wealth began to flow out of the treasury. Incredulously, chests, cupboards and boxes were opened and everywhere they found jewels, gold, fabrics, spices and treasures. The old king had taken everything he could lay his hands on and Henry immediately began to give it all back.

Almost immediately, Katherine conceived during those carefree days of constant celebration and entertainment, but it was a bad night for her on 31st January 1510, when she gave birth prematurely to a stillborn daughter.

Almost immediately, quiet rumours began to spread that God had not blessed the marriage. She had, after all, been married to Arthur before Henry and everyone knew that the Bible forbade this sort of thing. Margaret Beaufort's mood darkened even more and daring mistresses whispered in Henry's ear. Look! See! Remember the curse!

Then in 1511, a son was born on New Year's Day and Henry was jubilant. He was christened weeks later and named Prince Henry, Duke of Cornwall. Fifty-two days later, his little body was found blue and cold in his cradle.

There is never any comfort for losing a child and Katherine was no different than any other woman. Except there *was* one big difference. Her husband was Henry VIII and the dead child had been the future King of England and the future of the Tudor line. As Henry fell silent, everyone watched and waited in the uncertain stillness that spread through the court. Everyone was watchful, unsure of what would happen next.

Two years later, things changed dramatically again. The year was 1513, and it was the first time since the Hundred Years' War that an English army had campaigned in Europe. Katherine was blessedly pregnant again and Henry had headed off to France on a military campaign to reconquer

Bordeaux, lost sixty years before. In his absence, he named Katherine as England's regent.

While Katherine's father King Ferdinand invaded Navarre, a republic of Venice, the English expedition to Gascony was failing miserably. The English found that the style of warfare they had learned in the War of the Roses had become obsolete on the continent. Longbows and heavily armed mounted men were regarded as archaic and ponderous and both Ferdinand and the French employed professional infantry, both Swiss and Austrian, who advanced at a great pace in solid squares with eighteen-foot pikes bristling in every direction. As Henry's father-in-law, Ferdinand gave a great deal of advice to Henry and suggested that he should use his gathered wealth to procure an overwhelming professional force of his own.

Everyone knew that it wasn't in Henry's nature to take advice from anyone. He had a mind and a will of his own and more than anything, he wanted to prove his own worth on the battlefield. So as Henry reluctantly and slowly considered the advice, his army, unaccustomed to Gascon wine and to French tactics, was devastated by dysentery and quickly disintegrated. Facing the French army with dwindling numbers was something no one wanted and Henry's troops flatly refused to obey their officer's orders to advance. Instead they boarded ships for home.

Negotiations with France lasted throughout winter but in the end Ferdinand and the Venetians simply deserted Henry as he refused to compromise. With nowhere else to go, Henry reluctantly decided to take his father-in-law's previous advice and hire Emperor Maximilian's Austrian army to help him fight.

Although costly, the arrangement was brilliantly successful. Together, the English and the Austrian mercenaries whitewashed the French in August of 1513 at the Battle of the Spurs, so called because of the rapidity of the French retreat. Even Tournoi, the richest city in Northeast France, surrendered at the mere sight of the Imperial artillery. To add icing on the cake, Henry was ecstatic when he received a letter from Katherine saying that the Scots had invaded England and despite being heavily pregnant and outnumbered two to one, she had ridden north in full armour with some troops, and defeated James IV of Scotland, who had died in battle at Flodden Field. While she danced happily and London celebrated, Henry held the bloodied coat of the Scots king that Katherine had sent him.

His joy was to be short-lived.

It was too early, much too early, for the baby to be born. In the early hours of a cold November morning, Katherine woke up in a pool of blood and delivered a tiny baby boy. In her husband's absence, she named him Henry, Duke of Cornwall and hours later, he stopped breathing. They slapped him and shook him but his little body remained limp and still.

It wasn't until Henry returned home from France that he was given the news that Katherine had lost another son. Even worse news was that a 1-year-old boy had succeeded to the throne in Scotland as James V. The mother of the young king was Henry's eldest sister Margaret and there was now a new claimant to the English throne, adding to the growing list. As for Henry, he was yet to produce an heir.

In autumn of that year, the French were struggling and Cardinal Wolsey hired a Swiss army and pushed forward to invade Burgundy. When Dijon was captured, Henry had every intention of renewing his campaign in France until he found out that his father-in-law Ferdinand had been making his own separate peace with France and was trying to lure Emperor Maximilian over to his side, away from Henry.

Henry may have been unpredictable but he was always resourceful. He was quick to launch a counter-attack and he was quick to devise a plan. In the space of weeks, he strengthened his navy and openly planned an attack on Paris.

Seeing Henry's determination and the size of his new army, France was quick to make a peace treaty with Henry. Much to his delight, this new treaty secured him exactly double the amount of revenue they had paid to his father. The crowning event was Henry's insistence that his youngest sister, Mary was to marry Louis XII, King of France. Mary was 17, Louis was 52.

The story runs that Mary extracted a promise from Henry that if she married this one time for England, she would be free the next time to marry for love. And that is exactly what she did. Three months after the marriage, King Louis died and to Henry's intense displeasure, Mary cut short her widowhood by marrying Charles Brandon, the Duke of Suffolk.

In December 1514, Katherine delivered another stillborn son, another Prince Henry Duke of Cornwell and Henry, of course, was desolate. But this time his displeasure was somehow different. Subtle changes were happening.

By then, Henry had met Mary Boleyn, the eldest of the Boleyn girls, and within a few years, she had delivered a bouncing baby boy.

Then, two years later, as if God had finally decided that Henry had suffered enough, Katherine delivered a healthy girl they named Mary. She was christened three days later in a glorious ceremony at the Church of Observant Friars and to all of England, it seemed like the curse had been lifted. Two years further on, Katherine became pregnant again and England was ecstatic.

On 10th November, Katherine gave birth to another daughter. While England held its breath and waited for Henry's reaction, the child grew weaker and weaker. Seven days later, the child died.

Henry may have been growing distant from his wife but he hadn't changed much in his style of ruling. He was still a closed book and he still chose men of low incomes as his advisers. Thomas Wolsey was no different from any of them.

Wolsey was the son of a poor and rascally butcher from Ipswich who was reported as selling meat unfit for human consumption. Other advisers were Thomas Cromwell, a small attorney and Thomas Cranmer, an obscure ecclesiastic lecturer. Like his father, Henry distrusted hereditary nobility, preferring discreet men without a wide circle of friends.

Wolsey's job was to find money for Henry, and he was good at it. He raised taxes and carefully recorded all of them in order to build Henry's largest warship of the age, the *Great Harry*. This seven-tiered warship weighed 1,500 tons and boasted an incredible array of guns.

Up until then, Henry and Wolsey had been inseparable. But things were subtly changing. Henry became suspicious that Wolsey was withholding money from him and a visit to the new great college Wolsey was building at Oxford was arranged. When he arrived, he was astonished at the vast sums of money that were being lavished on the stonework. *"It is strange,"* he remarked to Wolsey *"that you have found so much money to spend upon your college and yet could not find enough to finish my war"*. They were words Wolsey would remember in the future as Henry began watching him even more closely.

Around 1525 Wolsey breathed a sigh of relief when he was put on the back-burner for a while. It was Katherine's turn to take up a lot of Henry's concentration. She was forty and a typical Spanish princess, maturing and ageing rapidly. And Henry knew for certain there would be no more legitimate children. He was faced with the realisation that either his favourite illegitimate son, 6-year-old Henry Fitzroy Duke of Richmond to Henry's mistress Elizabeth 'Bessie' Blount, would have to be appointed as the heir to the throne by an Act of Parliament (not an easy task) or his daughter Mary, now 9 years old, would be the first Queen of England in her own right since Queen Maud.

I think we should give Henry a little benefit of the doubt here. Sure, Henry's desire to provide England with a male heir was partly from personal vanity but it was also partly because he did not believe a daughter would be strong enough to strengthen the Tudor Dynasty or maintain the fragile peace that existed following the War of the Roses. The long clash had been a nightmare for England and he knew it would not survive another disputed succession.

There didn't seem to be much of a choice for Henry. What he needed was a boy, more to the point, a legitimate boy. But how was he to going to achieve that with an ageing wife? While he thought, he tested the waters and introduced Henry Fitzroy to his court.

Probably saying 'introduced' is a little mild. The 6-year-old actually travelled by barge from Wolsey's mansion down the River Thames accompanied by a host of knights, squires and other gentlemen. The barge pulled up and the party made its way through the palace to Henry's richly decorated lodgings on the second floor. Various members of court and nobility were already waiting, among them bishops, Duke of Norfolk, Duke of Suffolk, Earl of Northumberland, Earl of Oxford and the Earl of Arundel. While everyone watched, the child knelt before Henry and was created Duke of Richmond and Somerset. The double dukedom was the highest honour Henry could give him.

Katherine seethed after the ceremony when the child was presented at court. Not only was she anxious for her own daughter, Mary, the humiliation she felt at a time when it was clear to everyone that she would not bear Henry any more children was almost unbearable for her. Henry had become cruel in his treatment of her and was even heard to have called her *ugly and deformed*". He had even vowed he would never sleep with her again.

All this led to what Henry is best remembered for – his six wives. The significance of Henry's reign is, at all times, overshadowed by those marriages which can best be described as divorced, beheaded, died, divorced, beheaded, survived.

Now it's time for a new character in our story. Henry had met Anne Boleyn and things would never be the same again.

For two long years, Henry pursued Anne. And she remained steadfast. She would *not* be just another whore in his bed like her sister, she said. She would *not* sleep with him while he was a married man and she would remain a virgin for her husband on their wedding night, whoever that husband was, she stated.

Anne Boleyn was Mary's younger sister and a maid-of-honour to Katherine. Her dark looks, black eyes, lustrous hair and high cheekbones had totally enthralled Henry and early pictures of her show a happy, vivacious girl with the world at her feet. But if you viewed the progression of portraits over the years, those early joyous pictures would change slowly and they would catch wariness and watchfulness in Anne's eyes. There are many accounts of her personality but we can be sure that she was charming and very resourceful. And really, how does one refuse a king, especially when that king is Henry VIII?

The Boleyn family originally came from Blickling in Norfolk, fifteen miles north of Norwich. At the time of Anne's birth, the Boleyn family was considered one of the most respected in the English aristocracy. Among her relatives, she counted the Howards, one of the pre-eminent families in the land.

Since she had returned from school in France, she had grown into a vibrant, witty woman of twenty-four. Slender and frail, her eyes were almost black and her thick black hair was so long that she could sit on it. She wore it flowing loose over her shoulders as a mark of her virginity - something she knew would catch Henry's eye. She exerted a powerful charm on those who met her, though opinions differed on her attractiveness. The Venetian diarist Marino Sanuto, who saw Anne when Henry VIII met Francis I at Calais in October 1532, described her as *"not one of the handsomest women in the world; she is of middling stature, swarthy complexion, long neck, wide mouth, bosom not much raised ... but eyes, which are black and beautiful"*.

It was obvious to everyone that she was more than willing to provide him with the *legitimate* son he longed for. Which of course meant getting rid of Katherine.

Henry knew he needed help and Wolsey was the obvious answer. Putting his money issues aside, Henry held many meetings with Wolsey who was more than willing to have the limelight taken away from him and shine it on someone else.

Eventually they arrived at a solution. Henry's marriage to Katherine had to be declared illegal. She had been married to his brother Arthur and the marriage had been consummated. There were plenty of people who could attest to that. After the reception, there had been a bedding ceremony and most of the court had put the young couple to bed. And everyone knew that if the Church had known about this, they would never have given permission for Henry to marry Katherine in the first place. It was illegal in the eyes of the Church.

In one decree, Henry had made it possible to be free of Katherine and free to marry a younger fertile bride. The problem was not everyone agreed with that decision. After months of deliberation, the court decided that the marriage was in fact perfectly legal after all.

Henry was used to getting what he wanted so to say his mood became increasingly angry and he became impatient with his court is an understatement. While he lavished jewels and presents on Anne, animosity grew at court for the *"goggle-eyed whore"*.

But Henry was never one to accept defeat easily. There was always a Plan B. Knowing that his wife was a devoted Catholic, Henry decided that his next move was to convince Katherine that due to the consummation of her first marriage with his brother, Katherine and Henry had lived in mortal sin for eighteen years. However, the unspoken truth of this was it also meant that their daughter Mary would be illegitimate.

As you can expect, Katherine denied the marriage had been consummated and she flatly refused to go away. While the couple fought, Anne Boleyn watched intently.

Anne was playing a rather dangerous game. She constantly refused Henry's advances to seduce her, while all the while proclaiming her love for him. And Henry was absolutely smitten. He was so absorbed with her that he forgot to tell Cardinal Wolsey, who hated Anne intensely by the way, that they had secretly sent a special royal messenger to Pope Clement VII requesting that his marriage to Katherine be annulled so they could marry at once. Sir William Knight had been 'brought out of retirement' at 70 years of age to do so.

It was all rather bad timing for Henry. By then in 1527, the Hapsburgs had shocked Europe by seizing Rome. Italy had fallen and Pope Clement VII was practically a prisoner of Charles V of Spain, and Charles was determined that Henry should not divorce his Aunt Katherine. As a consequence of the siege, Pope Clement could do nothing but refuse to annul Henry and Katherine's marriage. To top it off, Henry was to be excommunicated from the church.

Henry threw a wobbler. In his tirade, he stated that he was the head of England both politically and religiously and he no longer wanted to be a part of the Catholic Church. The name of his new church would be called The Church of England and *he* would be the head. New counsellors were called in, the first being the Duke of Norfolk, Anne Boleyn's uncle, who was appointed as Secretary to the King. All sorted.

The decision was devastating for Wolsey. In October, Wolsey had a visit from Norfolk and Charles Brandon, Duke of Suffolk (then married to Henry's sister Mary), who demanded the Great Seal of England back.

Wolsey knew instantly that this meant he was no longer the Lord Chancellor. And he was right. Norfolk became President of the Council, Suffolk became the Vice-President and Sir Thomas More became the new Lord Chancellor. And it had all come about with the influence of Anne Boleyn. When they left, Wolsey totally broke down.

Anne was not satisfied with a simple breakdown. What she wanted was to totally ruin Wolsey. She had set her heart on York Place, the London residence of the Archbishops of York owned by Cardinal Wolsey, and it was perfect for her and her parties. Anne and her mother, Elizabeth Howard, took Henry to inspect York Place, and as with the college in Oxford, Henry was incensed by the wealth that Wolsey had accumulated. Henry demanded York Place be returned to him and promptly charged Wolsey with *"traitorous correspondence with the King of France without the King's knowledge."* Wolsey was to be executed. The King had spoken.

As chance would have it, on the way to London, the Cardinal fell ill and died.

It had taken six years after Henry's excommunication from the church, but in 1533 Henry finally draped Anne with a crimson mantle of velvet as a mark of his Queen and a mere six months later in September, she delivered a child.

A daughter.

Bonfires were lit throughout London but there was no rejoicing in Henry's heart. A male heir had been his one desire. That's what Anne had promised him. After all he had done, defied the whole world, perhaps committed bigamy, been excommunicated from the Church, and the result? Another daughter. He galloped away from Greenwich, away from Anne and his new daughter named Elizabeth after his mother, and in three days he reached Wolf Hall in Wiltshire, the residence of a loyal courtier, Sir John Seymour, who had a very clever son named Edward and a very pretty daughter named Jane, both of whom we will see more of later.

After the birth of Elizabeth, a question began to form in everyone's mind. If there was a choice between princesses, why then not choose Mary? She was after all the eldest.

During the summer of that year, Henry showed his savageness when two women of his household were stripped, beaten and had their ears nailed to a wooden post for saying *"Queen Katherine is the true Queen of England"*. One week later, Mary was stripped of her title of *"the King's daughter"* and was to be called *"The Lady Mary"*. She was then sent to Hadfield to act as lady in waiting to her baby sister, the rightful Princess Elizabeth.

But despite Henry's show of support for Anne, things were far from happy in the royal household. Henry and Anne were not as pleased with married life as you would have expected after waiting for such a long time and they fought incessantly. At one time, he was heard to say that he could lower her as well as raise her. They enjoyed periods of calm and affection, but Anne refused to play the submissive role that Henry expected of her. Henry expected absolute obedience and that was not Anne. The vivacity he had craved and made her so attractive to him as an illicit lover also made her too independent for a royal wife. It made her many enemies and on his part, he disliked her constant irritability and violent temper. Still he was confident that the next child would be a boy.

Three miscarriages followed.

In 2011, Catrina Whitley and her colleague Kyra Kramer wrote about the reasons behind Katherine of Aragon and Anne Boleyn's many miscarriages and stillbirths. Interestingly, they assert that it was not Henry's queens who 'failed' to provide the king with an heir, as history so often remembers them, and neither was it the women who were in some way physiologically responsible for the many miscarriages and stillbirths. Instead, the problem lay in Henry VIII himself. They argue that the same theory that explains Henry VIII's reproductive problems also helps explain why Henry VIII became a paranoid tyrant in his later years.

This new theory proposes that Henry VIII was positive for the Kell blood group and also suffered from McLeod syndrome. McLeod syndrome is a recessively inherited genetic disorder that may affect the blood, brain, nerves, muscles and heart.

They state:

"A Kell negative woman having multiple pregnancies with a Kell positive male will suffer repeated miscarriages and the death of Kell positive foetuses. This pattern is consistent with the pregnancies of Katherine of Aragon and Anne Boleyn. Additionally, Henry VIII may have suffered from McLeod syndrome, a genetic disorder of the Kell blood group system, which is a condition that causes physical and mental impairment consistent with his ailments."

Furthermore, they support their theory by tracing the reproductive history of Henry's maternal male relatives that also displayed the Kell positive reproductive pattern. You will also remember that Henry's great-grandmother was Catherine of Valois, whose brother King Charles VI of France was labelled as 'Crazy Charles'. And then there was her son, Henry VI.

It could explain Henry's transformation from gentle prince to terrible tyrant. Between 1534 and 1540, there was a genuine fear of speaking against Henry. Over 300 executions were ordered and many more people fled England when two carts full of friars drove through the street of London on their way to the Tower ready for the scaffold. A leading monk was partially hung before his heart was ripped out and rubbed in his face. His bowels were then pulled out and burned before beheading him and chopping him into quarters. There were three more who would suffer the same death in the space of three months.

On 7th January 1536, news reached Henry that Katherine of Aragon had died. He and Anne decked out in yellow, the colour of mourning in Spain at the time, but Henry was joyous.

Life seemed pretty good for Henry. He was free from Katherine at last and his beautiful young bride was heavily pregnant again. He fervently believed that this time the child would be the elusive boy. Life looked rosy until three weeks later when Henry had a nasty fall from his horse during a jousting tournament. As he lay unconscious for hours, Anne was distraught. A week later, she miscarried a male child.

Of course, Anne declared that it was Henry who was to blame for the miscarriage. She had been hysterical with grief that Henry could die, and that grief had caused the miscarriage. Again, she promised that there would be more children.

By March, less than two months later, Henry was courting Jane Seymour and things went from bad to worse for Anne.

On 24th April, calamity struck when one of the ladies at court spoke about the Queen's 'affairs' mentioning Mark Smeaton, a court musician. Henry heard the rumour and it took on a life of its own as his interest in Jane Seymour was increasing.

Jane Seymour's rapid ascent to queenship in 1535–1536, is usually seen as part of the intrigues against Anne Boleyn, assisted by her own family background and station at court. Her father, Sir John Seymour of Wolf Hall in Wiltshire, was a knight who stood high in Henry's regard. His connections and experience had enabled him to place Jane as maid-of-honour to Katherine of Aragon from 1529 until Anne Boleyn's time. Her mother, Lady Margery le Despenser, was the daughter of Sir Henry Wentworth of Suffolk, and Jane could trace her own descent back to Edward III's second son, Lionel of Antwerp. This meant that Jane Seymour and Henry VIII were related as fifth cousins.

But, as with Katherine, to marry Jane, Henry had to first get rid of Anne. In April 1536, Henry took the first step in that process and had Anne investigated.

It was a dangerous scheme and it would have been madness to implicate men in a plot that had no foundation. So the court was given a *very* strong case that implicated not one, but five men, including a gentleman from

Henry's privy chamber, Henry Norris, a young courtier, Mark Smeaton, and none other than her own brother, George.

What sealed her fate was a letter supposedly written by Anne and read aloud in court. The letter had been passed on to Anne's sister-in-law regarding a certain king's impotence. It stated, *'the king was not skilful in copulating with a woman and he had not virtue or power'*.

For a man as vain as Henry, this would have been the last straw. At least, the public statement would certainly have humiliated Henry and there would have been no doubt that Anne could expect the worst possible punishment. And she did. She was charged with high treason, adultery and incest.

The speed with which it all happened is astonishing. On 2nd May she was arrested and sent to the Tower of London, where she was tried before a jury of 27 peers, one of whom was her uncle, the Duke of Norfolk. Two weeks later, she was found guilty.

Anne received her sentence with dignity and watched from her tower window as Mark Smeaton and Henry Norris were hung alongside her brother George. Four days later, on 19th May, she walked calmly to Tower Green amid the jeers of the people. She took her jewels off and handed them to a favourite lady-in-waiting who was sobbing quietly behind her. As silence finally settled over the crowd, she placed her head calmly on the block and was beheaded.

Henry dressed in white for the execution and 10 days later, he married Jane Seymour.

Henry's anger at Anne Boleyn overflowed and he took it out on anyone he could. The week after the execution, he reduced Elizabeth to the same state as Mary. At the same time, at 15 years of age, Henry Fitzroy was married to 14-year-old Lady Mary Howard, the only daughter of Thomas Howard, Duke of Norfolk.

The English people had put up with a lot in the past. They had suffered famine and disease and they had watched as their priests were hung drawn and quartered for their faith. They were too scared to make a move in case they suffered the same fate. But when Henry began to lay heavy taxes followed by dissolving and ransacking valuable jewels and vessels from their churches, (he was in serious need of money by now) they'd had enough. They revolted.

Tenants began to rise against the lords, apprentices left their masters and the number of rebels swelled to 40,000 men, all intent on a battle. When one of Henry's chancellors was pulled off his horse and murdered by a mob, the message was clear and Henry knew he had a serious problem on his hands.

Henry had a few good points but one of them was not conciliation. His reaction was as usual: brutal. In every village or town, monks and abbots were to be executed. Many were hung from their own trees, and among them were many nobles who had spoken out against Henry's actions.

In the subsequent terror, the savagery worked and within a fortnight, the rebellion had stopped, although England was still seething with discontent. But Henry wasn't finished yet. Priests were dragged through the streets and publicly hung as Henry's new adviser, Thomas Cromwell, stood by and watched. And the plundering of churches then went up a notch.

Henry was always short of revenue and the Church properties offered a tempting prize. In England at this time, there were nearly 400 monasteries containing fewer than twelve monks each. The combined rent from their lands alone was a considerable sum. During the summer of 1536, Henry had commissioners tour the country, dissolving the monasteries and transferring the priests and monks to larger houses. Abbeys were robbed and then converted into bakeries, a naval depot, a place to store coal, taverns, stables and even a glass factory. Henry then kept the revenue they produced.

It was during this time that Henry was told his treasured son Henry Fitzroy had died. He'd been sickly for a while with suspected tuberculosis and had died at St James's Palace. With the news, Henry went into meltdown.

Thank goodness for the spring of 1537. Jane Seymour became pregnant and Henry was elated.

As a queen, Jane was said to be formal, gentle and proud. Her only reported involvement in politics was late in 1536 when she asked for pardons for the participants of the revolt against Henry when he had increased the taxes. Henry is said to have rejected this request immediately, reminding her of the fate her predecessor had met when she *"meddled in his affairs"*. After that, seventy more were hanged as traitors and when Norfolk seemed inclined towards compassion, Henry sent word that he desired a larger number of executions. Altogether some 250 were put to death.

Thomas Cromwell handled the dissolution with cold-blooded efficiency. The high nobility and country gentry were allowed to buy the estates that had been confiscated, at a price of course, and many local squires who had once been stewards now bought properties which they had managed for generations. Most of the displaced monks, nearly 10,000 of them, faced their lot with sadness, assisted by substantial pensions with some of them even marrying nuns. The dissolution bought lands into the Crown's possession worth at the time over £100,000 per year and by the sale of the rest, Henry gained another million and a half – a huge sum for those days.

Now, the poor, weak and ailing people, especially in the North, who only had help from the monks, were left destitute. They were to find that the new landlords could be harsher than the clerical predecessors.

On 12th October, St Edward the Confessor's name day, Jane gave birth to a healthy baby boy, the coveted male heir. The name Henry, Duke of Cornwall was quickly rejected, not so surprisingly when you consider the fate of the other babies who had been given the same name, and the tiny child was named Edward. The king wept with joy when he first held the boy.

Twelve days later, Henry heard that Jane, still in confinement, was seriously ill.

Her labour had been difficult and had lasted two days and three nights as the baby was badly positioned. On 24th October, Jane died, most likely from a massive haemorrhage caused by the retention of parts of the placenta in her womb, an oversight of the royal physicians who had banned experienced midwives from the delivery.

As his father had done, Henry went into overdrive into protecting his child. Floors were swept and scrubbed three times a day, food was tested for poison and only selected servants were allowed to touch him.

From the outset, Edward was a healthy baby who suckled strongly and his father was delighted with him. Henry was often observed *"dallying with him in his arms ... and so holding him in a window to the sight and great comfort of the people"*.

In the back of Henry's mind, there must have been the knowledge that he needed more sons. Henry's father was a prime example. He'd had three healthy sons and out of them all, Henry was the only survivor. As Henry dressed in mourning clothes and grieved for Jane, Thomas Cromwell and the Council began looking for a replacement queen for Henry. As they looked, the ulcers on Henry's swollen leg became blocked and for twelve days he lay scared to even breath in case a blood clot entered his lungs. He recovered from this episode, but it was a problem that would reoccur many times in the future.

In the search for a new bride, Cromwell, newly created Earl of Essex, strongly suggested Anne, sister of the Duke of Cleves. Henry was told that she outshone the beautiful Duchess of Milan as *"the golden sun does the silvery moon"*. Henry was given a portrait (painted in a flattering light) but was warned that although she looked beautiful, she could only speak German and apparently had no ear for music. Henry listened to Cromwell and finally agreed that despite her deficiencies, she was worthy of him. At the end of 1539, she was shipped off to England to marry her future husband.

Henry was so excited, he rode to Rochester himself to meet her. When she arrived in England on New Year's Day 1540, all embraces and compliments were forgotten. Henry mumbled a few words and left.

The woman who greeted him was decidedly unattractive. She was tall and thin, slightly pock-marked with a high forehead, heavy-lidded eyes and a pointy chin. His mumbled words to Cromwell were, *"I swear they have brought over a Flanders mare"*. He promptly demanded an annulment and declared he would never consummate the marriage.

But there was no getting out of it. He'd promised the Germans and there was no way that he could insult them without consequences. Anne lasted until 9th July that year. She was given a generous settlement to simply go away including Richmond Palace and Hever Castle, home of Henry's former in-laws, the Boleyns. The marriage was annulled on the grounds that there had been no issue. For some reason, Anne did not seem too upset at all. I'm sure she considered herself lucky that she did not have to suffer the same fate as Anne Boleyn.

In all of this, Cromwell had been the one to arrange the marriage and Henry was not about to forget that little point. By then, Cromwell's career was almost over and he knew it. As Henry seethed, Cromwell was making one last effort to put himself in favour with Henry. And in his sights, he had Margaret Pole 8th Countess of Salisbury.

Not too many things had changed for the Plantagenet's since Henry VII usurped the throne. It was still a dangerous world for them. Henry's father had deleted Edward Plantagenet from the equation but not so his sister, Margaret De La Pole, and her brood.

Margaret was the only surviving daughter of George Plantagenet Duke of Clarence and Isabella Neville. Her husband, Sir Richard De La Pole, had died in 1504 leaving her a widow with five children, a limited amount of inherited land, no salary and no prospects. To ease the dire situation, she devoted her third son Reginald to the Church at a young age, something he resented bitterly his entire life. He saw it as abandonment since his sisters had gone into service and his two other brothers remained with their mother at Syon Abbey with the Brigidine nuns. When Henry VIII came to the throne in 1509, her situation changed dramatically.

An Act of Parliament in 1512 restored some of her brother's lands, along with the earldom of Salisbury, to her and several years later again; she was appointed Governess to Princess Mary. But things began to unravel again for Margaret when Reginald finally broke with the king in 1536 after the 'Boleyn' incident and one year later, he was ordained a cardinal in Rome.

Cromwell's treatment of 68-year-old Margaret can only be called brutal. And let's not let Henry off scot-free. He knew everything that happened in his kingdom and he knew exactly what was going on. Within a couple of years, she had outlived one son who had been executed while another son sat in prison awaiting his trial for treason. She herself was being held in the Tower of London awaiting trial.

For two and a half years she waited. On the morning of 27th May 1541, she was told she was to die within the hour. There was no crime against her but despite her repeated requests to know the charges, she was dragged from her cell and taken to a low wooden block within the precincts of the Tower and in front of 150 witnesses was forced to lie down.

The first blow from the inexperienced executioner made a gash on her shoulder. Ten additional blows were needed to complete the execution. The Calendar of State Papers reports that the executioner was a *"blundering youth"* who *"hacked her head and shoulders to pieces."*

While Cromwell pursued Margaret de La Pole mercilessly, another woman had caught Henry's eye as his frenzy for more heirs continued. At 19 years old, Catherine Howard, Anne Boleyn's first cousin, was a young and attractive lady-in-waiting to Anne of Cleves. Catherine's father, Lord Edmund Howard, was the brother of Anne Boleyn's mother, Lady Elizabeth Howard, and both

Edmund and Elizabeth were the children of Thomas Howard, 2nd Duke of Norfolk. At 22, Catherine had auburn hair and hazel eyes and was the prettiest of Henry's wives. Immediately Henry's spirits revived.

Despite their close familial ties, Anne Boleyn and Catherine Howard had never met. Firstly, Anne was about 15 years older than Catherine. Secondly, the Norfolk family was a tangled collection of cousins (far too many to list here) and, since Catherine was one of many children of a poor younger son, her status was relatively unimportant in the mid-1530s. And she was a descendant of – you guessed it – John of Gaunt.

Third, and perhaps most important, Anne Boleyn had disliked Catherine's father, declaring him conniving, opportunistic, and arrogant. This perhaps affected her relationships with all her Norfolk cousins including Catherine. It had certainly affected her uncle, Duke of Norfolk, who was one of the men who had sent Anne to the gallows.

Henry and Catherine's quick marriage was a mere three weeks after the annulment from Anne of Cleves and reflected Henry's urgency to father more healthy, legitimate sons since he only had Edward. He showered his young bride with jewels, a gift of land and expensive clothes and as an added bonus, he had Cromwell beheaded for treason, heresy and corruption, believing the rumours that Cromwell had been plotting to marry Henry's daughter Mary. Cromwell's dance of death lasted half an hour as his two executioners *"chopped at the Lord Cromwell's head"*. His head was then placed on a spike on London Bridge for the carrion birds to feast on.

By then, Henry was nearly 50 years old and expanding in girth. He weighed around 21 stone or 140 kilograms and suffered from a number of ailments including a foul smelling, festering ulcer on his thigh that had to be drained of pus daily. Catherine soon became aware of his formidable temper as he flew into fits of rage and wouldn't let her into his presence for the first ten days after their marriage.

Catherine was young, wild and tempestuous and she was not very content with her new husband who was three decades older than her. Behind the scenes, gossip travelled fast. Rumour had it that Catherine was not even a virgin at their marriage and that she had even been married previously. And then, rather stupidly, she added fuel to the fire by beginning a romance with Henry's favourite male courtier, Thomas Culpeper, who was distantly related to both Anne Boleyn and Catherine. People had even witnessed her transgressions. Disastrously, Catherine then appointed another handsome man, Francis Dereham, as her personal secretary.

By late 1541, Catherine's indiscretions had become known to Thomas Cranmer, the Archbishop of Canterbury. At first, Henry disbelieved the allegations. Then he remembered that Anne Boleyn and Catherine had been cousins and he requested that Cranmer investigate. Within days, proof was found, along with the confessions of Dereham and Culpeper who had more than likely been tortured first in the Tower and on 10th December 1541, Culpeper was beheaded and Dereham was hung, drawn and quartered. Both heads were placed on top of London Bridge.

After two years of wedded bliss, Catherine was charged with treason and adultery. If Henry had simply annulled their marriage and banished her from court, she would have only been disgraced and impoverished. She may even have been spared execution. But sadly, that was not an option for her. Not in Henry's present frame of mind.

Catherine's family hastily began distancing themselves from her at all costs. At her arrest, virtually every member of the Norfolk family was taken to the Tower, except the duke. He sent a frantic letter to Henry that included insults of all his imprisoned relatives, most importantly the *"abominable deeds"* of both Anne and Catherine. He was certainly an unappealing character but, unlike so many others, he managed to survive in the treacherous Tudor court.

Catherine remained in limbo and in absolute panic until 7th February the next year. When the bill was eventually released, she was condemned to death for failing to disclose her sexual history to the king within twenty days of their marriage. This made her unequivocally guilty and on 13th February, looking pale and terrified, she climbed the scaffold and made a speech describing her punishment as *"worthy and just"*. Her final words were *"I die a Queen, but I would rather have died the wife of Culpeper."*

Henry did not attend the execution. Instead, he held a huge banquet with twenty-six ladies at his private table to celebrate. By this time in his reign, he had begun eating so much that his bed had to be enlarged to a width of seven feet. Henry had developed a binge-eating habit, consisting of a diet of fatty red meats and very few vegetables. His weight had ballooned even more and he was covered in pus-filled boils and suffered from gout. No wonder he had mood swings and a lousy temperament.

Through all of this, Henry still longed for female companionship and one year later, he stood confidently before Catherine Parr, or Kateryn Parr as she preferred to be called. She was a serious little widow at 31-years of age and when Henry proposed marriage to her, he fully expected her to swoon with delight.

Marriage to Henry was a definite improvement in Kateryn's current status as lady-in-waiting to his daughter Mary, but her own credentials weren't too bad either. Kateryn was a descendant of Richard Neville who was himself the grandson of ... come on, you know it ... yes, John of Gaunt. But it wasn't like she could turn him down either. He was after all Henry Tudor, King of England, notorious for his quick temper and sly mood swings and anyone who dared deny him what he wanted would see the inside of the Tower before losing their head.

She would have looked up at the huge man standing before her, as round as he was tall, and seen a sallow 51-year-old man with thinning hair who still thought of himself as a handsome virile young man, a golden-haired God almost, riding and jousting with the best of them, with not a woman in all of England who could resist him. She would have seen swollen lips smiling wetly down at her, not quite hiding his yellow decaying teeth and foul breath, sharp little eyes almost hidden under his fat eyelids and she would have known the reason why he leant heavily on one leg. His other leg was bandaged not quite hiding the yellow pus that bubbled into the dressing and not quite disguising the horrible odour the wound emitted. She would have dreaded the moment he would bend down to kiss her and she would have wondered how she could ever escape. She was, after all, still in mourning after the death of her second husband but more importantly, she was in love with Thomas Seymour, Jane's brother, and she had fully expected to marry him after the suitable mourning period had elapsed.

She showed little enthusiasm at Henry's offer of marriage, (she had after all watched the number of heads falling), but in the end she had no choice but to accept him. She would have shuddered as she smiled modestly back at Henry and she would have known that she was gambling with her life.

From the beginning of the marriage, Kateryn made an attempt to be a good wife. Her face was always wisely masked with concern for Henry and she kept her eyes filled with affection for her husband. She was experienced in nursing cranky old men as she had already nursed two previous husbands on their deathbeds, and she knew what was expected of her. So she nursed Henry's stinking ulcerated leg that grew steadily worse and rubbed balms on them to relieve the pain for the four years of their marriage, until his death.

The brilliant young, handsome king had grown old and wrathful in his advancing years. The constant pain in his leg made him bad-tempered with anyone who crossed him and at all times, people weighed up replies to his questions, never sure if he would change his opinion at a moment's notice. It was much safer to simply agree with him on everything.

At the time of his marriage with Kateryn Parr, the hostility between England and Scotland still smouldered along the border. When James V's mother, Henry's sister, died, the smouldering flickered once more into flame. The Scots made an alliance with France and defeated the English at Halidon Rig only to lose nearly 10,000 men under Norfolk's attack. News came that at the second battle at Flodden, James was killed, leaving the kingdom to an infant of one week, Mary the Queen of Scots. Henry was so jubilant that all the heaviness of his past wives left him. Temporarily.

At once the Scottish child became the focus of his struggle with Scotland and Henry claimed her as a bride for his own son and heir, Edward. But the Scots Queen-Mother was a French princess, Mary of Guise, and the pro-Catholic party declined the 'offer' from Henry. Talks began for marrying the infant Mary to a French prince instead and of course, Henry was furious at the insult.

By now, Henry was in a grave position. Without a single ally, he was faced with the possibility of an invasion from both France and Scotland. The cost would be massive and the crisis called for more taxes on the English people. Those who owned lands worth more than 40 shillings per annum were expected to contribute as their duty to their king. They dared not refuse or else they would find they had accommodation booked for them in the Tower for three months. To set a good example, Henry mortgaged his own estates.

Still seething from the Scottish insult to his betrothal suggestion, Henry ordered Edward's uncle, Edward Seymour Earl of Hertford, Jane Seymour's elder brother, to invade Scotland. Of course, the wrath of the king meant death and Seymour responded with the most savage campaign ever launched by the English against the Scots. The war, which continued into young Edward's eventual reign, has become known as 'The Rough Wooing' where 243 villages and monasteries were destroyed.

By 1546, Henry was 55 years old. He had become morbidly obese and ill and as a consequence, he had become harsh, egotistical and cruel. As a result, this enormous man was a nightmare for his advisers.

Despite his ill health, he made his usual progress that year through Surrey to Windsor. But by November, when he finally arrived in London, he would never leave the capital again. In these last few months, one question dominated all minds: the heir to the kingdom was known, a child of nine, but who would be the power behind the throne? Norfolk or Edward Seymour?

A sudden unexpected answer was given. Norfolk had been heard talking stupidly of a time when the king would be dead and he had mentioned his own personal descent from Edward I. The inference was that his name should be added to the list of claimants for the throne.

Henry remembered years ago, Norfolk had been put forward as a possible heir to the throne, and his son, the Duke of Surrey, had been suggested as one of the possible husbands for Henry's daughter, Mary. Their thoughtless words set Henry's mind working. With his suspicions aroused, he acted quickly. On December 12th, 1546, Norfolk and his son were arrested for treason and sent to the Tower. By mid-January, Surrey was executed and Norfolk was condemned to death at the end of the month.

It was Henry's last declaration. He had swollen to the point of bursting. He had become huge and out of his large face with double chins glowed small piggish eyes. The handsome man who in his youth had led armies, excelled in jousts and hunts had become so bloated he could not move.

What he didn't know was that every night as he slept, Edward Seymour, Duke of Hertford, young Prince Edward's uncle, paced up and down the gallery outside, scheming. He did not have to scheme for long. Shortly before midnight on 28th January 1547, the king died and as fortune would have it, Norfolk kept his head.

It is a terrible blot on Henry's record that his reign should be remembered for his cruelness and the number of executions. Two queens, two of his chief ministers, Sir Thomas More, numerous abbots, monks, and hundreds of ordinary people who dared to resist him, were put to death.

Almost every member of the nobility in whom royal blood ran perished on the scaffold at Henry's command. Roman Catholic and Calvinists alike were burned for heresy and religious treason. The sufferings of devout men and women, the use of torture and the savage penalties for even paltry crimes, stand in shocking contrast to the enlightenment England had expected when they welcomed the energetic, charismatic 19-year-old to the throne.

Financially, his reign was a near disaster for the English economy. Henry had inherited the staggering amount of £375,000,000 by today's standards, from his father but sadly for Henry, his vast wealth was exhausted by the mid-1520s due to war and his ambitions in Europe. After this, he had to resort to taking possession of monastic lands worth £36,000,000 (again by today's standards) a year. Henry expanded the Royal Navy from 5 ships to 53 and he loved palaces. Lots of them. He began with a dozen and died with 55 in which he hung 2,000 expensive tapestries and took enormous pride in showing off his collection of weapons, which included exotic archery equipment and 6,500 handguns. Taking all of this into account, it is not surprising that Henry died in debt.

Two weeks after his death, a solemn 9-year-old little boy walked down the aisle of Westminster Abbey.

EDWARD VI

Born 1537
Reign 1547 - 1553

Henry VIII's final extensive will, made on 30th December 1546, named sixteen executors who were to act as Edward's council. Henry did not want a Protector or a Regent for his son. He simply wanted a Regency Council to rule collectively for Edward until he reached the age of 18. Henry bequeathed his crown to his son and then to his son's children. After Edward, the throne would go to Mary and then to Elizabeth and then it would jump to his youngest sister Mary, Duchess of Suffolk, then her children. The will totally excluded the Scottish family of Stuarts into which his older sister Margaret had married. Henry's will was very exact in every detail. It was read, 'dry stamped' and sealed on 27th January 1547 when Henry was past speech, and within hours, he was dead. He just didn't sign it.

Before anyone knew it, Edward Seymour, Earl of Somerset one of Edward's uncles, had taken over and informed Kateryn Parr that she was to hand her jewels over to his wife. No doubt after having done a deal with some of the executors, thirteen of the appointed sixteen (the others being conveniently absent at the time) agreed to appoint Somerset as the Protector effective immediately. For Somerset, it had all been rather easy.

Henry's hearse was nine stories high and the road to Windsor had to be repaired to accommodate it. His ever-so-flattering wax effigy was displayed to the crowds dressed in crimson velvet adorned with jewels while his real body, already decomposing, was lowered into the choir vault of St George Chapel.

Somerset's relationship with his younger brother Thomas Seymour, who has been described as a *"worm in the bud"*, was always tense. It didn't improve at all when Thomas demanded that he be made governor to the young king, who was after all, his nephew as well.

Somerset tried to buy his brother off with a barony and an appointment to the Lord Admiralship, as well as a seat on the Privy Council, but Thomas would have nothing to do with it. He was after a far greater share of power than that and his plotting began in earnest as he began to ingratiate himself with Edward.

He began by telling him that Somerset held the purse strings far too tightly. It was making him a *"beggarly king"* and he urged Edward to get rid of his uncle within two years and *"bear rule as other kings do"*. But Edward was still far too young and innocent and he did not take the bait.

When this attempt failed, Thomas's next step was to write Edward a letter requesting permission to marry Kateryn Parr, Henry's widow. It was a clever, conniving plan since her household also included Henry's great niece, 11-year-old Lady Jane Grey, and Henry's 13-year-old daughter, Elizabeth. The letter was obviously dictated by Thomas for Edward's signature and when Somerset found out about it, he flew into a rage.

But it was already too late. The letter had been signed, sealed and delivered and the couple had not wasted any time with a lengthy courtship. They'd headed straight to the altar.

Thomas was not the only one with designs for an improvement in his personal situation. Three months after the coronation, Somerset began building his own palace at the top of the Strand, removing three bishops' palaces and a parish church to make room for it. Regardless of this, it seems Somerset didn't go out of favour with the council.

Perhaps it was because it was at a time when Scotland needed to know who was in charge. During Henry's reign, Scotland had turned its nose up at a proposed marriage treaty between their young Queen Mary to England's young King Edward preferring the French dauphin and the 'Rough Wooing' had begun.

Now with a 9-year-old on the English throne, England was feeling a little nervous about the relationship. By late spring, Somerset took matters into his own hands and troops were assembled and war was declared against Scotland. Again.

On 31st August, Somerset's infantry crossed the border at Musselburgh while cannons were fired from English ships off the coast. 10,000 Scots were killed that day and dead bodies lay strewn over the fields in the red mud known as Pinkie Cleugh. Some survivors had fled to Edinburgh and others hid in bogs with their mouths barely above the water line. But the Scots were not about to submit. Not by a long shot.

As Scotland regrouped, Somerset returned to England in a hurry, fearing firstly a French invasion on the southern coast and secondly, another scheme by his younger brother Thomas. If I had been Somerset, I would have been worried, too, because Thomas had still not abandoned his hope of advancement. What Somerset found shocked him.

With Kateryn Parr heavily pregnant, Somerset discovered that his brother, dressed only in his nightgown, had begun chasing Princess Elizabeth at night as she giggled delightedly during the playful romps. It soon became obvious that Elizabeth was smitten by her handsome uncle who spanked her playfully on her buttocks during the frolicking. Very soon, Kateryn had Elizabeth removed from the household to Waltham Abbey, near Cheshunt, but later had her sent on to Hadfield House. Months later on 31st August 1548, Kateryn died after delivering a daughter and Thomas renewed his attentions towards Elizabeth.

Rumours abounded that he had full intentions of marrying her: that is until Somerset heard about it. It was the last straw. By then, the regency council was becoming aware of Thomas's bid for power.

Perhaps we should give Somerset a little credit because it seemed he tried to save his brother from ruin, calling a council meeting so that Thomas might explain himself. Stupidly, Thomas did not show. Very soon, he would go one step too far.

On the night of 16th January 1549, for reasons that are not clear, (perhaps to abduct the young king into his own custody), Thomas was caught trying to break into the Edward's apartments at Hampton Court Palace. He entered the privy garden and woke one of Edward's pet spaniels. In response to the dog's barking, Thomas did the most appalling thing. He shot and killed it. The next day, he was arrested and sent to the Tower of London.

The incident, being caught outside the king's bedroom, at night, with a loaded pistol, was understandably interpreted in the most threatening light. It even cast suspicion on Elizabeth's involvement in the incident and the council sent agents to question everyone associated with Thomas, including Elizabeth.

Upon realising that Thomas would probably be executed, Elizabeth was noticeably distressed, trying to free herself and her servants from suspicion. For weeks she was interrogated, and the council found itself engaged in a sharply defined game of wits with the 15-year-old girl. She appeared to be perceptive and defiant but eventually the embarrassing details of the flirtatious incidents with Thomas came to light.

On 22nd February, the council officially accused Thomas of thirty-three charges of treason. He was convicted and condemned to death and executed one month later. Through it all, Edward seemed very indifferent to his uncle's death.

From this difficult experience, Elizabeth seems, for the first time in her young life, to have become fully aware of the serious, even deadly, nature of her succession right to the throne. When she made her first public appearance at court eighteen months later, she was just turning 17 and the young girl who attended was a very different person from the one who left.

Subdued and silent, this Elizabeth was dressed in a simple, drab dress with plain and unadorned hair, contrasting sharply with the other ladies who dressed in bright showy splendour, almost as if she was trying to live down something. It was an amazing transformation. In this supposed show of self-rehabilitation to restore her good name and reputation, she was largely successful.

In the short span of twenty-two months, from May 1547 until March 1549, when she was just 13, 14, and 15 years old, she had experienced the sexually charged flirtation with Thomas, (her sometimes *"uncle,"* sometimes *"stepfather"*), the unexpected death of her stepmother in childbirth, Thomas's sudden arrest and execution, and even herself accused of treason, through association with him. There can be no doubt at all that these experiences would have made a lasting impression on Elizabeth, and affected her personally. Some things you just don't get over.

Edward had begun to grow up as well in those years and he began to understand more and more government business although how much involvement he had in making decisions is not sure. His greatest influence was in matters of religion, preferring to take on strongly protestant ideals.

It would have been a nervous time for England. The treasury was empty and it was necessary to make a sort of peace with France. For three years in a row, the harvest was poor and the price of English woollens had diminished due to a glut in cloth in Europe. Money had lost half of its value with the death of Henry VIII and flour had doubled in price. In the summer of that year, the sweating sickness had even returned with a vengeance.

Sixteen seems to have been a dangerous age for the Tudors. Edward's uncle Arthur had died at almost sixteen and his illegitimate half-brother Henry Fitzroy had died at nearly seventeen. 16th century illness was a terrifying thing and it could often strike down a young man or woman who was otherwise in peak physical condition. The cold that Edward caught in February 1552 soon gave way to an agonising series of physical complaints described as measles and smallpox.

In a panic, his advisers moved him from palace to palace, trying the cleaner air of Greenwich, away from the dust and dirt of the city as well as inflicting a series of increasingly desperate medical 'remedies' on the young man, all of which prolonged his suffering, and plunged him into ever-worsening pain.

Those who hadn't seen him for months were shocked by his appearance. He was terribly thin and, oddly, his left shoulder seemed higher than his right. It was obvious Edward was suffering.

Thanks to his doctors, Edward's last few months in this life were positively hellish and lacking comfort or relief. As well as subjecting Edward to progressively crueller and riskier medical treatments, Edward's government were also resorting to dishonest and desperate attempts to hide the truth of the king's deterioration from the public and, in particular, from his sisters.

By Christmas, Edward was clearly dying and he began drafting a letter for his succession. His fetid sputum was sometimes green, sometimes black, but he was still capable of a Tudor tantrum. Edward knew that with his eldest sister Mary on the throne, she would have full control over the restoration of Catholicism with the same militant efficiency he had devoted to Protestantism. That, he would not allow.

Time would show us that he had underestimated Mary enormously on that point, but his general assessment was correct. It was this fear that tortured Edward as he lay dying. Weak of body, but sound in mind, Edward conspired fully with John Dudley, the Duke of Northumberland, and other members of the Council in disinheriting both of his sisters. Since Edward was the last of the pureblood Tudor males, he knew the Crown would have to pass to a woman. He also knew that he could not remove Mary from the succession solely on the basis of her religion (that would not be tried in England until the next century). He also realised that he could not bar Mary from her inheritance, without also doing the same to Elizabeth.

Despite all the affection that had once allegedly been between them, Edward displayed not one iota of hesitation in eliminating them both from his will. During his father's reign, Acts of Parliament had declared the marriages of both Mary and Elizabeth's mothers to their father illegal and it was this technicality that Edward declared made them both unentitled to inherit the throne when he died. Illegitimacy, after all, had been used as the excuse to sweep poor Edward V off the throne by his uncle Richard in 1483, why not try the same tactic now? His inheritance, he declared, would skip over his two half-sisters and pass instead to their second cousin, Lady Jane Grey, now rather conveniently married to John Dudley, the Duke of Northumberland's son, Guildford Dudley.

At 15 years old, Jane Grey was prim, devout, intellectually brilliant and ferociously Protestant. She was, in many ways, a female version of Edward. With Northumberland's assistance, she would be the ideal candidate to oust Mary from her position as heiress to the throne. Next after her, Edward named Jane's sisters Katherine and Mary Grey and finally Margaret Stanley Clifford, the daughter of Lady Jane Grey's aunt. Until Jane came of age, Edward nominated Frances, Duchess of Suffolk, his first cousin, and the daughter of Henry VIII's favourite younger sister, Mary.

This rather bizarre, complicated scheme shocked everyone into silence. Not so Northumberland. He had the cat in the bag with an innocent daughter-in-law as queen and his son by her side to help her rule England. He could hardly control his excitement. On everyone's lips was the question *"What will Princess Mary do when she finds out?"*

As death approached, Edward altered his will even further in such a way as to favour Jane exclusively because the marriage of either Mary or Elizabeth to a foreigner might undermine both *"the laws of this realm"* and *"his proceedings in religion"*. Edward regarded Jane as his only acceptable successor. Like himself, she had absorbed the *"godly learning"* of the Cambridge-trained evangelical reformers and only she could be trusted to carry forward his Reformation towards Protestantism.

Whether Edward's disinheritance of his two sisters was legal or not, hardly seems to matter. 16th century law was a minefield of interpretation, loopholes and confusion and often outright lies. Even though it meant over-turning the terms and conditions of his own father's unsigned will, which had named Mary as next-in-line if Edward died without children, and even though his decision seemed harsh, it was not strictly illegal. As the king, he had every right to decide whom he passed the throne to when he died and it was the new monarch's will which mattered, not the old one.

Either way, with Mary and Elizabeth stricken from the list and Jane's succession seemingly secured, the young man slipped back into the lengthy process of dying.

The imperial ambassador later heard that during the last two weeks of his life, Edward was forced to lie flat on his back at all times and vomited up everything he ate. As the numerous diseases and ailments began to consume him, gangrene set in on his toes and fingers. The medical treatments subjected to him had caused his skin to deform and blacken, whilst his limbs swelled and his hair began to fall out. Emaciated, ravaged by illness and in constant physical agony, Edward, the only son of Henry VIII and Jane Seymour, died on 6th July at Greenwich Palace in the arms of his childhood friend, Henry Sidney and in the company of his doctors.

No one knows now, or knew then, exactly what it was that led to Edward's horrific natural death. The Venetian ambassador to London believed it must be tuberculosis, since only that could explain the wasting away of the king's physique. Rumours that Northumberland had slowly poisoned him are part and parcel of the habitual paranoia of 16th century politics and hold no more truth than the idea that Anne Boleyn poisoned Katherine of Aragon, which had been suggested.

Two of his modern biographers, the late Jennifer Loach and Chris Skid-more, have offered slightly varying explanations. Loach, in her Yalepublished biography of Edward, suggested that Edward had contracted acute bronchopneumonia, which lead to a suppurating pulmonary infection and either lung collapse, kidney failure or septicaemia, the same disease which had killed his mother, if in very different circumstances. Chris Skidmore, whose work as a student at Oxford formed the basis for his biography of Edward, suggested that the young king had simply been spectacularly unlucky to contract measles and then smallpox in 1552, the year before his death, and before he had time to recover from either, his immune system was so weakened, that he contracted tuberculosis which would later kill him. All of it aggravated, of course, by the medicine his physicians and advisers chose to use on him, initially to save his life, but latterly to keep him alive long enough until he had authorised Jane's succession instead of Mary's. In any case, it was a horrific way for the young man to die.

Charming, brilliant, athletic, handsome and musically gifted, Edward could, and did, show himself to be ruthless and cold like his father in his attempt to create a Protestant monarchy in the British Isles.

As Edward's disfigured corpse was prepared for burial in the Henry VII Chapel at Westminster Abbey, the great crisis of *'The Nine Days' Queen'* and Mary Tudor's improbable, but heroic, triumph was about to begin.

For Lady Jane Grey, that week in 1553 was not going to be a good one.

LADY JANE GREY

THE NINE-DAY QUEEN

Born 1536
Reign 1553

Lady Jane Grey has become an iconic Tudor victim: virginal and sweet and known as 'The Nine-day Queen'. This is the story about the granddaughter of Henry VIII's younger, and favourite sister, Mary Tudor. Jane was a tiny, red-haired, red-lipped slip of a girl who accepted her new role wearing platform shoes to give her more height. Her complexion was freckled and her lovely smile showed off perfectly white teeth. However, within nine days, she was imprisoned by Mary Tudor, tried and convicted of treason, and at only 16 years old, through no fault of her own, she was beheaded on February 12th, 1554.

When I began my research, I assumed there would be very little to tell about this seemingly innocent girl, the image of female helplessness, who perched on the edge of the throne for such a short time. After all, what can you do in only nine days? But as my interest grew, so did a juicy story.

The traditional story is that Lady Jane Grey was born at Bradgate Park in Leicestershire in 1536. It was a magical place, surrounded by forests where red deer still roam today. She was the daughter of Henry VIII's younger niece,

Frances, and her husband Henry Grey, Duke of Suffolk, and in a time of religious turmoil, she was a Protestant from birth. When she was just 2 days old, she was already pushed out of the limelight with the birth of her cousin Edward. Not wanting to miss out on the royal celebrations, her father left to go to Court.

Jane's mother, Frances, bore a strong resemblance to her uncle Henry and was a stout, bejewelled woman who was determined to have her own way and greedy for power and riches. She ruled her husband and her daughters tyrannically and, in the case of the latter, often cruelly. A Tudor trait, it would seem.

Supposedly, Jane grew up a bullied child, beaten repeatedly by her unloving and greedy mother but by the time Edward was dying, Jane was an exceptionally well-educated young lady who shared her parents' intense religious convictions and had snubbed gifts from Mary Tudor, a professed Catholic.

John Dudley, Duke of Northumbria, was an ambitious man. He had been a trusted friend of Henry VIII and had even been nominated as one of the sixteen executors of Henry's will. And as such, he was a staunch supporter of Edward with considerable power over him. With so much power in his hands, everyone was very wary of him. John Dudley organised Edward's education, chose his friends and influenced him in many ways that made most of the nobles sit up and take notice. Some had even suggested that it had been Dudley who had coerced Edward to nominate Lady Jane Grey in his will instead of Mary. And they may have been right. He would also have known that if either Mary or Elizabeth were to take the crown from her, he would lose his job, and probably his head as well. So as Edward's health worsened, Dudley began to panic a little. Then a plan began to formulate in his mind.

Jane Grey was an innocent, unmarried 15-year-old and there was Dudley, a court wise, experienced advisor to the king, with two eligible unmarried sons, the eldest being Lord Guildford Dudley. All he had to do was hint to Jane's parents that their daughter could be the first eligible female in the line of succession to the throne and that Jane should marry his son to help her rule the country. He knew full well that with his son by Lady Jane's side during her reign, there was no end to the power their family would have.

It didn't take too much convincing and Frances agreed wholeheartedly, sure that this would endear her daughter to Edward.

Most young girls dream of a fairy tale wedding. They dream of that first kiss. That first chaste look and that first promise of everlasting love. For Jane, this wasn't to be a fairy tale wedding of her dreams at all. There was no courtship and no romancing and because of Edward's ill health, the wedding took place in a hurry. On 25th May 1553, wearing a gown of gold and silver brocade embroidered with diamonds and pearls borrowed from the royal Master of the Wardrobe, Jane married a man she barely knew. At the same ceremony, John Dudley's daughter Catherine, married the Earl of Huntingdon.

Jane found she disliked her in-laws perhaps more than she disliked her own parents. Instead of moving in with them, she moved in to a former monastery that her parents were converting.

Jane's mother-in-law was not happy at all with the arrangement. She told Jane that as Edward was dying, she must hold herself in readiness. She could be named as his heir at any moment. Jane said that this was the first she knew of it and accused the Dudleys of lying. They in turn accused the Greys of deliberately keeping the newlyweds apart.

Such petty conflict was the beginning of rougher waters ahead. In the end, there was no reason why Jane should not be with her husband and she resignedly moved into the Dudley residence, Durham House.

At the time, we wonder if Jane actually had any idea of Dudley's plans to make her queen. Even if she did, there was nothing she could do about it anyway. She was quite literally, trapped.

Jane was barely married for six weeks when Edward died and sure enough, he named Jane as his heir to the throne in place of his Catholic sister Mary Tudor.

Dudley had obviously spent a great deal of time planning exactly what he would do. When he heard of Edward's death, Dudley bullied the council to reject Princess Mary for three reasons. Firstly, it had been Edward's dying wish that Lady Jane Grey should be the Queen. Secondly, there was her mother's marriage annulment from Henry VIII to consider. And lastly, there was the matter of her religion: All valid and convincing reasons.

The Council agreed to keep the king's death quiet for a few days and sent a letter to Mary telling her how ill her brother was and that he wished to see her. Dudley's plan was to seize Mary en route and take her to the tower as a prisoner.

Mary fell for the trap and immediately planned her trip to London to see Edward. Fortunately for her, along the way she heard that her brother had died two days previous. She halted long enough to send a letter straight back to the council on 9th July stating that she was the rightful heir to the throne and asking why she had not been informed of her brother's death.

In the meantime, the council had summoned Jane to London.

On her first day, the earls of Arundel, Huntington and Pembroke, along with the Marquis of Northampton, greeted her. They knelt before her and kissed her hand and Jane blushed with embarrassment. Confused, she was led into the Chamber of State in a formal procession and informed by Dudley that the king's dying wish was that she should take the throne after him.

Jane was stunned. She trembled from head to toe as she stood speechless before breaking into tears. Her stomach must have been clenched in fear. Through the sobs she cried, *"The crown is not my right and pleaseth me not. The Lady Mary is the rightful heir."*

Regardless of her protestations, the following morning Jane was dressed in the green and white of the Tudors and her husband was adorned with white and gold. Between 3 and 4 o'clock on the afternoon of 10th February, a parade of barges took Jane and her attendants to the Tower where the crown jewels were placed on her head and her apartments prepared for her.

As she sailed past, the people along the shores were silent. They had only just learned that day that Edward had died and now, here was a young unknown cousin claiming the throne. She must have seen the fear in everyone's eyes that another fearsome family war was about to be unleashed on them.

Unfortunately for Jane, it seemed the country did not share Edward's love for the Dudleys. It also seemed that at least nine-tenths were in Mary's favour. Not only that, but since female rule was considered unnatural, it was assumed that Jane's husband and her father-in-law would take effective command. Leaving the widely hated Dudleys ruling England.

The Marquees of Winchester knelt to present the keys of the Tower to Jane, but Dudley quickly stepped forward and took them himself, making it clear who was the power behind the throne. Guns rang out in salute and silk flags waved in the bright afternoon sunshine as Jane proceeded to the White Tower. Like several of her ancestors, she would never leave again.

Inside the Tower, Jane sat silently amongst the councillors as they argued on top of each other, each voice louder than the next. Finally, in the mayhem, it was Winchester who stood up and bellowed for quiet. In the silence, he walked forward and handed the crown to Jane and insisted she wear it *"to see how it fitted"*.

It was with trepidation that Jane took the crown. As she placed it on her head, everyone breathed a sigh of relief. It was only after everyone had left the room that her husband showed his true colours. He stood in front of her and stated that he would be the king, not just her consort.

For a timid 16-year-old who had only been married for two months and a crowned queen for half a day, it must have been with exceptional strength that she steadfastly refused. It was probably then that Jane realised her royal blood was being used to maintain Dudley's control of England. She was outraged and angry and as a Tudor herself, she was as proud of her royal background as she had every right to be. The arrogant Dudleys had no right to use her.

Distressed, her husband ran from the room and returned with his mother who ranted at Jane for over an hour. All to no avail. She stood her ground. He would only be a Duke as she had proclaimed earlier.

On Jane's third day as queen, Mary had heard the news and was gathering supporters outside of Suffolk. As determined as Dudley was that Jane should have the throne, Mary was just as determined to have the throne for herself.

That evening, a messenger delivered a letter from Mary that had come to the Tower for Jane. Mary had declared herself the rightful Queen and asked for no bloodshed. The letter was read aloud and was followed by silence.

Jane did not reply and Mary continued her march towards London.

There is little recorded of what Jane did between 10th and 12th. She spent most of the two days locked away, sick with stress. On day six, the 13th, it was clear that the people did not support Jane and they wanted Mary as their queen. The council met and decided that Jane's father should go to lead the troops but because of his old age, Dudley was sent instead with a troop of 600 men, carrying an odd assortment of weapons that he had gathered together the day before. Crowds pushed to watch the men leave but no one wished him well. Instead, they cried out for Mary. After they left, Jane ordered the gates locked and the keys brought to her.

By the 7th day, no one knew what to do. Jane's father and Jane's mother-in-law argued bitterly over whether Guilford Dudley should be made king and Jane's eyes were red from crying. In the middle of it came news that the country outside the Tower was refusing to take arms up against Mary.

By mid-morning on Jane's 8th day, it was obvious that everything was hopeless. All but two of Jane's council had left her to save their necks. That evening at around 5 pm, Mary was publicly proclaimed the Queen and London erupted in joy. Everyone was celebrating by drinking to the health of Mary and lighting bonfires in the streets outside the Tower.

That night, as Jane sat alone and frightened, her father came and held his hand out to her. With a trembling voice full of emotion, he told her softly to step down from the throne. *"You are no longer queen,"* he told her. Crying gratefully, Jane hugged him and asked, *"Can I go home now?"* He did not answer. If only things had been that simple.

John Dudley's supporters had melted away but he was not subdued that easily. He had ridden out to take the field against Mary. Again, there were no supporters cheering him on and a few days later he returned. But this time, it was as Mary's prisoner. He would later be tried for treason and executed on the 22nd of August.

Mary arrived in London wearing purple velvet trimmed with gold and a chain encrusted with gems to the cheers of everyone. When she arrived at the Tower, Dudley's supporters were already on their knees. She kissed each one of them on the cheek and said sweetly *"You are my prisoner"*. In that promise, she included Jane, her husband and her father. The reign of Queen Jane was over.

Jane had not wanted the throne, but in taking it she had been guilty of treason although Mary never treated Jane as a prisoner. While waiting for her trial, Jane was well looked after and allowed to walk the gardens within the Tower precincts with her two maids. She was also offered her life in return for her agreeing to follow the Catholic faith. As expected, Jane refused. While her father Suffolk was pardoned, Jane and her husband were tried for high treason in November 1553. Jane pleaded guilty and was solemnly sentenced to death.

While Jane waited in the Tower, there would be a rebellion instigated by Thomas Wyatt, which we will read more about later, but the writing was on the wall. On 11th February, Jane was ready to die. Early that morning, a panel of matrons came to examine her to make sure she was not with child. Perhaps if she was, Mary may have spared her. But she was not.

On 12th February 1554, she put on the same black dress she had worn at her trial and stood at the window as Guildford Dudley was led away weeping to Tower Hill where he was to be executed. Not long after, she watched the cart come back with his body and head wrapped in white cloths. Then she saw the headsman return from the Tower and she knew it was her turn.

Jane walked to the scaffold on the arm of her gaoler, calm and brave, with her ladies-in-waiting following behind, in floods of tears. She climbed the steps and spoke to the crowd. She said she had been guilty of taking the throne but guiltless in wanting it. *"I die a true Christian woman,"* she ended before kissing the Abbot goodbye. The headsman tried to help her untie her gown but she refused. He then knelt and asked her forgiveness for what he had to do, and she willingly gave it. *"I pray you do it quickly,"* she begged and then she laid her head on the block. Seconds later the axe came down and it was over.

Her father followed them two days later for assisting Thomas Wyatt in his rebellion. In March, Wyatt would also lose his head. It was a troubling start to Mary's reign.

It isn't hard to picture a beautiful summer's day and imagine the sound of horses thundering by with the news that Jane would be Queen. And no one will ever know how England would have turned out under the rule of Queen Jane. One could only hope that it would have turned out less 'Bloody' than under the rule of her cousin Mary.

As it turned out, England would soon see that Mary had quite a bit of her father, Henry VIII, in her and not her gentle mother, after all.

MARY 1

Born 1516
Reign 1553 - 1558

When we think back about Mary, most of us will agree that she is mostly remembered for her consuming passion in restoring Catholicism to England after the short reign of her brother Edward. This passion earned her the title of 'Bloody Mary' during her short rule of five years. During that time, she had over 280 religious rebels burned at the stake, which earned her that title.

In her youth, Mary was regarded as a beautiful woman although a precocious child. She could read and write Latin and Greek and was doted on by her father, Henry VIII, who had potential future marriages negotiated for her. When only 2 years old, she was promised to the Dauphin, the infant son of King Francis I of France but after three years, the contract was withdrawn. At the age of 6, she was instead contracted to marry her 22-year-old first cousin, the Holy Roman Emperor Charles V. However again, within a few years, Charles broke off the engagement with Henry's agreement. Henry had also offered her to James V of Scotland, but James' French mother swiftly rejected this proposal as well, much to Henry's anger.

Mary's life was one of defiance and despair. She was well schooled in regal customs and educated by the best scholars but the fallout from her father's marriage to Anne Boleyn very nearly destroyed her. Beneath her brave exterior, was an anxious woman prone to debilitating illnesses in the glare of a fickle court.

By 1533, when her father had annulled his marriage to her mother Katherine of Aragon, Anne Boleyn was pregnant with his child and Mary's mother had been demoted to Dowager Princess of Wales. At the same time, Mary was proclaimed illegitimate.

As we know, another daughter was delivered to Henry, a daughter Elizabeth, and the line of ill-fated wives of Henry began. In between marriages, Mary acted as hostess although she was often sick with irregular menstruation and depression. Henry's last wife, Kateryn Parr, convinced Henry to return Mary and Elizabeth to the line of succession, placing them after his son Edward, born to Jane Seymour who died in childbirth.

By Edward's death, the sisters had not seen each other for five years. Even if they had, there would not have much in common and any get-togethers would have been tense, considering their very different religious beliefs.

The two sisters' relationship was complicated. They both had been influenced and changed by politics and they had both suffered similar circumstances of alienation and disinheritance from their father. On the surface though, everyone was cordial and amiable.

As the girls grew older, after the death of their father, they found they had even less in common. The division between them was less whether they really liked each other personally and more about their political alliances. Mary was aware that Elizabeth was the darling of the Protestants even though outwardly Elizabeth pretended devotion to her. Through all of it, Mary never trusted Elizabeth and always kept her under close guard.

At first, Mary was magnanimous towards Elizabeth and I can only imagine that this was due to relief that after so many uncertain years, her dream had come true and she was, in fact, the Queen. But even then, doubt and suspicion were creeping in. Mary would have known full well that *being* the queen and *staying* the queen were two different issues. Doubt would have hit her like a lightning bolt when she rode into London with Elizabeth riding in place of honour by her side as the jubilant crowds cheered, not just for her, but also for her younger sister. She would have suddenly been aware that she was 37, unmarried, almost too thin with a small mouth and piercing eyes. Beside her was the quietly confident 20-year-old Elizabeth with youth on her side, who was carefully playing the obedient sister. Up until then, she had openly held Elizabeth's hand at public ceremonies. It was never to happen again.

Suddenly for Mary it was vital that she find herself a husband and produce an heir. If not, it would mean that Elizabeth would succeed her to the throne at her death and Protestantism would win out. That was something that she could not let happen at any cost. A few prospective suitors were mentioned but her cousin Charles V of Spain convinced her to marry his only son, Philip. Apparently on viewing a full-length portrait of him, she declared herself desperately and madly in love with him.

The marriage was as unpopular in Spain as it was in England where ugly stories passed from mouth to mouth of Spanish marauding troops. Philip's courtiers refused to go to a *"chilly land of barbarous heretics"* and England feared that the marriage would make them dependent on the Hapsburgs. There were people in England who opposed Mary's Catholicism but what they feared more was Mary's proposed marriage to the Spaniard who would undoubtedly have an influence on English politics. Neither outcome seemed pleasant.

When Mary insisted on marrying Philip, all hell broke loose. Only one year before, the people greeted Mary with cheers and smiles. Now they pelted her with snowballs.

Thomas Wyatt the Younger was the son of the poet Sir Thomas Wyatt who had secretly been in love with Anne Boleyn, possibly even had an affair with, if some stories are to be believed. Wyatt the Younger was raised Catholic and his godfather, the Duke of Norfolk, had a significant influence on his upbringing. At 16 years old, he had developed an aversion to the Spanish that stemmed from experiences with the Spanish Inquisition, while accompanying his father to Spain. And he wasn't the only one. It seemed everyone had an aversion to the Spanish. So when he learned of Mary's decision to marry Philip of Spain, he came to a momentous decision and began making plans to rid England of her. Unfortunately for Elizabeth, he wrote her a letter stating his support for her along with details of his plans to head a rebellion against Mary.

Wyatt proved himself to be a popular leader, and those who had concerns of their own regarding Mary's marriage, soon joined him. Before long, Wyatt was commanding 4,000 men and his command headquarters were set up in Rochester.

In a world where spying was rife if you wanted to further yourself in a Tudor court, it didn't take long for Mary to become aware of Wyatt's plan. Initially, she offered a pardon to his followers if they retreated peacefully to their homes within twenty-four hours. Thomas Wyatt would have none of it and openly encouraged his followers to stay put. He told them that there was imminent support from France and they believed him.

Of course, it was all a lie. They were on their own and Wyatt knew it.

But he wasn't the only one lying. Almost immediately, Mary had changed her mind. She had offered to meet with Wyatt to discuss his demands only to give herself time to gather troops of her own. He was a disloyal traitor in her eyes and he needed to be treated as such. A lucrative reward of a valuable sum of land was offered to anyone who handed Wyatt over to her and by January, over 20,000 men had volunteered their help. Wyatt was now a wanted man and his plan for a March commencement had to be brought forward in a hurry. It was a decision he would regret.

January was the worst month in terms of weather. The roads they planned to use were almost unusable due to the rain. Carriages carrying equipment from Kent to London lost their wheels in the mud and Wyatt's men had to leave behind precious equipment that would have helped dramatically during the fighting. The roads to the city were also narrow and made it very easy for any small force to defend the imposing gates to the city. It would also make it impossible for a surprise attack. Secrecy was a big issue and many nobles with their own lands and titles in jeopardy, passed any information they had on to the government. All the odds seemed stacked up against Wyatt.

Upon entering Southwark on his way to London, Wyatt and his companions soon discovered the security breach that had taken place and as a result, many of his followers simply abandoned him. He carried on regardless into the city only to be cornered from all sides. After several scrimmages along the way, Wyatt's numbers dwindled continually until Wyatt finally had to admit defeat. He surrendered and was sentenced to death for high treason as had Lady Jane Grey, her husband, her father and the Duke of Suffolk before him.

But this was not to be the end for him. It would only be the beginning. While waiting for his execution, Mary had begun to seriously distrust her sister Elizabeth. She suspected Elizabeth's involvement with Wyatt but she had no way of proving it.

In the past we may have all felt a little pity for Mary. There was never a time when she did not feel insecure and rejected. But as time wore on, her strength began to show and she was determined never to feel those emotions again. It was the first time we see Mary in her true light.

She gave orders for Wyatt to be tortured so that he would admit that Elizabeth had been involved in the rebellion. Although he continuously refused to admit to Elizabeth's complicity, even on 11th April as his broken body was dragged to the scaffold, Mary did not believe him and any show of harmony between the sisters ended abruptly.

During the subsequent ninety beheadings of Wyatt's supporters, Elizabeth remained imprisoned in the Tower of London for two months, declaring her innocence the whole time. As Elizabeth protested, plans for Mary's marriage continued.

Within two days of meeting each other, Mary and Philip were married on 25th July 1554 and by September Mary had stopped menstruating. She gained weight and felt nauseated in the mornings and virtually the whole court, including Mary and her doctors, thought she was pregnant. In the last week of April 1555, Elizabeth was released from house arrest and called to a cheerful court as a witness to the birth, which was expected imminently. Meanwhile, Philip had ominously written a letter to his brother-in-law, Maximilian of Austria, expressing uncertainty as to whether his wife was pregnant at all.

It was in her joyous trimester that the first religious executions and burnings began. Mary had always rejected the break with Rome established by her father and recognised further by her brother, so when she and Philip persuaded Parliament to revoke the religious laws passed and return the English church to Catholicism, no one was really surprised. In February, the Heresy Acts were revived as Mary made a major decision. England would be Catholic and anyone not confessing their belief would soon know the consequences.

The first executions occurred over a period of five days in February and imprisoned bishops were forced to watch as many members of the church were burned at the stake. In the end, no one was spared. Butchers, bakers and priests all suffered alike. Their legs were crushed and tied to a stake and they were burned in full public view. One young farmer had a jar of tar poured over his head and it ran down his face as the flames flickered around his feet. Sometimes, friends would tie a little pouch of gunpowder around the victim's neck in case the wood was too green and did not kindle quickly. Many Protestants chose exile and around 800 left the country but all told, 300 were executed, most by burning.

May came and went and then June as well, and still Mary had not gone into labour. She continued to exhibit signs of pregnancy until July when her abdomen suddenly receded. As her husband had suspected, there was no baby after all.

Feeling disgraced by the false and prolonged pregnancy, Philip left England in August to command his armies against France, leaving Mary heartbroken, distraught and in a deep depression.

When Mary's father-in-law abdicated from the Spanish throne in January 1556, Philip became King of Spain and Mary became his consort, even though they had been living apart with Philip in Brussels while Mary stayed in England alone.

Then Philip paid her a visit and once again, Mary began showing signs of pregnancy. The baby, she declared, was due in March 1558 and if anything happened to her *"in the minority of her child"*, she decreed her husband was to be the regent.

Once again, she showed signs of a pregnancy and once again her abdomen receded. Finally, Mary could only accept the inevitable: her Protestant half-sister Elizabeth would be her successor.

Whether it was through ill health or whether it was intense sadness, Mary grew sicker and sicker. Childless, sick and deserted by Philip, Mary had become the unhappiest of England's monarchs. In November 1558, at the age of 42, Mary finally died from what we now believe was uterine or ovarian cancer.

As Mary had come to realise, it was Elizabeth who would sit on the throne of England after her death. And it was Elizabeth who inherited a bankrupt nation torn apart by religious discord.

But with Mary Tudor dead, there was someone else watching closely with mounting interest, waiting for the right time to step forward.

Many nobles remembered full well the contents of Henry VIII's will, stating that Edward was the only legitimate child and both Mary and Elizabeth were not. Most of them also knew that in France, there was a 17-year-old girl whose mother, Mary of Guise, had just died.

Even before Henry VIII's sister Margaret had her 6th birthday, their father Henry VII had thought that a marriage between his daughter and James IV of Scotland was a way to end Scottish uprisings. James V of Scotland had been their only surviving heir and he in turn had married Mary of Guise. Their daughter Mary was born on 8th December 1542 and six days later, she became the Queen of the Scots on the death of her father. At 17, she was the Queen Consort of France as well as the Queen of Scotland. The person watching Elizabeth closely was Mary Queen of Scots and she was alive and well in France. She was a Catholic and she was legitimate.

When Elizabeth came to the throne, she was already 25 years old, unmarried and unbetrothed. Mary Queen of Scots, on the other hand, was only 18 years old and she had many childbearing years left to produce heirs to the throne.

Many saw the similarity of the situation between the two Tudor sisters and England realised, as their only hope, a swift marriage for Elizabeth with a suitable husband who she could lean on for support and whose babies she would bear, was the only answer. It was a fact that was to curse Elizabeth for most of her reign.

Though loved by her people for bringing stability to their country that had not been a part of their lives for the past century, Elizabeth would rule alone through difficult times for half a century in an age regarded as 'The Golden Age'.

ELIZABETHAN ENGLAND

In art galleries, we are shown pictures of the Elizabethan countryside and what we see are ruggedly beautiful landscapes of sweeping meadows full of flowers and banks of lush green trees on hillsides. But most English people in those days saw England as anything but beautiful.

For most people, it was a gloomy place worthy of murder around every corner, and you wouldn't hang around for too long. In the countryside, dotted around you would see cottages but they were far from idyllic. Families were poor and their houses were dark. Few people could afford the luxury of candles. Most houses were basic dwellings consisting of one room with a single fireplace. It was gloomy and smoky and windows were no more than a hole in the wall so little light entered the house. Their only possessions were a few pots, a ladle, some plates and if you were lucky, mats on the ground to sleep on. At night, the only sounds would have been the crackle of the fire, raindrops on the roof and the soft breathing of the children. And vermin were plentiful. And of course, with vermin came disease.

You would have been very aware of the diseases that could affect your everyday life. There were so many diseases lurking in the shadows: the flu, dysentery, small pox, the sweating sickness, typhoid and of course, the plague. Thankfully, by the 16th century, the plague was not as prominent as it had been in the 14th century. In earlier days, half of the population of Europe was wiped out, although by the 16th century, a quarter of a million people would still die from this disease alone. If you had a swelling in your arm pits, if you were very thirsty, had a racing pulse, a headache or vomiting you knew you were in serious trouble. You also knew it was fleas that caused the disease so you made sure to air your bedding. But by then, it was way too late.

With the number of diseases so abundant, death was common in everyday life. Most children lost one parent by the time they had grown up and most parents lost half their children. In 1560 alone, there were 63 baptisms and 43 burials. Of course, added to everything else, sanitation was almost non-existent, and it would be another 300 years before wealthy people could afford a flushing toilet. Until then, you had to make do with squatting over a running stream. With that came the stench and most times you could smell a village before you saw it.

For most people, options for work were very limited and your best bet was to go from farm to farm asking for work. You grew your own vegetables if you could and you made your own clothes. The question of whether to marry or not was based on the whether you could earn enough money to feed and support a family.

At the heart of everything, was your church. In these days of religious upheaval, attending church was compulsory every Sunday and if you didn't attend, you were fined £20. In England's chequered religious history, there were Protestants and Catholics but a new religion was raising its head with members calling themselves Puritans. Everyone believed in a God and if you said you were an Atheist, it was like saying you did not believe in trees and you could expect to be hated for it.

Where there is population there is crime and after dark, it was terrifying. In a place where so many had so little, it is hardly surprising. Many people carried a dagger and they kept their eyes open and their wits about them especially as ale was the only liquid available to drink due to a lack of clean fresh water. The combination of tempers and alcohol produced a dangerous and volatile situation and everyone could expect to be punished severely if they were caught breaking the laws.

Punishments varied and the level of cruelty won't come as a great surprise. The first was straightforward hanging on a gallows; the second was being hung, drawn and quartered. The third was to be burned at a stake but the fourth was more severe and longer lasting. With this punishment, you were laid on the ground and a large rock was placed on your body. Blocks were added one by one until your body was crushed under the weight. It could take up to twelve hours to die.

It was an unbelievably painful, harsh time for most but it was a time of power and glory for a few others. Not everyone was at the bottom of the ladder. For the elite, it was a time of extravagance and wealth. In the same art galleries that depict a typical English countryside are portraits of noble men and women displaying these luxuries. When you look at these paintings what you see in their eyes is supreme confidence and a lifetime of privilege. But if you look a little closer and deeper, you may also see something else. Perhaps doubt and uncertainty. Perhaps fear? It was a dangerous time and it is worth remembering that those who possessed the most had the most to lose. Everyone liked to complain a little over a glass of wine or two, but you had to be very careful what you said and in whose company you said it.

To be accepted into the elite was to be accepted into the strict hierarchy of Elizabethan society. But all round, this was a very expensive exercise. At court, there were servants, visitors, courtiers and clergy and you wouldn't have any trouble telling them apart. All were distinguishable by their clothes. Courtiers bought back ideas and trends from Europe and these would be copied and reproduced for all to see. Gorgeous appearance was a must at court. At the beginning of Elizabeth's reign, both men and women started wearing ruffles over the tops of their shirts and tunics. The introduction of starch allowed the collars to grow even bigger until eventually 18 feet of material was used and it needed a circular board underneath to support all of it. If you wanted to show off vibrant colours you had to be a part of the elite as it became a law that only the aristocracy and gentry were allowed to use certain fabrics like cloths of gold and silver, blue velvet and purple silk. As for Elizabeth, her dress was mainly black and white meant to symbolise consistency, purity and eternal virginity, which she was keen to project. It was not a good idea to turn up at court dressed too vibrantly and risk upstaging her. If you were unsure, you could check yourself in a mirror, which was a rarity anywhere else. These mirrors were called by the Puritans as *"devil's glass"* reflecting only pride. Those that looked at them may be said to *"look in the devil's arse"*. Charming.

During Elizabeth's reign, her whole court was packed up on more than two dozen separate occasions and hit the road as she visited many of her nobles and selected gentry. She would be absent from London for many months at a time. Tapestries and paintings were removed from the walls and put in storage along with the silverware and other valuables, ready for her return. Even though this was supposed to be an exercise to show herself to her people, I can see how this would have been financially beneficial for her as well. The outings were a huge undertaking requiring around 2,000 men and women in her entourage. Also needed were 300 – 400 carts driven by 2,400 horses, all carrying what was needed, including 200 of Elizabeth's dresses. All of this was the Tudor propaganda of showing the people that she really was just like them after all.

To the nobles she visited, it must have been an enormously costly two-day visit. The grocery list for her entourage would have included 11½ cows, 17½ calves, 8 stags, 1200 chickens, 2,500 pigeons, a cart load of oysters and so the list goes on and on. Take into account an average cow in those days cost people around £2 each and was a labourer's wage for six months. And then there was something needed to wash all this down. Water was far too risky and anyway, Elizabeth's court liked something a little stronger. In two days, they would go through 2,500 gallons of beer alone. But that was not for the gentlemen. They preferred to drink wine, which was imported at great expense and regarded as a status symbol. For these gentlemen and ladies, they drank an average of 63 gallons of white wine and 378 gallons of claret. In just two days.

Manners were very strict on these royal visits. You must always wash your hands before eating, you didn't eat before your superiors and if you had to spit or blow your nose, you didn't do it across the table. You did it at your feet and you tread it out discreetly on the floor. And it was good manners to take your hat off if someone urinated in your company.

Elizabeth didn't travel too far as she only visited the parts where she was popular and she never went near the Pro-Catholic north. But if you wanted to keep up with her progress, you needed transport. Most people travelled by foot but as gentry, you would need a set of wheels. You would have had a coach drawn by horses and the cost of this could be enormous as it included paying a coachman to drive you and you would need to feed the horses, which could sometimes cost more than your own food. Your comfort, on these trips, was dependent on the state of the roads. Roads in those times were meant for feet and hooves not heavy coaches and the road ruts were deep especially during the wet winter months. Bridges were wooden and dangerous and the stone bridges were extremely narrow. But more sinister than a wonky bridge or uneven ground were the highwaymen.

The word 'highwaymen' conjures up characters like Dirk Turpin but these men were not so polite. In 1560 in Essex, there were sixty court cases alone relating to the theft of money and jewellery stolen on the highways and unlike the 18th century, these robbers were just common thieves. If you were unlucky enough to come across these ruffians, there would also be another group cutting off your retreat. They would not only take your money and jewels, they took your clothes as well. Some killed their victims but most were left tied up in the forest in such a way that you could work yourself lose in an hour or two and make your way to the nearest inn or town in your underwear. If you survived the trip, you would be grateful to arrive unharmed but even these establishments housed thieves and unsavoury characters. On the whole, it was much safer to make arrangements for accommodation at the house of a local gentleman. These gentry were sheriffs, magistrates and men who oversaw the militia. In parliament, it was the gentry who filled the House of Commons.

If you were the owner of such a manor, you needed to take care as well. If a gentleman came to your door and if a woman opened it, it was seen as gentlemanly behaviour to grab the woman by the arm and kiss her smack on the lips, even if she was the wife of the house. You might want to rethink that when the plague was in town.

Naturally, inside these houses, there was a lot more in common with the palaces than there was in the squalid homes of the poor. You would have seen carved wood, carpets and maybe even a mirror. And there would be weapons such as pikes, swords and shields hanging on the walls available if the lord of the manor was called to arms. There would be servants ranging from two to twenty depending on the gentleman's wealth as male servants cost £2 a year and female servants cost £1. Even though the servants were desperate for their wages, it was not unheard of for these gentlemen to over-look payments by several months, sometimes several years. Even taking this into account, servants were expected to be loyal. You would not be surprised to find that a lord was beating his servants, sometimes his wife. And he was expected to beat his children. Not to do so was seen as quite irresponsible as long as he stopped short of actually killing someone.

He would also have expected sexual favours even if he were married. This put the female servant into a terrible position. Should she risk refusing, she would be dismissed. If she agreed, she risked disease and pregnancy and she would be dismissed anyway and be ostracised by her church and her community as well.

Elizabethan England did not share our obsession with soap and water. In fact, they thought that using water could make you unwell through the pores of your skin. Looking at the rivers running with excrement, they had a good point. So the key to hygiene and keeping clean was not through water but through linen. Linen cloths were rubbed over the body and through their hair to soak up the sweat while shirts and undergarments were made of linen. So you kept yourself clean, not by washing, but by washing these linen clothes and by using perfumes to improve the smell of your clothes. While taking care of your body odours, you had to take care of your breath. There were no toothbrushes so you had to use a toothpick made of wood or bone or the quill of a feather. As to freshening your breath, you would have chewed cumin seeds or aniseed but most just rinsed their mouths out with white wine. Having done all your hygiene requirements, most gentry still believed that you should still take a bath once a month, whether you needed it or not.

Even after using these basic health care tips, you could also come across some illnesses like dysentery, typhus and scurvy. With dysentery you could die in as little as two weeks but with syphilis, you could live for twenty years, gradually and slowly going mad and at the end, dying from it.

For the rich it was a time when Tudor architecture blossomed with oak-panelled rooms, bay windows and gable roofs. Mining companies began setting up shop and began to distribute copper goods and crystal glass and Hardwick House was said to contain more glass than wall. Houses were filled with tapestries, curtains, covered chairs, chests and cupboards. Lace became the craze for both sexes from cuffs to ruffs, aprons and handkerchiefs. The appetite for luxuries was endless for those who could afford them.

Through it all, Elizabeth dazzled everyone with her clever wit, and even her enemies were enthralled. But it would seem that Elizabeth's sense of duty came at a great personal cost.

Six months before Mary died, a comet was seen blazing across the London sky, half the size of the moon. It streaked fire behind it and lit up the skies in glorious shades of red, white and gold for days, much the same colours as the Tudor rose. It was what England had been waiting for – a sure sign of better times to come. And heaven knows, they needed it. Under Queen Mary, they had suffered persecution worse than any generation before but hopefully this would mean it had come to an end. That queen was dead now and a new queen had come to the throne. Their future lay in the hands of this bright-eyed intelligent woman who promised a magnificent future for everyone.

What she hadn't promised was an heir and her words, *"I would rather be a beggar and single than a Queen and married"* niggled at the back of their minds. She had also said, *"This end shall be for me sufficient, that a marble stone shall declare that a Queen, having reigned such a time, lived and died a virgin"*. That had not filled them with confidence either. *"I am married to England"*, were her next words.

But what was to become of them if she died without an heir? Was Scotland their fate? Did she really have their best interests at heart after all? Hadn't her sister and father promised the very same things?

During Elizabeth's reign, England would see another two hundred Catholics strangled, burned or disembowelled.

From our Viking past, England walked, ran, stumbled and bled through the centuries to find a Virgin Queen. Ironically, Queen Elizabeth's birthdate was 7th September, the feast day of the Nativity of the Virgin Mary.

In Part 2 of England's story, **'Virgin to Victoria'**, we see Elizabeth grow into the legendary monarch she was. We travel through time with the Stuart dynasty and the Hanover dynasty until we come to Queen Victoria, another legendary monarch.

Victoria did not ask to be queen. It was thrust upon her by the accident of birth and then by a succession of accidents that removed others who stood between her and the throne. She assumed it reluctantly and, at first, incompetently.

Parliament was sure she could be relied upon to leave the job of running the country to the professionals.

Couldn't she?